BEAUTIFUL
VILLAIN

BEAUTiFUL VILLAIN

REBECCA KENNEY

sourcebooks
casablanca

Published by Sourcebooks Casablanca, an imprint of Sourcebooks
P.O. Box 4410, Naperville, Illinois 60567-4410
(630) 961-3900
sourcebooks.com

Cataloging-in-Publication Data is on file with the Library of Congress.

Printed and bound in the United States of America.
LSC 10 9 8 7 6 5 4 3 2 1

To my husband and kids, who support me with so much unfailing love and bright-eyed belief. And to anyone guiltily wondering if they dare move this book to the top of their towering TBR pile...
Of course you can.

In his blue gardens men and girls came and went like moths among the whisperings and the champagne and the stars.

—F. Scott Fitzgerald, *The Great Gatsby*

All I kept thinking about, over and over, was "You can't live forever; you can't live forever."

—F. Scott Fitzgerald, *The Great Gatsby*

1

THE FLASH OF GREEN LIGHT FROM MY PHONE IS TEMPTING ME.

I should be asleep. Ever since I graduated from UNC, I've been staying up way too late. It's after 2:00 a.m., and I already told myself I was done for the night.

The ceiling fan glides soundlessly overhead, round and round, big, leaf-shaped paddles pushing the artificially chill air through the room. I stare at it, pointedly ignoring that seductive text notification.

No more phone, Daisy. No more scrolling through social media checking up on everyone I know, all the faces of people I used to see every day who have abruptly scattered to this city and that, thrilled to start their exciting new jobs. No one warns you how much it hurts when the people you studied with, ate with, and partied with for four years are just—gone.

Me? I'm taking a gap year. Or a gap summer, I guess. My parents said I could come home for a few months and rest before I start looking for a job and an apartment.

I haven't told them yet how much I hated college, how close I came to failing. How terrified I am of forging my own path. There's an empty, echoing hollow inside me where my life plan should be, and it's not a place I like to visit.

The distraction of my phone could help me with that, could stop me wondering why, oh why I chose to be a communication studies major.

Because I didn't know what the hell else to do, that's why.

For a while in high school, I wanted to be a lawyer—the kind that actually helps people who are suffering. I thought I'd join the debate team, get some experience, maybe major in pre-law. But my mild-mannered, easygoing dad shut down the debate team idea so hard, I never brought it up again.

"Our voices have power, Daisy," he told me. "And I want yours to be heard, but in the right way. You've got to be careful how you use it."

He wouldn't say any more on the subject. But it felt like a weird echo of things my grandma used to tell me when I was really little, before she passed. "You've got the gift of persuasion, ladybug. It'll only get stronger as you grow."

She always seemed as if she wanted expand on the topic, but my dad would hustle back into the room, asking brightly what we'd been talking about. He never left the two of us alone very long.

That's as weird as my family gets, so I guess I'm lucky. Except for the fact that my dad's veto of the debate team and his clear aversion to the idea of me being a lawyer left me with a bland, all-but-useless major, and I don't know what to fucking do with it.

Turning my head on the pillow, I glance at the green light, and it winks back at me. There's some juicy little tidbit waiting, and if I don't check it, I won't be able to sleep.

I claw the phone off my nightstand with a sigh of defeat. A swipe and the press of a finger, and I'm in.

A bunch of texts from Jordan Baker fill the screen. Went to the BEST party tonight. You wouldn't believe this guy's place. He's our age, but he's a billionaire. I'm talking a whole room just for VR tech, five-star catering, pools and a lazy river, goodie bags packed with high-end stuff. Next week he's having another party and you HAVE to come.

Jordan Baker—the girl who decided to skip college. I knew her back in high school, when she was building her TikTok audience. Now she has millions of followers and patrons. People worship her parkour vids, so they invite her to all kinds of things. Best of all, she makes plenty of money with her stunts, so she doesn't have to chain herself to a desk all day.

Jordan and I kept in touch, off and on, although after four years apart I'm not sure we can say we're friends anymore. Even back in high school we used to argue a lot, mostly about the increasing riskiness of her stunt work. Still, I'm touched that she's inviting me, that she wants to reconnect.

This party could be just what I need to get past what happened with Tom.

Tom. Even in my thoughts, his name sends a twist of nausea through my stomach, the creeping sense of a nightmare made real. It's why I hate turning the lights off and going to bed. The darkness crawls right inside me and expands, a vast, gaping maw that I swear one night is going to swallow me whole.

Anxiety tightens my skin, singing along my nerves. I fling off the sheets and jump to the floor, my feet padding across the smooth, cool hardwood. While my thumbs fly over the keyboard, I pace the room, trying to purge the negative energy.

I'm in, I text Jordan. Can you tell me more about the party? Like what I should wear? What about the host, what's his story?

Can't talk now babe, she replies. Deets later.

She sends me a kiss-wink emoji, her usual sign-off. I'm bummed at the quick end to the conversation, but Jordan is probably exhausted. And I should try to get some sleep.

I set the phone back on the nightstand and slither deeper into the sheets. Instead of the gaping chasm of my future, or the sickening sense of betrayal that accompanies memories of Tom, I focus on Jordan's description of the party.

A whole room for VR tech? Five-star catering? High-end loot? Sounds like my kind of fun.

I drift off into dreams of mile-long catered buffets and lazy rivers—until I'm bounced awake by something large and gangly crashing onto my bed. When I open my eyes, the sun shoots into them. "Ow! Serenity, lower the shades."

The smart house obediently darkens the room. My parents named it for the spaceship in this random sci-fi show they watched while they were dating. It was either that or "Mikasa," which my mom thought was hilarious since it's the name of an anime character she likes and also sounds like *mi casa*. I vetoed that pun.

My parents are way too nerdy for this house—and this entire elegant neighborhood.

"So this is how Daisy Finnegan spends her summer? Sleeping through the best part of the day?" Nick, my long-legged, blue-eyed cousin, lounges at the foot of my bed, sporting a pale-pink BTS T-shirt and vintage acid-wash jeans.

"Nick," I groan, falling back onto my pillows. "Why are you screwing with my beauty sleep? Just...why?"

"I'm sorry, I think you mean, 'Ooh Nicky, my darling, how lovely of you to come and see me today!'"

I hurl a pillow at him, which he catches expertly. "You know better than to expect politeness from me before coffee."

"True," he admits. "I'm meeting Jordan this morning for a shoot, and I told her I'd bring you along."

I prop myself on my elbows. "Why?"

"Because she pays me, hon. I have the incredible honor of being the only white boy she allows to touch her hair."

"I know *that*, but why me?" The timing is odd. Why wouldn't she have mentioned it in her text last night if she wanted me there?

Nick purses his lips and looks away. "Well...your mom may have mentioned that since you came home, you've been in your room a lot. And also...not showering often."

"So this is what, some kind of intervention?"

"Not at all, babe. Think of it as family and friends checking in, making sure your summer rocks." He smiles way too brightly. "Now get up and shower."

"Hmm," I mumble, lying back and plopping the second pillow onto my face. "Don't have to shower. Will swim in pool later."

"Chlorine doesn't equal soap, precious. You need to cleanse and condition. Come on, out of bed." He wriggles one hand under the sheets to tweak my toes, and I yelp.

"Fine, I'm up," I growl. "Screw you."

"Love you too."

Nick has chosen my outfit by the time I get done showering—cute shorts, a blousy tank, and dangly earrings. I don't complain because he used to do that for me all the time when we were in high school together, and it's kinda sweet that he's trying to bring back the good old days.

I swap out the many studs in my upper ears for fresh ones in the shape of tiny stars and moons and shove my feet into flip-flops that are way too expensive to be scuffed around in red North Carolina dirt all day. I can remember a time when my flip-flops were from Walmart and my clothes came from Goodwill. That was before Dad developed the antibody therapy that made him one of the top medical researchers in the country. Shortly after that, he scored a new job, one we were sure he'd never get. But somehow, against all odds, they hired him, and that decision changed our lives. Now my parents live on Glassy Mountain in a sprawling, luxurious development packed with amenities; but even after eight years, none of us are used to being wealthy. I still have this sort of desperate feeling, like I have to enjoy it as much as I can, because it could all melt away as easily as it came.

"Earth to Daisy." Nick snaps long fingers in front of my face. He has painted his nails electric blue with dizzying swirls of purple. "Breakfast?"

"I guess."

My parents are long gone to their respective jobs, so the enormous kitchen is empty. I snatch a pastry from under the bell jar on the island and hand one to Nick. "I shouldn't," he says, but he takes it anyway and pulls me out the front door so fast I barely have time to grab my bag and sunglasses.

When we burst outside, the sun doesn't seem as offensively bright as it did in my room. There's a humid promise of sultry heat in the air, but it's not horribly oppressive yet.

"Gotta stop for gas," Nick says, vaulting over the door of his Fiat Spider and settling into the driver's seat.

"I'll grab coffee for both of us."

"From the gas station?" He makes a face. "You drink that trash?"

"They have cold Starbucks in the coolers."

"Fiiiine." He draws out the word to about four syllables as the car glides out of our driveway.

"Watch the speed limit until we get through the gate—they're really strict in this neighborhood," I warn him. "So what's Jordan's stunt for the day?"

Nick glances at me through the cinnamon curls blowing across his face. "She doesn't want you to know until you get there."

"Something super dangerous then."

"You know Jordan." He shrugs. "She didn't get her followers by sitting around."

"She's going to end up in the hospital. Or dead."

"Ah, here we go. High school all over again." Nick rolls his eyes. "I'm not getting into this with you, okay? Take it up with Jordan. Just do me a favor and argue about it when I'm not around."

I tilt my head back against the leather headrest and close my eyes, relishing the sensation of warm wind pouring over my face. The sun filters through the leafy trees skimming past overhead, and its dappled light plays across my eyelids. This is bliss—a summer glow on my face, a breeze across my skin, and music singing through me, its intimate beat soothing me right down to my very soul.

A long-forgotten memory sifts into my mind—my blond hair brushing my bare shoulders, someone's fingertips trailing over my sun-warm skin, slow and wondering. A boy's touch, tentative, unsure. Wide brown eyes searching mine, reflecting the same startled amazement that I felt in that long-ago moment. The sensation of awakening to something universal and frightening and thrilling.

My eyes pop open. I haven't thought about that boy in ages, not since I left him behind with the Walmart flip-flops and the thrifted clothes. I couldn't fold him into a moving box and bring him with me into my new life. He was like a new friend at the playground—one you vibe with intensely and then never see again.

Except that boy and I weren't just friends for an afternoon. Our lives intersected for years. And when I had to leave, he let me go. Didn't even *try* to stay in touch.

Nick nudges me with his elbow. "You're not yourself today, precious. What's up?"

"I'm... It's nothing, I'm fine."

"Thinking about the cheating bastard?"

Tom. "Actually I wasn't, but I am now. Thanks for that."

We roar into the gas station parking lot, skew into a spot in front of the pumps, and slam to a stop so hard my whole body jerks.

"Thanks for the whiplash, too." I slam the car door with extra force, and Nick winces.

"Careful with my baby!"

"You should take better care of your baby, and your passengers." I stalk across the parking lot and swing into the gas station. I shouldn't fuss at Nick. He's not the one I'm mad at. I'm pissed at men in general: the ones who screw you over, and the ones who let themselves fade out of your life—

I grab a pair of cold coffees from the fridge and turn toward the checkout counter.

But the sight in front of me stops me cold, a fist to my gut, and I suck in a pained breath.

Crimped blond curls, big blue eyes. Lips like bubble gum, and a chest that strains against her crisp uniform.

Myrtle.

How is she working here? She and Tom are supposed to be three-and-a-half hours away in Durham.

Unless...unless their plans changed, and they decided to move here after graduation—oh fuck no.

My brain devolves into a string of curses, punctuated by flashes of bare limbs and huffing breaths. Why am I picturing her tangled up with Tom? It's not like I actually caught them in the act. I was spared at least *that* much.

Acidic fury spurts in my chest at the thought, drowning out the flash of panic, but I suck in a breath to quell it. I'm not that girl.

I don't smash headlights with a crowbar or drag my keys along car doors. I don't bad-mouth people on social media.

I just burn and burn inside, while I smile sweetly because I'm freaking Daisy Finnegan—the nice girl, the fun girl, the one you want at all your parties, whether I want to be there or not.

More calmly than I feel, I set down the coffees on a random shelf and walk straight out the side door. It's a big place, so it's possible Myrtle didn't see me. God, I *hope* she didn't see me.

My skin is a frozen shell over the molten core of my soul. I slide into Nick's car and stare ahead, unseeing.

"Where's the coffee?" he asks.

"Myrtle works here."

"*What?*"

"Myrtle. Works. Here."

"The *hell?*" Nick gasps.

"She and Tom must have come back here, instead of staying in Durham." I press my shaking fingers to my temples. "Nick, I think I'm going to be sick."

"Not in the Fiat, please god," he says quickly. "I'm so sorry, Daisy. Look, I'll go in and get the drinks, okay? You still want coffee? Or maybe a ginger ale? Some vodka?"

I splutter a laugh. "Coffee's fine. Thanks, Nicky."

While he's inside, I hunch down in the Fiat, terrified that Tom is going to pop out of the pavement. My heart pounds, and I have to think carefully to regulate my breathing. I close my eyes for a few seconds, grounding myself with the feel of the leather seat under my palm, with the soft caress of the summer breeze off the mountain. I'm okay.

I'm going to be okay.

Within minutes, Nick returns, and we're off again. The cool, sweet slide of the iced mocha down my throat calms my stomach and quenches my internal inferno.

"She's so skanky." Nick shakes his head. "No idea what Tom sees in her. She doesn't do a thing for me."

I slant my gaze toward him. "That's because you're gay, babe."

"Oh. Right." He smirks at me, and I smile in spite of myself.

"You're the best, Nicky." I rub my fingertips along his shoulder. My voice sinks lower, quieter, deep enough in my throat that I feel it in my chest. It's the cadence I find myself using when I want to be sure I'm understood. "I didn't want to believe I needed an intervention, but—maybe I do. Just a little bit. Maybe I need someone to help look after me this summer." I clear my throat, shifting back to my usual tone. "Anyway, I appreciate what you and Jordan are trying to do."

Nick shivers slightly. "You know, you have the most hypnotizing voice."

I frown, withdrawing my hand. "Now you're being weird."

"No, it's true. Other people have commented on it, too. You get this tone sometimes, and it's, like, *irresistible*. Why do you think Jordan used to have you narrate some of her vids? She always got tons more views when you did the voice work. I wouldn't be surprised if she hires you to do some audio for her this summer."

The unexpected turn in conversation has me a bit flustered. "But she has a great voice."

"That's not the point. There's something musical about yours..."

"Jordan sings better than I do."

Nick taps his fingers impatiently on the wheel. "You don't get it."

"Nope." And with that, I shut him down and turn up the music.

I shouldn't have said that bit about needing an intervention. That was too much, too raw. I don't want Nick to know how much

Tom's betrayal is still gnawing at me, or worse, how stupid I must have been not to recognize Tom for what he was, and what he was doing to me.

Enough of Tom already. I just want to enjoy a gorgeous summer day and *not think*.

The rest of the drive is wind tangling my long hair into an inextricable mess and Nick blasting Glass Animals' "Heat Waves" on the radio. I sip the coffee, smooth, sweet, and cold over my tongue. We pass a guy cutting grass, and I inhale that fresh green scent deep into my lungs.

Finally we park along the side of a mountain road and trek to the swimming hole Jordan uses for a lot of her stunts. When she's not doing parkour in the West End of Greenville or along the back streets of Asheville, or touring the Midwest and bungee jumping into canyons, she's up here in the mountains stretching her body to the limit.

I hate to think what death-defying stunt she's cooked up this time.

2

"So I'm gonna ride the bike off that rock up there, jump off in midair, do a couple flips, maybe grab it again—might have to try it a few times to get it right. You just stand here and film, got it?"

Jordan grins at me, her dark skin gleaming in the shafts of sunlight glancing through the trees. If smiles were superpowers, she'd be freaking Wonder Woman. I've never met the person who can resist a Jordan Baker smile—except maybe our high school principal, Ms. Hammond. She and Jordan clashed a lot in twelfth grade because Jordan didn't see the point of school at all, and she let everyone know it.

"Why should I study stuff I don't care about when I already have a career?" she'd say, and then she'd tell everyone exactly how much her sponsors were paying her. Judging from some of the trips she's been on since then, she probably makes way more now. Some of her content is public, and some of it she puts behind a paywall so people have to subscribe. Kinda brilliant, except for the part where she almost dies occasionally.

I should probably protest this stunt, even though I'm already standing here on the edge of a cliff, holding the phone, ready to film. "This is messed up, Jordan. What if you hit the rocks or something?"

"McKee already checked it out for me yesterday. No rocks in the middle of the pool, so as long as I land somewhere in the center, I'll be fine. I trust my body, and you should, too. This is a throwaway video for me. I've done way bigger jumps than this." She grips my shoulder briefly before walking the bike toward the spur of rock from which she plans to launch herself. A thrill of horror shoots through my stomach at the mental image of Jordan's body cartwheeling thirty feet above the swimming hole.

"Nick," I say plaintively.

He throws both hands up. "Don't look at me. If you can't stop her, I don't have a prayer."

"Oh god," I whimper helplessly as Jordan reappears through the trees with her bike. Between us lie a few stories of empty air, with the glittering blue of the swimming hole at the bottom. To my right, a frosty veil of water sprays over the rocks, pouring down into the pool.

Jordan glances my way and gives me the thumbs-up.

"Nicky, I don't know about this." I adjust the focus for the phone's camera. "Why am I filming? Doesn't she have people to—"

"Not today. Now start filming," Nick hisses. "The sooner we shoot this, the sooner we can leave and go swim in a nice safe pool full of chemicals instead of algae." He shudders.

While I was away at college, I watched Jordan through a phone screen. It's better that way—feels less immediate and dangerous. I forgot how terrifying it is to watch her do this stuff in real life.

My heart lurches into my throat as Jordan's wheels spin and she rockets off the spur of stone. She's suspended in midair, her body arching in a graceful, controlled curve that tightens into one flip and then another. She straightens, grabs for the handlebars of the bike—and misses. She and the bike crash into the swimming hole.

I rush to the edge of the cliff, staring down at the blue water below, too alarmed to even think to stop recording.

Jordan breaks the surface, then sinks again.

"What's going on?" I clutch Nick's arm. "Why isn't she coming back up?"

Her wet hair glistens as she surfaces. She's struggling with the bike. The swimming hole is deep, and if she lets the bike go, it will sink to the bottom. "She's got to get herself and the bike to the edge. I don't think she can do it." I kick Nick in the shin. "You go help her."

"Me? But—you know I don't swim in mountain water."

"Nicky." I lower my voice to its most persuasive tone. "*Go.*"

With a screech of frustration, he jogs down the path. It takes a few minutes for him to get down to Jordan, so I watch her carefully to make sure she's still okay. When Nick gets to the bank of the pool, he hops on one foot to take each shoe off and then, with a dramatic groan that I hear all the way up on the ledge, he jumps into the swimming hole.

He helps Jordan haul the bike out of the water, and they begin the prep for the next take. Her sports bra and shorts are soaked, but they'll dry quickly. Nick pats her tightly braided hair with a towel and touches up the bit of makeup she's wearing. Then, with another flashy grin at me, Jordan rolls the bike back up the path to the rock spur.

It takes a dozen more attempts to get a take she's satisfied with. And then she tells me what to say for the voice-over—as usual, full of jokes I'd never think of on my own.

"My followers are gonna love you," she says, jostling my arm. "Some of them still remember you from a few years ago. Hey, we should sing together sometime."

"You're doing songs now, too?" I lift an eyebrow.

"Covers, not originals. A subscribers-only perk."

"I wouldn't have thought the daredevil crowd would be into that."

"Everybody loves good music. Come on, what do you say? Lil music video, you and me? Hey, maybe the guy who hosted the party last night would let us use his recording studio."

"He has a recording studio? Like, at his house?"

"Yeah, girl! Top-notch equipment, too. I'll introduce you, and you can ask him. Bet he can't say no to the Daisy Finnegan charm."

Heat crawls into my cheeks. I want to ask if this guy is hot, but that would sound a lot shallower than I want to be. And I don't like it when people constantly mention my "charm." Makes me uneasy for some reason.

"Maybe we can do one song," I say. "But I'm not rapping."

"Oh, hell no." Jordan splays her fingers over her heart. "That would be a disaster."

"Agreed."

The rest of the day is a swirl of glimmering heat and limpid water, the hot slats of the pool chairs at Jordan's house, and the crisp pop of soda on my tongue. By the end of it I'm deliciously tired, sunbaked down to my bones. I think I might actually be able to fall asleep at a reasonable hour tonight.

Nick drops me off in my driveway and I meander toward the front door, flicking through messages on my phone, its glow coating my fingers.

My parents texted they'd be home late—some dinner thing with colleagues, or friends, or both. Lately, with them, every social occasion seems to shift into a networking opportunity, a chance to climb even higher on the ladder of luxury.

Haven't we climbed high enough? I mean, they were able to pay for my college outright, and they live in this amazing neighborhood. But I guess people never stop striving for more. Unless, of course, you're me, and you have zero ambition or motivation.

When I was a kid, my dad used to tell me to "check my privilege." He'd say it constantly, whenever I complained or acted a little too proud of my achievements. At the time we had far less than we do now, yet he'd point out all the ways I was better off than others, all the opportunities I'd been given that others hadn't. He'd explain how our whiteness itself was an advantage. He'd tell me that sometimes we have to actively step back and put others forward, to reject that unjust privilege, even if doing so hurts our chances of reaching our own goals.

He used to say all of that, years ago. But he hasn't told me to "check my privilege" in a very long time.

I'm nearly to the front door when a dark shape emerges from behind a tall cedar bush. I yelp, and the figure claps a hand over my mouth. The faint scent of pineapple and bergamot wafts to my nostrils—Creed Aventus cologne, with base notes of stale cigarette smoke.

Tom.

Adrenaline spikes in my veins, and I wrench away from him. "What the hell are you doing here? I thought you were staying in Durham."

"The job fell through, so I came back. I'm living with my parents until I get a place." His voice is rough with emotion. "Listen, can we talk? About us?"

Several years' worth of memories are knotted between us, their aching pull irresistible. Lunch on campus, sitting on a low stone wall, sharing bites of his sandwich. Autumn wind dashing leaves around us as he leaned in, laughing, to kiss my cold-reddened cheeks. Both of us curled up on his bed, laptops open, doing homework. His hand playing through my hair.

When he's close to me like this, brushing my upper arms with his knuckles, bending his dark head toward mine, I can almost believe that Myrtle never existed.

I tilt my face up to his, and he cups my chin, his thumb grazing my lips.

"I came to tell you I'm sorry, Daisy," he says. "I broke it off with Myrtle a few days ago. She was a mistake—a terrible mistake. I–I was out of my head. I didn't understand what I was giving up."

For a minute I indulge in his beauty—crisp cheekbones, sharp jawline. A body sculpted by years of soccer and track. A line from an old song, a favorite of my mom's, drifts into my head. Something about a pretty boy with an ugly heart.

I have other memories, too. His eyes lingering too long on other girls as they walked by. His voice, insisting I eat a few bites of his lunch instead of getting my own because I was "putting on college weight." When we did homework together, I'd end up finishing his assignments for him.

I want to be touched, I do. But not by him. Never again.

I pull away and step back.

"You still have the fob I gave you, the one that opens the community gate," I say. "I'm going to need that back."

"Daisy."

"Where is it?" I extend my palm. "Hand it over."

"Daisy!" He grips my hand with such ferocity that I cringe back, alarmed. With a twisting tug he yanks me closer, his rings grinding against the bones of my fingers. "I'm trying to apologize here. Don't be a brat about this."

I smell it then, the whisper of whiskey on his breath. "You need to go."

He shakes his head. "I won't. I came here to get you back. I'm not leaving until you take me back, Daisy."

"Then you'll be camping on the lawn, I guess. Enjoy yourself." I try to jerk free, but his hand is like a vise.

"I miss your body, Daisy," he purrs, one hand sliding along my waist, over my stomach. "I miss how you made me feel. I need you."

I need power in this moment. My "charm," or something stronger.

Inhaling slowly, I sink into softer, darker tones—my persuasive voice. "Thomas Reagan Buchanan. Let go of me and leave."

His jaw flexes, and his blue eyes burn into mine. But then his fingers relax and he steps away.

That's a first. Tom doesn't usually back off for anyone. Maybe he has changed. Or maybe he's got some other agenda here that I don't fully understand.

Tom is still looking at me the way he always does, like he's sucking all the beauty and joy from me into himself, swallowing it down.

"I'll call you," he says.

"You shouldn't."

"I will." He backs up to the spot where his motorcycle sits on our lawn, half-concealed by a tree's shadow. If I hadn't been checking my phone, I'd have seen it when I walked up.

Tom tosses the community gate fob into the grass at my feet so I'll have to bend over to get it. When I straighten, he gives me a slow smile, the kind that used to melt my insides. "What are you doing this weekend?"

"I have plans with Jordan and Nicky."

"Plans? What plans?"

I stare him down, pinching my lips tight.

"So you don't want to tell me. Fine." He ruffles his shock of wavy black hair. "I'll figure it out. See you soon, Daisy. Be a good girl."

With a grin, he kicks off and rides away down the street. The growl of his bike fades into the endless sawing song of the cicadas. The glow of a swelling white moon silvers the lawn, touching the leaves of the bushes with liquid light.

I've always loved the soft, mysterious shine of a full moon, maybe even more than I love the bright cheer of the sun. I once knew a boy who loved the moon just as much as I do...who claimed he'd sipped moonlight. When I asked him what it tasted like, he said, "Your smile."

I haven't seen that boy in eight years. He probably doesn't care about moonlight anymore. Probably doesn't remember me at all.

3

"Don't add more lip stain now!" Nick leans forward from the back seat of the car to squawk at me. "If Jordan hits a bump in the road, your look will be ruined."

I ignore him and daub a little more crimson onto my mouth.

"Bump!" warns Jordan, and I lower my hand just before the car jolts.

"All good," I reassure Nick.

"Thank god." The leather squeaks as he shifts back again. "I don't know why I'm so nervous. I've been here before. Got the Evite and everything."

"Evite?" Jordan glances back at him. "I didn't get an Evite. No one gets an Evite, Nick. People just show up. It's word of mouth."

"But—that doesn't make any sense. I know I got an Evite." After a few seconds of silence he shoves his phone over Jordan's shoulder. "Look."

"Fool, I'm driving." She glances at the screen and shrugs him off. "So you're the only person in the county to get an invitation. Lucky you."

"Isn't that weird though?" Nick retreats to the back seat again. "I wonder why. It's not like I'm anyone special."

I wince inwardly at his words. Nick lives at the end of this very road, in a modest little neighborhood much cheaper than ours, tucked into a rocky cleft. The neighborhood has no view and a stormwater drainage problem, which is why my aunt and uncle were able to afford it. They're struggling artists with a few patrons in Asheville and Greenville and the surrounding area, and they barely make enough to hold the house. Nick's Fiat was a gift from my parents for his eighteenth birthday a couple years ago. If they hadn't been so generous, he'd probably still be taking the bus or riding his bicycle everywhere—and a bike is not an easy mode of transportation in the mountains.

As a kid, before our fortunes changed, I used to envy Nick. When my family would drive up to visit his, it was exciting, glamorous. He had a pool—an old, smallish one, but still, his family seemed unattainably wealthy in comparison to mine. After each visit, I had to return to our tiny two-bedroom in the Ashmore Valley apartment complex.

Ashmore Valley was a drab, treeless maze of tenement buildings in Easley, South Carolina, halfway between the lush, vibrant city of Greenville and the artsy mountain city of Asheville. The owners of the complex cared so little for improvements that the siding had long since faded from hopeful blue to the same sun-blasted gray as the cracked pavement. The apartment interiors were full of cracks, too—thin cracks in the drywall, wider ones along the baseboards, moldering cracks in the grout between the shower tiles, and thread-thin cracks through the porcelain of the sinks. The worst hid beneath the footworn carpets. Earwigs and centipedes slithered up through those crevices, searching for crumbs and respite from the sweltering heat. Since the air conditioning was broken more often than not, the bugs didn't improve their lives much by crawling into our home. I used to long for the rare weekends when I could play video games in Nicky's blessedly cool house, or swim in his pool.

Now I have my pick of the enormous, luxurious pools and other amenities in our community, and my parents' house is twice as big as Nick's. I enjoy my life, but I've always had an itching discomfort over the way our roles have reversed.

"You *are* special," I tell Nick defiantly.

"Thanks, precious. But it's weird, isn't it? That I'm the only one who was invited."

"A little strange," I admit. "Maybe the guy who owns the house has a crush on you. Maybe he saw you last time and decided he had to see you again."

"But I've never met him. And he doesn't usually show up to his own parties. Or if he's there, he doesn't introduce himself to anyone."

I frown, glancing at Jordan. "Is that true?"

"Yup." The gold paint on her cheekbones gleams in the light of a passing car. "I asked around. No one I know has actually met him."

"How strange."

"Maybe you'll meet him tonight." Jordan nods ahead. "Here we are."

I crane my neck for a better view as she makes the turn. The house is a bonfire of golden windows and smoke-blue shadows. A broad driveway sweeps around it on the right, and Jordan nudges her Jaguar into the line of cars inching toward the parking area at the back. When we find a space, it's far from the rear entrance of the house, but that doesn't matter because the party spills into the grounds, too, under white canopies and latticed gazebos strung with Edison-style bulbs. People flutter through the gardens, looking half-translucent as they cross the streaming paths of light. The house looms over it all, an incandescent monstrosity, the pulsing multi-story heart of a party that seems to sprawl for acres.

"Wow." I stare up at the shining windows. I haven't even stepped out of the car, and I can already feel the beat of the dance music throbbing in my bones. "This is really it?"

"Yup." Jordan throws the car into Park. "This is Gatsby's place."

Shock blazes like cold fire along my veins. "Wait, what?"

"Gatsby's house. The guy who hosts the parties."

"Gatsby—what Gatsby? I mean, what's his first name?"

Jordan quirks an eyebrow at me. "I'm not sure. He likes to go by his last name, I guess. Who cares?"

"I don't care," I reply hastily. "I just... I would have liked to know."

"O-okay." Jordan drags out the word, a clear sign she thinks I'm being weird.

And I am. I'm being ridiculous, because there's no way someone who owns this house and throws these extravagant parties could be the boy I knew eight years ago in Podunk Easley, South Carolina. That Gatsby wore secondhand sneakers and faded Beatles T-shirts. He drank moonlight and told fantastical stories and touched my shoulder with something like reverence.

This Gatsby coincidentally shares his last name, but they're two different people. They have to be.

Nick opens the car door for me and invites me out with a flourish. He gets super courteous when he's nervous, but for once I don't feel like teasing him about it. I unfold myself from the car slowly, tugging down the hem of my dress a little. It's a wispy, gauzy lavender thing that comes to midthigh, and I've got glittering flapper beads and a feathered headband, too. Jordan said the theme for tonight was Roaring 2020s, though how she knew that without an invitation is beyond me.

"Daisy." Jordan snaps her fingers in front of my face. "You're zoning, babe."

"This place is huge," I reply. "I was overwhelmed for a second, but—" I draw in a deep breath, inhaling the scent of heavy southern florals, burnt sugar, woodsmoke, and something meaty and savory. "Let's do this."

The best way to party is to hurl myself into it, like diving into a pool, and then flow with whatever current comes my way. Forget the name Gatsby, forget expectations and careers and futures. It's time for fun.

I clutch Nick's and Jordan's hands. "I want to dance. Come on, beautiful people—come dance with me!"

The music tugs at us, beating from the interior of the house, and I race toward it, pulling Nick and Jordan along. Jordan twists her hand free after a second, slowing her pace to a jaunty walk, but she laughs indulgently as Nick and I rush into the house. We sweep through rooms, past clouds of golden balloons and tables covered with catered delicacies that smell like spice and heaven. I'm floating in a haze of scent and sound, dizzy and delighted—and then we break out into the dance room, a cool cavern bathed in blue shadow, sliced with shifting beams of pink and purple light. At the head of the room there's a platform with a live band, a mix of guys and girls with wild hair, fake horns, and about twenty necklaces each. They're playing modern songs with a reckless jazz twist, and I'm so here for it.

There must be a hundred people in the space, which is perfect. At smaller parties, dancing can be so awkward. It's tough to push through your inhibitions, to stretch that film and pop through to the other side where you can feel the magic of the music. But with a big crowd like this, slipping into that zone is as easy as breathing. I maneuver myself and Nick deeper into the crowd, and then I let go.

A new song begins, and the music bursts over us like a sparkling wave, undercut with bone-deep, earth-melting bass. There are moments, magic moments, when everyone senses the spell of a song, when all the souls in the room quiver with desire, when a fresh flood of energy roars through our veins because the song is just right, synchronized to the rhythm inside us, promising something we desperately, desperately need. We aren't individual people anymore—we are a great pulsing heartbeat, throbbing faster and faster, reaching for that something at the crest of the music because maybe if we dance hard enough, fast enough, our souls will float out of our bodies and we won't have to worry about careers and ambitions and if the effort will even be worthwhile. The bass shivers and hammers underneath all those worries like an earthquake, until they crack and splinter into a thousand bits of shale, and we grind them into dust under our heels as the music carries them away.

I dance until my heart is booming like thunder through my entire body and there's sweat slicking my spine under the lavender dress.

"I need a break, Nicky," I eventually gasp, brushing my cousin's arm with my fingers. His dance partner is a black-haired guy with the delicate beauty of a K-pop idol—but there's an edge to the guy, too, a challenge in the dark eyes that meet mine. His lip hitches in a vicious half smile, daring me to take Nick away.

"You keep dancing. I'm fine," I tell Nick, and he nods gratefully, locking his fingers with the other man's.

I shrug off a slight sense of abandonment, an echo of nerves. I don't need an escort to find a drink. What is this, the eighteenth century? I'm Daisy Finnegan, and I can get my own freaking drink.

Tom used to insist on me staying right by his side wherever we went—or staying put wherever he placed me. He'd leave me with a kiss and a "be a good girl," and then return and snap his fingers when he was ready to leave. But he can't tell me what to do anymore, can't snap his fingers in my face or wriggle his way into my head and tangle up my thoughts until I'm not even sure what *I* want.

Now that I've stopped dancing like a wild witch on the solstice, I can see that I actually know a number of people here—former high school classmates or their younger siblings, and some people I've met at other parties, movie nights, or game nights. Looks like not everyone left the mountain for college and career. Not everyone worships at the altar of big cities and flashy jobs. Maybe I'm not such a weirdo after all.

"Hey, Daisy!" It's McKee, another parkour enthusiast who helps Jordan with some of her videos. I met her senior year of high school and we follow each other on TikTok. She and her girlfriend, Bek, have their arms wound across each other's shoulders.

"Hey, hotties!" I grin at them. "Did you see Jordan's latest video?"

"Yeah." McKee dismisses the video with a wave. "An easy day for her. But she got a lot of attention with it, thanks to somebody's way-too-sexy voice." She pokes my arm. "Bek and I must have watched it a hundred times, right, babe?"

Bek nods, smirking, and my face warms.

"Oh, that was... I just wanted to help out. Um, I'm gonna find the drinks. Be right back."

I move on, only to be captured by Ryden and Colton, two guys who were starting tenth grade when I graduated from high school. They had very obvious crushes on me back then. It was cute and a little annoying.

"Daisy!" Ryden's flushed face bears a smeary smile, and his hand flops onto my shoulder. He has clearly found alcohol somewhere and has overindulged already. "We're back from Clemson for the summer! Freshman year was just—just *awesome*. Oh my god, it's so good to see you. Thought I might never see you again after you graduated." His face crumples, and tears form in the corners of his eyes.

Colton winces and pulls him back. "Hey, Daisy. Sorry about him."

"It's okay." I pat Ryden's shoulder, and he looks heart-meltingly grateful, like he might drop to his knees and worship me. "Just don't drive home, Ry, okay? Promise?"

"He won't. I'm staying sober," Colton replies. "Besides, the guy who owns this place has like these watchdog servers everywhere, and if you take even one drink, you have to turn in your keys. They call a ride for you when you're ready to go and deliver your car to your house the next day, free of charge. It's fucking amazing. Hey, have you seen the VR room? The bowling alley? The pools? There's a lazy river, too. Like the ones at beach resorts."

Sounds like freaking Biltmore House. Who is this guy?

"I haven't had the tour yet," I tell them. "Hey, do you guys know anything about the owner? I mean, our families are well-off, right, but this is—"

"This is next-level, for sure," Colton answers. "I just know he's called Gatsby. They say his parents died when he was young, and he's got a rich guardian who gave him this huge trust fund."

"I heard he made his money off Bitcoin." Ry nods sagely.

"Bitcoin?" says a familiar voice behind me. Hands close over my bare shoulders, squeezing possessively. "No one makes this much money off Bitcoin. E-currencies are so over."

I shake Tom off and step beside Colton. I'm not interested in Colton or Ry, but they're sweet guys. I'd rather hang with them than with the bastard who cheated on me after a seven-year relationship.

"What are you doing here?" I ask Tom.

"Me?" He gives me a cruel smile. "I told you I'd figure out what your plans were for tonight. Anyway, it looks like everyone on the mountain is here. The place is tacky, don't you think? Too overblown for my taste."

"I like it." I tuck my arm into Colton's. "Let's go."

"You're here with him?" Tom's black brows sink lower over his eyes, a clear threat written in the rigid lines of his shoulders.

"They're showing me around," I say. "Come on, boys."

Open-mouthed, Colton and Ry move with me.

"Be good, Daisy." Tom's sneering voice follows me, itching in my ears even after we've left him far behind.

The guys and I stop for drinks first. Colton steers Ry away from the alcohol and convinces him that a cup of Diet Coke is actually a Cuba libre. Then we wander the first floor. The house has a couple of outflung wings, and along them are the recreational spaces—the bowling alley featuring six glossy lanes and a minibar, the movie theater stocked with plush chairs and a popcorn machine, a room with a ping-pong table, pool table, and board games, and a wide hallway lined with vintage arcade games and a Dance Dance Revolution station. At the end of one wing is the indoor pool, with a lazy river that flows through an archway and out into the gardens. There's even a hot tub, a booth where you can borrow swimsuits in any size, and locker rooms for showering and changing. It's a house designed to entertain people—lots of people.

"This is blowing my mind," Ry groans as the three of us sink into the hot tub together. My borrowed swimsuit is navy blue, and so are the guys' swim trunks. The heat of the tub bites into my flesh a little too sharply at first, but then it feels incredible. The tension of encountering Tom seeps away from my muscles, and I relax with a sigh.

"How long have these parties been going on?" I ask.

"Couple of weeks," says Colton. "It wasn't as crowded last time, but I think word is getting out that it's free and everything is fucking awesome."

"I'll bet the cleanup after an event like this is a nightmare." I close my eyes.

"I guess so," Colton replies. "I heard that Gatsby even lets people stay here overnight if they're too tired or drunk to get home."

"Really? Seems weird."

"Clearly you haven't been to many parties," Ry slurs. "There's always stragglers hanging around until the next morning."

I don't answer. Truth is, every time I started having some real fun at a college party, or drawing too much attention from a guy, Tom would insist we leave. I found out later that he'd go back to the parties by himself and keep the fun going, sometimes with other girls.

I thought his jealous streak was cute. I thought it meant he really loved me, like with an epic, powerful love, an alpha-male love. I thought it was hot.

Stupid of me.

"I've been to so many parties," Ry continues.

"You have not," Colton retorts. There's a splash and a jostle between the guys. "You've been to like three parties, dumbass."

"You're just as lame as me," Ry says indignantly.

"You're both lame." It's Tom's voice again, and my eyes pop open.

He stands above me, wearing borrowed swim trunks that show off his lean chest and stomach. He's leering down at my shiny, wet cleavage, which is barely visible above the surface.

I sink lower in the water. "Go away, Tom."

"It's a free country." He crouches beside me and slides into the hot tub.

"Come on, be cool, man," mutters Colton.

Tom fixes him with a hard look. "What's that?"

Cowed, Colton glances away and shrugs.

"Fine. Then I'll go." I lurch upward, springing out of the water, but Tom catches my leg and jerks me back down. My shin cracks against the underwater bench, and I bite my lip against the pain.

"I love it when you bite your lip like that," he whispers, his eyes on my mouth. His hand glides along my thigh under the surface, squeezing lightly. "You've gained a little weight, huh? Eating your feelings after the breakup? You should come to the gym with me sometime."

"Enough," I snap, climbing out of the hot tub. This time, when he tries to grab me, I kick him hard. I wasn't aiming for his throat, but I'm not sorry when my toes drive into his Adam's apple. He chokes a curse while I hurry away to the changing rooms.

There's an attendant at the door, and I point Tom out to him. "That guy was harassing me."

The man nods. "I'll have him removed from the premises. Mr. Gatsby doesn't allow that sort of thing."

In the locker room, I switch from the swimsuit back into my dress and toss my limp feathered headband in the trash. A stern-looking woman is cleaning up the soiled paper towels and empty soda cans littered across the floor. Feeling a little awkward—even after all these years, I'm not fully comfortable being waited on—I collect some of the garbage as well and place it into the bag she's using.

"Sorry you have to deal with this mess. People can be pretty inconsiderate, huh?" I smile at her.

She looks surprised, but she doesn't speak until I'm nearly out the door.

"Little tip," she calls to me. When I turn back, she says quietly, "Don't drink anything from the ones with the bracelets."

"Bracelets?"

"Thick metal bands." She points to her wrist. "Look for them, and don't drink what they give you."

"Um, okay." I hesitate, questions surging in my mind, but the woman clamps her lips together and moves into a stall, a clear signal that she's not open to further disclosure.

As I walk the hall, my gaze darts to the arms of the guests. There are bracelets of all kinds—braided twine, embellished leather, delicate gold, simple hair elastics strung in colorful rows.

And then I see an unusual one—a thick, smooth bracelet, maybe brushed titanium, on a girl's slim wrist. Probably a smart watch or something, though I don't see a screen. But who even cares?

And then I see another bracelet, identical to the first, this time on the arm of a burly dark-haired guy a handful of years older than me. He's got two girls draped on his shoulders, and they're all laughing hysterically as they sidle past me.

The matching bracelets freak me out a little, like maybe there's some underground-society shit going on here. But I'm not panicking. I've been to plenty of parties, and I know how to be careful. Besides, I have enough to worry about right now. I refuse to let paranoia ruin my fun.

Still, it wouldn't hurt to have backup I can trust, in case Tom shows up again. The staff guy said they would kick him out, but I don't know if they'll follow through, or if he'll stay gone. I have no idea where Jordan has wandered off to, but Nick might still be in the dance hall, so I head that way and look for him in the flickering purple dark, among the shifting shoulders and bending bodies. He's nowhere in sight, but the band is playing "Hallucinate" and I can't resist joining the dance again. Jordan used to make fun of me for liking Dua Lipa—too pop for her taste—but I don't care.

The music drives through me, racing faster and faster like a passionate heartbeat. The magic in the room is grittier now, the crowd all elbows and sweat and desperation, glory and grinding, fists raised and feet pounding painfully through heels, and none of us mind. Little pills shift from hand to hand through the crowd; a girl passes me one and the dilemma breaks my rhythm. The automatic, ingrained *no* resounds in my head, clashing with the beat. But I need something to take my mind off Tom—what's the harm, maybe it would feel good—so I nearly pop the pill in my mouth before it slips between my fingers and bounces away among all those rattling feet, and I smile because the choice was made for me and because I'm feeling pretty hyped up on nothing at all.

The song comes to an end, and with a brilliantly executed key change, the band brings up a jazzy version of "Gold Rush," from one of Taylor Swift's 2020 albums. There's an audible sigh of delight from throats all across the room because new music meant something more that year; it melted under your tongue and circled through your thoughts and softened the constant worrying.

I close my eyes and forget everything else except the side step, hip sway, delicate swirl of the lyrics, like a gold chain unspooling across the room—

My shoulder bumps someone, and I laugh an apology.

"No worries," a male voice responds, pitched low to be heard under the music. "Are you having a good time?"

"A great time," I answer. "I love this song."

"Well, who doesn't like a little Tay-Tay once in a while?"

I turn to look at the speaker, but he's in a dark spot of the room, where the ever-changing laser lights sweep past without touching him. He's tall and lean, I can tell that much. There's a lithe, buzzing energy about him, though he's barely swaying to the song.

"Not all guys will own up to liking her music," I say.

"I always own up to the things I like."

There's something familiar about him, like when you're watching an animated movie and you know you've heard the voice actor before, but you can't quite place them. "Have we met? Did you go to Blue Ridge High? I graduated from there about four years ago."

"No," he says. "I never went there."

"College, maybe? I went to UNC at Chapel Hill."

"I did my degree online."

"Oh," I say vaguely, because I just noticed the gleam of a thick metal bracelet on his wrist, and my warning sensors are lighting up. "So now that you've graduated, it's party time, huh?"

"Something like that." He's moving closer, and I ease backward, luring him into the path of the sweeping lights.

"I'm glad you came," he says.

A swath of violet light cuts across his face for one blinding, world-cracking second.

And then he's gone, vanished into the churning crowd.

"Wait," I whisper. And then, louder, "Wait!"

I'm paralyzed, turned to stone, while the dancers jostle and bump around me like boats caught in the current of the music.

4

IT WAS HIM. I'M SURE OF IT.

Actually, I'm not sure at all, because the light was weird and he didn't look like I remember and it doesn't make sense, because he was worse off than me, broken shoes and shaggy hair, thin as a light pole, and now—now he's got all this, and it's simply not possible.

Someone snags my elbow and I startle wildly, snapping around to face Jordan's surprised eyes. "Chill out! I'm just checking on you. You okay?"

She's trying to yell over the music. I can barely hear her, so I tow her to the edge of the room, through an arch and into a hallway. I'm looking for somewhere, anywhere—a quiet space.

"Daisy, you're scaring me. Did someone hurt you? Touch you? You show me who it was and I'll—" She clenches her fist, and her biceps bulge in her upper arm.

"Down, girl. Nobody hurt me." I push a half-open door and rush in, dragging her with me. For a second I lose my words, because the room is a library, full of floor-to-ceiling bookcases with an ornately carved rolling ladder for accessing the upper shelves. There's an immense free-standing globe, couches of shiny dark leather, and velvet tasseled pillows.

This luxury can't belong to the boy I used to know. There's no way.

I whirl on Jordan. "What do you know about the guy who hosts these parties?"

"Told you already. Nobody knows much about him. I heard he made his money selling drugs. He's some kind of genius chemist and he cooked up his own unique formula."

"And you believe that?"

Jordan shrugs. "Makes as much sense as anything else I've heard."

"Well, you're wrong," croaks a voice.

We both turn to see a dumpy little man flopped in an armchair to our right. He's completely relaxed and completely still, as if he ran out of energy and someone laid him there to recharge. He's the oldest person I've seen at this party—late fifties, maybe, with round black glasses much too big for his face.

"Do you know him?" I ask, desperate.

"Gatsby? No. But I heard he seduced a rich older widow and married her when he was only seventeen. She died a few months later and he inherited everything."

"Ew." I exchange disgusted glances with Jordan. "No way that's true. That wouldn't even be legal, would it?"

The little man shrugs and sucks a few swallows from a flask. His head rolls back against the chair.

Someone taps on the open door of the library. "Miss Jordan Baker?"

It's one of the ubiquitous staff members who have been quietly circulating through the house and grounds, providing drinks and taking keys. Since half the people at this party are under the legal drinking age, I'm surprised the entire event hasn't been shut down. Of course, not all the drinks here are alcoholic. I had one cocktail-looking thing, but I don't even feel a buzz. And maybe Gatsby has a monetary understanding with law enforcement. It happens, especially in areas like this where money can accomplish almost anything.

Jordan looks at the server curiously. "I'm Jordan Baker."

"If you would come with me, please."

"Why?"

"There's someone who would like to speak to you. Only to you," the man says pointedly as I move forward with Jordan.

"I can't let you wander off by yourself," I protest.

"I'll be fine. You go look for Nick." She shuts me down with a firm look as I start to object. "Seriously, Daisy. It's all good."

She follows the staff member out of the library. For a second I stare at the snoring little man in the chair, and then I peek out into the hallway. Jordan and the server are headed up a dimly lit stairway at the far end of the hall.

This party has been way more of a mindfuck than I expected, and even though I try to tell myself it's perfectly safe, I can't let Jordan disappear into the depths of this house, not after that woman's warning in the bathroom. Not after who I *thought* I saw on the dance floor. Not when there have been so many surprises tonight.

The best thing to do is to follow them and see what's up.

I trail behind them, keeping my distance so they won't notice. There are a couple of partyers right by the steps, huddling in a shrouded corner. The guy is pressed to the wall, head tilted and eyes closed, while the girl kisses his neck. A chunky silver bracelet shines on her wrist. Awkwardly, I move past them, up the stairs.

When I reach the top, I scan the hallway. The server or butler or whatever is ushering Jordan through a door. Once she's inside, he turns and walks in the opposite direction from me, probably toward another staircase.

Thick blood-red carpet deadens my steps. On the walls hang

dramatic abstract paintings, marbled, swirled, and textured in rich jewel tones. The wall lamps have shades of dark, faceted glass that don't yield nearly enough light. There's a definite horror movie vibe to this hall, and my stomach keeps tightening, twisting, like a warning. The air is thick with a heavy rose fragrance, like the potpourri my grandma keeps in her bathroom, only this scent has another layer, a metallic sharpness.

I sidle closer to the doorway where Jordan disappeared. I have zero qualms about eavesdropping, especially in this place full of questions and mysterious men who look like old friends.

The man downstairs resembled the Gatsby I knew—Jay Gatsby from Ashmore Valley in Easley. But the man downstairs didn't have the same thick southern drawl. He spoke crisply, and his face was more dramatic and defined. My Gatsby had wide brown eyes and cheeks like rosy peaches and all the sweet earnestness of fifteen. I loved that Gatsby—until I moved away and he never spoke to me again.

Maybe the two Gatsbys are related. They can't be the same person. And yet something about him was so very *my Gatsby*. If only the lighting had been better...less flashy and swervy...if only he'd come closer.

Jordan's voice, bright and strong, emanates from the doorway, and I pause, pressing myself to the wall. Not that standing against the wall will do me any good if someone happens to look out of the room—but it feels more covert.

"Happy to meet you," Jordan is saying. "My friends and I have heard a lot of things about you."

"Don't believe any of them." I can hear the smile in the male voice that answers her, and I almost gasp, because it sounds like him, the man from the dance floor. The maybe Gatsby. "Listen, you must think it strange for me to pull you aside like this."

"You in love with me or something?" Jordan laughs. "I've got my share of fans, and stalkers, and stalker fans."

He chuckles. "I'm not a stalker, though I am a fan. I follow you on TikTok, and I admire your fearlessness. But what you do is very dangerous. You could die anytime."

"There's risk, yes." Jordan's voice turns stiff, like it does whenever someone questions her choices. "But what I do is important to me. I'm good at it, I enjoy it, and it helps me feel alive."

"I get it, I really do. And that's why I want to offer you something. You see, I provide a kind of—insurance. Something to minimize the risk for you and the people you care about."

My shoulders sag with relief and disappointment. So he's just an insurance salesman. I had no idea insurance brokers could make so much money.

"Insurance, huh?" I can imagine Jordan crossing her arms. "You're not the first person to try to sell me life insurance. Forgive me if I don't want to spend my money on something that won't do me a lick of good once I'm dead."

"But that's just it." The man's voice is smooth and warm as rich leather. "This insurance takes care of you before death."

"Like health insurance? I've got that. And if you're trying to sell me something, let me stop you right there, okay? Let's not waste your time or mine. You throw a nice party, but I don't like salespeople."

"It won't cost you a thing," he replies. "You're Daisy's friend, right?"

My lungs tighten, and a thrill of shock pulses through my chest.

"Y-yes," says Jordan, slow and uncertain.

"I'd like to do this favor for you. For her sake."

For my sake? Is he really—

A cheerful, drunken holler from behind me draws my attention.

A cluster of the party guests are staggering along the hall, rejoicing in having made it all the way upstairs without collapsing. As the newcomers' noise increases, the door of the room where Jordan is swings shut with a decisive click.

I gnaw my lip, aching to know what the two of them are saying behind that door.

The drunken group passes me, and I notice that two of the women aren't just drunk—they're completely unconscious, being dragged along by the others. And the others are all wearing the same style of burnished metal bracelet.

Anxiety wads itself up in my stomach. I don't like to confront anyone, especially strangers. It makes me all trembly and tongue-tied. But given what I'm seeing, I don't have a choice. If I was one of those girls, being toted off to god knows where by god knows who, I'd want someone to speak up for me.

"Hey." I step forward. "What's going on?"

A bleary-eyed guy turns to face me, adjusting the limp arm of the girl he's hauling. He has shaggy blond hair, like some kind of hipster Thor. "Going to find them a place to rest."

My throat is dry with nerves, but I push through it. "And we're not touching anyone while they're unconscious, right?"

"Nah," he drawls. "Of course not."

"Hey." A girl in the group meets my eyes. Her moon-white skin practically glows in the shadowed hallway, and her scarlet dress plunges nearly to her navel. "They're my friends, and I'll keep an eye on things. Woman to woman. It's all good." She smiles, white teeth and red lips. "I'm Sloane."

"Daisy."

"Thanks for being so vigilant, Daisy." She's still smiling. "I'll let the girls know you were looking out for them."

And the group moves on, trickling into rooms farther down the hall.

Are those girls really okay? Did I do enough? Should I follow them?

No. Sloane gave me her name, which she probably wouldn't have done if she was trying to hide something. She looked me right in the eyes and said she's got it covered.

A tension headache is screwing slowly into the space behind my left eye, spiking the nausea in my stomach. I want to leave, and if I can't leave, I at least need some fresh air.

I have to find Nick.

Swimming through the crowd downstairs is harder now—the numbers at the party have swelled in the last hour. For thirty minutes or so I navigate the swarms and pods of people, throwing my best smiles right and left when people greet me, asking for Nick at every turn. I've been through every first-floor room and part of the grounds, and I can't find Nick or the guy he was with. He's not answering my texts.

Finally a text from Jordan pops up. Where are you?

I text her back. Rear entrance. Can't find Nick, looked everywhere downstairs. Can you check upstairs?

After more fruitless wandering and asking, Jordan and I meet behind the house. She keeps fidgeting with her bag, switching her weight from one foot to the other, plucking at the neckline of her dress. "Did you find Nick?" she asks.

"No, and it's nearly three. Do you think he's okay?"

"He probably just went off with someone."

"But he would have texted me."

"Really?" Jordan lifts her eyebrows. "He reports every romantic tryst to his cousin?"

"No, but—"

"It's fine. One of Gatsby's staff will call him a car when he's ready to go. Just text him that we're leaving, okay?"

My head is throbbing hard, and surges of nausea keep welling in my gut. I don't have the energy to argue with her. After texting Nick, I climb into Jordan's car and roll the window down, dragging in deep lungfuls of cool night air, beating back the sickness.

"You okay?" Jordan asks.

"Headache."

"But you had fun, right?"

"I did, until—"

"Yeah, sorry I got called away. I met Gatsby, though! He's hot and well spoken. And he told me things—god, Daisy, I can hardly believe it—but I can't tell you. He made me promise not to say a word to anyone. But it's life-changing, Daisy, honestly."

"Don't trust him," I say wearily. "We don't know anything about him."

"But he explained everything, and it makes so much sense. I really want to tell you. But I can't. I promised not to. Not yet..."

"Jordan." I can barely manage the word without gagging. "If you don't want me to throw up in your car, please let's just be quiet for a while. And drive slowly, for goodness' sake."

5

WHEN I WAKE UP, THE MEMORIES OF THE PARTY ARE A HAZY nightmare. Gatsby's face in the sweeping light of the dance hall. The unconscious girls being dragged along the second floor. The absence of Nick.

I fumble for my phone, but there are no messages from my cousin. And that scares me, with a jittery wretchedness that propels me right out of bed and into the first tank top and pair of shorts I can find. I scrape earrings off my dresser without even bothering to check if they match. I'm entering the kitchen before I realize that it's Saturday—the day my parents usually have brunch together before splitting up to do chores or hobbies.

My dad is flipping French toast on a griddle while Mom sips coffee and reads him memes and headlines from her Twitter feed. Her auburn hair is a match for my aunt Sarah's, but where Nick's mom has a wild mane, my mom's crisp bob is glassy smooth, even on a Saturday.

"You got in late last night," she says to me, with a half-smile. "But you don't seem hung over."

"I didn't drink much."

"That's my girl." My dad shakes the spatula at me so vigorously his glasses bounce on his nose. "That's what I like to hear. My daughter, being smart."

"Dad, I'm twenty-two. I can drink, and I do. I just...had other stuff on my mind last night."

My parents exchange a glance I know all too well. They're worried about me, which is why my mom prompted Nick to stage his little "reconnection intervention"—and now Nick is missing, and it feels like my fault.

"Join us for brunch?" Dad asks.

"Look, I'd love to, but I really need to find Nick."

"Didn't he go with you to the party?" My mother frowns.

"Yeah, we picked him up, but he didn't leave with us. We couldn't find him. I think he left with this guy..." My voice trails off as my mother rises, her dark eyes snapping.

"Daisy Faye Finnegan. Are you telling me you left your cousin at some stranger's house?"

"He's an adult, okay? And he was with someone," I protest. "We checked everywhere. Jordan and I both looked, and we texted—"

"I'll call your aunt Sarah and see if he showed up at home." She has her phone to her ear before I can say anything else.

Dad flips a couple slices of warm French toast onto a plate. "Eat up, sweetie." But he doesn't smile.

Their disappointment is a weight, bowing my shoulders. It's always like this with them—proud of me one second, pissed the next. I'm always getting close to their ideal, but never quite reaching it. I know they wish I'd had a higher GPA in college and graduated cum laude. That designation always looked and sounded kind of dirty to me, and I never really cared about it. All I cared about was getting through college so I could marry Tom, maybe travel the world with him—backpack through Europe and crap like that.

Tom was my whole plan. I should have known better. I mean, who makes her plans around a guy? Who calls herself a feminist and still does that shit? But I did, almost without realizing it.

I know my parents want me to have a plan for my life, now that college is checked off the list. But is it so wrong to just enjoy my summer without thinking about the next step? The whole cycle of "school, college, career, death" doesn't really do it for me. I'd rather meet interesting people, and travel, and try new things. But having the freedom and money to do all that is a privilege in itself, one I'll lose in a few months when my parents push me out of the nest. Might as well enjoy myself now.

I chew my French toast slowly, savoring the slide of melted butter and syrup over my tongue.

"Sarah says they haven't seen Nick." Mom sets her phone down.

So much for savoring my breakfast. "Okay. I'll head back to the party house to look for him."

"Your dad will drive you." Mom gives Dad a pointed stare.

"I'm not going to crash on the way over there," I protest. "It's not that far."

I stuff another bite of French toast into my mouth, set my dishes in the sink, and walk into the foyer to grab my bag. It's a soft, slouchy thing with a distressed texture, so scrapes and snags don't matter as much. I have, like, three dozen purses, but this one's my favorite because it's tough and it can hold everything, like Mary Poppins's carpet bag.

Mom comes into the foyer as I'm opening the front door. "I'm not comfortable with you going to a strange house alone."

I stare at her. "Mom. I've been on my own for a few years now. I think I can handle this."

"But you haven't really been on your own, have you?" She puckers her lips, glancing away. "You had Tom looking out for you."

"Right." My tone is dry as bones. "He did such a great job of that."

I know it's not fair, treating her like this. She only knows about the cheating, not all the other controlling, messed-up stuff Tom did. How could she know, when I avoid the topic every time she brings it up? But I can't talk to her, I can't, because I guess I'm still angry at her for letting me date him, for not seeing the signs and warning me. Wasn't she supposed to protect me from guys like him? And now I'm damaged inside, and I can't manage to heal, and I'm fucking pissed about it.

Obviously Mom and Dad aren't mind readers. Tom fooled them into believing he loved me as much as I loved him. They never realized how toxic he was. The closest my dad came to that awareness was my senior year of high school. Dad stopped me in our front doorway one afternoon right before I left with Tom, and he said, "That kid reminds me of someone I knew back in school."

"Okay," I replied, shrugging.

"I didn't like the guy," my dad said. "He couldn't see past his own reflection, if you know what I mean."

"I really don't," I said, and then I left with Tom.

Maybe I should have listened more closely to what Dad was trying to tell me. Might have saved me some heartbreak. Either way, it's not fair to put the blame on my mother. I was the one so deeply immersed in the relationship that I couldn't see how Tom had changed, and what he was doing to me.

Inhaling slowly to steady myself, I meet my mother's eyes. "It's fine, Mom. The guy who hosted the party is nice, okay? If it makes you feel better, I'll take Jordan with me." I have no intention of bothering Jordan at 10:00 a.m. on a Saturday, but my mom doesn't need to know that.

"Okay." She narrows her eyes. "Be careful. And stay in touch."

"I will."

My car is a Toyota Prius, a handful of years old. Dad refused to buy me anything too flashy or expensive because I'm a terrible driver. The Prius is my fifth car, and it already has a number of bumps and dings and scrapes. I've named most of them—Mailbox Crush, Post Problem, Fence-That-Shouldn't-Have-Been-There, Rainy-Day-Run-In, Acci-Dent.

I know roughly where the party house is, since it's so close to Nick's home. In a weird way, Nick and Gatsby are kind of neighbors despite the vast differences in their wealth, separately only by forested acreage and a rocky spur of the mountain.

I'm halfway to Gatsby's when my phone chimes. I'm so tempted to check it while driving, but for someone like me who can barely navigate mountain roads with my full attention intact, looking at a text would be disastrous. There's a gas station ahead—the one Nick stopped at the other day—so I turn in there and park.

The message is from Nick. Sorry I didn't text you. Weird stuff happened last night. Come over.

So he's okay—or at least, he's alive. I text back, On my way.

Some of the tension drains from me as I lean back in my seat. I don't have to panic-drive over there—I can take a moment to breathe.

Movement by the door of the gas station catches my eye. It's Myrtle, with her cloud of squiggly blond hair and her bubble-gum pink lips. She's leaning against the brick wall, and beside her stands a slender dark-haired man with cheekbones like knives. The sight of him stalls my pulse.

Tom's biceps bulge as he reaches up to light his cigarette. He flicks the lighter shut and slides it into the pocket of his deliciously snug jeans. My heart aches again at the beauty of him, at the memory of my hips pressed to his—the scent of pineapple and bergamot swirling in my nostrils. His lips on mine—mint and the faint after-taste of cigarette smoke. His fingers, laden with rings, dancing on the steering wheel to the music pounding from the speakers of his truck. Wind slapping my clothes as I rode behind him on his motorcycle.

And I remember him easing into me from behind, one hand planted on my spine, the way he liked it. "Say you belong to me," he'd pant, hips rocking against my rear, sending swirls of pleasure through my belly. Close, so close—

"I belong to you," I'd gasp. "Only to you."

"Mine," he'd groan. Sometimes he would smack my ass until it was red and sore, even though he knew I didn't like spanking. It made me feel weak and childish, made my own climax recede. I usually ended up frustrated and unsatisfied. But Tom said spanking me made him come harder, so I didn't protest much, because I loved him.

I loved him, and he broke me.

My car is half-tucked behind a big tractor-trailer, so Tom and Myrtle haven't noticed me. There's no one else parked on this side of the gas station, no one to witness the argument they're having. Either they're already back together, or Tom's trying to persuade her to come back—or he never actually broke up with her to begin with.

Myrtle steps forward, planting her hands on her hips. Her glossy white teeth are bared and snapping; her enormous candy-colored hoop earrings swing wildly with every sentence. I don't know what she's saying, but I recognize the hard lines of Tom's shoulders, the tension in his stance. He's approaching his limit, the place where he loses control. I used to be able to talk him down from those violent moments; I'd shift into my low, persuasive tones, as musical as I could make them, and I'd lure him away from that peak. It gave me a kind of thrill, knowing I could tame the beast, knowing he needed me. I had some romantic notion that my love empowered him to be a better person.

Absently I massage my own fingers, still sore from when he ground my knuckles together the other night.

Even when we were a couple, my powers of persuasion didn't always work. He hurt me several times, in small ways—twisting a pinch of my skin, squeezing my hand too hard, hustling me along a little too roughly. Maybe it was only a matter of time before it escalated.

Even as I think the words, Tom's free hand flashes. I hear the pop of his palm against Myrtle's cheek all the way inside my car, despite the windows being closed.

Then he looks around to see if anyone saw him hit her.

My first impulse is to hunker down so he doesn't notice me, so his anger doesn't refocus in my direction.

But I can't hide. That's not who I am. Or at least, it's not who I want to be.

I lunge out of the car and slam the door behind me as hard as I can. And I stare Tom down across the stretch of oil-stained pavement.

Myrtle is sobbing, clutching her face. I know he'll apologize to her in a few minutes—buy her a treat or a gift to make up for what he did. "You push my buttons, girl," he'll tell her. "You know exactly what to say to make me mad. It's a sign, you knowing me so well. A sign that we're meant to be together."

I should walk straight up to them and offer to call the police. I should offer to stand by her while she holds him accountable.

But I've pushed my courage to the max, and Nick is waiting for me. So I glare at Tom to let him know that I witnessed the slap.

A long moment passes, his eyes locked with mine, the ugly truth hanging in the air between us. Then he turns, without saying a word, and goes inside.

I take a few steps toward Myrtle. "Are you all right?"

"Fuck off," she snaps, and she pushes through the door into the gas station.

Sure. Fine. I can totally fuck off.

My fingers, my legs—hell, my entire insides are still trembling as I get in the car and drive away. I'm still shaking when I reach Nick's house. The Prius almost careens into the mailbox, but I manage to avoid it and park crookedly in the driveway.

Aunt Sarah is mowing the lawn in a cutoff T-shirt, her strong, tanned arms bared to the sun. She shuts down the mower and waves. "Nick's out back."

"Thanks." I skirt the house and head to the backyard.

As I walk, I breathe, and I refocus. I did what I could at that gas station—I faced Tom, maybe stopped him from doing worse to Myrtle. That was enough, for now. Tom and Myrtle aren't my immediate problem. I need to make sure Nick is really okay.

Their pool is small, and the concrete around it is spiderwebbed with thin cracks. The blue tile is faded and chipped. But what does it really matter? The water is the main thing. Nick is sprawled face down on an inflatable pool mat, trailing his fingers through the pool's limpid surface. His freckled back looks as if someone sprinkled him generously with cinnamon.

He turns his face toward me and grins, his sparkling blue eyes a match for the pool. I hope that cute face of his didn't get him into real trouble last night.

I kick off my sandals and swing my feet into the water. "You okay?"

"I am now."

"What happened to you last night?"

"To be honest, I'm not sure. I danced with someone named

Cody. Super hot. Said he went to USC. We danced a long time, and then we got drinks, and then we danced some more, until we weren't dancing so much as—" He clears his throat. "Grinding. It was... He was... Well, we found a place to make out, and had another drink... and I don't remember anything else after that."

"Oh my god." My stomach wrenches. "Did he...hurt you?"

"I don't think so. I'm not sore anywhere. There's no sign of anything, and trust me, I checked. Thoroughly. The only weird thing was a couple marks on my inner thigh. Two little dents, like I slept on something pointy. Which is possible. Anyway, when I woke up this morning, I was in one of the bedrooms in Gatsby's house. Second floor. The staff brought me this amazing breakfast—bacon, eggs, a yogurt parfait, fresh-squeezed orange juice, toast, the works. They barely talked to me except to tell me to eat up and drink a lot of liquids. When I was done, they called me a car and gave me a gift bag full of stuff—good stuff, like fancy cologne, Haus samplers, lotion and Summer Fridays lip balm and macarons."

"Did you see him? The Gatsby guy?" My heart quivers when I say his name—stupid freaking heart.

"Nope. Saw a few other party guests, though. A handful of girls, a couple more guys. They all seemed fine. They were squealing about the goodies in their gift bags. One woman said her dress got ripped the night before, and when she woke up, there was a new one hanging over the chair in her room. Similar style, her size and everything."

"Wow. So he's, like, super generous."

Nick slides off the pool mat without answering and swims underwater until he can tweak my foot. He resurfaces, water glittering in his auburn curls. "Either that, or he's the kind of guy who doesn't want trouble. With anyone."

I shiver. "Foreboding much?"

"Just keepin' it real." He plunges back into the water and does a lap before returning to me. "One more thing—there was another invitation from Gatsby in my bag."

"What? Why didn't you mention that earlier?" I kick water into his face.

"Yeah, apparently he's heading to Lake Keowee tomorrow, to take his boat out. He said I could come along, and bring someone. You wanna go?"

"Did he just invite you, or the others who stayed overnight as well?"

"I'm not sure."

"Well, I'm not letting you go alone, especially after the weirdness of last night. I'm surprised you're even considering it."

"I'm going because I want to meet him, and because I want to run into Cody again," says Nick simply. "And because I don't have a boat of my own. Come on, Daisy. It'll be fun. This whole Gatsby deal is the best thing that could possibly happen to us this summer. Lavish parties, hot guys, and a mystery to solve!"

His smile is infectious. "Fine, I'll go. But I'm bringing my pepper spray and my Taser just in case there are plans to ax-murder us and dump our bodies in the lake."

"Fair enough." He twirls in the pool. "You coming in?"

"No, I'm good. I didn't bring my suit, just rushed over here to check on you."

"Aww, so sweet."

I flick more water in his direction, and he dives.

I don't relish the idea of going out on a stranger's boat. But I desperately want the chance to meet this Gatsby face-to-face to find out if he's the Gatsby I knew, or is at least related to him. If they're related, maybe this Gatsby can tell me what happened to mine.

Although he won't be able to explain why Jay ghosted me after I moved away.

After we left our little apartment in Easley, I tried emailing, calling, and texting. Jay never responded, never reached out. His phone was a thirdhand gift from someone, and I considered the possibility that it died. I handwrote him two snail-mail letters, just in case.

No response.

I was only fourteen. I didn't know what love was back then. I'm honestly not sure I've got a handle on it now. All I knew was that one of my best friends had dropped out of my life with the suddenness of a snapped rubber band. It pissed me off, and underneath the anger was an aching hollow in the shape of him.

When I started out at Blue Ridge High, I went from tentatively optimistic to startlingly popular. It helped that Jordan immediately scooped me into her group, and that the sardonic and sexy Tom Buchanan started lounging by my locker every day, waiting for me. He gave me an Elsa Peretti open-heart necklace from Tiffany, and I felt like a princess opening that pale-blue box. I couldn't believe it. I wore that necklace every day.

I also wore a cheap little charm bracelet from Claire's, the one Jay gave me before we moved.

But eventually, I put the charm bracelet away. I don't remember exactly when—sometime between my first date with Tom and the day he picked me up in the high school parking lot and carried me over a puddle of ice and slush so my shoes wouldn't get soaked.

Tom could be so painfully, deceptively sweet.

Until he wasn't.

And Jay? I've put him away, like the charm bracelet, in a closed drawer of my life.

6

WE'RE NEARLY TO LAKE KEOWEE, AND I CAN HARDLY SIT still. I peer at my reflection in the black glass of my phone screen. "Do I look okay? Do I have anything in my teeth? Any mascara flecks under my eyes?"

"For the fifth time, no," Nick snaps. "God, Daisy. What's up with you?"

"Nothing."

"You want to impress this guy 'cause he's rich? I thought you were better than that."

"I am." I stuff the phone back into the little crossbody bag I brought. I wore my silky blue halter top and white shorts today, but now I'm second-guessing my choice. Is the color scheme too nautical, too on the nose? Is the shirt too revealing? I mean, my shoulders and half my back are bare. Am I wearing too much makeup for a day on the lake? I desperately want to ask Nick all those questions, but the set of his jaw tells me we're done talking about my appearance. After all, he's nervous too, hoping to see the pretty boy he made out with at the party.

"Come on," he growls, throwing the car into Park and cutting the engine.

As we jump out onto chunky gravel, a soft breeze from the lake grazes my arms. It's overcast today, the sky swathed in dull gray. I can barely see the glimmer of water through the belt of trees separating the lake from the parking lot. The air smells of spicy pine and sweet honeysuckle, of lake water and mulch.

My stomach is doing its best imitation of a panicked fish.

As Nick and I walk the path down to the dock, two dots of rain hit my cheek. And then a few more drops splash on my arm and my shoulder.

Nick swears. "Figures it would rain."

"Maybe it will just sprinkle, and then stop." I glance around for potential places to take cover. There's a picnic shelter not far away, but it looks as if it's been reserved for a wedding or something; it's decked out with lights and greenery, and there are a couple of people dressing the tables in heavy white cloths and huge vases of flowers.

We step out of the trees into the open space around the dock. The boat, a sleek ivory thing with a name I can't make out, bobs at the end of it. Two guys are standing on the boards, side by side, motionless and waiting. But before I can get a good look at them, the sky releases a deluge over us all—sheets of shimmering rain soaking me to the skin in a handful of seconds.

I squeal, and Nick shouts. The two men on the dock race toward us through the downpour, their feet thumping on the boards, heads bent against the rain. One is Cody, the black-haired man who danced with Nick—and the other...

He looks up, the rain a flickering veil between us.

The other is Jay Gatsby.

He stops a few feet away from me and just stands there, his hands clenched and his shoulders rigid.

It's him. I can see it now. Unmistakably, impossibly him.

His rain-slicked face has crisper lines, and his cheeks are taut instead of rounded. The raindrops bead on his arched upper lip and dribble down the full lower lip, before racing off the edge of his jaw.

Why am I staring at his mouth?

His eyes are the same—golden-brown and full of eager light. His hair curls in messy brown waves, rapidly darkening in the rain. He lifts a shaking hand to sweep the locks back from his forehead.

"You," I breathe.

"Me." He doesn't smile. Doesn't move. Nick and Cody have gone somewhere—or ceased to exist. Who cares?

I want to scream at him for so many things. I want to smack him, and shake him, and kiss him.

But I'm frozen, locked inside my body. There's a cosmic disconnect between my emotions and my reactions; I'm on autopilot now. I hear myself saying primly, "We should get out of the rain."

"There." Gatsby points to the decorated pavilion. "I had it reserved for us. I thought we could have lunch there before going out on the lake."

"A nice idea," says autopilot Daisy.

As we run toward the shelter, my brain spits out random thoughts—like how glad I am that my mascara is waterproof. How my sandals squelch with every step. How the rain on the surface of the lake looks like peppered glass.

We stumble into the shelter. Nick and Cody are already laughing, cracking open a bottle of something bubbly. Nick side-eyes me, clearly curious about the weirdness between me and Gatsby. He knew about my friend Jay back in Easley, but I don't think I ever told him Jay's last name.

A heavy odor of gardenias and roses infuses the air in our pocket of dry space under the pavilion, between the falling curtains of rain. Under glass domes are trays of gourmet cupcakes, platters of neatly sliced fruit, shrimp on ice, and tiny white sandwiches with layers of pink or yellow inside them.

Guys don't lay out a spread like this when they're taking their bros out on the boat.

I walk straight to Nick and grip the collar of his T-shirt. "Excuse me," I say to Cody with a dazzling smile. "I'm going to borrow Nick for a moment."

"Excuse you is right," Nick complains as I hustle him into a corner.

"Did Gatsby's note ask you to invite me?" I whisper fiercely. "Me, specifically?"

Nick winces. "*Maybe.*"

"You traitor. You didn't tell me!"

"He said he was an old friend of yours. I figured you'd want to see him, that it would be a nice surprise. Ow, Daisy!"

"A kick in the shins is less punishment than you deserve." I let go of his shirt. "I'll be back soon. Or never."

And I walk straight out of the pavilion into the rain. Well, I walk for a few steps, and then I break into a run, matching my frantic steps to the scattered beat of my heart.

I knew it was going to be awkward if the mysterious Gatsby turned out to be Jay himself, but I didn't expect this—the dramatic decorations, the fancy five-star lunch. He's telling me something he has no right to, not now, not after he dropped out of my life for eight years.

My sandals are drenched and sloshy, my clothes are thin wet rags, and my carefully styled hair is a wilderness of rivulets and tangles. I blink water out of my eyes and crash palms-first into a big tree, a magnolia whose waxy leaves shed rain as well as any umbrella.

Pressing my forehead to the corrugated trunk, I breathe. Rain whispers around me, and in the dreamlike quiet I could almost imagine the past few minutes were an illusion, equal parts delightful and distressing.

"I'm sorry, Daisy." Gatsby's voice comes from behind me. "I did this all wrong."

I speak without turning around. It's easier to talk when I'm not looking into those beautiful brown eyes. "What, exactly, did you do wrong?"

"I didn't stay in touch."

"You ghosted me, Jay. We were best friends. We were—" I can't say what we were, because there's no word for it in this language—maybe not in any language.

"I know. I'm sorry. My mom was arrested not long after you left, and I ran away rather than go into foster care. Things were really uncertain for a while." He says it so matter-of-factly, but my heart lurches with pain at the idea of him alone, with nothing and no one. I can't bear the thought that he went through that, and I didn't know, couldn't help him.

"You couldn't have emailed me from a library or something? Borrowed someone's phone for a quick call?" My voice is harsher than I intended, and I grind my lip between my teeth.

"I could have," he says quietly. "I chose not to."

"Because you were angry with me."

"Because I didn't want you to think of me as the impoverished runaway, the homeless boy with nothing. You would have pitied me, and I couldn't stand that."

"So it was a pride thing."

His voice comes nearer. "No. Maybe? Please try to understand. I didn't want to meet you again until I had something to offer you, until I'd made something of myself."

I whirl around. "You're barely a month over twenty-four, Jay. No one expects you to make anything of yourself yet."

He smiles, and my heart does the jitterbug for a second. His smile is devastating, dangerous.

"You remember my birthday," he says.

"Of course I do," I hiss at him.

And he repeats softly, "Of course you do."

Something inside me is breaking up, melting like ice under the gentle insistence of a warm rain.

"Can you forgive me, Daisy?" A flood of honest regret pours from his eyes into mine, trickling into my heart.

I suck in a shaking breath. "You'll have to work for it."

Jay's smile reappears, infused with hope. "Glad to."

The awkwardness of a thousand missed days hangs between us. We used to talk about everything—school assignments, music, politics, video games, books, random ridiculousness—and now I can't think of anything to say. The air around him smells and tastes different. He's not a short, skinny middle-grade boy anymore, with Juicy Fruit gum on his breath and the sharp artificial ocean smell of Walmart deodorant hovering under his ratty T-shirts. Now he's a shockingly tall stranger of twenty-four, and his dress shirt is slicked to his chest, and the faint scent of cloves and basil wafts from his skin—some decadent, unfamiliar cologne.

When did he get so close to me?

And why do I suddenly want him even closer?

The craving that digs its claws into my chest shocks me, as does the delicate flutter that spreads low through my body, my *clit*. For a second, I panic at my body's instant, instinctual response. We never got this far before, Jay and I—we were too young—and this feels strange and heady and uncontrolled, like being a virgin all over again. It's scary, and it's fucking amazing.

Eyes dropping to my mouth, tension mounting steadily between us, he steps even *closer*.

Experimentally I inhale his scent again, and feel the answering throb between my legs. It's hauntingly familiar and wildly different at the same time, like he's summoning a part of me he's never called to before. Great...just when I need a clear head, my freaking libido has to get involved.

I can't yield to this urge, not when Jay and I just encountered each other again. I can't go from "how have you been" to "pin me against this damn tree and fuck me until I scream your name" in the space of an hour, even if I desperately want to.

I shrink back a little, my fingertips brushing the bark of the magnolia.

"I'm hungry," I say in my soft, persuasive voice. "We should go get some food. Are you hungry?"

His eyes glaze over a little, and he leans nearer. "Yes, I'm hungry." His voice has gone vague and distant, and his upper lip hitches slightly. Were his canines always that distinctive? They give him a feral look.

He's coming even closer. Oh crap, is he going to *kiss* me?

If he kisses me, I'm going to kiss him back, and I won't be able to hide how much I want him.

"Jay!" I snap my fingers in front of his face.

He blinks. "Yeah?"

"Come on." I slip past him, beyond the magnetic pull of his body in an attempt to wrestle back control. "Let's head back to the shelter and eat."

He frowns, as if he's a little confused, but a second later he's back to himself—already on board with my plan, as coolly casual as if he hadn't been begging my forgiveness and almost kissing me just seconds before. His long legs take such big strides that I have to half jog to keep up. He hails the other two guys eagerly, a broad smile on his face. "Let's eat, lads!"

"Lads?" I giggle, settling back into familiar grooves. This Jay I know how to handle. "What, are you British now?"

"He's not," says Cody in a crisp accent. "But I am."

Nick grins at me with such obvious triumph and delight that I have to laugh. He has always loved British accents. To find a guy as hot as Cody with a sexy accent, too... It's like Nick's own personal kryptonite.

"So, you two are friends?" I gesture from Cody to Jay. When they exchange a glance full of secrets, my stomach clenches.

"I was Jay's temporary guardian until he turned eighteen," says Cody. "And we share the house."

"Cody's like a mentor to me," says Jay.

Mentor? Cody only looks maybe a year or two older, and not necessarily any wiser, but sure. Why not? As if that's not strange enough, both Jay and Cody are wearing the thick bracelets the cleaning lady warned me about.

I'm sure it's nothing sinister. The bracelets are probably just some fitness band or smart device I haven't heard about yet. Still, it's enough to kick me into caution mode again. Jay is an old friend, but we haven't been close in a very long time. I need to remember that.

"Nick, did you get a chance to ask Cody about that thing the other night?" I raise my eyebrows significantly at him. *You know that thing where Cody maybe drugged you?*

"It's fine, Daisy." Nick gives me a pointed stare. "I must have picked up someone else's drink. Or had more cocktails than I realized. Cody took care of me that night, made sure I got safely into a quiet room."

Cody's mouth curls at the corner, and the look he shoots me is both a challenge and a question. *Are you going to push this, or let it go?*

"Let's not have drama," Jay says cheerfully. "Have a sandwich instead." He's reaching for one when his phone trills a series of notes. "Excuse me. Work." He stalks away to the edge of the shelter to take the call.

Work, huh? What kind of work does a twenty-four-year-old rich guy do? And how *did* he get so rich, so fast, anyway? My ears strain to catch his half of the conversation, though I pretend to be listening to Cody and Nick banter about sandwiches.

Snatches of Jay's voice filter to my ears under the thrumming of the rain. He's speaking in a low, intense tone. "He has to pay. He doesn't get special treatment because of that." He listens for a moment, then says, more harshly, "If he doesn't pay, he doesn't get it. Money first, in full. He's got to have faith in the process. That's all I'm asking for. A little faith, and the full sum up front. Make sure he understands—" Another pause. "He can threaten all he wants. You think anyone will believe him? Tell him if he keeps this up, the deal's off. I'm starting to think I don't want his money. Who needs him around for that long, anyway? No, I can't right now. I said I can't, Cheadle. You handle it."

What the hell is Gatsby involved in? I really hope he's not a drug dealer. Maybe a hacker? He was always decent with computers—he used to collect other people's cast-off tech and get it working again, or sell the bits of precious metal from the insides. For a while, that money was all he and his mom had to live on. His other skill was chemistry. He and my dad used to mess around with chemicals on an old workbench in the back corner of the apartment complex parking lot. I joined them sometimes, but whenever I tried to help, things tended to explode, so I usually ended up riding my bike while they experimented.

If Jay is a hacker or some kind of genius rogue chemist, I can live with that. Drug dealing, counterfeiting, human trafficking, or weapons dealing—nope. Honestly, the drug thing is most likely. How else could a guy his age make this much money in less than a decade? But Jay always swore he would never drink or do drugs. Not after what substance abuse did to his family. I don't want to imagine him dealing that stuff to other people. I don't want whatever he's been doing to ruin my image of him, my memory of what we had.

Jay finishes with his call and strides into my peripheral vision, and though I can feel him looking at me, I don't turn. I'm still watching Nick, with a smile fixed on my face, while Cody feeds him a bite of egg salad sandwich. I used to love egg salad. Haven't had it in ages. I wonder if Jay ordered egg salad sandwiches for this picnic because he remembers I like them.

As if he can read my mind, Jay sets a sandwich on a plate and offers it to me. The plates are fine china, white and wafer-thin, with gold tracery along the edges. Totally wrong for a lakeside lunch.

"The egg salad isn't quite right," he says, taking a sandwich for himself as well. "I had several chefs make it, and I tested the batches. This one's as close to your grandma's recipe as I could find."

The thoughtfulness of it, the time it must have taken... I look up into his face, struggling for words. His skin is so much clearer than it used to be. He used to have terrible acne along his temples and between his eyebrows. He scratched, so some of the pimples left scars, tiny pockmarks. I couldn't have cared less because the glow inside him was the important thing. But I can't help noticing that his skin is absolutely flawless now, and nearly poreless. I've got to find out what skin-care regimen he uses.

"What?" he asks. "Do I have something on my face?" He bats at his cheek, nearly drops the plate, and does a swervy juggling thing to keep it balanced. "Sorry. Um—sandwich?"

I rescue the plate from him. "This is weird, right? I mean we used to talk all the time, and now...it's strange. I'm a little nervous around you."

He lifts his eyebrows. "You? *You're* nervous?"

"Very. In fact, I'm a little jealous of those two." I nod at Cody and Nick, who are pelting each other with bits of crust and laughing like idiots. "They make it look so easy."

"They do seem to be getting along well. But"—Jay's voice lowers—"you should tell Nick that Cody is distractable. He doesn't stick with one person for long. I wouldn't want to see Nick hurt."

"I think they're just having fun." I savor a bite of the sandwich. "Oh my gosh, this is amazing."

"Yeah?" He grins, brilliant and joyful.

"It's absolute perfection." I take another bite, and he does the same. For a second we chew companionably, and then our eyes meet and we both chuckle, dissolving a little more of the tension.

"So tell me, what do you do?" I steal another sandwich. "For work, I mean? All this—the money, the house, is it Cody's? He said he's your guardian, right? Or he was until you turned eighteen?"

"Yes, but all this technically belongs to me. Cody lives here for now, but he has his own house in Knoxville."

I hold his gaze, lifting one of my eyebrows slightly to remind him that he didn't answer my other question.

"As for work... Well, Cody gave me some money to help me get started, and I invested it well. That's all there is to it."

"Is it drugs?" I have to know.

He recoils as if I slapped him. "If that's what you think, you don't know me at all."

"I didn't think you would do that, not after..." I let my sentence trail off. "But I had to ask. You must know how it looks—so much money, and you're only twenty-four."

"It looks like I'm a rich guy enjoying himself. Just like everyone else in your life now." He cracks the caps off two glass bottles of sparkling water and holds one out to me. "A toast. To the unexpected."

The clink of the glass rings through me like a bell, and the bubbles fizz inside me long after the sip. Or maybe the fizz is just me feeling unsettled, uncertain how I should respond to the enormity of the gesture he's made by moving here, buying this house to be near me. Arranging this outing, this lunch, for me.

He's so smooth now, so studied and controlled in his manners and movements. Even soaked with the rain, he looks handsome and elegant, with drops beading in his hair and a wet gleam along his cheekbones and the line of his neck.

Eight years, and he feels so different. So far away from the friend I loved.

I want to shake him out of this carefully constructed new self and rile him up a little. But before I can think how to do that, a shaft of rose-gold sunlight bedazzles the air between us. Outside the pavilion, the clouds are breaking into fragments.

"Let's take some food and go out on the boat for a while," says Jay. "Before it gets too bright."

"It's already too bright for me," complains Cody. He takes out a pair of sunglasses and recoils from the incoming shafts of light as if they're lasers.

"You could use some vitamin D, precious." Nick catches Cody's hand and tows him into the sunlight. Cody winces, but he doesn't protest.

"Just for a little while," Jay assures him.

With sandwiches, chips, and wine in hand, we climb onto the boat. I can't imagine better weather—delicate veils of sunlight sifting through clouds, jeweling the lake's surface. The rain washed away some of the humidity, and the air has a fresh, clean scent that makes me want to inhale it right down to my toes. Cody steers the boat, picking up speed until the sheer pleasure of wind rushing over my skin makes me laugh out loud.

Jay stands beside me and points across the water. "See that house over there? It's owned by a client of mine. She and her wife have Jet Skis, and they told me I can borrow them whenever. We can try them out sometime if you want. Or I can buy a couple." His hand curls around the railing so tightly his knuckles whiten. "Have you ever water-skied? I tried that about a year ago. Not as fun as it sounds, but if you want to give it a shot, I can make it happen."

He still talks a lot when he's nervous. I remember long streams of conversation uncoiling from him after nasty incidents with his parents or trouble at school. I would sit and listen, patting his hand until he was done and could breathe again. We have years of long conversations woven between us. Followed by eight years of silence. But he still chatters like he did then, and a tremulous delight wakes in my heart, because I still *know* him.

I slip my hand over his, my fingers finding the notches between his knuckles and settling there. Jay stares at our hands, a flush coloring his cheeks.

Feeling self-conscious, I pull my hand back and start messing with my bracelet instead.

"You don't have to bribe me with Jet Skis," I tell him. "I'm happy to see you. And I'd like to spend time with you."

"I'm having another party this weekend," he offers. "A Met Gala theme. Dramatic costumes encouraged."

"You don't strike me as the dramatic-costume type."

"It was Cody's idea."

"Why doesn't that surprise me?" I glance back at Cody, who's currently gaping at Nick, who has taken his shirt off for no apparent reason.

"If you come to the party, I can show you around my house," Jay says eagerly.

"Fine, twist my arm." I nudge his elbow with mine. "I'll see if Jordan wants to come, too."

"If she's feeling up to it," he says, and then bites his lip and turns away as if he's said something he shouldn't.

His discomfort unsettles me, and I pluck nervously at the clasp of my bracelet. "Why wouldn't she feel up to it? Is she sick?"

"Not yet, but she might be soon. You know, big parties, lots of germs...circulating...um..."

"Shit!" I exclaim as the bracelet finally gives way to my fiddling, snaps open, and drops from my wrist.

"I'll get it!" Jay sounds almost excited, or relieved. He shucks off his shirt, hoists himself over the railing, and plunges into the lake.

I squeal in shock, and Cody halts the boat.

"Jay Gatsby, you idiot!" I yell at the rippling surface.

Pretty sure this isn't just about the bracelet. Something I said made him so uncomfortable he'd rather jump into a lake than stay on the boat another second. I'm tempted to try to figure out what it was, but I'm distracted because the ripples are fading, the water going still where it closed over Jay's head.

A long minute passes. Then another.

"Maybe he hit his head." I glance back at Nick and Cody. "Should one of us go in after him?"

"He's fine," Cody says carelessly.

Another minute passes.

Nick is looking very worried, but Cody only seems concerned about tucking every part of himself under the scant awning, the only scrap of shade on the boat. I guess I'll have to do the honors. I'm not about to lose my best friend right after getting him back.

Frantically I strip my sandals off, swing my legs over the railing, and launch myself into the water.

The surface shatters under me, then wraps itself over my head, burying me in lake water much deeper and murkier than I expected. I can't see Jay anywhere, not with the cloudy detritus stinging my eyes. He's been under for three minutes. How could he hold his breath that long? What if he drowns down here while I'm muddling through the dark?

Fingers dance up my spine, and I jerk, releasing a flood of bubbles. Jay grabs my wrist and tows me up until we break the surface. He's laughing so hard he can barely breathe.

"Jerk." I shove his head underwater briefly. "You scared me, you dork."

"Success!" He raises a wet fist, grinning. The bracelet gleams in his hand.

The crinkle at the corners of his eyes, the width of his smile— they're heartbreakingly familiar, warming every inch of me.

This is the Jay I remember. Less polished, more reckless.

"You absolute idiot." I shake my head, moving closer, my hair trailing through the lake behind me.

"I know, I'm the worst," he says, softer now. His leg brushes mine as we tread water.

I extend my wrist so he can quickly clasp the bracelet into place. "Thanks," I murmur, but more words weigh on my heart, hover on my tongue.

The boat has drifted away a bit, and I'm not mad about the semi-privacy. It gives me the chance I need to say what's on my mind.

"You should have called me." I keep treading water, letting each slow sweep of my arms narrow the distance between us. "Sometime in the last eight years, you should have called."

"I know." His breath is warm on my upturned face. "I'm sorry."

"I missed you, dummy."

"I thought of you every day, Daisy." His hand brushes my waist as we float together in the chilly lake, legs sliding against each other beneath the water. "Every damn day."

Droplets glitter in his lashes, on his shoulders, and across his collarbones. I always thought he was cute, but he's goddamn glorious now.

Jay runs his tongue over his lips, clearing the drops of lake water, and I inhale sharply. Just a small hitch of breath, but he notices. A seductive heat pools in his eyes.

I shouldn't encourage this.

I *want* to.

"You look so different." I let myself drift against the length of his body and shiver at the heat that unfurls low in my gut. How does he keep doing this to me?

"And you." His gaze drops to my wet halter top, which clings to every curve of my breasts. My nipples go tight.

A burst of laughter from the boat startles me, briefly pulling us apart. Clearly Nick and Cody have moved past worrying about us and are engrossed in each other again.

With a tight sigh, Jay pulls his focus back up to my face. He's trying so hard to be good...which makes me very much want to be bad. If Nick can find a boy to have fun with, no second thoughts, no doubts, then why can't I? Even if that boy is Jay Gatsby, he's also a beautiful stranger, and the combination of those two things is messing with my head, making me want to take risks.

To be wild.

"You can look," I murmur, moving my arms through the water to propel myself a little nearer again. "And you can...touch, if you want."

His eyes widen.

But he doesn't hesitate, as if he's been waiting years for permission.

I feel his palm at my waist first, sliding up to my ribs. Pausing under my arm, his thumb stroking the side of my breast. And then shifting over, until his hand is entirely covering my breast. Strong fingers splayed, the thumb stroking over my nipple again and again. He knows what he's doing. *Fuck*.

Jay bends toward me, angling his head a little. His breath whispers into my parted mouth. My entire self is waking up, coming online, and the power source is the steady glow of Jay's eyes on mine. Eyes like sun-warmed earth, like pinecones in a spice-scented evergreen forest. I want to crawl into those eyes and curl up, safe.

I need to keep treading water, but I also need to touch him. I need to feel his new skin, this grown-up body of his.

Tentative, I reach through the water until my palm presses flat against his chest. He huffs out a breath, soft against my lips, almost kissing me but not quite. Not yet.

Alarms are ringing in the back of my mind—questions that need answers, warnings that I'm moving too fast with him, that I don't fully understand who he is now, or why he's here. I ignore them for a few more seconds while my fingers slide over the contours of his pectorals. They are, in a word, magnificent. Someone's been working out.

What else has he been doing?

What am *I* doing? This isn't just some hot boy I met at a party. This is Jay.

Cody shouts from the boat. "Can we go? The sun's getting very intense."

"Sure, man," Jay answers, eyes never leaving me. "One second."

He's staring hungrily at my mouth. He's going to kiss me. And if I don't find a way to break this delicious tension soon, I'm going to let him.

"You sell insurance," I blurt out.

He blinks, startled, eyes meeting mine again. The moment effectively broken. "What?"

"You were trying to sell Jordan some kind of insurance."

Caution creeps into his eyes. "She told you about it?"

"No, I–I overheard a little of your conversation. And then I got distracted by something else. She wouldn't tell me the rest. But I think you should know that if you swindle her somehow, this"—I gesture between us—"will be over. Like that." I snap my fingers. I feel more in control again, less overwhelmed. The heat's still there, but it's receding. I made the right call to reroute things before they could go too far.

"Understood," Jay says, following my cues. There's distance between us again. "Trust me, I have Jordan's best interests at heart. She knows all the fine print, and she'll be completely satisfied with the results."

"But what exactly is involved with this insurance of yours?"

"It's a private policy. I promise I'll explain it one day, but not now, not here. We need to get Cody back in the shade, and honestly, I could use some shade myself."

While he swims back to the boat, I peer up at the sky. The sun feels good. Not oppressive at all. So why are these two so eager to escape it?

1

JAY AND I EXCHANGE NUMBERS BEFORE WE PART WAYS. IT'S AN awkward, tentative transaction, nothing like the goodbye between Nick and Cody, in which Cody buries his face in the curve of Nick's neck and inhales, as if he wants to draw my cousin's whole being into himself. It's awkwardly hot to watch. Cody whispers something into Nick's ear, and Jay's mouth twitches as he types his number into my phone.

"What is it?" I ask.

"I guess I'll be having your cousin as a houseguest tonight. Cody just invited him over."

"How did you hear that from way over here? You must have really good ears."

"You could say that." His gaze flicks up to mine and there's something sharp and dark in it, a thorn prodding my consciousness, a mental nudge from him to me. As if he is willing me to figure something out.

"What about the lunch stuff?" I nod toward the pavilion.

"I have people to clean that up. Don't worry about it." He hands back my phone. "Hopefully during our next get-together you won't be quite so wet. Um...your clothes, I mean. With the rain, and the lake." He stuffs his hands into the pockets of his pants. "Have a good afternoon." And he walks away, his shoulders stiff. After a few steps he kicks a pebble abruptly, a wordless swear, and I smile.

Curled on the couch that night, rewatching *Sherlock* with my parents, I break the news.

"So...Jay moved here."

"Hmm?" says Mom absently, playing with my hair.

"Jay Gatsby. Remember? My best friend Jay, from back in Easley."

Dad pauses the episode. "Of course we remember Jay. Great kid. I always felt bad about splitting you two apart when we left."

"That poor boy," says Mom. "He had it so rough. I hope we made his life a little better, though. Gosh, he was like part of the family. How's he doing, sweetie?"

"So much better. He has a new guardian, or he did until he turned eighteen. He's got a big house now and lots of money."

"A real Orphan Annie story, huh?" says my dad.

"Dad. Seriously. You need to watch something released in this decade."

"Annie's a classic," he says. "And I love the new version as well as the original, so lay off the old-dad thing. I've got little enough time for TV. Don't want to risk it on something I might not like."

"So you just keep watching the same old stuff over and over, to infinity."

"*And beyond*," he says dramatically.

I roll my eyes, but I can't help chuckling.

"Is that where you were today? With Jay?" Mom asks.

"And Nick, and another friend. I'm going to Jay's house this weekend, too. He's having a party."

My parents exchange glances of suppressed delight.

"That's wonderful, sweetie," says Mom. "You're getting out, making friends. This is good. This is really, really good. Isn't it great, Liam?"

"It's great," Dad echoes.

It's almost like they're high-fiving each other with words. *Look, Daisy is recovering! We're such great parents.*

Thing is, they really are. Sure, we've had our issues, but I never went through a phase where I truly hated them. Back in high school, my friends thought my parents were the coolest because they didn't ever forbid me from drinking. Instead, they taught me restraint. And since I honestly hate the taste of every kind of alcohol I've ever tried, it's not hard to keep myself in check.

Sure, I like the warm, buzzy feeling at the start, but I don't like teetering around, grasping for balance and having to think hard to form my words correctly. That loss of control, that vulnerability scares me, right down to the pit of my stomach.

Maybe I have trust issues.

Maybe they started when Tom cheated on me, or when my so-called friends kept his secret for months. Or maybe they began earlier, when a certain best friend said he would stay in touch and then cut me out of his life.

Maybe I haven't quite forgiven him.

The next morning, I text Jordan about the party, and she texts back a bunch of skull and vomit emojis.

Okay, I get it. I text back. Met Gala party, not your thing. Geez.

Her response pops up. Party = yes. If I'm feeling better by Saturday.

You okay?

Sick. So sick.

Can I bring you something? Soup, tissues, electrolysis? Dang it, stupid autocorrect. I mean electrolytes?

I've got everything I need. Just gotta ride it out. Ttyl.
  Sleep now.

I toss my phone on the bed and lie back, staring at the ceiling fan as I do.

How did Jay know Jordan was sick, or that she *would be* sick? Did he and Jordan...do something? Like, together? That would go against every signal he sent me at the lake, but I can't be sure of anyone or anything. Not anymore. People can't be trusted—not even people like Jay Gatsby.

To distract myself, I spend a couple hours browsing photos of celebrity outfits worn at the Met Gala, the annual fundraiser for the Metropolitan Museum of Art in NYC. My eyes pop when I discover that tables go for around $300,000 at the benefit. What the actual hell? My family might be in the high middle or upper class now—not sure where the line falls—but we're nowhere near that rich. The gowns and ensembles are stunning, though, and I start pinning photos to a Pinterest board. Seems like most of the guests go for startling silhouettes, dramatic structural pieces, bold colors, and surprising accessories.

After a long browsing session, I call up McKee to see if she and Bek want to go shopping for the party with me, since Jordan's out of commission. There end up being six of us in the group, including Catherine, a girl from our school. She wears her hair in a gelled mass of dark curls, with heavy eyeliner thickly applied at all hours of the day.

I'm not Catherine's biggest fan. We knew each other in high school, and she went to UNC at Chapel Hill, same as Tom and me.

At a frat party right before last Christmas break, she introduced Tom and me to Myrtle.

I had liked Myrtle right away—I used to like most people right away—and she seemed so unsure, so out of place. She didn't really have a friend group. I wanted to make her feel comfortable and welcomed, so I included her in things for months, right up until the day I discovered she'd been sleeping with Tom since the night after that holiday party.

The deeper I dug, the more "friends" I uncovered who knew about it—knew, and said nothing. Didn't warn me, didn't give so much as a hint. Just watched me float around on Tom's arm like a pretty little fool, like a moth dancing with flames.

After I found out, I didn't confront any of them. I kept right on smiling and being my sweet, friendly self. But in my heart, I crossed out the names of each friend who knew.

Maybe that's why it's so hard to still see them all on social media. It's not so much that I miss them; it's that secretly I want them to suffer like *I'm* suffering. I want something bad to happen to them, and I want to witness it, like they witnessed the destruction of my heart. And I hate that Tom's infidelity didn't just implode our relationship—it soured every other connection I made during my four years at UNC. Every single friendship I had was linked with Tom somehow, and when it came down to it, they all chose him.

So yeah. Having a close friend of Myrtle's along on our shopping trip isn't great, but McKee and Bek couldn't have known that it would bother me. I've been so very forgiving, so easygoing. I'm Daisy Finnegan, and I'm a fucking delight.

It takes our little group three full days to find the right outfits and the perfect accessories for the Met Gala party. After a trip to Asheville and four hours at the Gaffney outlets, we finally have everything we need for our looks. And the effort was so worth it because we are going to slay.

McKee borrows her dad's Escalade and picks everyone up for the big night. There's champagne, but I only sip a little from Bek's glass.

The line of cars on Gatsby's road is ridiculously long. We pass the time blaring Camila Cabello and Halsey, singing and dancing along in our seats. By the time we roll up, we're all flushed and laughing, and we have to quickly pat our hair and cheeks before the valet opens the door and we're ushered out into a world of sizzling light. A river of red carpet flows from the car to halfway up the front walk, where there's a photo background patterned with "J. G." initials. People are strutting up the carpet, posing in front of the backdrop, flashing smiles. I'm not sure who Jay hired to take the photos, but there's a crowd of people with cameras and phones, shouting and cheering like the paparazzi for each new arrival.

He wants every single guest to feel like a movie star.

"Oh my goddess," breathes Bek, gripping McKee's arm. "I think I love this Gatsby guy. Don't be jealous, babe."

"Nah, it's okay." McKee pinches her cheek. "Everyone loves him."

Catherine and the other girls are already sashaying up the red carpet, giggling and bumping into each other. An attendant makes the rest of us wait until they've had their fifteen seconds of poses and photos, and when he motions us forward, McKee and Bek flounce onto the red carpet together, doing their best runway walks. McKee has dyed her short hair purple and slicked it back, and she's wearing dark cigarette pants and a brocade vest embellished with swirls of dusky violet. Across her shoulders twines a scarf of lavender feathers. Bek wears a diaphanous blue cloud of a dress, with heels like skyscrapers, striped with zippers and crystals.

They pose, and pose. Then they're done, and it's my turn.

I don't have a partner to walk with, because the guy I like is somewhere in the sparkling mansion looming above me, and everyone's in love with him.

But I loved him first.

Someone in the crowd recognizes me and calls out, "Daisy! Daisy Finnegan! Look over here! Smile!" So I do, because it feels good to be noticed.

I hold my head high and my shoulders back, and I perform the fiercest walk of my life. I'm wearing a gown like a waterfall of crushed gold, with a sheer black bodice and sleeves. A spray of appliqué gold leaves sweeps across my breasts for coverage. My gold heels flash through the slit in my gown as I stalk forward, feeling both overexposed and incredibly bold at the same time.

I pause, and turn, and smile while the cameras flash. Once I'm past the backdrop, I scan the crowd for the girls, but they've already flitted away. I don't blame them, really. I told them I was going to wait around for Jordan. She texted me a few minutes ago, saying she'd be here, although I have no idea how she found time to buy a dress, sick as she was.

I step aside and watch the endless parade of people headed into the house. One man swaggers by in a long-tailed Victorian coat with sequined pants. His partner wears gauchos with gold-embroidered socks and a vest. There's a girl in a yellow cape, another person in a black velvet jumpsuit draped with silver chains, a woman in a sheer champagne dress with a massive wing of peacock feathers springing up from her right shoulder.

And then comes a tall figure in fiery red, her ebony skin glowing, her hair intricately braided and dotted with ruby pins. Jordan's gown clings to every plane of her trim body. The sleeves split at her upper arms and flare out, falling in great scarlet wings that morph gradually to the dark red of blood by the time they brush the ground.

She poses for a second, flashing a smile I can barely see from my angle, and then she ripples up to me in a river of ruby silk. Her eyelids and lashes are flecked with red sparkles.

"This is an incredible dress." I stroke the material. "Where did you get it?"

"Ordered it. Discount couture, baby. Paid extra for fast shipping." She lifts her arms, swirling the long sleeves. "Aren't these the most awesome kind of ridiculous?"

"You look like a goddess," I say fervently.

She catches my hand in a painful grip. "I feel like a goddess, inside and out, and it's all thanks to Gatsby."

A sick flutter pulses through my stomach. "What do you mean? Are you two... Are you guys involved?"

"Oh, no, honey, nothing like that. I'm just saying...he took away my last fear. With the special insurance."

"The insurance you can't tell me about?"

"Yeah."

I grit my teeth. "If somebody doesn't start talking straight to me, I swear—"

"He will, babe. He swore to me that he'd tell you everything. Give him a little time."

"Fine." I spin on one glittering heel and stalk away. "I'm glad you're better," I throw over my shoulder.

I'm going to find Jay Gatsby, and I'm going to make him explain to me what's going on. Either that, or I'm going to bribe one of his staff until they spill his secrets.

As I march toward the house, I look up—and the sight of the

place takes my breath away. Gold streamers flutter from the windows, and confetti cannons intermittently spurt glitter from the balconies. Pink and gold lights crisscross each other, sweeping over the faceted front of the building. The doors stand wide open, allowing the party to flood in and out, sending cascades of wild music into the cool air of the evening. It's the same live band as the other night, I think, though I can't see them from here. They're playing house music with a distinctive twist and a beat like an earthquake. People are everywhere, lifting bottles and glasses, toasting and joking. A low perpetual roar, woven of shouts and squeals and laughter, writhes out of windows, travels along the red carpet, and slithers into the crooked paths of the garden.

I thought the last party was peak Gatsby. I was wrong. There's a manic exuberance in the air tonight, a violent delight that triggers a ragged heartbeat inside me.

"Daisy!" The shout comes from somewhere above—the balcony overlooking the front doors.

From Gatsby.

His brown hair is artfully tousled. He's wearing a shirt the color of merlot and a dramatic gold jacket with a massive, curled collar. Apparently he's outed himself as the host, because several girls and guys are clustered around him, their eyes trained on him alone. I can sense their greedy desperation from here.

I'm not the jealous type. At least I never used to be, until Tom cheated on me. I don't want to let his betrayal ruin me, turn me into the kind of girl who's constantly jealous and suspicious. But I have a nagging fear that's exactly what I'm becoming, because I deeply, truly hate the colorful swirl of bodies circling Jay.

"I'm coming down," he calls.

"Good, because I have no idea how to get up there," I call back.

It's true—I'm still confused about the layout of this place. There seems to be a never-ending series of half-curtained doors, arches to duck through, narrow steps to climb, corners to turn.

Jay disappears from the balcony, while his entourage sags artfully against one another or against the balustrade, darting resentful glances my way.

I smooth my dress and wait, but before Gatsby appears, three other guys manifest in front of me. They're all vaguely familiar—I think I met them briefly at the last party—so I smile. "Hey there. Wow, you guys look great! Having fun?"

My innocent question opens the floodgates.

"Dance with me, Daisy!"

"Want my drink? I haven't touched it yet."

"Have you checked out the gardens? There's a hedge maze! Let's go."

"A hedge maze?" snorts one guy. "Really, dude? She's the kind of girl who wants to be in the middle of the action, dancing that cute little ass off. Come on, girl, I got you."

"This is a special party cocktail," says the second guy quietly, as if he's the only one speaking to me. He swirls the purple drink, and one of the strobing lights filters through it, glimmering on his bracelet—a smooth band of brushed metal. "You should taste it. It's delicious. They call it the Hairy Style."

"That's 'Harry Styles,' you moron!" interjects the man who invited me to the garden. "Come on, honey, let's get you away from these ignorant bastards."

I drop my voice, letting it slide under the music. "Actually, I'm waiting for someone. You should all move on, find some other women to hang out with."

The cocktail guy stares at me, his eyes turning oddly glassy. He cocks his head as I speak, as if he wants to savor the cadence of my voice. He turns and walks away without another word.

Odd. For a second, he looked like Jay did by the magnolia tree—dazed and entranced...and hungry.

If only the other two men were so easily dissuaded. "Aw, come on, girl," drawls one. "Your guy might never show up. Why not kill some time with me?"

"There he is now. Excuse me." I slip between them and head for the front doors. I haven't actually seen Gatsby yet, but I'd rather not deal with those two anymore.

I cross the foyer, heading for the dance hall. The music is thrillingly loud, and the harmonies are so bewitching. I have to see the band that's playing.

Standing on tiptoe, I catch a glimpse of horned heads. It's definitely the group that was onstage at the last party.

"They're called Klipspringer," says Jay from behind me.

"Klipspringer?"

"The band. That's their name." He shrugs. "It's also the name of some antelope in southern Africa. Cute little creatures. Lots of eyeliner."

"Speaking of which." I touch my fingertip to the corner of his eye, which is heavily outlined.

"Cody's idea." Jay's mouth twists wryly. "Too much?"

"I actually love it."

"And I love this." He spreads his hands, indicating my outfit. "You're stunning."

"A lot different from the old T-shirts and cutoffs I used to wear."

"I loved those, too. I remember one shirt was a really soft gray, with a skeleton angel on it."

"One of my favorites!" I exclaim. "I still have it. It's a sleep shirt now, though."

"I remember it used to slide off your shoulder a lot." Stiffly he reaches out, trails his fingertips along the sheer black gauze covering my shoulder. The touch brings back the memory of that moment almost nine years ago, when everything changed between us and we weren't just childhood friends anymore.

Suddenly I can't breathe. He barely touched me, and I'm asphyxiating, my skin alight, my heart swollen and pounding. It's everything I felt for him back then, tripled. It's familiarity blended with uncertainty, the urge to be reckless because I know, in my very soul, that I'm safe with him.

Jay is watching me, lips parted, a tender starvation in his eyes. "Can we go somewhere else? My ears are pretty sensitive, and the volume here is a bit much. Excruciating, actually."

"Of course."

"There's another place we can dance. Come on."

He catches my hand and tows me through the hallways, past a rainbow of dresses and suits. There's a guy in a blue gown, a girl in sequined underwear and a dazzling headdress, a woman with copper skin and a quivering crown of feathers.

"They're all so beautiful," I breathe.

"There are some bona fide celebrities here tonight, too. I'll introduce you later, if you want."

We round a corner and nearly crash into a cluster of people—Tom, Myrtle, and Catherine. I guess his ban from the premises was a temporary one—that, or he used another name to get into the party tonight. Although it's not like they check IDs—people just show up, uninvited, in swarms. A dark and sour tide rises in me, and the sound of Tom smacking Myrtle's face echoes in my head until I can barely hear Jay's voice. He's apologizing for charging around the corner and nearly colliding with them.

"It's fine, really," Myrtle says, batting at his chest with slick candy-colored fingernails. "You're such a sweetheart. What's your name?"

"I'm Jay Gatsby."

"Oh my god, seriously? Like, the guy who owns all this?" Her blue eyes open very, very wide, and I swear she flutters her lashes.

"Guilty as charged," Jay answers. "You like the party?"

"Oh my lord, yes!" Her nails travel to something at her neck, right above her ample cleavage, and my heart jerks. She's rolling an Elsa Peretti open-heart necklace between her fingers. It's just like the one I keep in a box in the back of my closet. The one Tom gave to me.

He clearly gave her one, too.

Why couldn't he have chosen a different style, at least?

"It's a lot, this 'gala' of yours." Tom makes sardonic air quotes. "I mean, a costume theme? Really? What are you, one of those rich chicks from *Gossip Girl*?"

"We've watched a couple episodes together," says Myrtle proudly. "Tom's favorite character is Chuck Bass."

"That makes so much sense." I give Tom my most baleful glare.

Tom ignores me and offers Gatsby his hand. "So what did you do, Gatsby? Win the lottery? Marry and murder a wealthy widow? Takes a lot of cash to run a big place like this, not to mention the parties."

"I'm into several things right now. Investments, insurance." Gatsby clasps the other man's extended hand.

"Are you involved with that Robin Hood nonsense? Screwing around with stock values?" Tom's grip tightens on Gatsby's fingers. It's a power move of my ex's, a stupid macho-male thing where he shows off his physical strength instead of shaking hands like a normal person.

"That's not your business, Tom," I interject. "Let's go, Jay."

"Sure." But Jay doesn't extract his hand. His fingers flex as he tightens his own grip—tightens it until Tom pales and winces.

"Sorry, buddy, did I hurt you?" Jay asks softly.

"Not at all, *buddy*," Tom retorts, massaging his hand. "How do you know Daisy?"

"We've been friends a long time. Knew each other as kids. I guess you could say we were childhood sweethearts."

My face burns.

"Is that so?" Tom sneers. "I dated Daisy for seven years. We had some really good times." He waggles his eyebrows.

"Okay, we're done here. Enjoy the party, you guys." I hustle Jay past the group and down the hall.

"Be a good girl, Daisy," Tom responds, and anger flushes hot through my body. I hate that phrase of his. So condescending. So annoying. So fucking misogynistic.

Once we're clear of them, Jay pulls me toward a large door fitted with a keypad. "Hestia, unlock Dance Room Three," he says, and the door unlatches with a faint whirr.

"Is that your AI? Hestia?"

"Yes."

"Nice name. Way classier than ours."

"What's yours?"

"Serenity."

"Of course it is." He chuckles. "I remember how much your parents loved that show. Here, I'll give you access, so the house will obey you, too." He presses the screen a few times, navigating through the menu, and then the house records a sample of my voice.

He's being impulsive, trusting me with control of his home. Has he given any other girls access? Or do I get special treatment as his *childhood sweetheart*? The thought of those words being repeated mockingly by Myrtle's stupid bubble-gum lips and Tom's sneering mouth makes me so mad I can hardly stand it.

"Now that's done. You're one of the admins." Jay rubs his hands together and grins at me. "Ready to see what's in here?"

"I can't wait." My response is only half-genuine, but Jay doesn't seem to notice.

He ushers me into a ballroom, smaller and less modern than the main dance hall. With its glossy floor, rich wallpaper, and creamy crown molding, the room feels like something out of a bygone era. Two big chandeliers twinkle from the ceiling, dripping frosty crystals. With the door closed behind us, the sounds of the party are muffled to a mere whisper. It's a relief to be somewhere so quiet, the eye in the middle of a hurricane.

Jay steps over to a big record player and begins shuffling through the shelves of albums beside it.

"Why'd you tell Tom that? About us being childhood sweethearts?" My cheeks are still burning.

"It's true, isn't it?" He examines a record without looking at me.

His response unspools a chain of memories: golden summer days spent side by side, shooting down sun-hot slides at the playground or riding shabby skateboards through empty parking lots; chilly winter afternoons huddled on my living room couch, doing our homework while our toes touched under a blanket; meals shared with my family because his dad was in jail and his mother was passed out in their apartment. A thousand cords of friendship woven together, long before the day his fingertips grazed my bare shoulder, when he looked at me with a new softness and I felt the tingle of something awakening inside me.

After that kaleidoscopic shift, even our tiniest touches were bathed in rosy color. Jay's hand in mine was the most exciting thing

I'd ever felt. His lips on my cheek set my heart pounding. We spent three blissful, innocent months that way, until my dad came home with the news of his new job and our impending move.

The baby romance between Jay and me was private and precious. Not something for Tom to sneer at.

"I didn't want everyone to know about it," I whisper. "And they will. Tom and Myrtle will tell everyone, and they'll make fun—"

"Let them."

"You shouldn't have said anything."

Jay has the record poised over the platter, but at that, he glances up. "You're ashamed of me."

"I'm not."

"Good." He settles the record into place. "I've worked hard to make sure you wouldn't have to be. I've made myself important. Powerful. No gossip of theirs can shake what I've built."

"That's not what I—I wouldn't ever be ashamed of you, even without all this. You're my oldest friend, Jay."

His gaze cuts me open. "So if I'd wandered up this mountain and climbed the fence into your beautiful wealthy community and come to you in my ragged clothes, without a dollar to my name, you'd have been just as glad to see me?"

"Yes! Seriously, Jay? You really think I'm that mercenary?"

"I think you live a different life now. And I've done what I needed to do to carve my own place in it." He poises the spindle on the record, and music unfurls, a sweeping melody. "Would you like to dance?"

With the wine-colored shirt and gold jacket, he looks like a beautiful prince, brown-eyed and earnest, blending perfectly into the vintage ambiance of this elegant room. I'm still upset—maybe at him, or Tom, or both—but the music is luring me, softening me.

I drift toward him, and he clasps my fingers and slips his other hand under my arm, his palm resting on my shoulder blade.

We've danced before, he and I. Silly, wild dances at my house, where we imitated the moves in music videos until we collapsed on the carpet, our stomachs aching with laughter. But we've never danced like this. Just the two of us, with romantic music swirling our insides, under the heavy awareness of what it means that he's here, on Glassy Mountain, in this house.

He's here for *me*. That's pretty fucking clear. And as much as I care about him, as flattered as I am, there's a magnificence to the gesture that overwhelms me.

"Do you know the fox-trot?" Jay asks. "Cody taught me. I'm pretty good."

"Mom made us all take ballroom dancing lessons as soon as we moved up here," I tell him. "I think she expected us to be attending a lot of very fancy parties. She had possibly been watching too many old episodes of *Dancing with the Stars* at the time."

He laughs, sweeping me into the long, swift strides of the dance. "I've always loved your mom. I'd like to see her, and your dad too."

"You will. I told them you're here. They were...surprised."

"And full of questions, I imagine."

"Uh-huh," I say vaguely. A scent twirls past my nose as we move—the sharp, sweet edge of alcohol. "Do you drink now?" I don't mean it to sound judgmental, but it does.

"No." He tilts his head with a light frown of confusion; then his brow clears. "Ah, the champagne. One of the girls I was hanging out with—Sloane—rubbed champagne into my hair when I told her I didn't drink. She said something about getting me drunk via osmosis."

"I do not think that word means what she thinks it means," I say in my best imitation of Inigo Montoya, and he laughs. I forgot how delicious his laugh is—bright and boyish, with a slight hoarseness that's just plain sexy.

"*Princess Bride* quotes, nice." He twirls me expertly, and I manage to follow the move semi-gracefully.

"Though maybe she *did* know what it means. Osmosis isn't just movement of a solvent through a semipermeable membrane," I murmur. "It can also be a slow assimilation of attitudes or ideas, sometimes without the awareness that you're changing."

Jay ducks a little closer as we continue to step—slow, slow, quick-quick. "I love your brain."

He used to tell me that often, even when my grades weren't great, when my parents' faces expressed their concern about my abilities and my future. I couldn't explain to Mom and Dad how my brain picks and chooses what it remembers. They don't understand how I can recall certain concepts in vivid detail and let others slip away completely, even if I've studied them. It's a quirk that yields some unfortunate test grades and a less-than-stellar college transcript.

But Jay always loved my funky, unpredictable brain, and his familiar words nestle in my heart. At least his opinion of me hasn't changed. But he's different, intangibly and irrevocably so, and it makes me sad.

The music is falling over me in layers of silk, cool and sweet. The light glints on Jay's gold jacket and pools in his eyes, and I'm desperately trying to keep step with him. He's so graceful, and grown-up, and glamorous, and I'm still just me, even in this shiny gown. I can feel myself cracking inside, my sinuses swelling, tears clustering in my eyes.

I'm going to start ugly crying, right now. Right in the middle of the dance. And I can't stop it.

With a burst of desperation, I break away from him and crumple to the floor, bowing my head so my curls hide my face.

"Daisy." He kneels beside me. "Daisy, what is it?"

"It's...it's this room," I struggle, my breath hitching. The tears are slipping out, one after another, wetting my cheeks. "I've never been in such a gorgeous room before. I can't dance here. I'm not this person, Jay. I'm pizza and UNC hoodies and caramel cold brews. I'm not glamorous like this—"

"Hey." He tips my chin up, swiping at a tear with his thumb. "You don't have to be anything you don't want to be. You are enough for me, always. Just you."

"How can you know that?" I push his hand away. "You're different now. You're so—perfect. Like you've turned yourself into some kind of hero out of a novel. Someone every woman would want."

"That was kind of the idea."

"But I just want *you*." The words burst out of me in a plaintive squeak, with another rush of tears. I have to stop crying; I can't break down like this in front of him, not here. Ugh, this is so embarrassing...

Someone opens the door at that moment. "Mr. Gatsby, there's a problem."

He doesn't turn away from me, empathetic eyes still locked on my face. "Not now, Henry."

"There's a glutton involved. I think you should come."

Did he say *glutton*? What a weird word choice.

Gatsby rises instantly. All I can see of him now are his crisp dark pants and gleaming black shoes. "Who is it?"

"Slagle."

"Damn it. Daisy, I have to go, but I'll be back as quickly as I can. Please know that I—" He groans in frustration. "I'll hurry back."

He leaves me sitting in the middle of the ballroom, alone under the chandelier glow and surrounded by the crackling of the record player.

8

WHAT THE HELL WAS THAT STAFF GUY TALKING ABOUT? A GLUT-
ton? There was plenty of food all over the estate—rich, decadent food,
mountains of it. Why would Jay care if someone was overindulging?

He wouldn't. Which means *glutton* has another meaning to him.

Behind the gleaming gables of the house, beyond the glittering
rooms, beneath the mesmerizing music and the luscious food, there's
something else going on. There's another layer, one I can nearly perceive, but not quite.

I wipe the tears from my cheeks and stand up. Now I'm curious
as well as angry. Why all the secrecy? Why does Jay feel like a lost
part of my soul and yet also a stranger? Why couldn't my parents
have been rich right where we were, instead of moving us all the way
up into the mountains and away from my best friend, and why is he
really here after all these years without a word?

I'm going to find answers. Tonight.

There's a bathroom a couple doors down from the ballroom, so
I check my makeup, irritated by the cherrywood gloss of the stalls
and the way the whole place is redolent with the aroma of roses. The
luxury taunts me, raising the same questions, over and over. Where
did Jay get his money, and how?

What is he doing?

Sweeping back into the hallway, I join the flow of spiced, spangled people. When I studied in high school or at UNC, I sometimes had trouble seeing the whole picture; my brain tended to latch on to certain details and exclude others. And in this slurry of humans, certain body parts stand out in sharp focus. A hand laced with delicate tattoos cupping a wineglass. The flex of a man's thick fingers. The tilt of a woman's hip, the swell of a breast through gauzy fabric. The nape of a brown male neck, the smooth graze of his fade. A ring flashing on a waving hand. Purple-painted lips, pierced near the corner. A spray of feathers from an arched shoulder.

I wander past tables lined with guests, past the chink of plates and the haze of savory steam. Past tables holding tiny golden bags imprinted with J. G.—party favors for Jay's guests. Hundreds of them.

I enjoy my family's newfound wealth, but I'm still a poor girl at heart, and the excess of this party is starting to sicken me—like when I saw this thing on TV about one of the world's richest people. I had to go for a run after watching that, to burn off all the churning anger.

This night was supposed to be fun—it *has* been fun. I could exert myself and find some people to hang out with, but I'm too tired to shine. Instead I go deeper into the house, taking the hallways less traveled, climbing the stairs less frequented. There's a man guarding the stairway up to the third floor, but as I hesitate near him, he sighs and marches off to shoo away a couple who are humping urgently against the wall.

While he's distracted, I hurry up the steps.

Jay's room might be somewhere on this floor. And I might find something interesting if I poke around in it. But that would be wrong.

Maybe I don't care.

The hallway is swathed in a dusky amber glow and its walls are deep red, contrasting beautifully with the dark hardwood floor. My fingers trail along the wall as I walk, and then they snag on a handle. I try a little downward pressure, but it resists. Locked tight.

The door is solid wood, heavy and glossy, with a carved decoration in its center, like a shield and vines. This isn't your average door—it's ponderous and ornate, important. Maybe it leads to Jay's room, or Cody's. Below the embellishment, it's fitted with a similar panel to the one downstairs, which makes for a weird blend of old-fashioned style with modern tech.

On impulse I say, "Hestia, unlock the master bedroom."

"I'm sorry," says a cool voice from the panel. "I didn't understand that request."

"Hestia, unlock Gatsby's bedroom."

"Okay," says the panel, and there's a click, not from this door, but from one a little further along the hall. When I approach and try that door's handle, it turns easily. The door slips open, and I nudge it wider. Lamps flick on automatically inside the room, and my stomach ripples with apprehension and triumph.

The walls are the color of a cloudy day, with furniture and bedding in burgundy and smoky blue-gray. There's a massive painting of a regal magnolia above the bed—Jay's favorite tree. This has got to be his space.

Slowly I sidle into the room. A green glass bottle of Ralph Lauren Polo cologne stands on the dresser. With my eyes closed, I sniff at it—basil and cloves, leather and oak. Jay's new scent.

The room is clean—I imagine Jay has someone to keep it clean for him—but it's slightly untidy. A pair of sneakers are tumbled by the bed, some clothes are in a pile by the nightstand, a book lies upside down on the pillow. I touch the cover lightly—it's called *The Future Is Faster Than You Think*, by Peter H. Diamandis and Steven Kotler. Something about converging technologies, business, and industry. Heady stuff.

On the wall over the dresser is a row of sketched portraits. I recognize a few thanks to my dad—Sir Humphry Davy, Marie Curie, Rosalind Franklin, Antoine Lavoisier, Alfred Nobel. Famous chemists and other scientists. So he's still interested in chemistry. My dad will be happy to hear that. And I'm happy to see the Lego model of the periodic table on the wall—out of place in this classy room, but a clear sign that Jay is still Jay, underneath all the glamour.

There's a laptop on the shiny cherrywood desk in the corner and several items in glass cases—collectibles maybe? But before I have a chance to see what Jay's been collecting, a sound outside the room sends my heart to my toes. Instinctively I cringe into the corner behind the bedroom door.

A split second later, I recognize Cody's voice. "What Gatsby and I do is our business. We've been over this, Wolfsheim. Just because you're my progenitor doesn't mean you get to boss me around. You're not the bloody ruler of us all." A pause. "You think you can decide that for everyone, just because you were the first? That's bullshit. You need to back the hell off. No, I'm done. I'm done with all of this."

There's a gusty sigh that hitches suddenly.

Did Cody notice the open door of the bedroom?

Yes, he did. He's coming in, stuffing his phone into his back pocket.

And he looks right at me, with a gaze so cutting I feel utterly naked. He's wearing an electric-blue suit that seems to shimmer into purple when he moves. A long earring dangles from one ear, and his blue-black hair is spiked up.

"What are you doing in here?" His voice is a cool blade, deadly and sharp.

"Um...I'm waiting for Jay."

He lifts an eyebrow. "Jay wouldn't bring you up here. Not yet."

"Maybe he would." I tilt my head, holding his gaze.

"But he didn't. Which means you're sneaking around, spying."

"Spying on *what*, though?" I move away from the wall, straightening my shoulders. "That's what I can't figure out. There's something going on here."

"A fantastic party."

"Something more than that. Nick said you took him to a room to sleep it off because he drank too much. At least, that's what you told him happened. But I wonder if you might have drugged him instead."

Cody's face remains perfectly stoic, nearly expressionless. "You think I'd do something like that?"

"Honestly, I'm not sure. I'd like to think not, because you're Jay's friend and he's a good person. But I don't know you at all, and I can't help feeling like you've done something to Nick—changed him somehow."

"Maybe I have," he says smoothly. "What are you going to do about it?"

Anger churns inside me. My hands clench into fists. "Oh, I'll think of something."

"I'd love to see that," he purrs. "You can't hurt me, little Daisy Finnegan. I have no idea what Gatsby sees in you. You're a white bread, milquetoast blond, interchangeable with any number of airheaded twentysomethings. Yet for some reason, no one else will do for him. He only wants you, the boring girl puttering around his room, asking her bland little questions."

My stomach knots painfully. In my darkest moments, I've told myself this is why Tom left me—because I was too boring, too bland, too insipidly cheerful and generically likable, because I didn't have enough of an edge. I had nothing to make me interesting.

But I know that's not true. Tom just didn't take the time to figure out the intricacies of me like Jay did.

I screw my courage tighter and step forward. "White bread, milquetoast blond, huh? Is that the best insult you can come up with? Seriously? I can't change who I am any more than you can. Should I be ashamed of it, then? Dye my hair? Do something wild so I stand out, so I'm 'not like other girls'? Jay and I have history, Cody. We know each other—knew each other long before he met you. And I'll have you know that nobody is boring, because no one is exactly the same as anyone else. We all have different flavors, like... like coffee beans."

The corner of Cody's mouth lifts. "Coffee beans?"

"Yeah, you know how they taste different depending on where they grow, and the weather conditions and the soil and whatever... I watched a documentary about coffee beans once. Honestly, I'm no expert so I probably shouldn't use that analogy, but I think you know what I mean."

He's actually smirking now. "So you're not white bread—you're coffee beans?"

"Um, maybe?" There's a smile flickering over my lips too, and the knot in my stomach is loosening. "Listen, I'm sorry for snooping. I just... I haven't seen him in so long, and he's changed so much. I guess I was looking for something to explain it. Or maybe something to reassure myself that he's still the same person."

Cody sighs, sinking onto the edge of the bed. "He's still a hopeless romantic, if that's what you mean. An impossible idealist. And he's worth more than the whole bloody bunch downstairs, that's for sure."

"You can't know that." I approach him and lean against the footboard, my fingers curled around the edge. "Each one of those people downstairs has layers and talents that you can't gauge just by seeing them at an event like this."

"You're way too kind to the human race. Like Gatsby." He stares at me, like he's trying to perceive my deeper layers. His dark eyes flicker as he leans toward me. "You smell good. What's your blood type?"

"My blood type?"

"It's a personality test thing, like your zodiac sign." He stares at me, unblinking, with an intensity that makes me nervous. Like he's starting to find me a little too interesting.

"I'm type O."

"Ah, the leader type. Outgoing, generous, resilient, passionate. You're loyal, but a little unstable. You can seem careless or selfish at times, but that's only because you don't like to think about troubling events, lest they affect you too deeply. And you hate confrontation."

I grin at him. "You just made up all that crap, didn't you?"

He splays a hand over his chest. "I would never. It's pure science."

After a mutual chuckle, Cody meets my gaze again, with the same curious intensity. "You didn't say whether you were O positive or negative."

"Negative."

"The universal donor. Exquisite." He breathes the word with relish. "You'll be a favorite on the blood donation circuit." He smiles, teeth glinting, and then he closes his lips again, all humor fading from his eyes. His mouth is small and plump, like a rosebud. I can see why Nick likes kissing it.

"Do you know where Nick is?" I ask.

"Hydrating," Cody says hazily, rising from the bed. He wavers a little.

"Hey, are you okay?" Instinctively I reach out to steady him.

His eyes flash to mine, and their depths are swirled with white, like cream drizzled into a cup of dark chocolate. His upper lip looks thicker now, swollen or something. He runs a finger along the bracelet on his wrist, and it flashes briefly yellow.

"I need to find Nick." He sways, turning his face aside, staggering toward the door. His breathing is frantic and shallow.

"Okay. Okay, we'll find Nick. But first, Cody, you need to calm down." He's scaring me. And the only thing I can think of to calm him, to help him, is to go to that place—to use that special tone of mine, the one everyone says is so musical, so persuasive. My voice lowers into its familiar timbre, like a guitar player shifting into a deeper chord. "Take a breath and relax."

Cody instantly draws a huge breath, and his shoulders sag as if the tension is draining from his body.

His immediate reaction clinches it, cements my vague suspicions, flashes through me like lightning. I can't deny it anymore. There's something different about me. About my voice. "Okay. Good," I tell Cody. "Now another breath—and you should, like, blink or something."

He inhales, blinking several times.

"That's better, isn't it?" I say softly. "Now we'll go find Nick, all right?"

"All right," he echoes.

He's calm now, and the weird thing with his eyes is gone. Maybe I imagined it? But he still isn't acting like himself. He went from verbally sparring with me to almost liking me, and then there was that moment where he looked way too intense. And now he's all glassy-eyed, like a zombie, following meekly behind me as we head down the hall. He's behaving the same way that guy with the cocktail did, when I used "the tone" on him. Dazed and compliant.

It reminds me of the stories my dad sometimes tells about my grandmother. He doesn't like talking about her career, because as a man devoted to science and logic, it embarrasses him. She was a medium, a mentalist, and a hypnotist—fairly well known in certain circles. She went on tour a few times, and she had a shop where she read tarot cards and held séances. She could hypnotize people, put them into a suggestible state and make them perform tasks. She even won some awards for her skills as a mentalist.

I've often wished she had lived longer. I only remember a few conversations with her—a handful of gifts I still cherish. She died when I was seven, and yet I've always felt more connected to her than to my mom's parents.

Years ago, after one of Dad's stories about her, I watched a documentary on hypnotism, and from what I saw, hypnotism and mentalism aren't inherited gifts. They have to be learned and practiced, like anything else. It seems silly to think that I could have hypnotized Cody without meaning to. Although according to the documentary, certain sounds and vocal rhythms can affect brain waves, making a person more docile and suggestible.

There's only one way to find out if I have inadvertently hypnotized my cousin's boyfriend. If Jay were here, he'd want to do the scientific thing and devise some tests of this phenomenon. Experimentation to confirm theories.

"Cody," I say quietly. "Pat your head."

And he fucking does it.

Okay.

This doesn't mean it's hypnotism. Maybe he's messing with me.

"Cody." I pause, carefully controlling my voice. "Turn around three times."

He revolves in place three times.

I stare at him, and he stares back, peaceful and expectant.

This is so, so freaky. And dangerous. And possibly morally wrong.

And also, what the *hell*?

"We're going to find Nick," I tell Cody, softly and firmly. "And we're going to pretend none of this happened, okay?"

"Okay," he chimes back.

"Stop it, Cody! Please, just...stop."

He frowns, his eyes clarifying, refocusing. "Stop what?"

"You were... I mean..." He's obviously back in control again. And I can't even begin to explain what happened when I don't understand it myself. "Let's just find Nick." I turn and head for the stairs.

"Sure." Cody inhales as if he's going to say something else, but when I look back, he only shrugs and descends after me.

The guy at the foot of the steps frowns, as if he's wondering how I slipped by him, but then his gaze flicks to Cody, and he lets us pass without protest.

My heart is jackhammering in my chest, and Cody keeps stealing glances at me. Finally, he says, "You seem nervous."

"I'm fine. It's nothing." Except it really might be something, and the only way I can figure it out is to collect more evidence. So here goes.

"I overhead a bit of your phone conversation," I say to Cody. "And I was wondering... Is Jay in trouble? Who's the Wolfsheim person you were talking to?"

He shakes his head. "Spying and eavesdropping. Naughty, naughty."

"Are you going to answer my question?"

"No. If you want answers, talk to Gatsby."

Okay then. Now I know this is a question he won't willingly answer. Which makes it the perfect control factor to test my "hypnotic voice" theory.

We descend the steps to the second floor, but when we reach the landing I step in front of Cody, look into his eyes, and say in my silkiest tone, "Tell me what I need to know, Cody. Tell me who Wolfsheim is."

His eyes drift instantly, sliding from mine.

Oh my god, is it actually working? "Cody, tell me who Wolfsheim is," I say soothingly. "Come on. You can trust me."

His voice is hollow, toneless. "Wolfsheim is the one who made me. He likes things done a certain way, the traditional way. Not the way Gatsby and I are doing them."

"The one who made you?" My excitement surges but I press it down, keeping my voice soft and lyrical. "You mean he's your dad? Or the one you got your money from?"

"He made me," he repeats. "He's not my father. And the money is mostly Gatsby's. This whole thing was his plan."

"What plan?" I urge. But at that moment Cody's phone chimes, and he frowns, confused, his hands drifting over his pockets as if he's not sure what to do.

"It's fine. Go ahead and check it," I say in my normal voice.

He's back to himself again, casually taking the phone out and examining the text. "It's Nick. He's waiting for me." His mouth curves, and I could swear he's blushing a little.

Either the introduction of a new sound or the return to my normal voice snapped him out of the daze. I'm not sure which it was, and honestly, I've had enough experimentation for now. I think if I don't dive into some kind of mindless entertainment, I just might start screaming or crying from sheer nervous exhaustion and too many fucking changes in my life.

"Before you go, would you mind telling me where the VR game room is? I don't want to go back into that crowd right now." The VR room might be a good place to hide out from Jay and to process the freaky, freaky weirdness that is me and my hypno-voice.

"I'll do you one better," says Cody. "I'll take you directly there. A virtual world is a good place to escape once in a while." He gives me a knowing look. Maybe we understand each other better than we thought.

And now I feel bad about whatever I did to him. I...compelled him, or something. That's what it's called in the vampire TV shows, anyway—compulsion. Or holding someone under your sway. That's a witchy thing, I think. But vampires and witches aren't real, so it's got to be hypnotism. My grandmother's gifts, resurfacing in me. *Thanks a lot, Gran.*

Cody leads me down some steps and along a hallway to a wide arch where a staff member stands with a tablet.

"Name?" asks the attendant.

"Daisy Finnegan," I tell her, and then I smile at Cody. "Thank you."

"No problem, Coffee Beans." He saunters away down the hall.

"Daisy Finnegan," repeats the attendant. "Ah, here we go. You're preapproved by Mr. Gatsby, so no need to leave a deposit or ID. Please go in and help yourself to the equipment. There are instructions posted in each cubicle."

Preapproved, huh? That's pretty cool.

The room beyond is immense, divided into a couple dozen cubicles, each about eight feet square—enough room for one person to comfortably play a VR game. Each cubicle has padded walls—probably in case players bump into them—and a narrow, cushioned bench at one end for observers. I walk past a few cubicles occupied by people in chunky headsets, swinging wildly at nothing. When I find an empty one, the screen on the wall activates immediately and says, "Welcome, Player." A short orientation video plays, and then a selection of games shows up. I choose a zombie one because I feel like fighting something. Come to think of it, there's probably a punching bag somewhere in this place that would help me release my inner tension, but then I might come away with bruised knuckles and I'd rather not. Zero-impact punching and swinging should do the trick.

The screen on the wall switches to the in-game display mode. If I had a friend along, they could sit on the bench and watch what I'm seeing. But I'm alone, and for now, I want it that way.

The gloves and visor sit in their own dock, on a small table beside the bench. I've tried VR stuff before, things like skydiving and kayaking, but never a game like this, and always with controllers rather than gloves. The headgear also feels lighter than the ones I've used. With a bit of calibration to adjust for my height, it's ready to go, and the game begins.

I'm in a ruined city, standing between walls of brick and concrete. There's rebar and rust, cracked plaster and dry grass poking out of splits in the pavement. The sky overhead is dark blue, streaked and swirled with clouds in a smokier blue, dotted with a couple stars. The attention to detail is killer. When I look down at my hands, they seem slightly larger than usual. The pads of the fingers are stained and smudged, and when I rotate my hands, palms down, there's dirt crusted under the nails and dried blood across the knuckles.

I move out of the little spawning alcove and into the alley beyond. A cat squalls and skitters across my path, making my heart jolt. The crate it jostled tips over, revealing a crowbar leaning against the wall behind it. Okay. I could use that. I reach forward and grab it, swinging it experimentally a few times. There's a light buzz through the glove, and that, together with the visual input, makes me almost believe I'm really holding the weapon.

A zombie lunges from the shadows, a glistening eye bulging from one socket, its gnarled hands outstretched.

It's so real and vivid that I jump back and scream, lashing out with my gloved fist. My iron bar bashes ineffectually against the zombie's shoulder.

"Aim for the head." A voice drifts into my new reality, and a chill floods every inch of my skin, raising goose bumps.

Jay's voice.

He's standing behind me. I can't see him because of the headset, but I can feel him, like a sailor senses an oncoming storm. I can smell the pine, leather, and cloves of his cologne.

How did he find me? The staff member at the door of the VR room probably ratted me out.

The zombie lunges at me again, gargling from its broken mouth.

"The head," Jay repeats.

"I'm trying, okay?" I jab forward and manage to spear the thing's skull. The haptic feedback provides the illusion of resistance, and a sickening squelch blasts through my headset as the bar sinks home.

"Pull the weapon out. Like this." A bodiless hand touches my arm. I look down, but all I see is the scarred ground of the post-apocalyptic world.

Jay guides my motions, helping me wrench my crowbar free of the dead zombie's skull. The corpse topples aside.

The press of Jay's hand disappears from my arm. There's nothing in front of me but the empty street—yet I can sense him, very close. "Where are you?"

"Here." His voice is faint through my headgear.

I reach forward, and where the game shows empty air, there's a solid something—fabric shifting over a firm chest.

"This so weirdly cool. It's like you're invisible. Touch me again." When Jay inhales sharply, I realize how it sounds.

I also realize, with a salacious thrill, that I don't care.

"Oh, there's another zombie," I gasp. "Move or I'll hit you." I hope he moved, because I need to swing the crowbar like now or be bitten. The bar arcs, striking the zombie's temple, and I jerk back as brain matter splatters my visor.

Two steadying hands brace my waist; Jay is behind me again. I move ahead in the game, climbing a ladder, ducking through a window, jumping to a lower floor. The house is cluttered with moldering furniture and bloodstained family photos. I round the corner and come face-to-face with another cluster of zombies. "Oh, crap!"

"There's a gun on the table in the kitchen," says Jay.

"Where's the kitchen?" I squeal, flailing with the crowbar.

"To the right, if I remember correctly—wait—left, not right, sorry."

I'm slashing violently, but I'm also hyperaware of his hands on my waist. When I move, my rear bumps lightly against the front of his pants, and each time that happens, a delicious tingle races between my legs because I can feel a rigid hardness against my ass.

When I've finally obtained the gun and dispatched the remaining zombies, I shift purposely backward so that telltale bulge presses into my bottom.

I haven't forgotten that I'm frustrated with him, that I need answers. But my pussy doesn't care about any of that, traitorous little fucker that it is. It's been so long since I've let anyone touch me... I haven't had the heart to even think about starting over with a stranger, trusting someone with my body and my heart again. But Jay... With all his newness and his unknowns, Jay is already mine.

I shouldn't play with him until I'm sure about this, shouldn't let arousal blur my judgment into a rosy haze. But I want him so badly, and I *ache*. I'm sore, deep inside, right in the crevice of my broken heart. Letting him ease one kind of soreness might help with the other.

I push my lower lip into a pout. "I'm not good at this."

"You're doing great." His voice sounds a little breathless. "You just need to relax."

"Maybe you should help me out with that."

His sharp exhale stirs my hair. No plausible deniability now... He knows I can feel him, and he knows what I want.

Jay's body is fitted to mine, moving with me, the heat of his breath ghosting across my ear now. His hands move lower on my hips, then slide forward across my lower belly, until his long fingers press lightly between my legs. Soft, ticklish quivers race through my clit at the proximity. He's almost, almost touching the perfect spot, but not quite, and I'm desperate, both in game and in real life.

I'm breathing fast and shallow, and everything's flashing red. "My health is low."

"I think there's a med pack in the next building. Sometimes it shows up in the food truck, though." His fingertips delve inward, pushing the fabric of my dress between my legs. Then he ripples those fingers, a quick, firm palpation that makes me gasp aloud. Between the game-induced adrenaline pumping through my veins and the waves of lush heat racing over my body, I'm riding a pretty dramatic emotional high in this moment.

Before Jay showed up, it had been weeks since I felt even the tiniest bit of desire for a man. I'd been Tom's for years—his to grope and squeeze, his to spank or pinch or fuck whenever he liked. He rarely took the time to tantalize me like this. But what Jay is doing—this slow, sensuous progression, the way he caresses my body like it's a treasure—makes me want to cry and scream for joy at the same time. I had no idea how much my body has been craving this kind of intimate touch.

Feeling his touch without being able to see him is wildly titillating—a new kink unlocked, one I never suspected I'd enjoy, but the slippery state of my underwear is a firm *yes* on that score. Jay keeps stroking between my legs, his erection hard against my ass, while in game, I clamber through some wreckage into the neighboring building, searching gloomy, foul bathrooms and bedrooms streaked with gore. "No med pack," I say, just as Jay's fingers arch, his nails scraping against the thin fabric of my dress, grazing my clit. I bite back a faint scream as thrills race through me, heightened by the sight of four more undead stumbling my way.

"Jay," I breathe. "This is so creepy and awesome."

"Speaking of creepy, is there a noncreepy way to be obsessed with someone?" His voice is husky, barely audible through the bellowing of the oncoming zombies. "Because I'm kind of obsessed with you, and I'm trying not to be weird about it." His nails keep grazing my clit, over and over, but now and then he curls his fingers, cupping my pussy, his palm giving me just the right amount of agonizing, intoxicating pressure.

My heart pulses, hot and bright, and I use the energy to rain dreadful havoc down on the zombies. "You're trying not to be weird about it, huh?" I manage between blows, while Jay holds me against him, anchors me with the press of his hand. "Look around, Jay. The money, the house, the parties—supposedly all for me? You've got to admit, that's a little much."

"I'll admit I bought this house to be close to you," he murmurs in my ear, while his fingers flex, coaxing another flare of arousal. Oh god, I almost came that time. "I was hoping you'd show up one night, because I was too nervous to come to your house. And you did show up, thank god. But the parties have another purpose, too."

"What purpose?" Viciously I stab a zombie through the chest and fling it aside; and then my spine arches involuntarily because Jay's other palm is skimming up, along my rib cage, over my breast. Thankfully I have a moment's peace between waves of attackers, because I can't do battle anymore. I can only lean helplessly against Jay's chest while his fingernail circles over and over the silky material in precisely the right spot, teasing my clit faster, faster... He's relentless, holding me captive while I gasp and squirm and *oh...oh...oh god, oh fuck...* An explosion of pleasure crashes through me, bathing my lower body in ripples of heat. My hips jerk forward, and Jay croons his satisfaction against my ear, his hand cupping firmly over my pussy while I struggle to hold back the cries I want to release.

As the orgasm fades, my common sense returns, and along with it the shocked awareness that I just came on Jay's hand in the VR room. Anyone could have walked by and seen us. Oh god, my panties are drenched. What if the wetness soaked through my dress?

Pushing away from Jay, I tip up the VR visor and straighten my skirt, relieved to find only two tiny spots of dampness.

The game may as well be over. I can't concentrate anymore. With trembling fingers, I remove the headset and strip off the gloves.

Jay watches me set the equipment back on its station. He's flushed, his pants bulging with what looks like an impressive erection, but he doesn't ask for relief. He's reading my expression, my body language. Tom wouldn't have respected those signals. He'd have considered my silence an invitation to get rough. He would have shoved me face down on the carpet and taken what he wanted, and I would have pretended to be fine with it, because I loved him.

I gave too many years of my life to that bastard, and I'm going to be damn sure about Jay before I let him in.

My gaze drops to his hand, to the long fingernails that teased me so skillfully. Strange...his nails look much shorter than they felt when he was touching me.

"That was—" I draw a shuddering breath and squeeze my thighs together.

"Not the answer you asked for," he finishes quietly.

"Enough with the secrets, Jay. Are these parties some kind of networking thing, so you can meet clients and pull them aside and make secret little promises about mysterious insurance policies?"

"Yes, exactly. And the events also serve the needs of my previous clients."

What the hell does that mean? My hands curl into fists, partly from anger and partly because I'm still shaky from the best orgasm I've had in a while. "Jay, I will put that visor back on and hit you with my invisible crowbar if you don't give me a straight answer."

"I don't think you're ready for the straight answer." He steps toward me, cups my cheek, and skims his thumb along my lower lip. "I want to tell you everything, believe me. But I need us to reconnect first, to pick up where we left off."

I scoff and whirl away toward the cubicle's opening. It's easier to tell the truth when my back is turned, when I don't have to watch the hopeful light in his eyes fading to sadness. "There's no way to rewind time, Jay. You and I are different people than we were eight years ago, and that's not going to change. We have to be honest with each other and start building again from here and now. We can't just pretend the last eight years never happened."

"I guess not." There's a fragile ache in his voice. I can feel him standing there behind me, with a careful distance between us now that I stepped away from him, because he heard my wordless no. He won't touch me again unless I let him, and that simple act of respect means everything to me.

"May I touch you?" he whispers, and I almost laugh, because I knew it—I knew what he was thinking. We're still connected, he and I.

I don't know what he wants to do, and I still haven't gotten the answers I need—but every nerve in my body is whimpering yes, and the soaked underwear between my thighs is a mute and desperate yes, and so I breathe, "Yes."

His fingertips start at my elbows and drift upward, halting at the dress's cap sleeves. "You have the loveliest skin."

"Says the guy who's trying not to be creepy."

Jay chuckles, a low masculine sound that shivers in my very soul. His left hand traces my collarbone and wraps lightly around my neck, his thumb grazing the corner of my jaw.

My breathing goes ragged and shallow.

Jay tilts my head back and kisses the space right under my earlobe.

I reach back, cupping his head with my arm, tangling my fingers in his hair. It's crisp with gel, not as soft as it used to be. I twist, letting my demand for answers slip to the back of my mind. There's a clumsy moment of chins and noses before our mouths find each other.

The first kiss is quick, tentative, a delicate brush of skin. The next is a little deeper, a little harder. A little throb between my legs lets me know that my body isn't done with Jay Gatsby, not tonight, and maybe not ever.

At the third kiss, I'm gone, lost in a flaming, roaring lust that sears us together, galvanizes my mouth to his, pours molten heat through my throat and skin and stomach. I lock both arms around his neck and he grips my body, pulling me tight against him. This kiss doesn't really stop. I'm not even sure how we're getting enough sips of air to sustain us, and it doesn't matter because this is Jay, *my Jay*. His mouth is soft and hot, his tongue traces mine in a slick languid roll that thrills me in the naughtiest way.

My brain is a fiery haze, and I'm liquefying on the spot, melting, pulsing. I whimper, crushing my hips against his in a shameless surge.

Something pricks the inside of my lip, a sharp dot of pain. I make a quick sound in my throat, and Jay pulls away instantly, turning his back to me.

"I'm sorry," he gasps.

"So you bit me a little. I don't mind. It just surprised me." I lace my fingers around his wrist and try to tug him back toward me, but he resists.

"Give me a second, Daisy."

"Oh." Is he about to come in his pants? Maybe I should offer to... No. No, I shouldn't. "Um, maybe I should go see where Jordan is." Because now that my head is cooling a bit, I realize I don't want to have sex with him yet, not until he's willing to be honest, and if we keep kissing like this, I'm going to forget that resolution again.

"Please—just wait." Jay's voice is thick, his words blurred. But the next second he's facing me again, looking perfectly normal. Through his smile I catch a glimpse of the sharp eyetooth that poked my lip. I've always liked guys with slightly longer canines—it gives them a sort of feral look that I love. Guys like Taylor Lautner, Christian Bale, Henry Cavill—I'd die to have them smile at me. I don't remember Jay's teeth being this sharp, though. Had I ever mentioned my little preference to him? Would he have gone so far as to have some kind of dental procedure done to enhance his teeth? Surely not. That would be too weird.

His lips close under my inspection. "Listen, Daisy, I'll tell you everything you want to know, I promise. Just give me a week, okay? Let's go on a couple of dates first."

I open my mouth to protest, because I have trust issues now, and I need the truth, and...and maybe it's not all about me. Jay's gaze is open, pleading, but there's a shade of caution in it, too. Maybe I'm not the only one with trust issues. I mean, his home life was a real mess. Physical attraction clearly isn't the problem, but maybe he feels the emotional distance between us, like I do. Maybe he wants to make sure of me, to confirm to himself that I really am trustworthy. That I won't vanish from his life again.

Maybe he doesn't owe me immediate answers.

Maybe I need to be patient.

I purse my lips. "Dates, huh?"

"We never had any actual dates."

"Right. We only hung out together almost every day," I say dryly.

"We could do that again, if you prefer it to dating." He looks so eager that I want to grab his sweet face and kiss him again.

"Tell you what, Jordan wants to check out this waterfall she heard about—Wildcat Falls. She might want to do some videos there. You can come along on the hike. You and Jordan are all chummy now anyway, right?"

"We're acquainted." A faint smirk hovers across his mouth, and a twinge of jealousy flicks through my chest.

"It's settled then." I try to keep the edge out of my voice. "Tomorrow, around noon. I'd rather go earlier in the morning when it's not so hot, but Jordan won't get up until late. There's no address, but there's a spot where you can pull off onto the shoulder of

Highway 215. I've been there a few times. It's pretty, and just rugged enough to be fun, and there are a few different trails..." I'm rambling, and I pinch my lips together to put a halt to it.

"I'd love to go. I'll pick you up." The way Jay is looking at me makes the words feel far more intimate than they are. Heat crawls up my cheeks, across my forehead.

"I'm thirsty," I blurt out.

"Let's fix that then."

He offers me his arm like freaking Mr. Darcy, and I shove it aside with a giggle. "Seriously?"

"I'm trying to be the romance novel hero, remember? Everything a girl wants." He's laughing, but he's serious, too.

"In real life, guys like that make us girls nervous," I tell him. "Those men don't seem genuine. And maybe we don't actually want that level of perfection. We're more comfortable with the guy who's occasionally clumsy, who sometimes burps or farts like we do, who messes up now and then. All we really need is a guy who is kind, generous, and absolutely comfortable with himself."

Uncertainty flickers across his face, but he keeps smiling. "Okay then. I'll need a big bottle of Coke so I can produce a generous burp for you."

"Now that," I say, poking his chest, "is the Jay Gatsby I remember."

9

W HEN J AY PICKS ME UP THE NEXT DAY, HE'S ALREADY GOT
Nick with him. His car is a bright-red Tesla Model S, with a race
car–style steering wheel and a sleek screen instead of a dashboard.

"Nice." I swing into the back seat and poke Nick in the shoulder.
"I notice you didn't offer me shotgun."

He cranes to look back at me, pursing his mouth. "Cody's not
coming. I think I deserve this seat as a reward for my misery."

"Cody doesn't like hikes. Especially not on bright, sunny days
like this." Jay's eyes meet mine in the rearview mirror.

I nod. "Too hot for him, huh? Wow, he really isn't the work-up-
a-sweat type."

"Oh, trust me, he is," says Nick. "Just doesn't care for too much
sun and heat, I guess."

"What is he, a vampire?" I giggle.

Nick laughs raucously. "Somebody's been watching too many
teen TV shows."

"Hey! There are plenty of grown-up shows with vampires, too.
True Blood, *V Wars*, *Being Human*."

"Like I said," Nick says smugly. "Too much TV."

"Shut up." I kick his seat.

Jay isn't laughing, or talking. In fact, he's been steadily increasing his speed, and I'm not sure he realizes how fast we're going on this narrow mountain highway.

I touch his shoulder, and he jumps. "Jay, you should probably slow down a little."

But it's too late. The unmistakable *whoop* of a siren shrills behind us, followed by rotating red-and-blue lights. Nick swears, but Jay pulls over immediately. From what I can see of his profile, he looks calm. Unconcerned.

When the policewoman arrives at the window, Jay rolls it down and says pleasantly, "Hello, Officer Sheetal."

The policewoman's eyes widen. "Gatsby! Sorry, I didn't realize it was you."

"It's my bad. I was going way too fast. I'm sorry about that. I'll be more careful."

"Of course." She bows slightly—actually bows. "I'll know your car and license plate next time."

"You're just doing your job. No need to give me special treatment. You feeling okay? Any concerns?"

"None at all! Orientation took care of all that pretty thoroughly. I feel great. So much stress off my shoulders."

"That's what we like to hear." Jay salutes her. "See you around."

"You too." She backs away and hurries toward her vehicle.

Jay angles back onto the road. Silence thickens in the car, and the weirdest part is that Nick, my over-expressive and over-curious cousin, says absolutely nothing and questions nothing.

"Jay," I say at last. "What was all that about?"

He clears his throat. "I have provided...insurance for some members of law enforcement around here. It helps them out, and they give me certain privileges in return."

"Like being able to host parties with underage guests and not get busted for serving minors alcohol…among other things?"

His eyes dart to the rearview mirror again, his brows slanted inward. "The other rich folks in this area have their own ways of shimmying out of trouble. Why shouldn't I do the same? Especially when what I'm offering can save lives?"

"Don't the police have their own insurance?"

"Yes, but this is like a bonus package. Supplemental, you could say."

"I know what supplemental insurance is."

Nick inhales as if he's about to speak, and Jay cuts him off. "We must be close. Where should I park?"

I don't press the issue, even though my brain is a whirlpool of questions, sucking my mood down. Jay's reluctance to tell me the truth is frustrating, but I'm not angry with him. Curious as I am, part of me doesn't really want to know everything he's hiding. What if the truth tarnishes the image I have of him, the one I cherish from when we were kids together? I always admired how good and true his heart stayed, no matter what happened to him. When I knew him, he had an unerring moral compass, a sweetness and hope that dimmed occasionally, but always came back even brighter.

Truth always forces a choice. Once I find out what Jay has done, or what he's doing, I'll have to accept it, and him—or I'll have to give him up. So the longer we do this noncommittal dance, the longer I can hold off the decision.

I'm so buried in my thoughts that I stumble on the rocky steps leading down to the head of the trail. Jay catches me, his hand cupping my shoulder. He does it so lightly, almost carelessly, as if I weigh no more than a twig. As if he has a great reserve of strength to draw upon. I can feel that strength thrumming through his fingers.

When I'm steady again, he lets go. "Careful there."

"Yup." I run lightly down the rest of the steps just to prove that I can. At the bottom, Nick pauses to look anxiously back at me.

"There are more people than we planned on," he says significantly, nodding toward the group waiting for us by the stream.

There's Jordan, looking vibrant and goddess-like as always—and McKee and Bek, and Catherine (ugh), and a teenage boy I don't recognize—and Myrtle and Tom.

"What the hell," I hiss to Nick.

He winces. "I don't know. Did Jordan invite them?"

"She wouldn't do that to me."

"Must have been Catherine then."

Jordan spots us and stalks over on those impossibly long legs of hers. Her movements are quick and tight, brimming with half-restrained energy. "Daisy, I'm so sorry," she says in an undertone. "I invited McKee and Bek, and Bek invited Catherine, and Catherine invited Tom and Myrtle. And Myrtle brought her little brother. It's a mess. I'm so sorry." Her eyes leave mine, latching onto Jay. "Oh, Gatsby. You're here, too."

"Is that all right?" he asks.

"God yes, I'm thrilled to see you!" She grabs his hand. "Feel that? I'm so much stronger now!"

"As promised." He smiles back.

I narrow my eyes, looking between them.

"Oh, uh... He told me about this new workout regimen," Jordan says. "Well, since Gatsby's here, you'll be fine, right, Daisy? He can keep Tom at bay. Let's go! I've got so much energy, and I haven't even had a drop of coffee!"

She bounds back to the others. Nick, Jay, and I follow her slowly. Here at the start of the path, the stream is a wide, clear belt, burbling over smooth dark rocks and pooling in sandy shallows.

There's a stubby waterfall glistening nearby, but it's only the great-great-grandchild of the big waterfall we've come to see, whose source springs straight from the high heart of the mountain.

Tom is already straddling two rocks midstream, arms crossed and head canted, posing, like he often does. Beyond him, at the top of the muddy bank, the trail twists away through lush forest thick with rhododendrons and oaks and maples. This clearing by the stream feels like the inside of a stained-glass window, all emerald and gold, with hazy sunlight sifting through the leaves, heating the air and lifting earthy, spicy scents from the undergrowth. If Tom and Myrtle weren't here, I'd be in heaven.

I love nature like I love parties. They're both immersive and multifaceted experiences—you can throw yourself into the flow of them, lose your way and wander, forget about expectations and futures. At a party or in nature, your attitude determines your reality. That's what I like—not grades and metrics and structured career paths, but the freedom to let my personality and my inner strength determine my place in the world.

Not sure what kind of career allows for that.

Tom is staring at me, oblivious to Myrtle's glare. Objectively, he looks magnificent, his black hair curling across his temples, his sharp face dappled with sun and leafy shadows. His biceps swell beautifully, which is no doubt why he has crossed his arms.

I used to worship him. But once I found out he'd cheated, that veil of worshipful love evaporated, and I realized that he wasn't mysterious and moody, but sneaky and sour. He wasn't thrillingly dangerous—he was just plain cruel.

Jay's hand grazes my inner elbow, a light touch to let me know he's here, and he's got my back.

"Check it out, Daisy," Tom says loudly, turning his head and pointing to his ear, which has a couple additional hoops along the edge. "Got two new piercings. And this." He points to a stud glinting above his eyebrow. "And these." He rakes up his T-shirt to show a tiny bar through each of his nipples. "Hot, right?"

I avert my gaze, refusing to feed his vanity. "That's one word for it."

"You look like a fucking prince, babe," coos Myrtle.

He ignores her and leaps the rest of the way across the stream. "Are we checking out this big-ass waterfall or what?"

"Let's go!" Jordan skips across the rocks and bolts up the trail.

"Good lord," says Nick. "She wasn't kidding about having energy."

The rest of us trickle after Jordan and Tom, filing up a path laced with roots and studded with rocks.

After several minutes of uphill progress, Tom lags, dropping back to walk near Myrtle and her brother, George, a skinny white-blond kid of maybe fifteen. When I glance back at them, Myrtle is sagging on Tom's shoulder.

"God, it's so hot." She plucks at the neckline of her tank top. Sweat glistens along her cleavage. "Why are we doing this again?"

"Because," Tom growls, with a significant look at me, and I quickly face forward again. That look of his was a not-so-subtle hint that he came on the hike because he knew I'd be here. Unbelievable. He's hiking with his girlfriend, yet still angling for my attention. He just can't let it go.

"My mouth is parched," Myrtle whines.

"Here," Tom says, and from behind me comes the sound of a bottle cap unscrewing. "Drink this and shut up. You make the heat worse by bitching about it."

Jay is walking ahead of me now, tension lining his shoulders.

There's a firm quickness to his steps that tells me he'd rather be running ahead with Jordan.

I tap his back, right above the pack he's carrying. With a start, he turns.

"Want to run ahead? With me?" I say, low and soft.

An odd glaze drifts over his eyes, and I think back to my encounter with Cody at the Met party. I'm going to have to be more careful about my tone if it's going to affect Jay in a similar way.

"Whatever you want," he says.

I glance back at Nick, who's lagging behind Tom and Myrtle. Catherine, McKee, and Bek are even farther back, barely visible.

"Run with us, Nicky," I call in my sweetest tones.

"Fuck you, darling," he responds.

"I'll run with you," offers George.

"Okay." He's Myrtle's brother, but he seems nice enough. Quiet. Overshadowed, maybe, by his sister's bombastic personality.

"Fine, I'll run too," grumbles Nick. And he shoves by Tom, rockets past me, and bolts ahead, up the path.

Jay makes a low sound, like an excited growl, in his throat. Which is very odd, and I've never heard anything like it from him. He's off like a shot, chasing Nick. George shoots past me next.

I run after them, full out, skipping over the roots and ridges, grabbing the occasional branch to haul myself up the slope faster. I dart off the path through the brush to get past George, and the brambles scratch my bare calves. My thighs are burning, and my lungs are starting to hitch and ache, but it doesn't matter because I'll catch up to the other guys if it kills me.

Up ahead, Jay has overtaken Nick. He reaches out for him, claws extended—

Wait, what?

I blink, peering at Jay again. He has passed Nick now, and he's too far ahead for me to see his fingers clearly. For a second there, I could have sworn he had claws. Which is impossible. Maybe I shouldn't be running in this heat.

Nick is flagging, and I push myself harder, skidding on the forest litter as I skirt around him. I give him a sassy two-fingered salute and charge ahead, aiming for Jay's back.

But he's too fast. How is he that fast when he's carrying the pack with our water bottles? My muscles are rioting, straining, and my lungs throb with each frantic breath. Sweat courses down my back, drips between my breasts, and films on my forehead.

Spots are dancing in front of my eyes. I need to stop.

Jay glances back and sees that I'm the closest one to him. The approving grin on his face is the only trophy I need, my permission to quit before I pass out. I collapse against a tree, hauling in ragged lungfuls of humid air.

Jay circles back to me, holding out a water bottle. "Nice running, klipspringer." When he winks at me, my heart does a quivery, ecstatic dance—which in my current state is not a great thing. I might be about to freaking swoon. Except I live in the 2000s, not the 1800s, and I refuse to faint. Just flat out refuse. Won't happen.

"You okay?" Jay leans in.

I look up at him and say softly, "I think you need to carry me."

His eyes gloss over for a second, and without another word he scoops me up so fast I nearly drop my water bottle. "Jay!" I hiss at him. "What the hell? I was *kidding*."

He strides on, ignoring me, his lean arms locked around my body. The scent of him envelops me, a tingling aroma of sweat and grass and spices, mixed with something masculine and indefinable. Or maybe it's very definable—pheromones, pure and simple. Can pheromones be smelled? I'm getting even hotter, and more flushed, and very tingly.

Jay obeyed me. Without thought, question, or embarrassment, he obeyed my voice instantly. And now he's acting grimly purposeful, a ferocious energy rolling off him even though his eyes are oddly distant.

He ducks his head, breathing in slowly, like he's inhaling my scent. A faint ripple of sound rolls from his throat.

Did he just fucking growl? And did my pussy just quiver at the sound?

I have this breathless fear that we are a few seconds away from him charging into the woods with me, hitching my legs over his hips, and fucking me senseless. And while part of me would love that, I just can't go there with him. Not yet.

"For goodness' sake, put me down, Jay," I gasp again.

He doesn't.

I wonder...

Taking a deep breath, I switch to that low-pitched, musical tone that had such a weird effect on Cody. I lay my palm against Jay's cheek. "Jay, stop carrying me."

Immediately he sets me down.

"God, Jay," I say in my normal voice. "This is really freaking me out."

Jay's eyes clear. "Are you all right?" Then he frowns, as if realizing he's already asked me that.

"I'm fine." I peer at him. "Are you?"

"Uh...yeah." He rubs the back of his neck and rumples his brown hair with his fingers. A few wavy locks cling to his damp forehead.

Nick and George jog past us, their steps heavy with fatigue.

"We...we beat you," Nick pants. "Screw you both...for

suggesting…a run…in this heat." He slows, arching a brow at our proximity. "Or maybe you should both just screw each other. I'm sure there's a mossy nook…somewhere around here where you can—"

"Nicky, darling," I say in my sweetest voice. "Shut up."

"—hump to your heart's content. You have my permission, Gatsby. You may ravish my cousin."

I charge at Nick, and he ducks away, pelting up the path with renewed vigor.

Apparently that tone doesn't work as well with my cousin as it does on Cody and Jay.

Why?

What am I?

A sickening knot twists tighter and tighter in my gut as we continue the hike. In the middle of that anxiety is a growing certainty, confirmed by other little moments that float to the surface of my memories like ocean debris after a storm.

The summer of junior year, I applied for an internship. During the interview I spoke as persuasively and skillfully as I could, and the guy conducting the evaluation became flushed and told me I got the internship before I'd even finished talking. I knew he wasn't supposed to announce the recipient yet, and that scared me. I thought he was trying to get me to sleep with him in exchange for the spot. Right away I declined and got out of there.

But now I wonder if that event, like so many other tiny incidents throughout my life, might have a different explanation.

10

THERE'S A PART OF THIS TRAIL I'VE ALWAYS LOVED—LESS OF a location than a moment, really. Not the moment when you begin to hear the waterfall, or the moment you realize the path isn't making your thighs ache anymore, that it's starting to slant downward. Not the moment when you pass through a muddy dip and the foliage curls in close around you like the translucent emerald shell of an egg.

It's the moment when you break out of it all, when the leaves give way to rock, and the waterfall bursts into view, a multitiered veil of frosty white. It's like waking up on a day that's full of exciting plans, a day that you know is going to be wonderful.

Jordan is already beside the falls, taking photos. Nick and George collapse onto the rocks, panting and groaning. They don't seem to feel the magic of the moment.

But Jay looks at me, his brown eyes wide and warm. The smile that curves his mouth is gentle with wonder.

That look of his sinks right through my flesh and bone, down to my heart, where it thrums and glows.

My love for him awakens quietly, like drifting out of a nap, like remembering the lyrics to a song. I love him differently than I did when I was fourteen, and differently than I loved Tom. This love pulses harder, more insistently—and it feels deeply essential to my existence. I'll always need it to live, whether I'm ever happy again or not.

Tom, Myrtle, and the others emerge from the bushes, a collection of humid bodies, sweating and sulking, but Jay keeps watching me, as if I'm more beautiful than the waterfall. Phrases form inside my head, silly poetic things I could never say to him out loud. A few sparse words are all I can manage.

"You look so cool." My voice is a drifting current, barely audible over the ongoing susurration of the waterfall. "How do you always look so cool?"

Tom does a double take. He eyes Jay's unadorned ears and fingers, his basic jeans and gray T-shirt, his tumble of sweaty brown hair. There's a natural grace to Jay's stance, a generous openness to his face. It's the only accessory he needs.

Then Tom shoulders his way between us, stinking of sweat and jealousy. "You call this a waterfall? It's a lot shorter than I expected."

I crane my neck to look up the rocky cliffs to the top of the falls. "Really, Tom?"

"I think it's perfect." Jordan steps to the edge of the path, staring down into the churning froth. Then she looks up at the cliff. "I can climb this. Maybe slide down part of it, or do jumps across the falls."

Horror vibrates through me. "Jordan Baker! No way. You really will die this time if you try that!"

"Oh, no I won't." She grins at Jay. "I've got my insurance policy." And she leaps for the slick black rocks beside the falls and begins to climb while we all gape at her. She's always been athletic, but the speed and strength with which she scuttles up the cliff is something else entirely.

"Oh my god," Myrtle whispers.

Tom shrugs. "It's not that steep, and there are lots of handholds and footholds. I could climb that thing, easy."

"So could I," Myrtle's brother pipes up.

"Shut up, George," Myrtle snaps. "Your arms are like skinny little Popsicle sticks. God. Don't be stupid."

George shrinks under his sister's words. I throw him a sympathetic glance and then focus on Jordan, just as her foot slips on a wet rock. Her body jerks for a second, as if she's going to fall—and then she finds her footing.

"Someone needs to go up there and help her—make sure she doesn't hurt herself," I gasp.

"She'll be okay," Jay assures me. Somehow he ended up at my side.

I grab his arm. "She thinks you're her insurance policy or something. Talk to her, Jay. Maybe she'll listen to you."

He chuckles, and there's an intense light in his eyes, the gleam they used to get when he had an exciting secret. "The rest of you definitely shouldn't go up there. But trust me, she can do it. And so can I."

He starts to climb, fast as a spider scuttling up a wall, hands barely gripping the black stones before he's reaching again, hauling his lithe body upward quickly, higher and higher. He's already gaining on Jordan.

My fingers flutter to my mouth. "Show-off," I whisper.

What if he falls? What if Jordan falls? I'll lose two friends at once.

"He's something, isn't he?" Myrtle giggles, elbowing Catherine. "I could watch him climb all day."

Tom grabs her hand roughly. "Let's go find somewhere to cross."

He drags Myrtle toward the pool beneath the falls, where large rocks create a path to the other side. McKee, Catherine, Nick, and

Bek follow them. But I stand rooted, watching Jordan and Gatsby scale the cliff like a couple of free-climbing experts.

"I could climb it, too," says a voice at my elbow. Myrtle's brother, George. His face is flushed with heat and shame. "My sister never thinks I can do stuff."

"Myrtle doesn't know everything," I say, barely listening.

"Right? She doesn't know what I'm capable of. No one ever does."

Part of me resonates with those words, on a deeper level than he could possibly know. I'm at a different stage of life than he is, but I feel just as frustrated, just as lost, just as desperate to discover my "thing" and prove my worth to the world.

"I'm sorry you feel like that." I reach over and squeeze his shoulder for a second, and he blushes deeper. "But you don't have to listen to your sister about everything. You should follow your instincts and be brave. Show people what you can do."

I let my voice trail off as I spot Jay glancing down at me from high above, with a grin of wild glee on his face. He never used to be this athletic, and I'm not complaining, exactly, but I'm not sure I can have *two* daredevils among the people I love.

By watching this, I'm encouraging both of them.

"Risk your neck if you want," I yell up to Jay. "But I don't have to stand here and witness it."

Deliberately I turn my back to the cliff and focus on the glitter of the sun-dappled pool and the frothy foam of the waterfall. Tom is showing off too, crowing about how fast he can spring from rock to rock across the pool.

I don't want to attract his attention, so I walk a little farther downstream and occupy myself by tossing a few pebbles from the bank into the water, enjoying each satisfying *plop*. Then I pick out a different crossing for myself—a chain of smaller stones and a falling log that juts out from the opposite bank. I step to the first stone, spending only a second on its uneven surface before I move to a flatter rock with better footing.

It's a struggle not to look back at the cliffside, to check on Jay and Jordan's progress. *Please be okay, please be okay...please reach the top safely...* Oh god, and then they'll have to come back *down...*

I hop to the next rock, watching the glossy flow of the water over the pebbled floor of the pool. Everything's fine as long as I don't hear anyone scream...

Screw it... I have to look back and check on them. I have to know they're okay. I'm poised on a jutting stone, so I have to turn carefully or I'll lose my balance.

Jay has just reached the top and is hauling himself up to stand next to Jordan...

And George Wilson is about halfway up the cliff.

Shit.

Did the kid think I was telling him to climb the cliff to prove himself, or to spite his sister? That's not what I meant at all... I was giving life advice, not urging him to do something incredibly dangerous.

I'm too far away to try my persuasive voice on him. It requires a low, gentle tone, and he wouldn't hear me from this distance. I want to yell at him to get down, but I'm petrified that a shout from me might startle him and make him lose his grip.

I clench both hands, my nails digging into my flesh in an agony of suspense. George isn't as athletic as Jordan and Gatsby. He's going to fall.

Myrtle is standing on the bank with her back to the cliff, pulling the heads off flowers. She gives me a scornful look. "What are you gawking at, Daisy?"

I can't speak. I don't dare.

Something in my face must tip her off, because she turns around. Sees her brother clinging to the rocks. Above him, on the lip of the cliff, Jay kneels, his arm extended, speaking words we can't hear.

"That Gatsby is egging him on!" screeches Myrtle. "He's going to get my brother killed! George Wilson, you get down from there this instant!"

Her shrill tone spears the humid quiet of the forest, slicing through the rush of the water.

George turns his head to look at her.

Misses a foothold.

Claws at the slick rock.

He bucks, flailing in panic, and peels away from the cliffside, his body arched like a falling angel.

I'm moving, yelling—bounding across the rocks to the bank—but it's already too late, because the boy's keening shriek ends with a wet, sick thud, a crack, and the hollow drumlike bounce of his skull off rock.

George lies several feet from me, his neck at a strange angle. His blue eyes mirror the sky, unblinking.

Myrtle screams, and I want to scream too, but her screams are sucking away all the air—I can barely inhale enough to stay clearheaded.

This isn't happening. No. It's just...not happing. Not possible. We're on a hike, for fun. It's supposed to end in a picnic, not like this, not with a pale-haired boy cracked and broken at my feet, leaking his life into the dark seams of the rocks.

Slowly, dizzily, I force myself to approach George and press two fingers to his throat. I try not to think about the odd angle of his head, and the crimson lake spreading from the back of his skull.

No pulse.

Mechanically I lift my phone and dial the three numbers I've never before had to dial. I'm not here anymore—I've withdrawn deep into myself, where my raging emotions can't affect anyone else. Autopilot Daisy is in charge. She answers the emergency operator's questions and explains what happened.

Jay is somehow at the foot of the cliff again, stammering, "I can fix this. I'll fix it," and pressing his wrist to George's mouth—to see if he's breathing, maybe? Autopilot Daisy watches Jordan hugging Myrtle, holding her together, watches the other members of our group arrive and scream or swear as they realize what happened.

Jay turns, his forearms smeared in blood, his eyes desperate. He says to Jordan, "It's not working. He's already gone." Autopilot Daisy was too busy talking to the 911 people to see what he was doing. Trying CPR, maybe?

The next hour is sticky with sweat and blood and endless waiting. Then come the professionals with questions and reproachful looks. As if we forced George to climb that cliff. As if we caused his death. Maybe we did. Myrtle keeps screaming at Jay, shrieking that climbing the cliff was his idea, that he egged her brother on. None of that is true, but autopilot Daisy is barely keeping herself calm and doesn't have the energy to defend Jay.

I don't remember who takes me home, only that Jay grips my upper arm briefly before I get into the car. "I'm so sorry," he says, and then he is whirled away, hustled aside by two police officers. One of them is Officer Sheetal, the woman who stopped him for speeding earlier.

When I walk into my house, my parents are already there, white-faced. They wrap me in two sets of reassuring arms, and the inner Daisy trembles with grief, with relief, but autopilot Daisy is still firmly in charge, and she says stonily, "I want to take a shower."

In the shower I allow my two selves to merge again, until I'm no longer inside Daisy and outside Daisy, but one whole broken Daisy who can finally cry.

You should follow your instincts and be brave. Show everyone what you can do.

Why didn't I pay more attention to what he was saying? Why didn't I use my words more carefully? Why didn't I react faster to stop him?

You should follow your instincts.

Be brave.

Show everyone what you can do.

Oh god.

Oh god oh god oh god.

It's my fault.

Why can't I rewind, reset, respawn?

Show everyone what you can do.

I did this.

My voice, my power.

What comes with power? Not responsibility. No.

With power comes a spine arching in midair, and a cracked skull leaking blood onto stone.

11

WHEN JAY TEXTS ME THE NEXT DAY, I TELL HIM I NEED TIME.
A few days.

I understand, he replies. But you have to know—you're not to blame for this. I heard everything the two of you said. It's not your fault he took it the wrong way.

He heard everything we said? But he was so far up the cliff already, and George and I were talking quietly. There's no way he could have heard. He's just trying to make me feel better.

I text back a single word. Thanks.

For a handful of days, I bury myself in YouTube videos and anime shows, avoiding TikTok because it reminds me of Jordan and cliff climbing and death. She texts me too—sad, regretful texts, but she doesn't feel George's death the way I do. To her he was a dumb kid who shouldn't have followed them. Not that she thought he deserved to die. But Jordan could be harsh sometimes, and though she doesn't reference Darwin's law, its echo hovers in the spaces between her texts.

The survival of the fittest.

I suppose I'm one of the fittest. For now. Can someone stop being one of the fittest? Can you be worthy to live one day and not worthy the next?

From what I've seen of the world and the people in it, a lot of folks survive who aren't the fittest or worthiest.

None of us are invited to George's funeral. I didn't expect to be, didn't want to go. I'd just met the guy. If only Myrtle hadn't brought him along that day. Does she blame herself, now that she's had space and time to think? I hope not. I hope she realizes that blaming Jay is ridiculous, too. I hope she gets some grief counseling.

On the morning of the fourth day, Jay sends me another text, pleading to see me, with a sad emoji and a GIF of some little anime critter with sparkly begging eyes, and I can't help giving in. I need to talk to him anyway about what happened when I asked him to climb the cliff. I need to know why he felt compelled to do it, even if I already suspect the answer. Even if I don't really want to know.

Something I've always had in me is growing stronger, twining through my insides like a golden cord, lacing through my throat and lungs and turning them into terrible instruments that can play on other people. For some reason, those instruments manipulate Cody and Jay more strongly than anyone else, and I need to understand why.

My dad is off on a short business trip, and my mom is working from home because she might be coming down with a cold, but I know it's really to keep an eye on me. My parents are afraid I'm going to slip back into my postgraduation, post-Tom depressive phase.

I pause in the kitchen doorway and watch my mother for a minute as she hunches over her laptop. The two little dents between her eyebrows drive deeper every year. I wish I could smooth them out with my fingers and keep them from coming back. When our lives changed and we suddenly had more money than we could use, we all felt delighted, relaxed, freed from the financial stress we'd lived with all our lives.

And then the demands and responsibilities started mounting higher for both my parents. More income, more taxes, more complications and bills and debts, more projects to complete, deadlines to meet, pay raises and promotions to strive for.

Are we really better off now?

I sidle up to my mom and lay my hand on her shoulder, over the cool silk of her blouse. With a tired smile, she presses her fingers over mine. "Hey, sweetie. How're you feeling?"

"Better. I think I might go over to Jay's for a while. Not sure how long I'll be there...could be a while." I hesitate, then forge ahead, because I want to cover all the possibilities. "Maybe overnight."

Awareness registers in her gaze. "So you two have gotten close again? You *like* like him the same way you used to?"

I study the pattern of the marble-topped island, tracing its creamy swirls with my finger. "What are you talking about?"

She chuckles. "I'm your mother, Daisy. I saw what you two were like back in Easley. And I saw what it did to you when he ghosted you." Her smile vanishes as she sinks back into protective mode. "I don't want to watch you go through that again."

"It's different this time. He's got money now."

She raises an eyebrow.

"No, I just mean he doesn't have that barrier anymore. He can do what he wants."

"Where did he get all this money?"

"Um..." I search for an answer that will end her questions. "Bitcoin."

"Oh." As expected, her curiosity fades. She doesn't understand the entire concept of Bitcoin; not that she couldn't grasp it, but she doesn't want to bother trying. "Okay. Well, have fun. Stay safe." There's tension in her eyes, like she wants to keep me from walking out the door. George's accident hit her hard, too, and I can tell she's struggling to let me go.

But I'm not a teen anymore. I'm twenty-two.

Sometimes I wish I could go back to when things were simple, to the days when I was newly popular and newly rich, just starting to crush on Tom. But even then, there was something missing—so if I could go back, I think I'd rewind to the Ashmore Valley Apartments, when I wore thrifted clothes and spent all my free time with a brown-eyed boy.

I'm still chasing that feeling, that wonder and ease we had together. I felt an echo of that on the night of the Met Gala party, and if I'm honest with myself, I'm hoping to feel it again today.

Not that I deserve it, when a good kid like George died right in front of me because of something I said.

The time at the waterfall belongs in the void at the back of my brain, along with the hollow, empty chasm of my future and the oily pit of my seven years with Tom. Seems like the ugly, painful, scary zones of my mind are multiplying, expanding. Is this what adulting feels like? Because if so, I don't want it. No thank you. I'd like to return it for a full refund, please.

When I arrive at Jay's house, he's pacing the front walk. There's a stiff-looking man standing near him—the same one who called him away the other night to deal with the glutton—a tall, serious man who looks doubtfully at my haphazard parking job. "Would you like me to repark that for you, miss?"

"Why?" I say innocently, glancing at the rakish angle of my wheels. "It's fine."

Jay lets out a breathless, nervous laugh. "Don't worry about it, Henry."

"Of course, sir. I'll just go run those errands. And remember, Lillian and Armand have the day off."

"It's no problem. Daisy and I can take care of ourselves," Jay says.

Henry looks me up and down before walking toward a gray car sitting farther along the drive.

"He doesn't approve of me, does he? Your butler?"

"He's more like a manager. And don't worry about it. He doesn't approve of me either." Jay's long fingers twist together. "I, um, was out here checking the lawn. The landscapers cut the grass today."

"Looks good."

"I'm so sorry, Daisy." He turns to me, desperation in his eyes.

"For what?"

"For climbing up that cliff after Jordan. I shouldn't have. I didn't know the kid would follow me. I don't even know what came over me. I just suddenly felt this compulsion to climb." He shakes his head.

"Compulsion, huh?" My stomach drops. "Interesting choice of words. That's kind of what I wanted to talk to you about. I think you climbed up there because of…because of me."

His head tilts. "What do you mean?"

"Well, I've recently discovered that I can be very persuasive."

"You always were." He sweeps open the front door of the house, allowing me to pass inside. It's strange to be here in the daytime, when the place isn't swarming with colorful flocks of noisy guests. The foyer is so clean and crisp and airy—and empty. The rooms opening out from it on either side are hollow shells, frozen vistas furnished in fawn and cream colors, a blank canvas for the next party. At the far end of the foyer are the double doors leading into the dance hall. They're closed now, and silence seeps from them, filling the space between me and Jay.

I force my way through that silence. There's been enough of it.

"Persuasive is one thing," I say. "But being able to compel

someone, to Jedi-mind-trick them into doing what I want? That's something completely different."

I bite my lip, watching his face for his reaction.

"Ah," he says, glancing away. "Cody suspected you could do something like that. I thought he was paranoid. He's sometimes paranoid, and with good reason, considering his background, but this... Wow."

Okay, he's not running for the hills. That's a good thing. And Cody told him about our encounter, so he's not completely shocked either. "You're being very chill about this."

"Let's just say I've met a few people with interesting traits and abilities since you and I last saw each other. Sometimes this kind of thing takes a while to develop, or doesn't show up until adulthood. So yeah, I'm surprised, but... I've gotten used to dealing with the unexpected." He gives me a rueful grin. "What do you know about your ability so far?"

"Not much. I'm not even sure how it works, just that I'm slightly more persuasive or compelling than the average person when I speak in a specific tone. Most people are only moved a little bit by it, but you and Cody... It affects you two a lot more. You go into a kind of trance, and in that state, you'll do whatever I want."

Jay's eyes slant to mine, and his lip hitches in a half grin. "So what have you made me do? Anything fun?"

I smack his arm lightly. "It's not a joke! You should be a lot more upset at me for using my voice on you."

"But you weren't really sure about it, right? You didn't know exactly what you were doing."

"I started to figure it out when I was with Cody. I thought maybe he was extra suggestible to hypnosis, and maybe he'd taken something that increased the effect of my voice—some type of drug?"

"Cody doesn't do drugs. The occasional joint, but no hard stuff."

"Then we're back to my hypnosis theory. I'm no expert on hypnosis, but I watched a documentary on it once, and my grandmother was into it for years. My dad tells stories about her making people do ridiculous things during her shows."

Jay looks at me sharply. "Your grandmother was a hypnotist?"

"Yeah. She read tarot cards, told fortunes, and did mentalism stuff, too. But her big thing was hypnotism. My dad hated everything about her work. The kids at his school used to make fun of him because of what she did. It's one reason he's so firmly grounded in all things science."

"What was your grandmother's name? Did I ever meet her?"

"No, and I barely knew her myself. She died when I was seven."

Jay's sharp canines rake over his lower lip, and a subtle warmth surges inside me. I want to move closer, to kiss that pretty mouth of his and test the edges of his teeth with my tongue—to forget the things that flash through my brain at random moments. The smack of Tom's palm, his fingers digging into my flesh, the hollow bounce of George's skull, the moment when someone handed me my diploma, the moment when the scripted part of my life ended and everything turned foggy and terrifying.

I must look as wretched as I feel, because Jay squeezes my shoulder, and his voice turns even more gentle. "Let's go sit by the pool. It's still shady this time of day, and we can do some research on my laptop."

"Research? About my grandmother? You think I inherited some kind of ability from her?"

"It's possible."

"But how would that explain the fact that you and Cody are so vulnerable to it?"

"Do you remember when I told you that my ears are really sensitive?"

"Yeah..."

"Cody's ears are the same. Jordan's are too, now."

"Okay, and why is that?"

"Oh god." He rubs his forehead and rakes his fingers through his hair. "I've told this to so many people, but it feels extra weird saying it to you. You're going to laugh. Or maybe scream and run—" He releases a sharp, breathless chuckle.

"Just spit it out."

"Let me get my laptop first, okay? You go sit by the pool, and then we'll...we'll have that talk I promised you. The big one. All the secrets, yours and mine. We'll sort everything out."

I want to know right now. My stomach keeps knotting and untwisting, and my fingernails are digging deep into my palms. Before I can answer, Jay's phone buzzes.

"I have to take this." His beautiful brown eyes meet mine, pleading for patience, and I can't resist.

"Go ahead, answer it. I'll wait for you outside."

He nods, flicks his finger over the screen to accept the call, and walks around the corner to the stairs. I turn toward the back hallway, the one that leads to the side door and the pool area. But then I hear Jay's voice, threaded with irritation. "Parke? Again? That guy is becoming a serious problem. We can't have any more gluttons running around the mountain. It'll wreck everything."

Slowly I edge toward the sound of his voice. He's headed upstairs, but I manage to catch a few more sentences.

"Remind him of the contract he signed. He agreed to certain rules, and if he keeps breaking them, I'll do what I have to do."

I've never heard him use a tone so dark before.

A pause, and then, "I can and I will. I've done it before. I'm not as soft as you think, and you should keep that in mind, Keziah."

The threat sends a shiver over my skin. I strain to hear his next words, but he's all the way upstairs now.

Frowning, I meander along the hall toward the pool area. The back door opens into a screened porch draped with sheer white curtains that whip and waver in the breeze. I walk between them, feeling as if I'm passing through a bank of pale clouds into another realm, a place where everything is different and anything is possible. Whatever Jay has to tell me, and whatever we discover about my power, those things are going to alter our reality. It's up to us whether they dissolve our relationship or make us stronger.

The pieces of the puzzle are drifting together in my mind, but they're moving too slowly. The brain fog I've felt since George's death hasn't quite lifted yet. Honestly, I've been off my game ever since I found out Jay was here on Glassy Mountain. I know I've got some bad shit to deal with, but is it also possible to be traumatized in a good way? Because I think Jay's reappearance has traumatized me. And that, along with the added trauma of Tom's return and George's death, is slowing me down, keeping me from seeing the truth. If only I could brush away the mental fog like I brush aside these curtains.

I step outside onto the patio. It's a stunning sweep of glittering white concrete, with the pool nestled like an enormous blue jewel in its center. Curved lounge chairs sit in neat rows, each with a fat white towel folded on the seat. Tropical plants drape themselves over the tiled edge of the low wall, and at the far end of the pool, a fountain bubbles endlessly, sending ripples across the surface.

It's a beautiful place to share secrets. And Jay is about to share his with me. He's going to tell me everything, answer all the questions that have been burning in my mind since he came back—

A ringing blow to the back of my head shatters my thoughts. My eyes spark white, my breath sticks in my throat—I'm already falling when someone shoves me, hard. When I hit the patio, my head bounces off the concrete. *Just like George*, my brain whispers muzzily.

My skull is full of bright, hazy pain, but I'm not unconscious. I can't control my movements, though—my limbs are slow and useless. Someone rolls me onto my stomach, and thin frantic fingers wrap a length of rough nylon rope around my wrists, around and around and then a knot, and then around again a few more times and another knot.

My vision is clearing, but all I can see is the white concrete of the patio and a diamond-blue sliver of pool. My attacker jerks my head back, stuffs a ball of rough cloth between my jaws, and whips another strip of cloth across that, working it back until it's drawn tight against the corners of my mouth, knotted at the back of my skull. The wad of cloth touches the tender flap at the back of my mouth. My throat and stomach revolt together. Suddenly I realize why it's called a gag. I inhale through my nose, because if I vomit now, I'll choke and probably die.

"I didn't expect you to be here. I thought it would just be him." The taut, panicked voice is Myrtle's. She tugs at the ropes around my wrists. "Not my best work, but it'll have to do." She pushes me over onto my side. Her blue eyes are bright, glassy with tears. "Tom said this was the only way. See, Gatsby *told* my brother to climb that cliff. Egged him on, when he knew George couldn't make it. George will never get justice because Gatsby has money, and that's all that matters to the crooks in law enforcement."

The weird thing is, she's right about the crooked cops, at least the ones around here. But she's wrong about Gatsby's guilt. If she hadn't gagged me, I could have explained that the person who sent George up that cliffside was *me*. My head is starting to clear, but when I try to move, to buck against the ropes, a searing white-hot pain races through my neck and skull. I whimper and go still.

"Why did you have to be here?" Myrtle gasps with effort as she drags me behind the grill, triggering more flashes of pain in my neck. "Fuck...fuck... This is all wrong, this is so messed up... Shit, I don't know what to do!" She pinches her lips together, then swipes a tear from her cheek with the back of her trembling hand. "Look, I don't want to shoot you, but... Fuck, why isn't Tom here? He promised he'd help me with Gatsby's body afterward, so I guess...I'll just tell him we got a two-for-one deal." She laughs suddenly, a shrill bubble of nerves.

Okay, so she and Tom have a sick Harley and the Joker thing going between them, and I'm pretty sure Tom plans to leave Myrtle holding the losing hand. There's no way he's helping her dispose of any bodies. I had no idea she was this deluded, or disturbed. But I guess grief can twist what's already there and make it worse. And who knows what manipulative crap Tom has been feeding her to work her into this state.

Myrtle backs away from me and pulls a handgun from the back of her belt. I think it's a Glock, but I hate guns, so I don't really know much about them.

"You understand that I don't *want* to do this." Her eyes are wide, bloodshot, fractured with pain. "I *have* to. Otherwise he gets away with it, like all these rich fucks get away with screwing up everybody else's lives. And you're here now, you're a witness, so that means... You know." She grits her teeth, hissing sharp breaths through them. "I got no choice. I'm not going to prison for doing what's right."

I have to warn Jay. He's going to walk out here any minute with his laptop in his hands and those innocent brown eyes in his beautiful face, and then she's going to shoot him for something that wasn't his fault.

I shift my body, even though more agony spears through my brain and neck. My hands writhe, scraping and squirming against the rope.

Myrtle has backed farther away, but my movements attract her attention. "I should hit you again, knock you out for real this time."

She takes one step toward me—and Jay's voice wafts from the doorway of the screened porch. "Myrtle? It's Myrtle, right?"

"That's right, bastard." Myrtle's voice breaks, but she snaps the gun into position, bracing it with both hands.

"What's going on, Myrtle?" Jay says. I can't see him yet, but I can hear him—calm and cool.

"You killed my brother, you piece of shit. You told him to climb that cliff."

I want to scream at Myrtle, to tell her Jay wasn't the one who prompted George to climb. But with the gag sawing the corners of my mouth, scraping my tongue, I can't do more than choke and moan and writhe. Tears run hot down my cheeks, soaking into the fabric.

"You know I didn't kill him." Jay's voice is moving, as if he's slowly circling the pool's edge. Myrtle moves too, maintaining her aim, keeping the water between them.

"Words can kill," she says. "You egged him on."

"I encouraged him when he was already more than halfway up. I wanted him to make it. I didn't want him to get hurt."

"Stop moving, or I'll shoot you."

"It's okay," Jay says softly. "We're just talking, you and I. Tell me, Myrtle, where's Daisy?"

"Maybe she's dead. How would that make you feel?"

A throaty growl rips through the air, and for a second I wonder if Jay has a dog I don't know about. And then I realize the sound came from him.

"You didn't kill her," he says. "I can hear her heart beating. But she's frightened and in pain, and someone will have to pay for that."

"You're such a freak." Myrtle is still moving, inching closer to where I'm lying behind the grill. I wrench at my hands, wishing I knew how to dislocate my thumb bone or whatever people do in movies to get out of ropes.

"Tom's been doing his homework on you," Myrtle says. "He knows you're up to something bad. Probably raping and murdering the people who come to your parties. You've got a basement full of body parts, don't you, you sick bastard?"

"I'm not the one threatening murder here."

I twist, craning my aching neck, and there's Jay, rounding the edge of the pool, prowling toward Myrtle. Myrtle stands with her back to me, no longer circling. She's caught, cornered. The roles have shifted, and Jay's the hunter now, stalking slowly nearer.

"Stay where you are," Myrtle croaks. "Or I'll shoot you."

"You're going to shoot me either way, right?" he says quietly. "You really shouldn't, though. I promise you'll regret it. Think of your own future. Are you ready to go to jail for life?"

"Tom will help me. We won't get caught."

"Oh, Tom will help you? Because he's *so* reliable. I'll bet he talked you into this, didn't he?"

"No. I mean, he wants justice for George. For me."

"And justice is shooting me and Daisy?"

"Because of you, I lost my brother!" Myrtle screams, tears thickening her voice. "He was all I had, do you understand? The only person who cared."

"Interesting. Doesn't Tom care about you?"

"Shut up! Just shut up! You dared George to climb that cliff. You didn't stop him. You basically murdered him."

"But your voice startled him. That's why he fell."

"You're blaming me?" Myrtle's voice shrills with anguish.

Jay is still walking the edge of the pool, half a dozen steps from her now. "I'm only telling you the tr—"

The shot cracks the air. Short. Brutal. *Final.*

Jay stands as still as a tree, the breeze fluttering through his shirt and hair.

Dark blood spreads slick across his chest, blooming wider like a malignant rose. I whimper against the gag and lurch forward, bucking savagely against the ropes. Pain flares through my wrist bones, but I twist harder, and one hand pops free of the loop.

Jay wavers, takes a staggering step, and falls backward into the pool, arms wide and eyes unfocused. I tear away the ropes and fight with the gag knotted at the back of my head, but I can't pick it loose. Myrtle has her back to me. She's frozen, the gun still raised. When I struggle to my feet, pain forces a tiny cry from my throat, and she whirls, aiming the gun at me. But I'm blind with grief and reckless rage, and I throw myself at her in a tackle worthy of a linebacker. We crash to the ground, and the gun skids away. My nails find her face and her throat, clawing, shredding. I grind my teeth into the gag until pain shoots through my jaw.

I want her to hurt.

I want her to die.

Twisting a fistful of her hair in my hand, I slam her skull against the cement. Once is enough; she's out cold, and I crawl backward, off her body. My fingers tremble with the urge to smash and smash her head against the patio.

But I have to help Jay.

Sobbing around the gag, I crawl to the edge of the pool.

Jay floats in a cloud of his own blood, delicate crimson swirls unfurling around him like spectral wings. His face under the blue surface is unbearably beautiful—dark lashes on pale cheekbones, lips parted over white teeth.

I have to get him out. I have to help him.

Scooting to the edge, I'm about to leap in when Jay's eyes flash open. They're milky white from corner to corner, irises erased, pupils a mere pinprick of black. His face contorts in a snarl. Maybe it's just the ripples, but it looks as if his canines are elongating, like rapiers sliding from hidden sheaths. His spine arches, his hands splaying rigid while dark claws extend from his fingertips.

He soars from the water like a ball shot from a cannon, and he crashes to one knee beside the pool, droplets raining around him, his claws screeching against the white cement.

Screaming through the gag, I scuttle backward, away from him. He looks up at me and cocks his head with inhuman suddenness. A second shriek dies in my throat. A knot of terror is tightening in my brain, and if it bursts, I think I might never recover my senses.

Jay rises to his full height, touching his wounded chest with delicate black claws. "Damn it, I've lost a lot of blood." The fangs slur his words a little. "I didn't want you to find out this way, Daisy. I was going to tell you gently, I..."

His head whips back toward Myrtle, like he can't help it, like something is summoning him, something more primal and needful than his desire to explain himself. He stalks toward Myrtle's body, kneels beside her, and slides his claws under the back of her neck. His jaws part wide.

I know what he's going to do a split second before he does it.

His fangs sink into Myrtle's flesh, and the slurping, sucking sound that follows drives nausea through my stomach.

Jay Gatsby—*my* Gatsby—is a vampire.

Holy freaking hell.

Whatever happened to vampires confessing their secret quietly during a walk in the woods, or in a meadow of flowers or whatever?

Whatever happened to vampires staying in TV shows and novels where they belong?

What is...what is *happening*? What the hell is happening right now?

Jay extracts his fangs from Myrtle's neck and licks the marks he left. Then he sighs with something like relief. And turns to me.

No. No no no. I can't look at him, not when he's like this. But I can't *stop* looking at him.

He crawls toward me—actually crawls, with frightening grace.

"Let me take care of that." He reaches for my cheek, wriggles one sharp nail under the gag, and slices through the cloth.

I rip the fabric out of my mouth. "Did you just kill Myrtle?"

"No more than she killed me." He smiles, fangs shining with blood.

"Don't smile," I snap. "Why are you smiling about this?"

"I don't know. Because I'm nervous?" He laughs hoarsely. "I know this isn't funny, but I can't stop."

"Is that so?" Rage bubbles inside me, and I smack his cheek, as if smacking him hard enough might possibly restore him to a previous timeline where he's not a vampire. Though in that case he'd be lying in the pool, a tragically murdered human. Fine, I guess the vampire version is better than the completely dead version.

But he wasn't a vampire eight years ago, when I knew him.

"When did this happen?" The words tumble out of me, toneless and raw.

He flexes his fingers, and the claws slide back into their sheaths. His fangs seem to be receding as well. "After you left Easley, I felt so angry and lost that I started getting into trouble. Then my mom got arrested for dealing again. I was coming home one day when I saw them putting her in the cruiser, and I knew I'd have to go into foster care, so I ran away. Hitchhiked to Charleston, where I met Cody. I was spending the night in the shadows of a dune on the beach, and I saw him going out to swim in the dark. I watched him stay underwater for a full five minutes, until I thought he must be drowned. When I swam out to try to save him, I discovered that he was perfectly fine. So I told him I wanted whatever power he had, and I'd do anything to get it. He could have drunk me dry right then, but he didn't. I guess he was impressed with me for some reason. He gave me a place to stay, and we became friends. On my twentieth birthday he turned me."

"With your permission?"

"Absolutely with my permission."

"But why—why would you want—what are—how does—"

"Daisy." He lays a hand on my shoulder, and I flinch away. Hurt flares in his gaze. "I'm still the same person. Still the same guy you knew."

"You're really not."

"Okay, there are some physical differences, sure. But inside, Daisy, I'm me. Same as ever."

The earnest glow in his eyes reassures me a little. But my body is trembling all over, uncontrollably, and my teeth have started to rattle. I clench my jaw to keep them still.

"I think you're going into shock," Jay says gently. "Let's get you inside, and once you're all snug in some blankets, we'll talk."

12

JAY CARRIES ME INDOORS AND LAYS ME ON A COUCH. WHEN he goes outside for Myrtle and settles her on another couch with nearly equal care, my nerves ease, and the knot of horror in my brain uncoils.

A vampire, but not a murderer. A monster, but not cruel.

Jay sweeps a blanket over me and goes to change his clothes. When he comes back with a glass of water and some painkillers for me, Myrtle is stirring and groaning.

"Wh-what happened?" She stares around, bleary-eyed and shivering. "What did I—Oh no, oh god—" She starts to whimper incoherently.

"It's all right, Myrtle. Here, put this on." Jay winds a light scarf around her neck, covering the puncture marks from his teeth. "You tried to shoot me, but you missed. So the good news is, you're not a murderer. I'm going to get you some help, and you're going to be just fine."

I huddle in the blankets while he talks on and on, low and soothing, first to Myrtle and then to one or two other people on the phone. Someone arrives to take Myrtle to the hospital for observation, and then Jay converses with a policewoman, the same one who pulled him over on the day of the hike. As they talk, he points to Myrtle's gun beside the pool. I'm not sure how he explains the reddish tinge of the pool water, but the policewoman merely collects the weapon and leaves without even asking me for a statement. The only acknowledgment of my presence comes when a paramedic checks me over briefly and nods, apparently satisfied that I'm in no danger. She touches the red marks where the gag dug into my cheeks, but she doesn't ask about them. She explains about concussion symptoms and which ones might require a doctor's attention.

Then everyone is gone, and the house is empty again.

It's scary that someone as young as Jay holds so much power, that he can smooth over an event like this with a few calls and quiet words.

The house is silent as a tomb, motionless as a corpse. I can't help thinking of the other way this day could have gone. If Jay wasn't a vampire, he would have died in that pool. And I would be the one screaming incoherently and vowing revenge—or more likely clamming up and withdrawing deep inside myself, into my own private vault of pain.

But Jay is alive. I'm alive. And Myrtle is going to get some help. So that's all good, and I should feel relieved, but I'm mostly shaken and confused. And very, very curious.

Jay perches on the edge of the coffee table, concern shining in his brown eyes. "Do you want to talk? Or would you like me to take you home so you can rest?"

"Are you kidding?" I haul myself upright, tugging the blanket tighter around my shoulders. "I will not be able to rest until you tell me everything. Starting with—how are there actual vampires?"

"There weren't. Not until four decades ago, when a guy named Dr. Clarence Endive started working on a new kind of gene therapy. He thought if he could create self-healing cells, or speed up the body's natural regenerative processes, he could cure a whole slew of illnesses and genetic disorders. He worked on the formula until he thought he had it just right. But he lost his funding, and his entire lab was shut down. So he went underground, got funding from some shady sources, and began conducting tests of his gene therapy, first on animals and then on desperate humans. And it worked—to a point. He was able to alter people at the genetic level, so that their cells would repair and regenerate at an incredibly fast rate—which meant resistance to diseases and aging. In some cases, he could even reverse genetic disorders like muscular dystrophy.

"But as with most good things, there was one drawback. The people he treated could no longer produce their own blood cells. The human body makes 259 billion blood cells daily, and none of his subjects could do that anymore, so they died. Dr. Endive altered the formula a bit, tried a new set of test subjects—and they started manifesting physical alterations, like fangs and claws. It's possible Endive blended some animal DNA into the mix—Cody doesn't know, and Endive died years ago."

"So he single-handedly created the first generation of vampires."

"Yes. And before you ask, there's no garlic or crosses or stakes involved." He smiles tenuously.

I give him the tiniest smile in return. The grin that floods his face is like sunshine. Which reminds me... "What about sunlight?"

"Ah, that. Well, we don't sparkle or burst into flames, but we are photosensitive. If I'm out in the sun for more than a few hours, I start feeling sick. The older the vampire, the worse the sun sickness is. Cody can't handle more than an hour of full sun, and even that much is uncomfortable for him."

"That's why we had to go home when we were on the lake and the sun started coming out."

He nods.

"So it's a side effect," I say. "Like when they advertise a medication on TV, and then list a million things that might go wrong with you if you take it."

"Exactly. But the payoff is healing from deadly wounds within seconds, and looking young and healthy for a very long time, so it's kinda worth it."

"How long do vampires live?"

"We don't know. Like I said, we've only existed for a handful of decades. Cody has met two people from the original batch— one was his progenitor, Meyer Wolfsheim. Cody says Wolfsheim was twenty-five and terminal when he signed up for the gene therapy, and he still looks twenty-five. Strong as a grizzly, and just as mean."

"So vampires are strong. Stronger than humans?"

"Nice fresh healthy cells tend to do that, yes. I'd say we have about the same level of strength as a human bodybuilder or heavyweight champion, and that's without hours of working out. And we're fast, but we don't have superspeed."

"Bummer. I was hoping for a speedy piggyback ride through some misty forest in Washington."

He arches an eyebrow. "That would make me the Edward in your scenario, and I object. Strongly."

Hysterical laughter bubbles in my throat. Aside from the horrifying blood-drinking bit, it's funny—really and truly hilarious—that the first boy I loved came back to me as a fucking vampire. And he's a billionaire as well—which he still has not explained, along with a number of other concerning things.

"Where do you get your blood?" I ask. "And if you actually drink it, how does it get from your stomach into your bloodstream?"

"Vampires have two stomachs and two hearts. The extra organs are for handling the intake of blood."

My eyebrows lift sky-high, and Jay winces. "Yeah, it's weird. But cows have like four stomachs, and squids have three hearts. It's not unheard of in the natural world."

"Point taken," I answer. But the idea still makes me squeamish, and my eyes drift over Jay's body. Where does he even keep an extra heart and stomach? He's so lean, so human-looking.

He keeps talking, apparently oblivious to my anatomical curiosity. "Like I said, we can't replenish our own blood cells, so when our blood supply is low, we start to feel achy and irritable. There's a special kind of hunger that kicks in, stronger and more painful than regular hunger. If we're near a live blood source, our fangs are triggered, and they start to elongate. The claws come out too, sometimes. And that change reroutes the internal systems."

"Like how food and air go down the same throat, but they end up in different places," I say.

"You got it. The blood we drink goes into its own reservoir, our smaller stomach, and our second heart pumps that blood into the regular vascular system, to be used as needed. We can go for a number of days without drinking any blood, but if we wait too long, we start to get sick—shaky, clammy, and weak. Then the headaches begin, and eventually, if the blood supply in our bodies gets too low, we start having seizures and go into cardiac arrest."

"So you *can* die."

"Of course. We're not undead. We're still alive, just changed. Genetically mutated."

"And how does someone become a vampire? Is Myrtle going to be one now, since you bit her?"

"The genetic catalyst doesn't transmit through saliva or other fluids, only by blood ingestion or transfusion. There's another component to the process as well, but we don't need to talk about that yet."

"So it's like the old legends then." My voice is way shriller than I'd like. "You drink a vampire's blood, and you become a vampire. Cool, cool, cool. Supercool."

Jay winces, cocking his head. "You're freaking out, aren't you?"

"Nope. Just...processing. A lot of processing going on here. Um, I guess my next question is where do you get your blood supply?" I cringe, afraid of the answer. "Please say stolen blood bags."

"We do sometimes conduct fake blood drives," he says. "But that blood only works for us if it's super fresh, drawn within the past two or three hours. Beyond that, we can't use it. Makes us sick. So live donors work best." He stares at the surface of the coffee table, tracing the whorls of the wood. "That's what the parties are for."

A chill races over my skin. "You and Cody drink from your guests."

"Cody and I aren't the only vampires in town."

"You're not?" I swallow hard. The puzzle pieces are shifting in my mind, notching together.

"We offer a service, you see. Immunity against disease, superior healing, youth and beauty, for as long as it lasts—which, considering the rate of our cell regeneration, is probably going to be a very long time."

"Your insurance policies," I murmur. "You're selling vampirism. Turning people into vampires in exchange for money. That's how you got all of this." I bark a laugh, gesturing to the elegant room around us and the entire house beyond. "You must charge quite a lot per customer." Then I clap my hand over my mouth. "Oh my god—Jordan. You turned her, didn't you?"

"I offered her protection. A safety net. She's a daredevil, Daisy.

You and I both know she'd have gotten herself killed eventually. Now she has extra strength and speed, plus incredible healing abilities. You saw how fast I healed. Myrtle punctured part of my heart with that bullet, and it repaired itself within a few minutes. Jordan is a vampire, which means she's safe. She can keep doing what she loves, without worrying the people who care about her."

"And how much did you make her pay?" My cheeks are burning, my heart swelling with anger.

"Not a thing. She's your friend, so she got the friends and family discount." He smiles hopefully at me, but the expression fades when I give him a thunderous frown.

"So she drinks from people now? At your parties? How does that work? Why aren't there guests running around shrieking about vampires?"

"Some of our clients have loved ones who provide them with blood. Those who don't are taught how to carefully choose their donors, people who won't be missed for a few hours. We dose the potential donors with sleep medication and take them to private rooms on the second or third floors. Each vampire only drinks enough blood to top off the tank, so to speak—not enough to hurt anyone. And they're under strict orders not to touch the donors beyond what's necessary for taking the blood."

Wait a second. Wait a fucking second. "That's what happened to Nick! He was drugged and someone drank from him. Cody, that rat bastard. I'll *kill* him."

"The first time, Cody drank from Nick without his knowledge, yes. But they have an arrangement now."

"Oh my god. So Nick knows."

"He does."

"You told him before you told me."

"Cody wanted to tell him, and it wasn't my business to interfere. I waited to tell you because I wasn't sure how you'd react. I kind of figured it would be something like this. The anger, the questions..." He sighs and musses his hair with his fingers.

"So sorry to inconvenience you with my questions," I snap. "And just because Nick is cool with it now doesn't change the fact that there was a major consent issue the first time."

"There's also a survival issue," Jay retorts. "I told you, we can't use the stale stuff from blood bags. It doesn't have the same potency. And we can't explain the vampire thing to all our donors. There aren't enough of us yet for that kind of exposure. We wouldn't be safe."

"Have you thought about what will happen if you keep turning people? Eventually everyone will be vampires and there won't be a large enough blood supply."

He sighs. "You sound like Wolfsheim. He's always fussing at Cody and me for turning people."

"It's a legitimate concern. You do realize your fountain of youth has a flaw, right? If you let too many people drink from it, eventually they will all die."

"That's why we're making people pay dearly for the privilege."

I can hardly keep from screaming at him, from slapping him again. "How could you? You and I know what it's like to be poor, Jay. To have less than everyone else, and to hurt because of it. What's wrong with you, selling eternal life to the rich? It's disgusting."

"I've given it away, too," he says stiffly. "To medical professionals, law enforcement, and some terminally ill people—those at high risk of disease or death. But as you say, not everyone can become one of us, and setting a premium price is the easiest way to control the demand. Why is it so hard to explain this to you? I'm trying to do a good thing here."

"And you're just a few generations away from a global vampire takeover and blood farms packed with human slaves."

"Do you really think I'd allow something like that?" His brown eyes practically spark with anger. "I have a plan, Daisy. I have teams working on ways to preserve the potency of drawn blood, to create blood substitutes, to fabricate viable cloned blood cells. We've started requiring candidates to spend some time as blood suppliers before they get transformation approval. That's what Cody and I did. He drank from me for years before he changed me."

The idea of Cody with his lips pressed to Jay's skin turns me hot and jealous. But now is not the time for hormones to take over. I need to focus on what I've learned.

It sounds as if Jay and Cody have thought this through carefully—or at least Jay has. I swear he is the mastermind; the entire plan is rank with his signature blend of boldness and precision. He and Cody have earned a lot of money doing this, and they've hired people for the scientific work to help them create the infrastructure they'll need as vampirism expands—as it takes over the fucking world.

The ramifications are far-reaching beyond anything I feared or imagined. My voice-control ability seems far milder and less dangerous in comparison. "Let's get back to your victims for a second."

"Donors," Jay says sharply.

"Don't they notice the bite marks when they wake up?"

"Our saliva has healing properties that activate during a feeding session, so any marks stop bleeding within minutes, and disappear within hours. When our donors wake up, they feel a little woozy, but that's it."

"So you could go around licking people who are hurt and healing them?"

"No," he says patiently. "That enzyme is only triggered when we're feeding. And it only works for clotting blood and healing skin layers quickly. It can't fix deep-tissue wounds, or broken bones, or diseases."

We stare each other down, while my brain churns over everything I've learned.

I can't really be angry with him for not telling me right away. The transformation was his choice, something he did while I was out of his life to give himself power. He went from a lost boy huddled on a Charleston beach to a wealthy young man with more money than a lot of people twice his age and a sure way to make more. Although come to think of it, if making vampires is as easy as consuming vampiric blood, why can't Jay's "clients" just go out and sell immortality themselves? There must be something else involved, a part of the process that's not easily replicated. The "other component" Jay mentioned. I hope it's nothing sexual. If he's been sleeping with all the people he's turned…

"It's not sexual, is it?" I blurt out.

"Excuse me?" He flushes, and it's so cute I almost laugh.

"The other component of the transformation. You said it was more complicated than drinking a vampire's blood."

"It *is* more complicated, and no, Daisy, it's not sexual."

"Good. Because I was picturing you having sex with all those other people."

"Picturing me…having sex?" His mouth tips up at the corner.

My cheeks turn hot. "I wasn't—I mean—if you had to do that with everyone you changed, it would bother me more than the fangs, the two stomachs, and the other stuff." My voice trails off, and I focus very hard on the plump cushion of the sofa arm, tracing the creases of its puckered edge.

"It would bother me, too. But thankfully that's not part of the deal."

Silence invades again, but my racing thoughts don't decelerate. Is it weird that deep down, I'm not actually mad at him? That despite all of this, I still want to find a way to fit into his life? Even now, I can feel myself making space in my soul for the morally gray zone he inhabits, realigning my ethical boundaries to include what he must do to survive.

Is that even okay?

"I don't want to talk or think about this anymore today," I tell him. "I want to make it a tomorrow problem."

"That's fair." He laces his fingers and studies them. "You've been through a lot."

"So have you. What with the dying and all."

"True."

"You can eat like a normal person, right?"

"You've seen me eat."

"Well, getting cracked on the head, being tied up, and watching my boyfriend get shot made me ravenous. I demand dinner, and I think I deserve to have it brought to me. Right here. While I sit comfortably on this couch."

"Of course." Jay leaps up. "Anything you want. Just tell me what sounds good, and I'll—Hold up. Did you just call me your boyfriend?"

"Is that not a term vampires use?" I pluck at the blanket, avoiding his eyes, my heart throbbing.

His fingers curl at his sides, tight and tense, like coiled springs. "That's absolutely a term vampires use."

Again with the silence. Is he waiting for me to say something? Why isn't *he* saying something? Was I too impulsive? Maybe I assumed too much. He might not even want that kind of relationship with me.

"Daisy," he says faintly. "Don't tease me."

I look up, and up. He's so fucking tall, and there's a stormy aura surrounding him, a mounting tide of emotion.

"Come down here," I say softly, skimming dangerously close to the tone that will make him my puppet. But I don't go there. That is a morally gray space I'm not comfortable with, at least not until I understand more about what I can do.

Jay isn't the only one who's different in a supernaturally unexpected way. Maybe we're two of a kind, he and I. More of a match than we ever suspected.

I reach for one of his hands and pull him down beside me, until he's kneeling on the rug while I sit on my throne of couch cushions and blankets.

"We've both changed," I tell him. "My family's whole situation changed. And you—your change is, like, *way* out there, superhard to wrap my head around, but people keep changing throughout their whole lives, right? And after each change, their friends have to decide whether or not to stick with them. I have to be honest. I feel like you didn't stick with me after we moved away."

"I've apologized for that, and I'll do it again. I'm sorry." But there's a shadow over his words.

I frown at him. "You're not sorry. Or at least, that's not the only thing you feel about it."

His brown eyes lock with mine, a stormy swirl of pain. "You left me, Daisy. You were the only person I had, and you left me behind with nothing. You can't imagine how that felt—to have my second home ripped away, the place where I had meals, the place where I made all my good holiday memories, where I studied and played. You all treated me as part of the family for years and then, when your dad got his new job, you left." He lunges to his feet, his voice rising, strained with repressed fury. "You abandoned me, and all you can think about is how it affected you. How you didn't get emails, or calls, or texts. You tore away everything that mattered to me, and you expected me to remind myself of that rejection by *staying in touch*? Screw that."

"What was I supposed to do?" Anger trembles in my heart, in my voice. I throw off the blankets and rise to face him, ignoring the lingering pain in my head. "My parents were in charge. I had to move with them. What the hell did you expect me to do?"

"Fight for me! Ask them to get custody of me."

"You know that would never have worked. No judge would have given you to us."

"They might have! Your parents had enough evidence of my mom's neglect. They didn't even try."

"Because you told them not to go to Child Protective Services! You didn't want to end up in foster care, and that's what would have happened if they'd spoken out. We weren't related, Jay. Mom and Dad could never have gotten custody of you—and even if they had, is that what you would have wanted? To be my foster brother?"

"Hell no!"

"Then what, Jay, what? What did you want? I was fourteen. What more could I have done?"

"I don't fucking know!" he bellows. The blaze in his eyes and the force of his shout sends me back a step.

He sucks in a quick breath, his face drawn taut, his eyes so wide with horror that I forget my anger. He sinks onto the edge of the coffee table, and I sit opposite him, on the edge of the sofa.

"Jay. Are you okay? You look like...like you killed someone."

"I don't yell like that." The words leak between his stiff lips. "That's not me."

"It's okay."

"It's not. I promised myself I wouldn't, that I would never—" He looks as if he's about to smack the table, but instead he curls his fist against it with studied control. "This is how it starts, with the yelling. The arguments. I want us to be different, you and me. I don't want us to ever get like them."

He's talking about his parents. I slip my fingers over his fist, settle them between his knuckles. "We won't."

"We might." He pulls away. "I thought I was ready for this, for us, but apparently I still need to work on myself. You deserve that. You deserve the best."

The finality in his tone is terrifying, like he might actually leave this house, this mountain. Whatever happens, he can't leave. Not when I just got him back, not when he just revealed his whole secret life to me.

"You don't have to be perfect, Jay," I whisper.

He stares at me, incredulous. "Oh, Daisy, of course I do. Of *course* I do. We live in a world where one mistake can destroy someone's reputation forever. We all have to strive to be perfect."

"Perfect to whom, though? Because people don't all have the same standards, you'll never be perfect to everyone. The lines are all drawn in different places. Even people who agree on one thing will eventually realize they disagree on something else. Perfection is impossible."

He gives me a crooked smile. "If there's one thing I've learned in the past eight years, it's that nothing's impossible." He stands again, pulling out his phone. "And you asked who I'm trying to be perfect for, but I think you know the answer. It's always been you. You've been with me through every moment, every decision I've made. Even when I hated you for leaving me behind."

"I'm sorry." I breathe the words straight from my soul, even though I know they can't fix his pain.

"It's okay," he says. "I forgave you already. Now tell me what you want for dinner, and I'll make it happen."

13

I'm warm, so warm, drifting on a sea of spice and heat, rising gently on a swell and then sinking again. Except this ocean isn't liquid, it's firm, covered in soft cotton fabric—

I blink slowly, and there's a lean muscled arm inches from my nose, a strong hand draped over my shoulder. My own hand is curled around a fistful of Jay's T-shirt, and my hip is nestled between his legs. Beyond the curve of his arm, I can see the empty containers of the Thai takeout we ate last night.

I must have fallen asleep on his chest. And he didn't move me.

Cautiously I sit up, trying to wring some order from my mass of blond tangles. It's no use, so I tug an elastic from my wrist and knot the whole mess on top of my head. My breath probably smells awful. There's water in a bottle on the table, so I drink a few swallows.

Jay is still out, completely relaxed. I've seen him asleep before, but he was just a kid then. He's so much bigger now. His angles have sharpened, while his chest and arms have filled out. I want to trace the curve of his lashes, the arch of his dark eyebrows, the line of his nose. His brown hair is smushed against the armrest of the couch; he's going to have the cutest bedhead when he gets up.

A vampire with bedhead. I smother a hysterical snicker as everything I learned yesterday rushes back in.

I spent the night with a vampire.

I spent the night with a man, and my parents will know. When I get home, I'll have to deal with their questions and comments. I hate feeling like I'm back in high school again. Easy and comfortable as it is at Mom and Dad's, I need to be out of there by the end of the summer.

I find a bathroom and wash up. Jay's still asleep when I return, so I walk out back to the pool area. My stomach clenches as I approach the spot where Myrtle struck me from behind. I make myself stand there and breathe through the anxiety, until I can move past it and think about the clear pink of the morning sky, the twitter of birds in the bushes, and the quiet gurgle of the fountain at the end of the pool. The concrete feels fresh and cool under my bare toes.

A whistled tune and a murmur of voices surprises me, and my heart starts to race—but it's only a couple of guys in T-shirts that say, "Schrader's Pool Maintenance," carrying several pieces of equipment and a length of hose. One of them nods to me. "Morning, miss. This the pool you need cleaned?"

"Um...yes." Because my vampire boyfriend bled into it yesterday. He must have called them to take care of the contamination. "Yes, thank you."

"Right on." They start setting up their equipment, and judging from what I can see, the pump's going to get noisy, so I pad along the path leading into the garden and pull my phone from my pocket. It's about time I talk to Jordan.

Luckily I have twenty percent battery left. I usually text her, but I think this conversation warrants an actual call. She's probably still asleep, but frankly, I don't give a damn.

She answers on the third ring. "Girl, you better be dying if you're gonna call me this early."

"Interesting choice of words. Jay died yesterday."

She swears, loud and long, and I wait patiently until the string of f-bombs has ended.

"Yeah, Myrtle shot him through the chest. Nicked his heart. Funny thing—he didn't stay dead."

A long pause. Then Jordan says, "So you know."

"I do. Apparently you now have a second stomach and heart, like a freaking cow-squid thingy. And the reason I didn't see you much at the Met party is because you were off guzzling some unconscious person's blood."

"More or less. Look, I'm hearing a judgy tone and I'm gonna tell you right now, I'm not in the mood, okay? It's way too early for you to be this morally upright."

I sigh, touching the peach-colored petals of a rose. There's a whole section of them in Jay's gardens—fat ones as big as my fist in colors ranging from lush pink and velvety red to buttery yellow and creamy white. Their scent is a delicate swirl in the morning air.

"Daisy?" Jordan's tone is sharp. It reminds me of my own special tone, and how Jay was about to tell me why he and Cody were more susceptible to my voice. It's because they're vampires, with extra-sensitive hearing. Which means Jordan should also be susceptible. I've never tried doing this over the phone before—but in the name of scientific research, I should probably try. Just to see how far my powers extend.

"I want you to tell me how it works." My voice drifts low, rising and falling like a song. "Tell me what Gatsby's special process is, the one he uses to turn people into vampires. Why can't anyone else replicate it?"

Jordan answers immediately, in a curiously toneless voice. "It's something he and Cody worked out together. The process used to be painful and clumsy, and the subject would be deathly sick for weeks while the new organs were growing. A lot of humans would die or give up and kill themselves to escape the pain before the change was complete. Gatsby found a way to ease the process, a special drug to help the subject's body accept the genetic changes."

"So Jay developed a safer, more comfortable transformation process. Is that what you're saying?"

"Yes."

"So people could theoretically become vampires without paying all that money, if they were willing to do it the old way, and go through the pain, and risk dying from the transition."

"Yes."

It changes things, knowing there's another way for people to become vampires if they really want to, even if they don't have enough money to pay Cody and Jay. Like any shrewd businessman, Jay is providing not just the product, but a premium service. An experience. A more comfortable transformation, plus the benefit of an orientation into the world, blood access at the parties, and an ongoing membership in a community of fellow vampires. It's kind of genius, actually. He's the vampire version of Steve Jobs. The thought makes me giggle, and that sound snaps Jordan out of her obedient mode.

"Did you hear me, Daisy? I don't like being judged."

"I'm not judging you. I'm a little mad you didn't tell me, but I understand why."

"Great. I'm so relieved," she says dryly. "Now I can go back to sleep."

"I have more questions. What's a glutton?"

But she's already hung up.

I guess that went about as well as could be expected.

I think about texting Mom, but I really don't want to field her questions about what happened with me and Jay last night. The answer is pretty boring anyway; I fell asleep after dinner and nothing happened. I kind of wish something *had* happened. But with everything I went through yesterday, all the emotions and the headache, it wouldn't have been a good idea. My head feels way better today, and my neck is only a little stiff. There's still a sore lump on my skull, though.

The sun is rising, casting nets of golden beams over the rosebushes, picking out the glittering dewdrops on every leaf and thorn and petal. Its warmth on my bare arms is like a familiar touch. No matter what else has changed, the world is still turning, and the sun is still shining. I'm alive to see it, and so is Jay.

He could have died. The moment I thought he was dead is tangled in the back of my mind like bristling black vines. Remembering that sense of raw, wretched panic kicks my heart into a faster rhythm. My soul was shredded in those moments, and even though it healed up again almost instantly, there will always be faint scars, the echo of what it felt like to lose him.

An unreasonable anxiety crawls through my bones, itching along my skin. I need Jay. I need him right now. I need to be touching him, making sure that he's really here. Existing. Whole.

I race back through the rose garden, past the entrance to the hedge maze, through the pool area, hopping over the big hose and covering my ears against the noise of the pump. I fight my way through the ghostly sheers blowing across the screened porch, and I hurry along the hall, into the room where I left Jay asleep.

He's standing there, casual and beautiful, checking his phone. I slam into him, wrapping him in my arms as tightly as I can.

He staggers a little, and his free hand lands on my head, a gentle pressure. "Hey there. You okay?"

"It doesn't matter," I murmur into his shirt.

"Huh?"

"It doesn't matter, any of it. The vampire stuff—it's all just logistics, something we'll have to work out. You're alive because you're a vampire, so I can never be mad about that, ever. I'm grateful, Jay. So, so grateful." Tears are streaming from my eyes, and I press my face further into his chest, listening to the thrum of his heart. It's got an odd cadence—the expected double-thump, with an offbeat echo. His second heart is working away somewhere deep inside. It's strange, and it's him. I accept it. I accept all of him, because underneath every choice he's made, questionable or not, he is good. He's got a head for strategy and a heart full of goodness and eyes full of hope, and I love him.

Of course I can't actually say any of that. It would sound dumb and sentimental, and I'd probably cry. So I just hold him, grip him like he might slip backward into that blood-tinged pool and sink forever.

He drops his phone on the floor and closes both arms around me, setting his chin on the top of my head.

After a moment, I tip my face up to his, rising a little on my toes. He meets me halfway, his soft smile pressing to my mouth. The kiss is tender, sweet and warm, like melting chocolate.

Being here like this, with my body molded to his, wakens the familiar flush of arousal over my skin. Last night, the vampire concept was too new in my head, and though I was turned on, it was a cautious sensation, less urgent than what I usually feel with Jay. This morning I've accepted it all, and every part of me got the memo. It's like I was temporarily locked down, and now the right password has been entered, so I'm open again.

My hands follow the slope of Jay's back down to his tapered waist, then to his backside. He's got the most squeezable, bitable ass, honestly. I wonder what sound he would make if I bit him there. Pretty sure I'd shriek with delight if he bit mine.

Palms against his butt, I pull him tighter against me. He's hardening against my lower belly, a thick length that sends a thrilling tingle into my pussy.

He huffs an eager breath against my lips and kisses me again—a fervent crush of a kiss, scorching and hungry. My tongue quests over the points of his teeth, slides into his mouth, and twines with his tongue. He moans low in his throat, gripping me tighter.

"Fuck, Daisy," he says hoarsely, each word a hot breath between my lips.

His hands find the hem of my shirt, nails scraping my skin lightly, fingers sliding up beneath it. He pushes the bra up, out of his way. It's wireless and stretchy, so it yields to him easily. My breath hitches at the glorious rush of Jay's warm hands over my bare breasts, and for a second I forget where I am, what he is, everything but the long fingers enjoying my skin, the thumbs stroking over my nipples.

He takes my mouth again, and I abandon my fondling of his ass to weave all my fingers into his hair. I open wide for him, gripped by a reckless need to be closer to him—to nestle inside him, or swallow him into myself.

But then we hear the distant voice of a pool cleaner, raised to shout instructions. At the same moment a door closes somewhere above us.

"One of the staff," Jay whispers apologetically. "We could go to my room, or...we could wait until we have more time, more space." He brushes his lips across my cheek. "When I can really savor you."

"Oh god, yes." He's right. We probably shouldn't get it on right here. But we can satisfy a different kind of hunger. "Breakfast?" I suggest.

He makes a wry face, but nods. "Breakfast."

I follow him through a doorway and down a hall. "Where's Cody, by the way?"

"I'm not sure. He's been going out a lot lately. Maybe he's with Nick?"

"Probably. They've been spending a lot of time together."

"Yeah. I haven't seen Cody quite this devoted before."

"Nick's a good guy," I say. "And he's family. I don't want him to get hurt."

"I can't guarantee that." Jay ushers me into the kitchen, a gleaming white-and-silver expanse of islands and counters and appliances. "Cody can be unpredictable. He's been through a lot. Like I told you, he was turned by Wolfsheim, one of the first-generation vampires, and Cody served as his boy toy for a while. He was dependent on Wolfsheim for blood sources, for protection. Wolfsheim abused him in a lot of ways."

"That's horrible. Why does Cody still take calls from him?"

Jay pulls open the fridge. "He doesn't."

"Yes he does. I overheard Cody talking to him on the phone at the Met party."

"You overhear a lot, don't you?" The ghost of a smile curls the corner of his mouth, but his eyes darken with worry. "You're sure it was Wolfsheim?"

"Yeah, that's what Cody called him." Briefly I outline what I heard of the conversation.

A muscle tics along Jay's jaw. He sets a carton of eggs on the counter a little too hard. "He should have told me Wolfsheim called. He shouldn't have to deal with that bastard alone. Wolfsheim is the most powerful of the First Gens. He believes in turning people the original way, slow and painful, to see who survives. It's like a ritual, so that only the *worthy* become vampires."

"Seems elitist."

"It is. But the other First Gens follow Wolfsheim blindly. He's been threatening Cody and me for months, demanding that we shut down our operation. For him, vampirism is like a religion. He and his people are fanatics, demanding that everyone fall in line with their rules."

"I've never enjoyed people like that." I take a pan from the rack over the island and place it on the stovetop. "Got butter?"

He tosses me a stick, and for a few minutes we focus on getting a nice scramble going, complete with chopped bacon, cheese, onions, and tomatoes. Then we perch on barstools and shovel all the warm deliciousness into our mouths.

"I could eat this forever," I moan. "So good. By the way, what's a glutton?"

Jay chokes on his food and has to guzzle half a glass of water before he can answer. "God, Daisy. How do you know that?"

"You and the Henry guy talked about it right in front of me. After our dance, remember?" When I lost it and crumpled on the floor in a mess of tears.

"Oh." He seems relieved. "A glutton—well, a glutton is..." He tilts his head and examines me, as if he's gauging my tolerance level. "I could tell you, or I could show you. If you think you can handle it."

I swallow hard. "I've handled a lot already."

"Is that a yes?"

"It's a tentative sort of maybe."

"You'll be fine. I'll be right there with you." He stuffs the last bite of eggs into his mouth and jumps up. "Come on. Let's visit the dungeon."

"The dungeon?" I mumble through a mouthful of eggs. "You have a dungeon?"

"I bought this place from a guy who was really into bondage stuff. He built the dungeon, but I remodeled it."

"So you had a sex dungeon. Tom would have loved that," I sneer.

Tom tried to push me beyond the spanking thing when we were dating, but I resisted. No shame for people who like that stuff, but it wasn't for me. It's probably one of the reasons he decided to cheat. I get the feeling he really wants someone who's a blend of me and Myrtle—my popularity and money, with Myrtle's amenability to his every whim.

I collect my plate and carry it halfway to the sink before Jay says, "You can leave it. I have people who clean up around here."

I cock an eyebrow at him. "You should take your plate to the sink, too."

He flashes me a sharp-toothed grin. "Make me."

And then the smiles drop from both our faces, because we remember that I actually *could* make him do it.

"Go ahead," he says. "Make me."

There's a now-familiar shift in my throat as I slip my voice into that special cadence. "Jay Gatsby, take your plate to the sink. And wash both plates—no, *all* the breakfast dishes—right now."

I sit on a barstool at the island and watch while he mechanically collects and washes every pan, plate, and utensil we used. He even walks over and takes the half-full juice glass right out of my hand, empties it, and scrubs it down.

When he's done, he just stands there, staring into space.

It's fucking scary, seeing him like this. Knowing what I can do, what it means.

It means that I'm not quite human. I'm something else. There is more to the world than I ever knew, and I can either tumble into helpless pieces or suck it up and deal with the frightening, fascinating reality.

In a way, isn't this what I've always wanted? A different future than the one society laid out for me? Something unique, something exciting? A gate swinging open to a path no one else can take?

From that perspective, I'm lucky. And I'm also fucked.

At least there's someone in my life who doesn't fear the power I possess. I'll make sure he knows his trust in me is justified.

"Wake up, Jay," I tell him.

And then he's back. He stares at the pile of clean dishes on the counter. "Holy shit. I don't remember doing any of that."

"You even stole my juice glass before it was empty." I pout.

A crease forms between Jay's eyebrows. "Daisy..."

"I will never use this on you without your permission."

His forehead smooths again. "And I will never drink from you without your consent."

My heartbeat jolts into a quicker pattern. "Okay," I breathe.

"I've scared you," he says. "Your heart is beating really fast."

"Not scared, exactly. More apprehensive. Or...excited."

"Excited, huh?" His mouth curves.

"Get over yourself, vampire." I flounce off my stool, collecting my phone from the counter and slipping it into the back pocket of my shorts. "Let's go see your dungeon."

14

THE DUNGEON IS IN THE BASEMENT, BECAUSE OF COURSE IT is. Nobody ever sets up their dungeons in pool houses or second-floor bedrooms. Maybe in garages or attics, but the basement is the standard choice.

Jay goes through a series of codes and handprints and facial recognition crap before the door opens. He has to create a guest profile for me, too.

"So you really do keep people down here. Good thing someone has friends on the police force," I say wryly.

"Only people who deserve it," he says. "And yes, it helps to have people on the force who owe me for their immortality."

"And you think that's a good thing? Removing the fear of death for people who already have a disproportionate amount of power?"

He pulls the heavy door shut behind us, and my eyes follow the swell of his biceps through the motion.

"Are we going to argue this now?" he says. "I already told you, I turn other people, too. Doctors, nurses, terminal patients who are young or have families. I have to be careful who I propose the change to, though. Scientifically minded types tend to be less accepting of the whole vampire concept."

"And the cops just swallow it whole?"

"Not at first. They usually need proof. But then they're typically eager to accept my offer."

"And in exchange they cover for you and your vampires whenever you need it."

"There are rules every new vampire agrees to follow. They're not exempt from regular human laws. If they make a mistake, sure, the police can help out a little so we're not exposed. But the police only do that as long as we hold up our end of the bargain—no human deaths or serious injuries. If that happens, Cody and I take matters into our own hands. And that's where the dungeon comes in."

He yanks open another door, an elaborate barred monstrosity that looks like something from a medieval castle. I stare at it, and then at him.

He flushes in the foggy glare of the overhead light. "Yeah, I ordered this one from a castle in Normandy. So?"

"You wanted to look the part." I smother a grin. "Dangerous vampire lord with a spooky dungeon."

"What if I did?"

"Do you have a big, black trench coat too?"

"What if I do?"

"Oh my gosh, you *do*! I want to see it."

He gazes at me with mock haughtiness. "I don't wear it during the summer, Daisy."

"You'll put it on for me later. Just for a little bit."

He shakes his head, laughing. "So demanding. Come on."

A sharp bang from the dim hallway ahead startles the smile from my face. "What's that?"

"A glutton." Jay isn't smiling now either. His fingers flex at his sides as we walk, and he cracks his neck briefly, as if he's preparing for something.

"Does your dungeon have to be so dark?" I eye the dim bulbs overhead.

"Gluttons are extra sensitive to light. We deprive them of it so we can use it as a training tool later."

"A training tool?" That sounds very not good.

Another loud bang and a moaning rattle.

"He can smell you," Jay whispers. "Stay behind me."

We continue along the hall to a row of reinforced doors. They've each got a vent-sized iron grate in the lower section, and latched panels in the upper section. I can't tell exactly how many doors there are, because they sort of melt into the darkness as the hall marches on into the indefinite underground.

"I don't like this place, Jay," I whisper.

"Almost there," he says reassuringly. "So, about gluttons... Cody and I teach our clients to drink only as much as they need to live, no more. But like anything else, the taste of blood can become addictive. When our tank is full, so to speak, we feel really good. Powerful, capable of anything. Pleasure is heightened. Some vampires start chasing that feeling of fullness and power, and they begin overindulging, taking too much blood. That puts our donors in danger, so it's not allowed."

"But how do you know if you're drinking too much?"

"See this?" Jay holds up his arm, showing me the thick metal bracelet I've been so curious about. "Every new client gets one. It uses pulse and blood pressure sensors to gauge how much blood we have left and how much we need to consume." He presses a fingertip to it, and a glowing bar shows up. "Mine is in the green right now. If it goes up to blue or purple, I've had too much blood. If it slides down to yellow, that's a warning I need to drink. Orange means I'm dangerously low on blood, and red... Well, at that point I might as well be dead, because I'd probably be having seizures and couldn't drink anyway."

The mental image of Jay on the ground, eyes rolled up, limbs spasming and jerking, terrifies me to my core.

"But you're good now," I say, to reassure myself. "Green is good."

"Yeah."

The glowing bar disappears, and I tap the metal, trying to make it show up again.

"It's coded to my fingerprint," Jay says. "I'll add yours too, if you want."

"I do want. I want to be able to check on you if I need to." I look up at him, and our gazes lock. In this corridor of rough concrete and shadows and cool stale air, we are the only warm, breathing, pulsing things, and the energy humming between us is vivid, magnetic. My thoughts swirl and refocus in a single refrain through my head, through every thump of my heart. *I love you, I want you. I love you, I want you.*

Another eardrum-shattering bang, and a loud roar rising to a shriek. The tension between Jay and me dissipates, and he hurries ahead. "Sorry about all the noise. This guy is fresh. I had to put him down here during the Met party. He hasn't had time to relearn his manners yet."

He stops in front of a heavy metal door and unlocks the cover on its window. "This glass is basically bulletproof, so don't worry. Just keep an eye on the grate lower down. He likes to stick his claws through there and poke at people—don't you, Slagle?" Jay sweeps his hand toward the window, dramatic as a circus showman. "This is what happens when someone can't control their bloodlust. It gets worse the longer it goes unchecked."

Cautiously I peer through the window, careful to keep my shins clear of the grate.

A face smashes against the glass—bloodshot eyes and stringy hair and slavering fangs. I yelp and jump back, slamming into Jay's chest.

"He can't get to you," Jay assures me.

A voice moans from the cell. "I'm starving, I'm starving, Gatsby. Let me out, let me out!"

"You're not starving, Slagle. You drank plenty the other night. Check your bracelet, and you'll see that you're fine."

"Damn the bracelet!" shrieks Slagle. "It's broken, I'm telling you. Malfunctioned. I need more, Gatsby. I'm dying in here, dying!" The man presses his face to the window again, fixing his eyes on me. Dried black blood cakes the corners of his mouth. "You, girl—you look too sweet to let a man die right in front of you. I need blood. This creep"—he points to Jay—"is trying to starve me. I feel sick!"

"That's because you filled both your stomachs with blood, Slagle," Jay explains patiently. "You broke the rules. And now we have to see if you can be rehabilitated."

"And if not?" growls the man.

"You know what happens. You agreed to it when Cody changed you," Jay says. "We can't have vampires running around ripping humans apart. Lucky for you, you haven't actually killed anyone yet, or I'd have finished you off already."

He says it so calmly that I cast a sharp glance at his profile. His face is as calm as his voice. He's done this before. He's had to kill people he or Cody turned, people who went wrong. How did he do it? Rip their heads off? Did it even bother him, or was it just another necessary step toward his goals?

I thought I had I settled into acceptance, but this revelation shakes me. How well do I really know this new Jay?

Slagle shudders and moans, his claws screeching down the glass.

"A glutton can't control his appearance like a regular vampire can," Jay says. "He's stuck in feeding mode."

"And you can control your fangs and everything?"

"Sometimes it's harder than others, depending on my blood level and the strength of the stimulation. But usually I can. Watch."

His upper lip rises, and his canines elongate, slipping from their hidden sheaths in his gums. The lower canines grow too, though they're not nearly as long as the upper ones. Jay's brown irises swirl cloudy white, and when he lifts his hand, claws emerge from above his fingernails. They're pointed at the tips, their shafts curved to match the arc of his nails. Like a second set of fingernails on top of the first one.

"They don't look that strong," I say, touching one of the claws lightly. "Do they ever break?"

"Sometimes, but they grow back. And they're stronger than they look." He scrapes them over the concrete wall and slashes them through the air.

The monstrosity of his appearance strikes me in the gut. The difference between him and the glutton in the cell is so thin, separated by a mere sliver of choice and opportunity.

"So who deals with you if you turn gluttonous?"

"Cody," he says, pronouncing the name carefully through the fangs. "And I would do the same for him."

"And if both of you turn glutton at the same time?"

"Then the staff know who to call at the police station, and they would come. A good shotgun blast to the brain or a swift beheading would do it."

"So all your staff are in on it?"

"Yes, and I pay them well for their service and silence. A few of them provide blood from time to time, in exchange for the promise that I'll turn them eventually if they request it."

The man in the cell speaks again, a guttural snarl. "You're torturing me. She smells so meaty, so savory. I can taste the salt of her blood. Let me have a little, please. Just a nibble."

"Eww. I'm not a piece of meat," I tell him.

"Yes, you are. The best kind of meat. Fresh, firm flesh. Leg and thigh, neck and breast, best places to sink my teeth—sweetness and salt, lick you clean afterward, I promise, *I promise!*" He ends with a shrill whine, crashing against the door again.

"All right, time's up." Jay slams the window cover shut and snaps the padlock in place. "That's all the exposure therapy he can handle today."

"Wait—you were using me as part of his treatment?"

"You wanted to know about gluttons. I killed two birds with one stone."

"Not sure if I like being that guy's bait."

"But you did so great." Jay winks at me.

I elbow him in return. "Does he have a family?"

"Yeah, a wife and a couple of teen kids. They think he's at a rehab facility, which he sort of is. When you're telling people lies, it's best to stick as close to the truth as possible."

"Wisdom from the great Jay Gatsby," I say dryly. "I'll keep that in mind."

Coming out of the dungeon feels like turning off the TV after watching a horror movie. The disconnect between the rabid man downstairs and the quiet, pristine rooms of the house is so startling I almost feel sick for a second. Or maybe I feel sick because of what the guy said to me. I stand in the first-floor hallway, watching specks of dust drift through a streak of sunlight from the window. The rays shimmer like a golden veil, so touchable that I trail my fingers through the light, half expecting to feel it. But there's only a faint warmth, nothing tangible. The illusion only exists as long as I don't try to grasp it.

"So...um..." Jay stuffs his hands in the pockets of his jeans. "I'm going to grab a shower. Do you want to shower too? I mean, not with me, but in your own shower in one of the guest rooms. Not that you need to shower—you don't smell bad—no, I meant... Oh hell..."

I turn and walk him backward to the wall, pressing him against it with my body and drawing his flushed face down to mine. His breath is faintly metallic, but it doesn't matter. All that matters is the enchantment I feel right now. All I want is this, the sensation of his mouth quivering against mine, the pressure of teeth through lips as I kiss him harder, as his hand creeps around the back of my neck and his fingers spiral through my hair, cupping the back of my skull with rigid eagerness. When his fingertips brush the sore lump on my head where Myrtle struck me, I flinch, and he quickly shifts his hand lower.

When we break apart to breathe, he studies me, his thumb stroking my cheek. "You're so beautiful," he says. "You were always beautiful, but you've gotten even more gorgeous. It's hard for me to process sometimes."

I still have some body insecurities—thanks, Tom—and I don't want to shave and soap down in front of Jay just yet. I accept the compliment with a smile and another quick kiss. "After showers—separate showers—could we try to investigate my voice power? Like we were planning to do yesterday?"

"Yes!" His eyes light up, and he pulls me toward the stairs. "I'm very curious."

"Doesn't it worry you, though? I mean, I could make you do anything I wanted, whenever I wanted." A lot of possibilities there—very dangerous and seductive ones. "I promised I wouldn't control you, but how would you know if I did?"

"I trust you to keep that promise. But even if you did command me, it makes no difference." He bounds up the stairs with an energy I can't muster without coffee.

"Why doesn't it matter?" I climb slowly to the second-floor landing.

"Because I would do anything for you anyway, even without being compelled." He flashes me a grin, then continues up the stairs to the third floor. "Hestia, unlock the Lavender Room." The door clicks, and he throws it wide. "You can use the bathroom in here. It's got a big rain shower and lots of towels. There are probably some clothes that'll fit you in the dresser if you want to change. We keep spares around in case someone gets blood on their outfit."

He's gone again before I can thank him.

Hot water is a blessing I will never take for granted. It washes away the phantom roughness of the gag, the scrape of Myrtle's fingernails on my wrists, the film of panicked sweat when I thought Jay was dead, that he would never come out of that pool again. It cleanses me of the glutton's avaricious gaze, and the grungy feeling of sleeping in my clothes on the couch.

I massage fragrant shampoo gently over the sore spot under my hair, and I use one of the disposable razors in the little basket on the shower shelf. There are some sample packets of makeup by the sink, so I help myself. From the closet I select a breezy, floor-length maxi dress with skinny straps and just enough bust coverage. Without my usual products, my hair is going to be all wild, bouncy, untamed curls today, and the dress fits the mood. Since my sandals are still downstairs, I pad into the hallway barefoot and cross to the door that I know is Jay's. It's standing ajar, like he wants me to come in. He must not mind if I wander in and poke around his things. If he's hiding anything else mysterious or incriminating, it's probably in some secret office behind a bookshelf. As a kid he was always hiding his special possessions in random unexpected places except for his money. He usually gave that to me to keep it safe for him so his mom couldn't find it.

When he was twelve, he made a list of resolutions. Things like "No drinking, drugs, or smoking. Work out every day. Save five hundred dollars. Try to be vegetarian." He'd eventually crossed that last one out as an unachievable goal. He'd also adjusted his financial goal to "Save one hundred dollars."

What would preteen Gatsby think of what he has become? If he and I met for the first time now, without any previous history, would I still love him? I hope I would. I want to believe that there's a mystical tie between us, deeper than our years of playgrounds and homework and shared meals.

My mother always says that falling in love is part coincidence, part familiarity, and part sexual attraction. I'm not sure she's right about all of that. My friend Hannah is ace and totally in love with her partner, though she couldn't care less about the sex aspect of relationships. Besides, I feel like there's something missing from Mom's definition. An affinity or a connection that can't be explained just by familiarity, or attraction, or chance.

When I enter Jay's room, the bathroom door is open, spilling warm light and steam into the bedroom.

Maybe he was hoping I'd come in and share the shower with him after all. My cheeks warm at the idea.

And then he walks out, dressed in a pair of boxers and nothing else, his skin still damp and glowing, tendrils of wet, wavy hair dripping water onto his broad shoulders.

"Hey," he says. "You look incredible."

I have no response because I've never seen such well-carved abs

outside of TV shows. I knew they existed in real life, somewhere.
Tom had a nice set of abs himself, but Jay is in another league when
it comes to fitness. He's got an unfair advantage, of course, being
a vampire with super cells and altered genetics or whatever. But
still—wow.

"Could you throw me a shirt?" he says. "In the dresser behind you."

"Okay." Reluctantly turning my back to him, I drag a drawer
open and inspect the rows of neatly rolled T-shirts. "Which one
do you want?"

"Any of them."

I pick one at random and throw it over my shoulder.

"Not this one," he said. "Doesn't go with the shorts."

"Right." I take a quick glance and choose another that looks like
it might coordinate. "Or maybe this one." I toss the second roll, and
he lunges to catch it. And then, with a twinkling grin, he throws the
first one back at me.

Oh. So that's how we're playing it. I snatch another from the
drawer and lob it straight for his face—but he's too quick and
sidesteps.

"It's no use," he says, still grinning. "You might be a quick little
klipspringer, but I'm the cheetah."

I whip shirt after shirt from the drawer and sling them at him,
and he dodges or catches every single one, until the floor and the bed
are draped with them—T-shirts in every color, some plain, others
with band logos or colorful designs or monochromatic patterns. I
leap forward, scoop up an armful, and charge at him, bearing him
down onto the bed and heaping shirts on top of him while he laughs
himself helpless.

Somehow I end up sitting astride his hips, draping a T-shirt over
his hair like a bonnet. "Do you surrender?"

"Always."

And just like that, the mood shifts and tightens, heat pooling between us. Jay's lips part, and suddenly he's hard against my core, his length pressing through the fabric of his boxers. And I'm wide open, every sensitive part of me wakening, tingling. Tentatively I shift, rubbing myself against him, and a crisp burst of pleasure trickles along my folds. Jay's head tips back, his lashes hooding his eyes, an unspoken moan shaping his mouth.

Slowly I push the pile of T-shirts off his chest. Then, heart racing, I trace a slow circle around one of his nipples with my fingernail. His cock throbs hard under the shorts, pushing against my center.

His hands find my waist and he starts to sit up, but I push him back down.

Shifting back onto his thighs, I part the flap of his boxers and slip my fingers inside, circling the hard, thick length I find there, easing it out into the open. He's big, and warm, and velvety-smooth.

When I glance up at him, there's utter vulnerability in his brown eyes. The predator who leaped from the pool and rattled his claws across the concrete of the dungeon wall is gone. It's just Jay now, my Jay, helpless and yearning in my hand.

I adjust my position, bend, and take the head of his cock in my mouth.

He cries out, fingers grasping handfuls of the bedspread. I slide my lips down, taking more of him into my mouth. He's so big I have to extend my neck and open my throat, and even then I can't fit all of him. In this case, I'm glad I've had experience giving head. But I won't think about how I got that experience. No, this is all about Jay, and I won't let any malevolent presence from my past mar this moment.

I pull back, letting my lips slide along Jay's entire length until they release his cock head with a soft *pop*. I lick him then, savoring the salty arousal beading at his slit.

"Daisy," he gasps. "You don't have to—"

"But I want to. And I'd much rather do it now, right after you've had a shower," I say truthfully.

"Oh god," he chokes out, as I lick up the underside of his cock and nibble at the groove right beneath the head. "I've dreamed about this. More times than I can fucking count. I can't believe you're really here... That I... That *we*—"

"Shh, Jay." I reach up, pressing my fingers over his mouth. "Don't think. Just feel."

He quiets, and I move my palm to rest over his heart while I take him in again, as far as I can. I curl the fingers of my other hand around the base of his dick and begin the sucking, bobbing motion I've performed many times. But with Jay it isn't the same rhythm, or the same taste, or the same scent. He smells like pine and oakmoss and fresh grass, and his low moans thrill me so much more deeply. I swirl my tongue over his sensitive skin, caressing him with it as I slide his length through the warm tunnel of my fingers, my lips, and my throat. I tell him I love him over and over, with my mouth and my tongue, until he huffs two sharp breaths and yells out, every muscle in his gorgeous body tensing at once. His release spurts into my mouth, coating the back of my throat. I pull off him and swallow, helplessly wet at the thought of Jay's cum staying inside me.

"You goddess," Jay says faintly, reaching for me. "Come here."

I crawl on top of him, settle against his body, and kiss him tenderly.

"I can taste myself in your mouth," he whispers. "Why is that so fucking hot?" I giggle against his lips, and he smiles. There's a predatorial gleam in his eyes as he tumbles me off him, onto my back among the T-shirts. His fingers curl into the fabric of my dress, dragging it upward along my thighs while I lie absolutely still, my breath short and shallow with anticipation.

His palm smooths along one bare thigh first, then the other. Then he sits up, takes hold of the panties I put on after the shower, and slides them down my legs and off my feet. I'm bare now, hot and helplessly wet. My fingers sink into the T-shirts, gathering fistfuls as I try not to squirm, not to beg. *Touch me, touch me right there...* His fingertips brush my clit, and I let out a quiet whine of need.

"Yes," he croons, leaning in to kiss me while his fingers repeat that same delicate motion. Then he shifts on the bed and brings his mouth down to replace his fingers.

His tongue is slick, sinuous magic, gliding over me, through me. He's giving my clit little kisses while his fingers sink inside me, while his thumb traces the sensitive outer lips of my pussy. I was already wild for him, and all those tiny sensations happening at once tip me right over the edge. I come hard against his open mouth, quivering against the wet caress of his tongue.

Even as I'm gasping through the shivers of pleasure, he's bathing me with that tongue, soothing me with those fingers. When he sits up, he's smiling, revealing sharp eyeteeth, and my breath catches a little because they were so close to some very tender parts of me. But he was careful, so careful.

The sight of those teeth snaps me back to a question that's been lingering in my mind—one I've been shoving aside until I had more information. The obvious question anyone would ask, once they discovered a way to become deathlessly beautiful.

"What if the klipspringer wanted to become a cheetah some-day? Not yet, but sometime?"

His eyes brighten. "The cheetah would be honored to make that happen."

"Whenever I want?"

"Whenever you want."

"You're not going to brood and fuss about the loss of my humanity?"

"You won't lose your humanity. And you'll be a lot safer as a vampire. I won't have to worry so much about you getting into a car accident, or a rogue vampire sucking you dry, or a piano being dropped on you—"

"All very likely to happen."

"Just your average daily risks."

Sighing, I stand up and pull my panties back on. So far, it seems we can't be intimate without getting interrupted or without me feeling anxious, frustrated, even a little angry. Not because of Jay himself exactly, but because of everything that has changed—myself included. A month ago I would never imagined him coming back into my life, or coming *back* to life after being shot. I'd never have pictured myself considering vampirism, or debating the pros and cons that go along with it.

"I won't like the blood-drinking part," I say.

"You might be surprised. It doesn't taste nearly as bad as you might think, and the experience can be...enjoyable."

"Because you're drinking from helpless, unconscious people and it gives you a power rush?" I start rerolling a shirt. It looks awful when I'm done.

"It's more complicated than that. And just so you know, I usually drink from one of the staff members here."

"Who?" I'm suddenly, unreasonably jealous of whoever it is, or anyone he has ever interacted with that way.

"Henry, sometimes, or Lillian. They don't mind. Henry doesn't want to turn, but Lillian says she'll take me up on the offer once her kids are older. You know, you don't have to roll up all these shirts. Lillian is just going to redo them. She likes things a certain way."

"Well, I wouldn't want to make Lillian unhappy," I say sweetly.

Jay rises amid the rumpled shirts and catches my chin in his hand, inspecting my face. "Hmm. Interesting. Very interesting. I think I have a diagnosis for your sudden mood change. You're jealous."

"Put some pants on," I hiss. "And a shirt."

"Why? It's summertime. Maybe I want to walk around without a shirt."

"And yet women don't get that option."

"I'm happy to allow you that freedom, in the spirit of equality and fairness."

"You wish." I flounce off the bed and stalk to the door. "I'll be downstairs researching my weird voice condition, if you care to join me. Oh, and I'll need a phone charger. I assume you have extras around here?"

"You assume correctly. Check the room you used earlier, top drawer of the nightstand."

I'm in the Lavender Bedroom, drawer open, reaching for the cable when Jay rushes in, his face tense with worry. "Just got a text from Nick. We need to go to his house, now. Something's wrong with Cody."

15

THE DRIVE TO NICK'S HOUSE TAKES FIVE MINUTES ON A GOOD day—two minutes the way Gatsby drives. He careens into the driveway at breakneck speed and yet somehow manages to park perfectly straight, without bumping into anything.

"Will becoming a vampire make me a better driver?" I climb out of the car, patting my stomach to make sure my insides are all still there and not stranded somewhere along the road.

"Nope. Well, your reaction times will be a bit faster. But you'll still have to practice to get good at it." Jay gives me an apologetic wince. "Also, the first rule of vampire club—"

"Don't talk about it where people might hear. Right. And also, I hated that movie."

"I know you did. I was there."

"I can't believe you made me watch it."

"Such fun though, right? The two of us, huddled in the closet of your room so your parents wouldn't see what we were watching, sharing a pair of earbuds between us—good times." He sighs and slams the car door. "Let's go see what Cody has done to himself now."

"Now? You make it sound like he gets in trouble often."

"Not often, but sporadically." He raps on Nick's front door. It pops open almost instantly. Under his freckles, Nick is white as salt.

"We fell asleep by the pool. It was shady at first, and then there was sun—and now Cody won't stop throwing up, and he won't"— Nick shoots a cautious look at me—"he won't drink anything."

"Where is he?" Jay charges through the living room.

"In the bathroom, the door on the left—"

"How long was he in the sun?"

"Couple of hours, maybe?"

Jay curses, forging into the bathroom. Now that I've stepped indoors I can hear the retching—long, horrible sounds, like hollow, drawn-out groans.

Nick's fingers are twisting together, trembling. "I couldn't help him. I tried. I didn't know..."

I collect his fingers in mine and draw him to the couch. "It's okay. It'll be all right. Jay's here now. He'll know what to do."

"Cody's, um, photosensitive," Nick stammers.

"You don't have to explain," I say. "I know about the vampire thing. I found out yesterday."

Nick presses a shaking hand to his lips. "Gatsby told you?"

"Well, no. Myrtle tied me up and shot him in the chest, and I found out when he came back to life and bit her throat."

"Oh. Wow. You have to tell me everything. You must be so—" He struggles for the words.

"Hush, Nicky. You don't have to worry about me, okay? You're always such a good listener, so supportive, but this time I need to be here for you."

"I should go see if they need anything."

"I'll go. You sit here and try to breathe, okay? I'll come right back."

"If he needs blood, I'll give him blood. As much as he needs. All of it." Nick's eyes are brimming with tears.

"Don't talk like that," I say. "Never do that, you understand? What would your parents do if you—speaking of which, where are your parents?"

"At an art show in Spartanburg. They have a booth there."

Another wrenching gag from the bathroom, and Jay calls sharply, "Daisy!"

I run to the doorway. Cody is slumped over the toilet bowl, his skin a sickly gray, his delicate features coated with glimmering sweat. His black hair has lost its usual gloss, and there are open lesions along his arms and across his chest.

"Sun poisoning," Jay says. "I'm going to need blood in a glass, since I can't get him calm enough to bite. And I need ice, all the ice they have."

"Does...does blood type matter?" I squeak.

"Our bodies can use any blood type, but when we're weak like this, O negative is usually better. Gentler, like chicken soup when you're sick."

I nod, my heart pounding. "I'm O negative. I'll do it."

"Don't cut your wrist or your palm," he warns. "Not too deep. Please be careful."

His warnings fade as I race to the kitchen, grab a short tumbler, and yank a knife out of the block. Then I stare at my arm.

I can do this. I can do this. I can cut into my own skin and muscle and bleed into a glass for my cousin's boyfriend.

I can set the blade of the knife to my skin and just press in—until it starts to hurt. *Ow, ow, ow!*

No. I can't.

I can't make myself do it.

On the brink of tears, I run back to the bathroom, carrying the knife and the glass. "I can't do it, Jay. You have to cut me."

Swearing again, Jay takes the knife from me, but before he can cut, I have an idea. "Wait!"

Jay pauses, with the tip of the blade against my skin.

Closing my eyes, I try to block out the sour smell of vomit and the reek of sweat, the echoing rasp of Cody panting into the toilet bowl, the faint sobs coming from Nick in the living room. I let my voice meander through my lowest tones, a lingering melody just for me and Cody. "Cody, sweetie, you're going to stop panicking. You're going to breathe, and you're going to believe that you will be all right. All you have to do is bite me, okay? Bite me, and drink what you need to survive this."

Opening my eyes again, I hold my left arm out, and with my right hand I grip Jay's shoulder.

Cody's panting fades into slow, even breaths. He blinks at my wrist, curling soiled fingers around it, and then, with frightening suddenness, his fangs whip out, and he sinks them in deep.

It hurts. It hurts so bad I can't help whimpering, can't stop the tears from escaping my eyes. But the pain recedes quickly, resolving into a slight ache and a gentle sucking sensation. My eyes meet Jay's, and he's looking at me with so much gratitude I think my heart might burst.

"Thank you," he whispers. "He's like my brother."

I nod, loosening my death grip on his shoulder. "You should get the ice. I'm okay."

He leaves, and for a few long minutes it's just me and the sun-poisoned vampire—the vampire I was able to physically quiet, using just my voice. An image breaks into my mind—the glutton in Jay's basement, thrashing and throwing himself at the door of his cell. Could my ability be helpful to him, too?

Cody sucks feebly at my wrist, tears and sweat slicking his cheeks. Has he ever gotten this ill from the sun before? He's decades older than Jay, so he's way more sun-sensitive—but that means Jay will eventually get to this point too, where a couple of hours in the bright outdoors could nearly kill him. I guess that rules out spending sunny days together on the beach. I can always go to the beach with human friends, though—if I have any human friends left after Jay and Cody are done with this area. And of course I'll be a vampire myself at some point, and I won't be able to relish the sun after that. Not like I do now.

Sun sickness, blood consumption, and a couple extra internal organs. Three side effects in exchange for perpetually perfect skin and good health, extra strength and speed, and immunity to disease and aging.

It's still a good deal, no doubt about it. A deal most people would take in a heartbeat. It's no wonder people are eager to take Jay up on his offer, no matter how much it costs. He has ensured that he will never have to be sick again a day in his life. He found a way to become essentially immortal.

But he doesn't look immortal when he returns with a huge Ziploc bag full of ice cubes and a couple of smaller ice packs. He looks like a scared boy who almost lost someone dear to him. He turns on the faucet in the tub, dashes a few towels in the stream of cold water, and slaps them out on the bathroom floor. I can feel his anxiety vibrating in the air, and I want to soothe him, to calm his nerves with my voice, but I don't. I haven't quite decided when it's okay to use my power, and when it's not. I still don't know what it is, where I got it, or why I have it. It's strange how obstacles keep cutting across my path every time I try to learn more. As soon as we've got Cody stabilized and safely back at Jay's house, I'm doing some research. No interruptions.

Jay touches Cody's shoulder. "Time to stop, buddy. You've taken enough of her blood."

Cody moans, gripping my arm tighter.

"Cody," I murmur. "Go ahead and stop drinking now. You need to rest."

Immediately he unlatches, licks the puncture marks on my arm, and lies flat on his back on the cold, wet towels. Jay places the ice packs on Cody's chest, then lays a wad of gauze over my arm and tapes it in place. "The healing enzyme in his saliva may not be as potent right now, but I'll check your wound later and make sure the holes are closing." His fingers linger over mine. "You saved his life, Daisy."

"Cool," I breathe. "I've never saved anyone's life before. I'm sorry I couldn't do the whole slicing-my-arm thing. I wimped out. They make it look so easy in movies."

He chuckles. "It's okay. You thought of a better way. You know, I'm good at brainstorming, planning, and logistical stuff, but in moments of crisis, my brain doesn't always navigate to the best solution. I'm really glad you were here."

"You were good during our crisis yesterday with Myrtle."

"Thanks, but it could have gone better. After you fell asleep, I sat there for a while, thinking of everything I could have done differently before and after George's death." He sighs. "But we can't repeat the past, can we? Now you should go hydrate, and eat something, and sit down. Let me know if you feel faint."

I raid Nick's fridge for a cheese stick and a sparkling water. "Cranberry-lime," I say, saluting Nick with the can as I take the other end of the sofa. "My favorite. Open it for me? I'm kind of one-handed at the moment."

Nick barely looks at me while he cracks the can open. "Did you feed him?"

"Yes. I had to use my voice thing to calm him down first."

"Your voice thing?" Nick cocks his head, confused.

"Oh, right! You don't know about the voice thing. Okay, so remember when you mentioned my 'hypnotizing voice' or whatever? Turns out you were on to something." Quickly I explain, delighted at the way Nick's eyes spark with interest. News of my ability is taking his mind off Cody, which is awesome. Before I'm even done talking, he has his phone out and he's typing in a search term. "We need to figure this out," he says. "The vampires must be more susceptible because of their enhanced hearing."

"That's what Jay said. What search term are you using?"

"Voice magic. But I'm getting results for voice-changing apps and *The Voice* and demo voice effects." He shakes his head. "We're going to have to dig deeper."

16

Nick and I are nestled together with our phones, buried in a research hole, when the two vampires enter the living room. Cody is still sickly pale and leaning heavily on Jay, but at least he's alert now and mobile, and the sores on his body are smaller. Jay dumps him into a recliner and cranks up the footrest so sharply that Cody swears.

"Cody is very sorry for scaring everyone," says Jay crisply. "He is also sorry for being an idiot, lying by a pool where there was a risk of sun exposure. It is no one's fault but his own. Cody promises not to do something so stupid ever again."

"Like you've never done stupid vampire stuff," growls Cody.

"I'm only a few years old as a vampire," Jay retorts. "You've had decades to learn, and you're still being careless. Like the phone call the other night. Talking to Wolfsheim? Really, Cody? I told you to let me handle him."

"He's my progenitor, and I'll talk to him if I please," Cody says.

"He's an abusive, manipulative psychopath. He tricks you into sharing information he doesn't need to know about us and our people."

"But I didn't give him anything," Cody protests. "I stood up to him. I told him to leave us alone, that he has no right to tell us what to do. Daisy knows, she heard me. And by the way, Coffee Beans, thank you so bloody much for tattling on me." He glares in my direction.

"Coffee Beans?" Jay frowns.

"It's his nickname for me. We bonded that night, after I eavesdropped on his phone call." I smile sweetly at Cody.

"Yeah, and then you mind-controlled me," Cody retorts. "I knew you were trouble."

"Right. And remind me—when exactly was I causing trouble? When I calmed you down with my voice so you'd stop puking? Or when I fed you my blood so your body could heal?"

Cody winces, practically writhing in his chair until the words finally work their way out of his mouth. "Thank you."

"That gratitude looked super painful." I lean forward, frowning in mock concern. "Are you okay?"

"Shut up."

"This has been such fun, but I actually have work to do." Jay smacks Cody's knee. "Rest, idiot. And make sure you cover up on the way home to keep the sun off."

"My boyfriend has a convertible," grumbles Cody.

"So buy him another car, with a roof and tinted windows." Jay glances at me. "Are you coming, Daisy?"

"Sure." I nudge Nick. "I haven't found anything remotely plausible related to voice magic. Have you?"

"Not really." He runs his fingers through his cinnamon curls. "You've got sirens, mermaids, banshees, all kinds of female temptresses. Then there's the alkonost in Russian folklore—part bird, part woman, with a beautiful voice. She's apparently a messenger between this world and the Otherworld. The Celts have their versions of the

Greek muses, the leannán sídhe. There's the gamayun from Eastern Slavic lore, another bird-woman who communicates with the Other Side. Hindu myths have the gandharvas, nature spirits with gorgeous voices. Lots of lore and pop culture with vampires compelling people to do their will, but I've seen nothing about a human girl being able to compel vampires. I guess you're the only one."

"Well, I don't like it," says Cody.

"No one asked you," Jay says smoothly. "You should stop talking before you hurt your brain as badly as you screwed up your body."

Cody glares at him. "Don't forget, I'm your fucking progenitor. I could take you down right now, you little wanker."

"In your condition?" Jay's brown eyes widen innocently. "You really think so?"

"Come on, you insufferable ass. Let's do this." Cody struggles with the lever on the recliner, jerking it angrily and unsuccessfully until he gives up and collapses in a pale, sweaty mess. "I'll beat you up later."

"Looking forward to it, buddy." Jay smirks, but when he turns to Nick, his expression is sober. "Watch over him for me."

"I will," Nick promises. "And you take good care of my Daisy girl." He blows me a kiss as Jay and I head out the door.

"What kind of work do you have to do?" I ask him.

"Some emails and a website update. I'll talk to Slagle again and see if his thirst has lessened at all. And Jordan texted me a few minutes ago, trying to find you. She wants to do a tribute song for George, and she wants you to sing it with her. Her follower count has dropped since his death, and she's getting some pretty negative comments because he fell while she was scoping out a location. I think she's hoping the tribute will help restore her image."

"Jordan knows about Myrtle. I told her this morning."

"Ah." He starts the car, but he doesn't back out of the driveway. "You didn't tell Cody."

"I will, when he's feeling better, and once I'm sure everything has been properly handled. Officer Sheetal, the woman you saw the other day, is one of ours. A vampire. She and her partner and the chief will cover the incident."

"And Myrtle? How long can they keep her at the hospital under observation?"

"I don't know. That's one of the calls I have to make—to ensure they don't let her out before she gets the help she needs."

"She needs ongoing help, Jay. Grief counseling, therapy, maybe medication. And as much distance between her and Tom as possible." I shudder over his name, and Jay notices.

"He's a cruel guy." He pulls backward out of the driveway in a swift, startling curve. "I don't like the way he looks at you. Like he thinks he still owns you, even though I know he never did. You never loved him, and you should make sure he knows that. Maybe then he'll back off."

He doesn't sound vindictive, only sad and matter-of-fact.

Something inside me shrinks from admitting the truth—that I did love Tom. I was addicted to him, the way I get addicted to candy corn at Halloween, because it's pretty and sugary and chewy, and even though I know it's bad for me and it's going to make me sick, I just keep popping the little kernels in my mouth, one after another, and crushing them into sweet sediment between my teeth.

Part of me never wants Jay to know anything about my relationship with Tom. There were moments of sheer delight, and moments so dark I don't like to think about them or analyze them too deeply. But if Jay and I are going to rebuild our mutual trust, I have to be honest. I have to tell him the uncomfortable things as well as the interesting or enjoyable things.

"I did love Tom," I say in a very small voice.

A muscle pulses along Jay's temple. He doesn't reply.

"It wasn't the same kind of love. If that helps."

His eyebrows lower, and he says, between clenched teeth, "You slept with him."

"Yeah, Jay. We were together for years."

Jay's face is pale and rigid. "But it wasn't good for you. You didn't enjoy it."

"Sometimes I did."

Jay winces, inhaling through his teeth as if I'm causing him actual physical pain.

"You're upset."

"No, it's just...I always thought you and I, that I would be the one—"

My face roars with heat. "Seriously? You disappeared for eight years, Jay. Did you think I would just sit around and have exactly zero relationships until you showed up again? I thought you were out of my life for good, so yes, I moved on, and I had sex. Sue me."

"But the first time is—"

I halt his words with a warning hand. "Don't be one of the weirdos obsessed with taking a woman's virginity! I'm not some freaking continent you didn't get to plant your flag on!"

"I know!" He whips his head toward me, eyes burning. "I'm sorry, okay? It's your body. Your choice. I just...imagined everything playing out differently in my mind." He stares ahead again, his fingers clenched on the steering wheel.

"You've done it too, right?"

"A few times, with a couple of Cody's friends. I always hated myself afterward. I felt like I was cheating on you."

"But you weren't. You were being a normal man with physical needs." I lay my hand on his shoulder. "It doesn't bother me at all."

"So your thing with Tom shouldn't bother me either. Is that what you're saying? Emotions don't work like that, Daisy. I feel what I feel. But I don't blame you, of course. He deceived you, manipulated you into thinking you wanted him."

"Stop trying to blame it all on Tom!" I snatch my hand from his shoulder. "I knew exactly what I was doing. Tom was the hottest guy in school—handsome, sexy—and he wanted me, and I made a choice, Jay. A conscious choice. Sure, he messed with my head later on—screwed with my confidence—but he didn't force me to be his girlfriend."

"And you...loved him."

"In a way. But it wasn't the same."

He nods, quick and sharp. "I understand. I can deal."

But it seems as if he really can't, because he doesn't say anything else, not even when we've parked at his place and we're heading up the walk to his front door. Without all the people swirling in and out of the entrance, the massive doors look even more imposing—gleaming dark wood inset with crystal panes, furnished with ornate bronze handles. There's a scrap of blue-gray shade across the sun-baked front step, thanks to the second-floor balcony.

"Do you want me to leave?" I nod to my car—which has been neatly reparked, probably by the fastidious Henry.

"No." Jay stares at the door handle without touching it. "But I'll be working, so if you'll be bored—"

"There's plenty to do at your house. And you said Jordan's coming over, right?"

"Right." He purses his lips.

"Jay, do you want me here?"

He looks at me, incredulous. "Of course I do."

"Okay."

"It's just hard." He focuses on the door again. "Knowing it wasn't the same for you as it was for me."

Knowing that I wasn't entirely devoted to him during those eight years, as he obviously was to me. He knows it's an irrational expectation, but he can't talk himself out of his emotions because he's an incurable romantic, as Cody said. He hoped that I would be just as incurably romantic.

The most I can be is incurably honest.

"I thought about you often," I tell him. The words are so pathetic, such a pale shadow of how I felt. I don't know how to tell him that I was lost, that I ached inside, that his absence was a cavernous ravine in my life, that the longing was part of what drove me to Tom. But all of that gets swirled up on the way to my mouth and comes out as, "I missed you a lot."

Jay opens the door and moves aside, holding it for me.

I can't say what I feel, but I can't let him suffer either. I have to distract him, to shake him out of this mood.

"I thought of something earlier." I step inside, and he lets the door fall shut. "I'd like to try using my voice to help your glutton."

"Like brainwashing him out of his gluttony?" Jay cocks an eyebrow.

"More like soothing him so you can reason with him."

He shrugs. "Worth a shot. Text Jordan about the song, and we can try your voice thing on Slagle before I start working. And we should test a few other things about your ability—how long it lasts, and how far you can physically move from your subject before your influence fails. Whether or not other sounds can break them out of your sway—that kind of thing."

"You're talking like a scientist."

"Yeah, so?"

"It's cute." I smile tentatively at him. "I remember how excited you got every time Dad came up with an experiment for you to do together."

A half smile curves his mouth. "I miss your dad."

"You should come for dinner soon. What about this weekend? Tomorrow is Friday, right? What about tomorrow night?"

"I'm having another party tomorrow."

My mouth falls open. "Jay. Seriously? So soon after George?"

"These parties aren't impulsive, Daisy. Each one has been in the works for weeks, and people expect them now. Even if I announce that I'm not hosting a party this weekend, most of the guests either won't get the memo or won't pay attention, and they'll show up anyway. Plus, you know these events give my people a chance to get the fresh blood they need without hurting anyone."

"Something I still don't quite agree with, I'll have you know."

"It's not a perfect system. Would you rather they start biting people in the back alleys of Asheville? We don't have handy little mind erasure or compulsion powers, you know." His lip curls. "That's the stuff of TV shows."

"That would be so convenient though, right?" I sigh.

"Real life is much more dangerous and interesting," he says softly. "Because it gave you, a girl fresh out of college, the power to control vampires like me."

He reaches out, trailing his fingertips along my cheek. He's adjusting, moving past his mood, fixing things between us. I reach up and curl my hand over his.

Tension quivers in that touch, and desire licks through me, quick and sharp. Here in the cool, shadowed foyer, there's no one to see, no one to know what we do, no pool guys to interrupt us—

"Mr. Gatsby." A plump middle-aged woman with bright black

eyes stands on the landing of the stairs. One fist is propped on her hip, and the other hand holds a clump of Jay's shirts. "Mr. Gatsby, what did you do to your room? Shirts everywhere! I know you can be messy, but this should not become a new habit. This is why I roll the shirts, so you can see what they are and make your choice without flinging them all over the room!"

"Sorry, Lillian." He gives her a sheepish grin. "And I've told you to call me Jay."

She shakes her head and waggles a finger at him. "Don't you try that pretty-boy charm with me. Tell me this will not happen again."

"It won't happen again."

"Good." Her eyes travel to me, and Jay draws me forward a step. "Lillian, this is Daisy. Daisy Finnegan. The one I told you about."

"Hi," I add. "Nice to meet you."

"Ah, Daisy!" Lillian's face relaxes into a smile. "So glad to see the two of you together! Don't let me keep you, Mr. Gatsby. I'll do the shirts. You go and have fun!" She bustles upstairs again.

Giggling, I tip my forehead against Jay's shoulder. "Should I have told her that the T-shirt thing was my fault?"

"We wouldn't want to mess up your flawless first impression." He nudges me playfully. "Come on, let's find you a rabid vampire to play with."

The glutton Slagle is crying when we enter the dungeon, but his sobs die out as we approach. When Jay opens the window in the cell door, Slagle's mottled face is already there. Snot, tears, grime, and blood streak his skin, and his sweaty hair is stuck to his scalp.

"You really need a shower," I say, wincing.

"Tell that to the sadistic monster who locked me in here," Slagle hisses.

Jay raises his eyebrows. "Oh, *I'm* the sadistic monster? Okay. I guess it was me out behind the gardeners' shed, gorging myself on the blood of two unconscious girls. And I guess it was also me who took an actual *bite* out of one of their thighs. Do you know what I had to do to make that go away, Slagle? Do you know how expensive plastic surgeons are?"

"That's nothing to you," says the glutton. "You can afford it. You can afford everything, including your pretty little escort there. How much do you pay her per hour? Must get expensive."

Jay's fangs flash out, and he crashes against the window, snarling a hideous threat. My heart jumps into my throat.

The glutton cringes away, whimpering. "I'm sorry, I'm sorry. I'm just so hungry, so thirsty. I'm dying in here, and you don't care, so of course I lash out."

"I could kill you, you know." Jay speaks through the mouthful of fangs, drawing a single claw down the glass. "It would be so much easier than trying to rehabilitate you. I'm very tempted, in fact. But lucky for you, Daisy wants to test her mind control on a vampire, and you're the perfect candidate."

Jay turns to me, still vamped out, all claws and fangs and swirling white eyes. There's a manic energy buzzing around him—the air practically crackles with it.

He takes in my expression and mutters, "Sorry. Did I scare you?"

"I'm not a bit scared," I murmur, my pulse kicking into a frantic pace as he steps closer. "And you're going to think I'm sick, but...this aspect of you is actually super hot."

He grins, and my heart flips.

"I don't think you're sick at all," he whispers. With the tip of a claw, he touches my mouth, tugging my lower lip down just a little. A tingling heat spreads over my body, and my breaths turn quick and shallow.

"What do you mean, mind control?" whines the glutton. "What are you talking about? You're both crazy."

"That's an offensive word, Slagle," I say, with my eyes still locked on Jay. "You may want to cover your ears so this doesn't affect you too, Jay."

"I'm okay," he says. "I want to see if you can control two of us at once. If it becomes an issue, you can order me to cover my ears."

"All right then." Carefully I shift into the lower register of my voice, the timbre that's becoming more familiar each time I use it. "I want you both to calm down and breathe slowly. You're at peace, and you're content. You don't need to drink blood or fight right now, so let the fangs slide away, and the claws slip back in, okay?" I keep my voice soft and musical, even as my excitement rises because the two of them are completely mesmerized, staring at me while their claws and fangs recede. They're breathing slowly, heavily.

"Good job, boys," I coo to them, while my mind races frantically for the next command, something to test the extent of my abilities. "Such a good job. Now I want you to, um, to pat your heads and your stomachs at the same time. Great job! Keep doing that, okay?"

I retreat down the hall, all the way to the heavy dungeon door. It's not an extensive test of the boundaries for my ability, but I don't want that big dungeon door between me and Jay, even if he did give me access to the system. I'll wait here a while, and then I'll go back to my vampire boyfriend and see how obedient he really is.

17

AFTER A FEW MINUTES I COME BACK, AND BOTH VAMPIRES ARE still patting their heads and stomachs. I take a quick video to show Jay later, and then I play several different sounds on my phone. They both react mildly to them, but they don't stop the motion I ordered. It's like the strangest game of Simon Says ever.

"Okay, snap out of it, both of you," I say sharply.

Jay frowns, shifting his stance and looking at his palms. "What just happened?"

"Apparently I can control two of you at once. And only my voice will snap you out of it." I show him the video.

"I want to see, too," says the glutton. "Bring those tasty little fingers over here."

"Ew." I glance at Jay. "He sounds more like a zombie than a vampire."

"Like I said, he took a chunk out of a girl's thigh. But I think it has less to do with the vampire deal and more to do with some preexisting tendencies."

"What do you mean?"

"Apparently he's a fan of movies and shows featuring cannibalism," Jay says grimly. "Most people who enjoy that sort of entertainment would never actually carry out the act, but he's the exception."

"And you didn't find this out before you turned him?"

"I didn't. We do a thorough background check, a psych evaluation, and multiple interviews—but occasionally someone slips through that safety net."

"Well, a secret inclination for cannibalism isn't something Slagle would want to share."

"True. He checked out fine and his money was good, so we went for it."

"You might need to adjust your approval process," I say.

"The problem is, anyone we deny tends to get vindictive," Jay replies. "You know, threatening to expose us. We usually get around that by putting them on indefinite probation, giving them hope that maybe one day they'll be approved for the transformation."

"And then you never approve them? That's so mean!"

"Never is a long time, Daisy. We just started this thing. Every new business has its kinks to work out, policies to adjust. It's fine."

"Well...the cannibalism thing sounds like a deeper issue than I'm qualified to deal with. I don't think I can just mind control him out of that."

"I'll have Miriam come talk to him soon. She's a psychologist I turned at half price because she does pro bono work for people who can't afford mental health care. In return, she helps us out from time to time."

"I don't want to talk to Miriam," groans the glutton. "I want to hear this little snack talk again. Such smooth, pretty words. Her voice sounds so warm, so liquid and red. It sounds like—"

"Her voice sounds like blood," Jay says abruptly.

My eyes go wide, and I stare at him.

He grimaces. "Sorry, but it's true. I can't remember what you made me do when I was under your sway, but I remember your voice, how it felt. When you talk in that tone, I can't help listening because it sounds like everything I crave the most. Like sex, and love, and blood, all melted together. Like the one thing that will fill me up and make me perfectly satisfied."

"Yes, yes, yes. Her voice is full of blood," sings the glutton.

"Thanks for that." I make a face. "I guess I should put a directive in place for him, and then we can leave and see how long it lasts. Jay, go wait at the end of the hall and cover your ears so you won't be affected."

He hesitates. "I don't like leaving you alone with him."

"He's locked in, right? And I'm in control. He can't hurt me."

"Fine." Jay claps his hands over his ears and stalks away, cursing.

"He's worried about you," says Slagle. "Concerned for his little love button. You must be the tastiest thing he's ever had in his mouth. I'd love to have a taste, too—just a lick, just a little finger."

"You're a disgusting creep, you know that? I'm beginning to think Jay should just finish you off."

"But then my family gets a refund, see? And Jay doesn't want that," Slagle says. "He needs my money. Millions of dollars, that's what he takes from each of us. A small price to pay, he says, for eternity. I took out a second mortgage. Lots of years left to pay it off, see? An eternity to get myself financially sound again. At least that's what I hope for. Gatsby says nobody knows how long we'll last. But I'd rather not live with this hunger, this thirst, and no one kind enough to temper it for me. All I need is a drop of your sweet, sweet blood on my tongue, Daisy, my fresh little Daisy. Come on. You can spare a few drops, and he'll never know."

I advance to the door, leaning close to the window. "I may be blond, but I'm not dumb."

"Not dumb, huh?" He leers into my face, the thick glass the only barrier between us. Then, quick as a thought, he ducks, and something slashes across my shin. I yell, stumbling back. The creep stuck his claw through the grate and made a shallow scratch on my leg. He pulls the claw back and licks off the blood that beaded on it.

"Mmm." He moans so lecherously that I feel sick. And I feel stupid too, because Jay warned me about the grate, and I just...forgot. I suppose after everything I've been through lately I'm allowed a mental slip-up, but it still stings—literally and figuratively.

"You're a sick man, Slagle," I croon in my special voice, and the glutton stops chortling over his taste of blood. He rises, eyes glazed, watching me through the window. "I want you to understand that your lust for blood and flesh is wrong. You will only drink enough blood to stay alive. You will control your desires and impulses. And—" I need something visible, a control that we can observe when we come back to check on him, but not something that will harm him if he does it repetitively. "I want you to pat your head three times, once every five minutes. Starting now."

His hand rises slowly and taps his head three times.

Satisfied, I close the shutter over his window. Without the dim light from his cell, the gloom of the dungeon seems to thicken and crawl like a living thing. I try to walk calmly, but after a few steps I break into a run, racing for the rectangle of pale light that marks the exit, where Jay is waiting for me. I rocket out of the dark, and Jay slams the door shut behind me before catching me in his arms.

"What happened?" He presses his chin into my hair. "Are you okay?"

"I got too close to the grate and he scratched me."

"I'm so sorry—"

"It was my fault. I wasn't thinking."

"You're exhausted. You should take a nap while I'm working," he says. "There are a bunch of bedrooms, dozens of couches—sleep anywhere you like."

"Is there a couch in your office?"

His brown eyes soften with pleasure. "Yes, there is."

"Then I'd like to be there."

"I'll be talking on the phone. It might disturb you."

"It's fine." Because eight years was enough separation. Because I'm making up for lost time. Because even though he's introduced more danger into my life than I've ever experienced before, Jay makes me feel safe in a way Tom never did. When I'm with Jay, I am cherished. Not coddled or treated like a fragile little ornament—not weakened or subdued when he needs to feel strong. I am cherished, like something powerful and beautiful and worthy of respect.

Everyone should have a person who makes them feel like that.

Curled on the couch in Jay's office, lulled by the mellow tone of his voice, I doze off for a while—maybe an hour. When my consciousness slowly resurfaces, he's sitting on the low table beside me, gazing at me with all the golden warmth of his beautiful soul shining in those brown eyes.

I uncoil myself, stretching. "You always did like to sit on floors and counters and tables. Even when there were perfectly good chairs around." He doesn't say anything, and my eyes drift to his soft lips, his crisp jawline. "Did you get all your work done?"

"Most of it. Jordan will be here any minute. Are you sure you're up for this? I know it's been a rough week."

"Rough? That's an understatement. I saw somebody die, Jay, and I have a feeling it won't be the last time." I scrunch my curls with my fingers. "And you've killed people before, haven't you? With your own hands."

His jaw tightens. "I killed gluttons who were out of control. People who didn't follow the rules they agreed to, who put everyone at risk."

"And how do you feel about that?"

"I'm not sorry." He clears his throat, glancing away. "But I dream about it, sometimes. You know me, Daisy. I'm not a violent person."

"But you could be."

"Anyone has that capacity. It's all about controlling your responses, making sure you're mentally fit to handle the stress."

"You're only twenty-four, Jay. You shouldn't have this much pressure on you."

"Says who? All the smartest, most successful guys start young."

I contemplate him, with my head tilted in thought. I know him so well—we have mutual memories—and yet he has inner sanctums I haven't touched yet, deep wells he hasn't let me peer into. Maybe because he's afraid of himself, and what he is capable of.

"I can't be your savior, Jay," I tell him. "I tried that with Tom, and it didn't work. I can't save you from yourself."

His mouth curves, a gentle smile, a glow that suffuses his eyes. "I would never expect you to save me. I did all this so you wouldn't have to. We're on equal footing again, and now I can give you everything—even immortality. When I first met Cody on that beach, and discovered what he was— Well, I won't pretend I had it all planned out then, but I could see flashes of the path that would lead me back to you. Becoming a vampire and developing the new transition process was my key to giving you everything you could ever want."

"Maybe what I want is a lot simpler than you think," I say softly, leaning toward him.

"'Sup, monsters," Jordan says from the doorway. Then she looks from me to Jay. "Oops. Did I interrupt something? I can wait out here for a minute if y'all want. Only a minute though, because I want to nail this cover song. Busy, busy, you know how it is. Chrystie and Ismay are already waiting for us in the studio."

"I'm coming." I rise from the couch reluctantly.

Judging by the constant interruptions, I must be fated to never kiss Jay again.

18

I'VE DONE A LOT OF THINGS IN THE PAST EIGHT YEARS—THINGS I never thought I'd have the chance to do before my dad scored his new job. But I haven't been inside an actual recording studio before. I guess I expected something more glamorous, but it's actually kinda plain. I suppose the real magic is in the walls, the soundproofing, and the acoustics, and in the digital spell that the soundboard casts over the raw music. Two friends of Jordan's, Chrystie and Ismay, will handle the recording and processing part of things. They're both human, as far as I can tell—no special bracelets. Chrystie is skinny, with lank blond hair, a beanie, and rows of bracelets covering half her arms. Her fingers are so laden with heavy rings it's a wonder she can manage the soundboard controls so deftly. Ismay is a soft, quiet person with purple-streaked hair, a skull T-shirt, and a black stud in their nose.

I'm not feeling too confident as Jordan runs through trills and mouthy noises that are supposed to limber up her vocals and lips for the song.

"Should I be doing all of that?" I ask her.

"Not necessary. I just need your sweet little voice as a counterpoint."

"So I'm your backup singer?"

"You cool with that?"

"Relieved, actually."

"Sweet."

We look at each other, really look, like we haven't in a while. I thought we'd see more of each other over the summer, but so far that hasn't happened. Breezing in and out of each other's lives doesn't really count.

Jordan's eyes drop to my bandaged arm, then flash up again, widening with understanding. "So..."

"Yeah. Cody got into some trouble with the sun, and he needed—you know."

"Right." She nods, puckering her lips. She's in her usual jaunty stance, one hip cocked and her hand at her waist. She's one of those people whose strength is immediately obvious, from the muscles rippling under her dark skin to the confident way she moves, seamlessly comfortable in her body. But right now, there's an edge to her movements. She's tapping her fingers, working her lips.

I was pretty judgmental on the phone when we talked earlier, and she's clearly not over it.

"Can they hear us in here?" I nod to Chrystie and Ismay behind the glass.

"Not yet." She points. "When that light goes on, yes."

"I think it's great you're a vampire," I offer.

Her gaze whips back to mine, hopeful. "Yeah?"

"I don't have to worry about your safety so much anymore. It's actually a huge relief." I allow a smile to creep over my mouth, and she grins back.

"For me too," she says. "I still get the adrenaline rush, you know? Because if I fall, there will still be pain. But I don't have the panic anymore. It's good."

"And you're feeling okay?"

"I feel amazing."

"Not physically, Jordan. You had a literal transformative experience. That's gotta throw your mind for a loop, at least a little bit."

"You know I don't do feelings talk, babe."

I consider her for a minute, then open my arms. "Come on."

She narrows her eyes. "No hugs."

"It's the least you can do after turning yourself into a vampire without telling me. Come on, girl."

She relents and steps in, letting me fold my arms around her. She's so hard, muscle and determination, ambition and drive. But she softens a little bit as I hold her.

"Love you," I say. "You know that."

"Hmm. You too."

It's the most I'm going to get, so I let her go. "Okay, feelings talk is over. Let's do this."

The song is a duet arrangement of Lana Del Rey's "Young and Beautiful." Jordan's smooth, rich voice slides over the lyrics, strong and glowing, and I'm the ethereal echo, the quiet harmony. Chrystie and Ismay are handling the soundboard behind the glass, but a few bars into our second run-through, another figure slips into the room with them. Jay stands there, watching us—watching me. His mouth is parted, his eyes glazed with a distant enchantment. My stomach flips, but somehow I manage to stay on key, to maintain the right pitch as my voice glides along behind Jordan's.

We do another take, and another, each one better than the last, and Jay doesn't move the entire time. Finally Ismay gives us the thumbs-up and says, "We got it."

It's only then that I realize Jordan is sweating. She wobbles as she rises from her seat.

"Are you okay?" I touch her arm, and she looks at me, wild-eyed and startled. "Whoa. What's up?"

"Your voice has changed," she says. "It's so dang beautiful that I just wanted to sit there and listen to it. It took everything I had just to keep singing my part, and I was only able to do it because I knew you wanted me to."

"But...your voice is way better than mine."

"I know," she says, her fingers curling with frustration. "Objectively, I know that." She shakes her head.

I cast a quick look at Jay, behind the glass. He's frowning faintly, pinching the bridge of his nose. Chrystie and Ismay are discussing the music, and the light on our side of the glass is off, so they're not listening.

"I promise I haven't used it on purpose...except to test it a little, but apparently my voice has a weird effect on vampires," I say quietly. "Something about your sensitive hearing and a specific tone I use. It, like, hypnotizes you guys. Makes you suggestible and obedient."

Jordan stares at me. "What the hell?"

I grimace. "Yeah, I'm not exactly sure what it's all about yet. It sounds similar to what Gran used to do—you know, my grandmother on my dad's side?"

"Right, you said she was a hypnotist and a mentalist."

"Yup."

"Well, babe, you gotta ask your dad about her. Get more details." Jordan picks up her bag. "Can't have you running around mind-controlling people."

"Well, at least you were able to resist it when I was singing. Not so much on the phone earlier, though."

"Hold up. You mind-controlled me over the phone?"

"Just a little bit. Just to see if it would work during a phone conversation. I asked you what was so special about the way Jay transforms people. I'm sorry... I should have explained first. I won't do that again, I swear."

"Good. You better not." She observes me for a second. "How does it feel?"

"The mind control thing? It's scary, and I feel guilty about it. I'm having to be a lot more careful with my tone, especially around people who might be vampires."

"But I bet it feels good, too."

I tug my lip with my teeth, slanting a glance at Jay. "It's fascinating, for sure. I've been so conflicted about it that I haven't really let myself admit this, but—yeah, it feels really, really good, having that level of power over someone. Does that make me a terrible person?" I cover my mouth with my hands. "It does, doesn't it?"

"Wanting power? Loving the way it feels?" Jordan chuckles. "You're not terrible. In fact, I'd say you're aggressively normal. Who doesn't want to feel powerful and in control? Why do you think I got into the whole stunts scene? I love the way it makes me feel. Where you have to be careful is when your power starts to hurt other people." Her smile fades, and I know we're both thinking about George. Strictly speaking, his death wasn't our fault, but there's a sense in which we both share some blame. She climbed the cliff first, and I told him to show everyone what he could do. Those combined influences were all the impetus he'd needed.

"I'll hold myself accountable," I tell her. "And if you're willing, I'd love for you to keep me in check, too."

"Like a sober coach, so you don't get drunk on all this power."

"Exactly. You call me out when I need it."

"You know I will."

Jordan stays for a light dinner, salads topped with grilled chicken or smoked salmon, depending on preference. Chrystie and Ismay join us as well, so we can't talk openly about vampires or superpowers.

After dinner Jay pulls me aside and gives me fingerprint access to his blood bracelet. Since Jordan arrived, Jay has barely spoken to me. Our conversation about immortality was left unfinished.

Jay can't know for sure that vampires are immortal. Cody definitely stopped aging when he turned. He's been a vampire for a few decades and he still looks like he's in his early twenties. And I suppose logically it makes sense that they would continue to exist indefinitely, as long as their regenerative abilities stay in place. But the blood supply thing might become an issue, if not soon, then a couple hundred years from now, and I can't help feeling that Jay's being a bit shortsighted in that respect. Like maybe he's putting too much faith in whatever research teams he's got working on a blood substitute. I've seen the movies, and that never works, at least not for everyone. There will always be vampires who prefer drinking straight from the vein.

"That should do it." Jay takes my finger and passes it over the bracelet. The lighted bar shows up, the indicator near the edge of the green zone. "And this is how you access my heart rate and other stats, pressing here. There's an admin app we use to track everything, but you don't need access to that right now. Eventually you'll have it, though. I want you to be a part of all this. If you want, I mean."

"Sure."

He shoves his hands deep into his pockets and leans against the wall, looking at some random point on the floor. I can't quite read his mood, and that unsettles me.

"Okay, we're off." Jordan breezes past us, jingling her key fob. "Misbehave, babies. Make me proud." She gives me a wink and links arms with Chrystie and Ismay as the three of them leave the house.

Ismay barely has time to throw a "thanks for dinner" in Jay's direction before they're all sweeping outside, and the door closes behind them.

We're truly alone now, Jay and I. No more pool guys or household staff. Just the two of us. The thought sends a shiver of anticipation over my skin. But I shrug it off and fake a yawn.

"I should go home," I say. "I've been in your hair for, like, a couple days now, and you're probably really sick of me, so—"

"Never." He bites out the word. "I could *never* be sick of you."

"Hmm." I survey him, drawing on my years of experience with Jay's body language. Seemingly casual pose. Hands in pockets, head down. Avoiding direct eye contact. He wants to say something or do something, and he's holding himself back for *reasons*. He used to get this way after something terrible happened with his family. A sort of bad day made him chatty; the really wretched ones made him quiet and jumpy. And the only thing that loosened him up was physical activity.

I grab his wrist. "Come on. Let's take a walk before I head home. I keep hearing about the hedge maze in your gardens. Can't believe you still haven't showed it to me."

He lets me pull him toward the back door. "During the parties, the maze becomes hookup central," he says. "I didn't think you'd want to see all that. You wouldn't believe the number of used condoms my poor cleaning guys have to retrieve."

"Gross."

He shrugs. "At least they're being safe, I guess."

"Still gross. Why don't people clean up after themselves? It's not that hard."

We pass through the screened porch and give the pool a wide berth. I don't know if I'll ever be able to swim in it again without having a flashback of Jay, spread-eagled and unconscious in its depths, his blood swirling around him.

I tighten my grip on his wrist. "I'm so glad you're a vampire." The words break free, colored with a ferocity I didn't know I had.

"So am I," he says, with a glance at the pool. "Can you imagine if I had made my money some other way, and come here, and gone through all of that—reuniting with you and everything—only to be shot?"

"That would have been seriously tragic."

"Way too tragic."

We walk between flower beds, past a fountain, to the entrance of the hedge maze. Tinted lamps, angled toward the hedges, illuminate them in green light. Moths and night insects flutter near the bulbs. A mosquito whines past my ear, and I wave it away.

Then I let my fingers slip from Jay's wrist. "I noticed, when we were on the hike, that you like to run. To chase people."

He kicks the ground. "It's like an animal instinct, a predatory thing. That's one reason Cody suspects Dr. Endive used some animal DNA in his formula. Our primal urge to hunt is way stronger than a normal human's."

"Cool." My heart is thrumming twice as fast as usual, and I haven't even started running yet. "Give me a ten-second head start."

"What?" His eyes widen.

I take his chin in my hand and stand on tiptoe to kiss him, a quick tempting brush of my mouth on his. "You're going to chase me."

And then I run.

I plunge into the maze, straight ahead for a couple seconds, then a right. Then a left. I run full out, eyes open, an exhilarated glee pumping through my blood. It feels so incredibly good, after everything, to just let go. I don't even care that my sandals weren't made for this and that I might have a blister or two tomorrow. My feet are winged, light as air, and I let myself laugh out loud because there's no one around to hear—except for the vampire chasing me.

I hear him before I see him—a thrum of quick steps, the ripple of a growl. Goose bumps rise on my skin and I leap forward, propelled by an instinct old as time.

He's right behind me, steps pounding nearer, his breaths heavy with predatory intent. Somehow I sense the moment he pounces, and I skid aside into a right-hand path. He crashes into the corner of the hedge and I laugh again, breathless, redoubling my pace.

Another second, and then I break into an open space with a fountain. I run halfway around it and turn, just in time to see Jay stalking out of the maze. His fangs and claws are out, and fear flickers behind my excitement. What am I doing, tempting the beast? I'm not super familiar with his vampire side yet. And I know it's possible for vampires to lose themselves in bloodlust. What if this game was a very, very stupid mistake?

Jay's tongue glides over his teeth. He starts to circle the fountain, and I move in tandem, keeping it between us. The spray is a glittering veil across his prowling figure. As the fountain lights change color, he sparkles in shades of pink, yellow, and green.

"You're playing a very dangerous game, Daisy," he croons.

"Maybe I like danger."

"I don't remember you being a thrill-seeker."

"Maybe I picked it up from Jordan."

"Maybe you need to think more carefully about how this could end." His tone carries the weight of real concern. He's talking about more than this game. This is a throwback to our earlier conversation about the future.

"That's what your mood was all about tonight," I say. "You're worried being around you puts me in danger."

"You could have been killed during that whole Myrtle show-down. You were hurt, for sure. I'll bet that lump on your head is still sore. And then today, you had to feed your blood to my friend. I wasn't thinking clearly when I pulled you into this, Daisy. I was being selfish, and that has to stop. I have to set you free of this mess while I still can."

My whole body rebels at the thought of freedom being anything but *this*. Freedom is the hectic heat coursing through my veins, the violent rhythm of my heart, the way I feel so exquisitely alive. It's the warm, ticklish thrills between my legs, the greedy ache in my soul, the wild abandonment of every inhibition. "That's not your choice to make anymore," I tell him. "It's mine. And honestly, I'd rather be with a guy who loves me enough to let me go, instead of the guy who cheated on me and still thinks I belong to him."

"Who said I love you?" Jay gives me a crooked grin.

My pulse jumps. "It was heavily implied."

"And here I thought I was hiding it so well." He's walking faster now, and I have to pick up the pace to keep the fountain between us. I'm going to have to run for it soon.

"Remember when we used to play tag at the park with the fish slide?" I ask. "We used to circle the merry-go-round just like this."

"And you were usually the winner."

"Not always. You were all legs back then. Still are, just with a little extra muscle."

"Your legs are longer than I remember." He trails his gaze up my body, and my skin heats. "And you've got more in other places, too. Curves that are positively delicious." His claws drag against the stone edge of the fountain. "I think the stakes are a little higher than a kids' game of tag. Have you thought about what happens when I catch you?"

I'm burning up, my heart pounding faster. *You'll fuck me. Fuck me hard, make me scream when I come...* But I just flash him a smile, then run straight for the opening of the maze behind me.

I only get a few paces along the passage before his body collides with mine, bearing me down to the grassy path. My breath leaves my lungs in a half laugh, half shriek. I'm on my stomach, with him half on top of me, bracing himself on both arms. I stay there for a moment, relishing the press of his hardness into my bottom, savoring the thrills racing through my lower belly.

I can hear him panting heavily above me, each breath thickened with a growl, and for a second I tremble with anticipation of what I'll see when I roll over to face him. This isn't a fairy tale. The beast doesn't turn into a prince through the power of love—it's the other way around.

I always preferred the beast anyway.

With a quick inhale, I twist, rolling over beneath him until I'm face up, staring into his brown eyes. They're shot through with white, and they blaze with triumph and desire. He ducks his face against mine, nosing along my cheekbone and temple, and I go perfectly still except for my frantic breaths. A louder growl grates from his throat, and there's the lightest scrape of a fang against my cheek. His claws travel along my collarbone, over my shoulder, snagging the thin strap of the dress.

"Jay," I whisper.

"Daisy." His lips press lightly against my neck, right over my pulse point.

I'm trembling, not with terror but with the frenzied hunger tearing through my blood. I need him. I need him so badly I think I might scream. I've needed him for years, for ages...forever.

One claw hooks into the strap, and—pop! Jay rips through it. His claws slide across my chest to the other strap and slit that as well. Then he drags the bodice of the dress down, inch by inch, looking into my eyes the entire time. My heart thunders through my ribs and my skin is incandescent with heat. It's all I can do not to lunge for Jay, not to writhe and arch to get my body against his—but a primal part of me recognizes the predator in him, awake in this moment, and I stay still, so very still, because any movement could make him snap.

Maybe I want him to snap.

I'm not wearing a bra under the maxi dress, and when Jay rakes the material down to my waist, his gaze drops to my breasts. A low moan issues from his lips. "Fuck," he whispers. "God, Daisy, you're beautiful."

His fangs skate along my skin, and my nipples tighten to eager nubs. Jay chuckles, low and breathless. "I love the way you react to me. I could tell, you know. Right from that moment under the magnolia. You've been wet for me ever since."

My body clenches in response, and my hips surge upward, an involuntary movement.

This is different from anything else we've done so far. My need for him goes deeper this time—it's ferocious, visceral. Even if someone came to interrupt us, I wouldn't want to stop. I'd let them watch while I fucked him anyway.

"Come here," I hiss at him. "Stop playing around."

He grins, a glittering vision of fangs, and my breath stops. But the next second his fangs recede, and the swirling white of his irises alters to black again. His lips look fuller, swollen and flushed, as he ducks his head and mouths my breast, teasing the nipple with his tongue.

With an urgent whimper, I sink my fingers into his hair, drag his face up to mine, and yield to the bliss that is kissing him. His fragrance soaks into my consciousness—pine, leather, and a fresh hint of basil. His crisp shirt presses against my bare skin, and I can feel him burning, burning through his clothes, his body hard with tension. He's as feral for me as I am for him.

The evening air breathes over us, stirs my hair as Jay slips his tongue into my mouth. He's cautious about it at first, until I tighten my grip on his hair and thrash my tongue against his, releasing a hoarse whimper into his mouth. I want him so badly I can hardly think. The sweet soreness in my pussy is so much worse—I ache to have him there. I can't wait another second.

"I want you inside me," I gasp. "I want you deep, as deep as you can get. I want you to fucking *break* me, Jay."

"In a minute," he whispers. "Just...give me a minute." His fingers glide over my bare skin, flexing, caressing my flesh as if he wants to memorize the feel of me. I shove my hands under his shirt, running them up his sides and around to the muscled expanse of his back.

Shifting his position, he rakes the maxi dress up my thighs and his fingers nestle at my core, probing my soaked underwear. The claws return, their sharp points dancing along the hollow of my hip, and then there's a raw rip of material as Jay destroys the panties.

I gasp with momentary terror that he might plunge those sharp nails into me—but I know he won't, because it's Jay. He stops kissing me for a moment while he focuses on retracting the claws—and then his fingers are back, sliding through my folds, swirling and circling. I arch into the touch, struggling to get the pressure I need, but he just keeps teasing, relishing my neediness.

"I've wanted to do this to you for so long," he whispers. "To watch you come undone for me, Daisy. I loved making you come in the VR room and on my bed, but this is even better. I can see you now, all the tiny changes, the expressions of your sweet face as I touch your clit, as I stroke your pussy right through here, and then down here...ah, you like that better, don't you?"

I can't form coherent words, but I lace my fingers at the back of his neck and pull him down to me. I crush his mouth to mine, swirling my tongue between his teeth. When he relaxes against me, bracing his hands on either side and settling his hips against my center, I reach down between us and graze my fingers along his length, through his jeans. I capture his throaty gasp with my lips, savoring it.

"Take these off before I bite you myself," I whisper.

He climbs off me long enough to shuck off his clothes and expose his entire lean, beautiful body to my sight. I prop myself on my elbows to get a better look at him. "Jay Gatsby, you are goddamn gorgeous."

Jay grins, his eyeteeth glinting. That feral smile of his prompts a naughty impulse, and I rise, sliding off the maxi dress so I'm entirely naked, just like him.

He's hard for me, dripping for me. I want to lick him so badly, to taste the desperation beading at the tip of his cock. But he made me wait, so I think I'll do the same.

"Looks like the chase isn't over yet," I say, and I flee into the maze again.

The air has cooled, but it's still soft and warm from the heat of the day, like cloudy fingers brushing my bare skin. Part of me can't believe I'm racing naked through a garden. I never do things like this—I never get any kinkier than doggy-style and spankings. I was always afraid that if I went any further with Tom, if we tried any of the other things he wanted to do, he'd take me deeper than I wanted to go. Some secret part of me never trusted him enough for that.

So why am I so trusting with Jay, who is an actual vampire with claws and fangs? Running naked from him through a hedge maze is the most reckless, erotic act I've ever indulged in—and yet I feel completely safe. He showed incredible control when he tackled me a few minutes ago—retracting the claws and fangs at precisely the right moments. I know he won't hurt me.

And if he does, I think I might like it.

Maybe that's the difference—the trust. Even when I loved Tom, some deeper instinct of mine kept me from yielding completely. The pain that came from his hands stemmed from rage or selfishness; but any pain Jay delivered would be laced with tenderness, sweetly synchronized with his love for me.

As I pelt past the opening of another corridor, Jay rockets from the adjoining path and slams into me, his bare skin hot against mine. We tumble into the soft, short grass with him heavy against my back.

"Got you." He bites my earlobe lightly.

I shift under him, lifting my bottom, trying to position myself so he can slip inside.

"No." His hands close around my body, turning me over. "I want to see your eyes when I make you come."

He pauses, one hand spread warm across my thigh. "Do we need a condom?"

"No, I'm protected," I say. "And I got tested for STDs after Tom. I'm fine." But I don't feel fine, not with Tom's name souring my tongue. I turn my head aside, staring into the hedge, biting my lower lip.

Why did I give Tom so much of myself? Why does he have to be here, ruining this moment for me? Tears pool hot in the corners of my eyes as I lie limp and splayed open to Jay.

He leans over me, brown eyes searching mine. "What are you thinking?"

Many things. That I don't regret my years without him, or what I chose for myself during that time—and yet I still have longings. Wishes. Things I would change now, as I'm looking back on it, knowing what I know about Tom. I feel like I'm coming alive again, returning to the best part of myself, and it's because of *me*, but it's also because of Jay.

"I wish things had been different," I whisper. "I wish I'd done everything with you."

Something breaks in his eyes, a tender pain that mirrors my own. "I know, baby," he says softly. "But it's all right now. Everything can be like it was supposed to be."

His mouth cradles mine, warm and sweet, flooding my sore heart with relief. I hum against his lips, latch my arms around his neck.

And I make the choice to banish Tom. To only feel what is happening right here, right now, with the beautiful man who made himself a monster for my sake.

I press the kiss deeper, probe between his soft lips, claim Jay with my tongue. My hands move from his neck to caress his shoulders, his arms, his back. "You're mine," I say fiercely, quietly, against his mouth—but not in *that* voice—not ever. This tone isn't some inherited gift from a mythic past; it's a special one, just for him. "Mine," I repeat, while my arms tighten around his body.

"I always have been," he breathes. "Helplessly, wickedly, wretchedly yours. Yours when I was alone, and yours when I was surrounded by dazzling crowds. Yours in every choice I made, and the ones I will make."

He kisses me, inhaling as he does it, like he's breathing me in. And then he shifts back, cups my ass, and lifts me slightly, easing his cock into me.

Finally, finally, oh god...

The rushing fullness of him is glorious. My head lolls back, my eyes fall shut, and I relax, every muscle loosening, every part of me hazy and hot and liquid.

Yes, yes.

Jay kisses my throat, teases the delicate skin with his teeth. Then his breath shudders, like he's on the brink of losing control, and he starts to move, gliding in and out of me.

"Faster, Jay, deeper," I whisper. "Please, please..."

With a groan he doubles his pace, and it's blessed friction, mind-melting wholeness. How does he feel this *right* inside me? Like he and I grew to fit each other exactly. Or maybe this sense of perfection isn't because of anything physical. It's because this is my Jay, my curious scientist, my playmate, my best friend, the biggest loss of my life, and my greatest rediscovered treasure.

With every name I devise for him I'm coiling tighter inside, heat building and rising and *god* this is incredible—

Jay is on his knees, one hand bracing my leg as he surges into me. His wavy brown hair is tossed and tousled, his cheeks are flushed, his lips parted. There's a glazed glory in his eyes and a tension to his toned body that I instinctively understand. He's close, and so am I, but I need something. I need to be anchored.

I reach for him, and he leans forward to grab my hand, a convulsive grip. He pulls it to his mouth, kisses my knuckles, then pins my hand to his chest while he fucks me harder.

I close my eyes, straining for this, desperate for both of us to get there together, because we deserve it, after everything. I'm concentrating so hard I barely notice when his other hand moves from my ass.

Then his thumb skates across my clit, stroking it with a quick, rough rhythm that sends white-hot fire through my veins.

He knew I needed more.

"Yes!" It's a squeal, a breathless scream. "Yes, Jay—"

"Daisy." His voice is deeper than usual, anguished and enraptured all at once. He leans into the rhythm, driving me closer to the peak.

My eyes fly open.

"Gatsby," I breathe, and then the avalanche comes, cascading along my nerves, glittering white. It rips me apart and heals me again, and I let myself shriek aloud with the joy of it, the utter relief of being finally his—all his, in all the ways. My pussy throbs around Jay's cock, and he gives a harsh, deep groan as he follows me in a pulsing release.

He collapses forward, arms braced on either side of me, and I have the delight of watching his knitted brows loosen, his taut features relax as his orgasm fades. His lashes blink apart, and he looks at me, perfect joy in his eyes.

We belong to each other. There is no truth more foundational than that for us.

We stay like that for a long moment, bodies locked tight, our gazes threaded together. Breathing. Blissful.

And then a mosquito dodges between our faces with a strident whine.

Jay bats it away. "Damn bloodsucker."

I giggle, cupping my fingers over my mouth. "God, Jay. Did we just have sex in your garden, like a couple of your horny party guests?"

"I guess we did." He chuckles and eases himself out of me. I lie there, limp and sated, savoring the warmth he leaves behind. Admiring the lean lines of his body as he stands up. Grinning when he sways a little, almost losing his balance.

"Damn." He glances down at me, wonder and joy in his gaze. "That was unbelievably good."

"No kidding." I release a satisfied sigh—which is interrupted by the whine of another mosquito. "We really should put some clothes on and get away from these bugs."

"Hang tight, I'll get our things."

I stand up, brushing bits of grass from my backside. When Jay returns, I slip on the maxi dress, which thankfully is tight enough to stay up without the straps, as long as I don't move around too much.

"Damn, I need my own clothes." I hitch the dress higher. "Much as I'd love to stay... I think I need to go home. I've spent one night away already, and texts can only hold my mother off for so long before she worries enough to hop in the car and drive over here."

"I get it." Jay nods, cupping my waist and pulling me close. "Though I'd keep you here forever if I could."

I melt against him, sinking into the comfort of another kiss. Then, fingers interlaced, we walk together through the maze to a side exit.

All the lights along the drive are on, illuminating every bump and dent on my poor car.

Jay traces one of the scratches with his knuckle. "Drive safe."

"I will."

"Daisy, I mean it."

Impulsively I rise on tiptoe and kiss his cheek. "Don't worry about me."

He holds the car door open for me, but before I duck inside he says, "You'll come tomorrow night? To the party?"

"Of course. I have to check on our pet glutton, anyway."

He leans over the car door, and my lips meet his halfway. After a few seconds I pull back, panting, my insides quivering and molten. How am I this aroused again? Geez.

"I should go."

"You said that already." Jay kisses me once more, harder this time, his hand cupping the back of my skull. There's a vibrating intensity to his kiss, a suppressed urgency that's not completely sexual, and when I pull back for air, I notice the milky white swirls in his eyes again.

My heart jumps.

Jay backs away a step, shaking himself like he's trying to dispel the hunger. His cheeks are flushed, his brown hair messy from my fingers raking through it. But his fangs are sliding out again, sharp and feral. His control is slipping.

"You should go," he says hoarsely.

Maybe I should offer to let him drink from me. But after everything I've been through today, and giving some of my blood to Cody, I just can't. It's too much, and I'm exhausted.

"Tomorrow," I promise.

"Go," he grits out, and I slam the door, pressing the button to start the car.

I guess, when your boyfriend's a vampire, you've gotta know when it's time to say good night.

19

WHEN I WALK INTO MY HOUSE, IT'S DARKER AND QUIETER than I expected. Usually Mom and Dad are still up at ten thirty, half working and half relaxing either in the kitchen or on the couch, with the TV running in the background. But tonight there's only one light on—the cold, stark ray over the sink.

I toss my keys into the basket, slip off my shoes, and drop my bag on a chair. First I swing by my room to pull on comfy pajamas, and then I shuffle back out to the kitchen. Not that I need a snack. If Tom were here, he'd tell me to skip the calories and go to bed. Maybe I should, but I want something warm, something comforting—something that feels like Jay.

"Hey, Sunshine." Dad's voice startles me, and I gasp, clutching my chest.

"Sorry," he says, wincing. "Didn't mean to scare you."

"You're back! How was the trip?"

"Long lectures, but I met some interesting people. It was good."

"Where's Mom? Everything okay?"

"She had a migraine. Went to bed early. I was reading, but I got peckish."

"Peckish, Dad? You guys watching British TV again?"

"Hey, it's a good word."

"I want something too," I mutter, peering into the fridge. "Something hot. But I'm not really hungry."

"How about some tea?"

"Ugh, you're totally going British."

"Fine. How about some hot chocolate?"

I snap my fingers. "That's it. That sounds perfect."

"I'll make it," Dad says. "You sit. I want to hear about Jay. Your mom said you two, um, spent the night last night?"

"Dad."

"No judgment here," Dad says, his head buried safely in the fridge as he pretends to look for the milk that's right in front of his face. "As long as you used protection, and he was good to you."

"We're way past the age when I needed that talk, Dad. But yes— he's good to me."

"So you really like him then." Dad withdraws from the fridge but keeps his back to me. This is how he handles tough or embarrassing conversations. When I was a kid, we'd always have them in the car, with me in the back seat. Or, these day, in the kitchen while he's fixing something or other at the stove. No eye contact.

"Well..." I settle onto a barstool at the island. "He has changed. Or I've changed. But he's still...him."

"And you guys talked. About what happened after we left Easley?"

"Yeah. He ran away from home."

Dad whips around to stare at me. "*What?*"

"His mom got arrested, and with his dad still in jail and no other relatives, he knew he'd have to go into foster care. So he ran away. But this guy Cody somehow got guardianship of him. I have no idea how they managed it." Bribery or threats, most likely. "And now Jay's an adult, so he's free to do what he wants. He still lives with his guardian, though. Or his guardian lives with him. They're friends, like brothers. It's complicated." I grimace, realizing how weird it must sound to my dad.

But he only nods, stirring the milk and sifting in cocoa powder. "Sounds like he had a rough time."

"Yes, but he's come out on top. He has his own business."

"The Bitcoin thing. Your mother mentioned it."

Oh crap. I forgot about that lie. "Yeah, there's that, and he does some investing, insurance, other stuff."

"Well, he was always a smart kid. Did he go to college? Study chemistry?"

"He did college online, I think. As for his major, I'm not sure. Why don't you ask him? We could have him over sometime."

"Absolutely." Dad sets a mug of hot chocolate in front of me. "Talk to your mother about it. She knows which nights are free."

"Speaking of which, I'll be going to his party tomorrow night."

Dad raises his eyebrows. "Another one?"

"He has them every weekend."

"Hmm." He blows on the steaming surface of the liquid. "Sounds like he's turned into a party hound."

I choke on my sip of hot chocolate. "What the hell is a party hound?"

"Someone who parties a lot? Chases parties? Has a nose for parties?" Dad smiles placidly. "A buddy of mine used to make a drink he called the Party Hound, but I think the correct name is the Racing Greyhound. I believe it is also a drink composed of Red Bull, grapefruit juice, and vodka."

I fake a gagging sound. "That sounds like literally the worst drink ever."

"You're not wrong." He chuckles, but then his eyes turn sober. "Does Jay drink a lot at these parties?"

"No. Not at all."

"Good. I'm glad that hasn't changed. Addiction can have a genetic element, and I'd hate to see him slip into the same bad habits his parents had. Letting any substance control your life is a recipe for disaster."

His words trigger a twist of guilt and worry inside me. What would Dad think about what I can do? The way I can control Jay and others? He always expressed such disgust over Gran's "powers." I could tell he despised the people who would allow themselves to be manipulated that way, whether in reality or pretense.

"Dad." I wrap my fingers around my mug, drawing courage from its warmth. "Remember the stories you used to tell about Gran?"

"Yep. I'm the one who told them, so..."

"Was there anything else?"

Am I imagining the tension of his shoulders? He clears his throat. "Anything else?"

"Yeah, anything..." God, why is this so hard to say? Why does it sound so ridiculous when I verbalize it?

"Was there something different about her? Something that made her especially good at what she did? You know, the hypnotism stuff?"

"Don't tell me you believe in that crap now." His voice is tighter, almost annoyed.

"Okay, I'm just going to come out and say it. Could she control people with her voice? And could that kind of skill be passed on to a relative?"

The panicked dart of his eyes to my face reveals volumes. Everything freezes inside me, and for a second, he and I just look at each other. He has assumed his usual placid expression, but it's too late, and he knows it.

"There was something supernatural involved, wasn't there?" I say quietly.

"Daisy." He shakes his head. "Let's not go there."

"Too late. You already gave it away. And now you have to tell me everything."

"Nope, I don't, because I'm the dad. Good night."

"Dad, please." Desperation slips through my tone, and he turns back to me, frowning.

"Why are you asking about this, Daisy?"

"Because...I've been noticing some things about myself."

"That's not possible."

"Why not?"

"I just... I was told... Ah, screw it." He massages his forehead with his fingertips, then returns to the island, seating himself on a bar stool. "The gift gets weaker with each generation. You shouldn't be able to notice anything."

The gift.

So he's admitting it, acknowledging that this thing is real. I knew it was real, but hearing my dad speak those words aloud—it shifts everything, changes my perspective of him, like a colored lens snapping into place.

"I didn't realize it for a long time," I say slowly. "When I use a certain tone, people pay attention, and sometimes they're more easily persuaded, but it's barely noticeable. And then with other people, the effect is really dramatic and obvious. They're completely under my control."

"How completely?"

"Like, I can make them do whatever I want. They stay under my sway or whatever until I change my tone, and that snaps them out of it." What I can't tell him is that the people most vulnerable to my sway are actually vampires, with ultra-sensitive hearing that renders them powerless to my voice. That's not my secret to share, not yet. Besides, a vindictive part of me is pissed Dad kept this from me and doesn't mind keeping something from him in return.

"I don't believe it," Dad murmurs. "They said as long as I married a human, like your grandmother did, the gift would die out within a couple generations. That's why I didn't tell you about it. I didn't think we'd have to worry."

It's the bombshell I've been psyching myself up for since I did the mythology research with Nick. I've seen this moment in dozens of movies—the moment when a person discovers they are something beyond human, or other than human. I've played it out in my head a few times, ever since I compelled Cody. But none of that was enough preparation for the cataclysmic earthquake of my father's answer and the giant ravine he cleaved through my worldview in just seven words.

As long as I married a human...

I try my best to speak calmly, evenly. To not freak out. I handled Jay being a vampire; I can handle this. "Married a human? So we're not human then? What the hell are we?"

"Breathe, Daisy." He releases a long, slow sigh, taking his own advice, and maybe giving himself extra seconds to form a response. "You're mostly human, all right? So don't worry about that. But we're *more* than human, I guess. That's the best way I know how to say it. On my side of the family, we're descended from an ancient bloodline—the result of intermarriage between two mythical races from Irish lore—the merrows and the leannán sídhe."

"The *who what* now?"

He sighs. "It sounds dumb, I know. In Celtic myth, the merrows were the sirens of the sea."

"So I'm descended from mermaids. Am I going to sprout a tail?"

"No, nothing like that. The ability to shift into aquatic form has long since been lost."

"Is that because the merrows slept with the—the leaning shee?"

"Leannán sídhe," he corrects. "And yeah, that's why. Many generations ago, a group of merrows and leannán sídhe lived in the same coastal town for a while, and there was some intermarriage. The mixing of the lines caused interesting effects in the offspring. Both merrows and leannán sídhe have a vocal element to their magic, so their children and grandchildren ended up with hybrid abilities that enabled them to influence humans with their words. Those descendants have all but died out now, and the gift decreases in potency with each generation."

"So you have it, too. Have you used it on Mom? On me?" With fresh, painful clarity I realize what an invasive power it is. How could Jay react so graciously to it? He must have felt violated when I used it on him, even with his permission.

"I have never used it on you or your mother," Dad says. "Not that I haven't been tempted. But I swore I'd never use it to influence anyone, and I've stuck by that vow—except...except once, almost nine years ago."

"When you got the new job," I say softly. "Oh my gosh."

"You can't tell your mother. Please." He leans toward me, anguish in his eyes. "We were in debt, Daisy, and you were about to enter high school. I wanted to give you everything you needed, so you could have a good high school experience. And I wanted to be able to pay for your college, wherever you decided to go. I had the best intentions. I only used a little bit of my ability—the rest was legit. My accomplishments were real, my research was sound, but they were going to give the position to someone else, a friend of the director, and I couldn't let that happen, not when I was so close. Not when I deserved it just as much, maybe more. We'd struggled financially for so long."

I want to tell him I understand, but my heart is sinking like a scuttled ship, and my image of him is crumbling like the shattered figurehead on its prow. Is no one who they seem to be?

"I guess you forgot to check your privilege, huh?" I murmur.

"Daisy—"

"I get it, I do. I just thought things had unfolded differently, and it's hard to mentally adjust to this. How much does Mom know?"

"She knows about your grandmother and our ancestry. But she thinks my gift is dormant."

"And you want me to hide this from her. About your job, and how you got it."

He sighs. "You make me sound like one of those awful parents in TV shows, forcing their kid to keep their secrets. I don't want to put you in that position, so...I'll tell your mother everything tomorrow."

The slump of his shoulders hurts my heart. Mentally I try to imagine my dad, my rational, gentle, quiet father, living with this power, swearing never to use it—and then breaking that vow, just once, for us. For his family. And he's going to confess to Mom, for my sake. Because he won't be the person who lays that burden of silence on me.

I'm disappointed in him, and a little angry, but I love him. He's the one who taught Jay how to be a decent man. Goodness knows there wasn't anyone else around to be Jay's role model.

Telling Mom is the right thing to do, but I ache for Dad, having to admit that to her. I ache for her, having to deal with it.

"What if she asks you to resign from your job? What if we lose everything and we have to leave here?"

"If that's what your mom wants, that's what I'll do."

"You're going to put that decision on her? Is that really fair?"

Dad rubs the scruff along his jaw. His eyes are wrinkled at the corners, and he looks tired, so tired. "I messed up, Daisy. And there's no perfect solution now. That's what using your powers will do. It'll put you in a no-win situation where every option is some shade of moral gray. I can't go back and change what I did, so we have to find a way to move forward. If that means giving up my job to keep your mother, I'll do it. If she thinks we should stay here, I'll do that, too. And I'll have to live with the unfairness of what I did to get where I am."

I'm about to protest, but Jay and I talked about something similar recently—how we can't go back. We have to move forward from where we are now.

As for me, I've already dipped my toes into the morally gray pool, unintentionally at first, and then as a test of my ability. I want to believe I won't go any deeper, but who knows? Who am I to judge my father when I'm venturing into the same waters myself?

"Lots of people do questionable things to get ahead," I tell him. "I'm not saying it's right, and I don't think you should ever do it again—but honestly, I don't blame you. Though I think you should find a way to pay it forward."

Dad's eyes are glittering with tears, and that troubles me more than anything else he's said tonight. "I hate that I haven't been the best example to you."

"You're only human, right?" I give him a shaky smile, and he answers it with the ghost of a chuckle.

"We should get to bed. But Daisy, I hope this is a lesson for you. Don't use your abilities, unless you have to protect yourself or someone you love. Our voice power is cheating, and cheating to get ahead never ends well."

He shuffles down the hall, and I go to the sink to rinse my mug.

He's right. Cheating doesn't end well.

If you get caught.

20

THE ATTENDANCE AT GATSBY'S PARTY THE NEXT NIGHT ISN'T
so much a crowd as a flood. Everyone who is anyone—and a bunch
of people who are absolutely no one—have descended on the place,
filling up the hallways and the rooms and the garden paths and the
pools. Jordan, Nick, McKee, Bek, and I arrive together, tumbling out
of the car into a whirl of color. Jay said it was a carnival theme, and
there are giant cutouts of animals everywhere, built of wood and lav-
ishly painted. Every so often, glitter spurts from somewhere above—
from the lampposts, the eaves of the house, the trees—wherever the
staff could hide a confetti cannon. The ground is already speckled
with it, the fountain is flecked with it, and it flutters through the
air, settling on hair and noses and bare shoulders. The air smells of
buttered popcorn, grilled hot dogs, and the sharp, bitter smoke that
follows firecrackers. Music trickles from the outdoor speakers—a
calliope's shrill, hollow notes coiling together with organ music and
percussion.

    Jay and Cody said they would meet us in the private lounge
adjoining the second-floor balcony. Since only Nick, Jordan, and
I are invited, we make a vague excuse and slip away from Bek and
McKee. Nick knows the way to the balcony, so we follow him up a

half-hidden set of stairs, through an archway, and past an attendant into a parlor I've never seen. It's dressed in artsy luxury—edgy furniture, dramatic paintings swirled over the walls, sculptures crafted of metal and wood.

One entire side of the parlor is French doors opening onto the broad balcony, and they're all wide open. Their sheer, wind-tossed curtains remind me of the screened porch at the back of the house, but this room is richer, uplit with lamps that paint the walls in swaths of amber and gold.

Cody is draped on the balustrade, his languid frame half-hidden by the fluttering curtains, smoking a joint against the blue-black sky. Nick goes to him immediately and Cody breathes smoke into his mouth.

On the couches and lounge chairs there are people, all of them wearing bracelets like Jay's. I recognize the girl Sloane, with the black hair and white skin, the one who assured me the unconscious girls wouldn't be molested. And there's the guy who offered me a cocktail and a walk in the hedge maze the other night. He waves nervously at me, with an anxious glance at Jay. I'm guessing he had his eye on me as a blood donor and didn't realize Jay had a previous claim. Clearly this guy is no longer under my sway, so there's a distance or time limit to my ability—maybe both.

Jordan sashays over to a young man with brown skin and a crown of thick dark hair sprinkled with blue glitter. He springs from the couch he was lying on and twirls her around. "Feels like I've been lying there since 2020, waiting for you," he complains, and she gives him a playful shove.

"There you are," says Jay from behind me. Where the hell did he come from? As far as I can see, the balcony and the stairs are the only exits from this room. Maybe there's a hidden door.

Tonight Jay is wearing eyeliner again, and he's dressed like a derelict ringmaster, in long ragged coattails and striped pants mottled with patches. He's even got the hat, though its tattered brim and drooping feathers are more Mad Hatter than P. T. Barnum. His outfit pairs perfectly with the Gothic look I chose for tonight— fringy black lace and puffy sleeves and a ratty multilayered skirt of black lace over holey leggings. Very Helena Bonham Carter.

Jay pulls me forward, and his words magnetize all the eyes in the room, drawing them to me.

"Everyone," he says. "I'd like you to meet Daisy Finnegan."

"Is she the one who knew you as a kid, Gatsby?" asks a pink-haired girl. "Daisy, you have to tell us something about his past. He won't talk about it at all, and it's so annoying."

Jay gives her a tight smile. "I'll tell you everything. I was born up north, and my parents were oil tycoons, but they're both dead now."

"Relatives?" asks a mustached man.

"All dead. Gas explosion. Very sad." Jay edges toward the balcony.

"See, he's being cagey again. I don't believe a word of it," the pink-haired girl pouts.

Jay and I sweep through the curtains into the evening air. Confetti is raining down around us, and two aerialists are climbing up and down the side of the house, hanging from long shiny sashes, whirling and dancing perpendicular to the walls. Dazed, I watch their limbs twist and untwist, always secured by loops and coils of the sashes. They're perfectly synchronized and heavily painted, with wide smiles fixed on their faces.

"Talented, aren't they?" Jay tosses his hat onto a lounge chair and leans on the balustrade with a nod to the aerialists. "Since circuses fell out of favor, a lot of these people have trouble finding work. But I'm paying them well."

"Those people in there, your vampire friends… Why don't you tell them your real story?" I ask him.

"I don't owe them the truth."

"I suppose not."

"I have to retain a bit of mystery. Helps me keep a grip on all this."

He's right, of course. Most charismatic leaders and celebrities maintain an aura of unknowability, of distance, from all but their closest friends. The people in that parlor are already more privileged than the mass of guests swirling below. They know who Gatsby is, and they have his favor. But I get to be the one who knows him best.

"How's our gluttonous friend?"

"I checked on him this morning and gave him some blood. He's looking good. Out of your sway, apparently, but he keeps asking for you."

"You let him sink his fangs into a human, without knowing whether or not he can be trusted?"

"Of course not! I let him drink from me."

"You can do that?"

"It's risky, but yes, vampires can drink from each other. I'll top off later tonight."

I don't ask who he's planning to drink from. Does he expect me to offer? Maybe I should…

"Mr. Gatsby." It's Henry, Jay's house manager. "There's a young man downstairs, very agitated, yelling about vampires."

"What the hell?" Jay mutters, and strides back through the parlor and down the stairs so fast I can barely follow him.

Halfway down the steps, Jay cants his head, listening. "You might want to stay upstairs, Daisy."

"Why?"

"The guy who's shouting about vampires? It's your ex."

"Tom?"

"He could be dangerous."

"I know. He's the one who convinced Myrtle to shoot you." I snatch at his arm, but he's already out of reach, moving unnaturally fast. "I'm coming with you," I whisper, knowing he'll hear it.

He doesn't reply, but forges through the shifting crowd into the dance hall, which isn't dark and laser-lit tonight, but bathed brightly from floor to ceiling and festooned with streamers, spangled balls, and strings of sequined flowers. Three more aerialists are swinging and twisting and twirling above the heads of the guests. There's a different band tonight, but I don't have time to inspect them because Tom is swaying in a little circle of cleared space, while the guests draw back from him with looks half-amused and half-alarmed. Tom clutches a beer bottle in one hand, and his long legs are braced apart. He looks like a mad drunken prince, cheeks red and lips wet with the liquor, his black hair in disarray.

"Ah, there you are," he roars as Jay emerges from the crowd. "The great Gatsby. I've been investigating you. Checking up on you. And do you know what I found out? People who come to your parties wind up a lot poorer than they were, scraping for cash. Maybe you've got a secret gambling den around here. Maybe you're convincing them to invest in risky stuff. Maybe you're a straight-up thief." He lurches a step closer to Jay. "At least, that's what I thought at first. But then...then I did some real digging. Twisted some arms. I have my ways, you know." He winks sloppily at the guests. "And you know what I figured out?"

"Dying to hear it, buddy," says Jay dryly.

"'Dying to hear it'—that's a funny thing to say." Tom's eyes narrow. "Because from what Myrtle tells me, you should be dead. Yeah, I visited her at the hospital you put her in. She's a great shot, you know. Been shooting since she was little. She swears she got you right through the heart, and yet here you are." Tom spreads his arms. "So I wondered, what's this guy's secret? I asked around. And someone finally told me the truth."

"You should lie down, buddy," Jay says. "Before you fall down."

Tom bares his teeth and smashes the beer bottle against the floor, drawing startled gasps from the guests. He stalks forward and takes a handful of Jay's shirt. "Call me 'buddy' one more time, bro."

Jay leans in, his voice a predatory hiss. "I think you've had way too much to drink...*buddy*."

Tom hauls back his fist, but before he can strike, Jay twists his wrist, flips him around, and tucks him into a headlock. He nods to Henry, who steps in to shoo the guests away. "Move along, please, folks. We'll get this glass cleaned up and this gentleman calmed down."

Jay hustles Tom into the library Jordan and I entered on the night of my first Gatsby party. I close the doors behind us and on a whim, I say, "Hestia, lock the library." I'm rewarded with a cool affirmative response from Hestia, an answering beep, and an approving nod from Jay. He throws Tom onto one of the leather couches, and Tom bends over, gagging, feeling his throat.

"Sorry about that, Tom." Jay tugs at the cuffs of his shirt to straighten them. "Couldn't allow that kind of violence at one of my parties."

"I know all about the violence you allow at your parties, vampire," Tom wheezes. "And I won't be quiet. I'm going to tell everyone."

"That's right. Tell everyone about the vampires." Jay gives him a cocky smile. "Tell them how your girlfriend, who's in a mental health facility, swears she murdered me. I'm sure that will be all the proof they need. They're sure to believe you."

"I've got more on you than that," Tom says.

"Oh, Tom. Buddy." Jay sits beside him and grips his shoulder. "You really shouldn't tell your enemies things like that, especially not when you're completely at their mercy." He glances up at me for a second. "Daisy, do you want to leave?"

"Nope."

"You should stay, Daisy," Tom says hoarsely. "See what your new boyfriend is really like. He pretends he's so fancy and gallant, but he's nothing. He *has* nothing. No family, no legacy, no future. He's just a poor little boy playing dress-up, throwing parties so he can feel big and powerful, when he's actually a no-good swindler and blackmailer, a piece of white trash, a little redneck shit who's not even worthy of my sloppy seconds—"

Jay is on him in a flash, one clawed hand crushing Tom's windpipe, white fangs gleaming a breath from Tom's nose. Tom whimpers through his constricted throat.

"You don't talk about her like that," Jay snarls. "You don't say her name. You don't even look at her, understand? Or I swear I'll tear your fucking throat out. I'll..." A sound like a growl rips from his throat, and he forces Tom's face aside, baring his neck.

Jay's head tilts sharply, his jaws parting wider. He's tense, like a snake about to strike.

"I should do it," he says, his voice thick with craving, with rage. "I should rip your head off, right now, for the way you've treated her."

"Jay," I choke out. "Don't."

"Do it," gasps Tom. "Show her what a monster you are."

I don't try to interfere; I couldn't stop Jay if I wanted to. I need to witness this, to know if the man I love is also someone I can trust, someone with the self-control to tell himself *no*.

Jay hesitates for another few seconds, his shoulders heaving.

Then his jaws close. He pushes himself off Tom, stalks across the room, and sinks onto a chair, propping his elbows on his knees and putting his face in his hands.

He's disappointed with himself. Heartbroken that he let himself go that far and nearly murdered my ex. I know exactly how he's feeling, because I understand him almost as well as I understand myself. I also know Tom, and I'm sure he'll perceive Jay's restraint as weakness. Which means it's my job to handle this for Jay's sake, and my own.

Slowly Tom sits up, feeling his throat. "You fucking animal. I'm going to ruin you," he rasps.

"No," I say, stepping forward. "You won't. Because you might think you know everything about Jay, but I know everything about you. What you did to me, and how you hurt Myrtle. I know what's on your phone and your laptop." I really don't. It's a shot in the dark, but it hits home. Tom's eyes widen with apprehension. "Jay might be too noble to really hurt you, but I can take you down, Tom. And I will. You're such an idiot, honestly, to come swaggering in here, shouting about the secrets you think you've discovered. Guess what I've recently discovered? I can make vampires do whatever I want, just with my voice. I could order Jay to drain all your blood, right now, and he'd have to do it." I stalk toward Tom, and he actually shrinks back. He shrinks away from *me*. The thrill I get from that is better than sex.

"Do you know how many vampires are in this house, right now?" I continue. "Do you know what I could make them do to you? And not just here, not just tonight, but anytime I want, because I know where you live, and I know all your favorite places. So you'll go away, and you won't say a word to anyone, because if you do, we'll know. And stay away from Myrtle, too. That girl has enough issues without you making them worse. Maybe with you out of her life, she can deal with her grief and find some peace." I raise my voice. "Hestia, unlock the library."

And then, just for good measure, I snap my fingers at Tom. "Go. *And be a good boy.*"

Tom wobbles out of the room with a frantic look at me before the door closes behind him.

"Hestia, text Henry. Tell him to have Tom Buchanan escorted off my property and permanently banned," says Jay, but he doesn't take his eyes off me. His claws and fangs have receded again, and he looks unusually pale.

My entire body is shaking. I collapse into a chair, knotting my trembling fingers to keep them still.

"That was the most powerful thing I've ever seen," Jay says.

"Well, he had it coming."

"I know." He perches on the arm of the chair I chose. "You've changed too, Daisy. You're a little sadder somehow, but a lot stronger."

"And that's a good thing?"

"A very good thing." His voice is rich with admiration, with respect—for me. "Thank you for taking care of that when I couldn't."

"Do you think he'll keep quiet?"

"I'll have my people keep tabs on him. But I think you made your point." A smile spreads across Jay's face. "Now, why don't we have some fun? It's a party, after all. What would you like to do?"

"I was in the hot tub the other night with a couple of guys from school. It was pretty relaxing before Tom came by and ruined it. I think relaxing would be good for both of us."

"Agreed."

As we leave the library and navigate the crowded hall, Jay

drapes his arm across my shoulders and leans down to my ear. "I guess I'm supposed to ignore the part where you were in a hot tub with two men?"

"Just some innocent fun."

"Okay. Well, in the interest of full disclosure, I'm planning on some not-so-innocent fun with you in the hot tub."

A flutter passes through my rib cage. I can't find words to answer, but I look up at him with a small smile, so he'll know I'm on board with that.

In the pool area, we change into swimsuits and slip into an unoccupied corner of the hot tub. Nobody in the immediate vicinity knows who Jay is, and I don't recognize anyone either. It's kind of nice, being incognito and unnoticed, with the heat of the bubbling pool pounding away the stress in our muscles. I'm starting to feel soft and melty, and very much affected by the glimmer of the hot tub lights on Jay's wet skin. I scoot a little closer to him, along the bench under the water, and he wraps one arm around me. My head drops against his shoulder.

After a few minutes I tip my face up, and he's watching me, his eyes so deeply shadowed they look black. His mouth is parted, just a little.

So, of course, I kiss it.

He makes a soft, blissful sound, angling his body toward mine, hauling me closer with a hand at my back. In the warm steam and the golden glow we kiss, again and again, until my whole world is alive with thrilling sensation, rippling through me from lips to toes. There's so much of his body pressed against mine, but I want more. I want to be overwhelmed and enveloped by him. I want to soak him in until we are the same entity and can never be truly separated. It's wild, way too sentimental, and violently true.

"Do you realize," I say, breathless, "how lucky we are to be both best friends and also this intensely attracted to one another?"

"So damn lucky," he whispers against my mouth.

"Not everyone finds this kind of thing."

His teeth graze my lip. They feel sharper than normal. Longer, too. "Oh crap," he hisses, pulling away. He hunches down in the hot tub, turning his face toward the edge. But people are passing by, humans with bare wrists and laughing faces, so he bends his face to mine to hide the fangs from them. He can't close his mouth all the way when they're elongated. He swears in a low voice, his chest heaving, and his slick shoulders tense.

I pull his wrist from the water and run my finger along the blood band. It lights up, the indicator hovering between yellow and orange. "Oh my god, Jay."

"I know. I waited too long to feed. I need to find Henry. Or Lillian—but she's probably gone home by now."

I pull his hand to my chest, and he stills instantly, his eyes widening. "You don't need to find either one of them. I'll do it."

He shakes his head. "I can hear how fast your heart is beating, Daisy. If it scares you, I don't want you to do it."

A shivery laugh breaks free. "I'm not scared." I move closer, until his wet hair drips onto my cheek. "I'm excited. And, um, aroused."

"That makes two of us, unfortunately," he whispers back.

"I'll get you a couple towels. One for your waist, and one you can drape over your head, to hide the...you know." I nod at his teeth. "Then we can sneak out. Do you know a dark corner somewhere nearby?"

"It's my house, sweetheart." He grins, all fangs and flushed cheeks. "I know all the dark corners."

21

Gatsby tells Hestia to let us into the maintenance room near the indoor pool. It's like a glorified closet, full of wire shelving and the acrid smell of chemicals, but at the back there's a tiny office with a desk and chair and a shiny new filing cabinet. We're both still dripping everywhere, so I push the keyboard aside so no water gets flung into it. A pointless move, since Jay could easily afford to replace it. But frugal habits are hard to break.

He's breathing heavier now, the white spirals in his eyes more dramatic.

"Why do your eyes do that?" I whisper.

"Some kind of temporary chromatic effect," he says. "I don't know. I've tried to figure it out, but there's no comparison for it anywhere in the natural world that I can find."

"What if it's not scientifically explicable?" I say, dabbing at the soaked ends of my hair with the towel. "You vampires think you're all science-y and stuff—a result of gene therapy or whatever. But this thing with me and my voice—turns out, it's something else entirely. Like there's actual magic involved—or if not magic, at least myth. Maybe your existence isn't as straightforward as you think. Who knows what that research guy put into his original serum? Maybe he found something mystical that he added to the formula. I mean, science can't explain how fast his original subjects developed fangs and extra organs, right?"

Jay stares at me. "You're incredible, you know that?"

"It's just common sense."

"But I hadn't thought of it that way. And you just opened up this whole new perspective on what we are and where we came from. A scary perspective that will require an ass-ton more research on my part, but still—incredible."

"I'll take the compliment. But, Jay, you're kind of drooling."

He snatches the towel from his head and wipes his mouth. "Damn it."

"It's okay." I ease into his space, slipping my arms around his neck. He looks down at me, lips parted over the fangs, his eyes nearly white. His chest shifts against mine with each labored breath. Every muscle in his arms and torso has gone rock-hard, and his claws have extruded, dull black and sharp as death.

"Daisy." My name is a plea, slurred through his mouthful of teeth.

I nod reassuringly. "Go ahead. It's fine."

"It's easier if you're asleep. No pain. I could get you the meds we use on the others."

"I want to be awake for this." My skin prickles with anticipation. Fear and lust swirl together in my chest until I can't tell one from the other. "Just do it already. Where do you usually bite? Do you have, like, a favorite spot?"

"Cody likes the inner thigh. I usually do wrist or neck. Although with you, I might want to try a few other places sometime."

Oh god, yes.

"Whatever you want," I whisper.

He wraps one arm around me and delicately scrapes my wet hair off my neck with his claws.

My heart is throbbing so hard I think I might pass out. But I won't pass out. I won't.

"Breathe." Jay's teeth graze my skin. "Breathe, Daisy."

"I *am* breathing."

"I'm only going to take a little, since you just gave some to Cody. I won't risk your health."

"Okay."

A moment of horrible suspension—*Breathe, Daisy, breathe*—and then his forehead sinks against my shoulder. "I can't do it. I can't hurt you."

"Seriously?" I push his face away. "Stop this, okay? You're Jay Gatsby, the vampire who has turned dozens of people and drinks from his staff regularly. You are not wimping out on me. I appreciate that you don't want to hurt me, but I offered, all right? I don't want you biting anyone else, only me, until I turn. And then I guess we'll both have to feed from other people. But for now, when you need blood, I'm the one you come to. Is that clear?"

"Until you turn?" he says.

"Yes. You said you would make me a cheetah—give me immortality, or at least as close as we can get to that in the real world, if this even is the real world and not some wacky alternate dimension I've slipped into—"

"Daisy."

"Fine, we'll talk about the turning thing later. For now, you either drink from me of your own free will, or I'll make you, so you don't die."

He hesitates, milky eyes narrowing, a soft snarl in his throat.

I give him my most wicked smile. "Come on, Jay. Bite me."

He grips my shoulders and his fangs plunge into my neck.

It's terrifying, because I feel incredibly, helplessly fragile in his powerful hands, but at the same time I know I'm safe and the man I love is taking part of me into himself, which if I'm being honest is pretty hot.

The jolt of pain fades to a deep sucking sensation, like it did when Cody drank from me. At first I don't care for the suction—it sets my teeth on edge and sends a chill over my bare skin. But then Jay gives this low, delighted moan, and a flush of heat soars through me, erasing every bit of the discomfort.

His damp hair tickles my neck and jaw, and his scent wafts to my nose—spicy cloves and oakmoss and freshly mown grass. His fingers clasp my shoulders tightly, but not painfully.

When his bracelet vibrates, his fangs slide out of my flesh—and then his tongue passes over the area, sealing the punctures with long, slow licks.

"There's a shot we give to some of our regular donors to help them replenish their blood volume faster," he says. "You'll need one, since both Cody and I drank from you."

"Okay." I feel kind of floaty and strange, maybe because of the blood loss, but also because I'm wearing a thin, wet swimsuit, and my bare skin is still pressed to his. We're both taking ragged breaths, heat pulsing between us. When Jay starts to move away, I grip his arm and tip my head up, my profile skimming his.

His mouth grazes mine, a delicate brush of smooth skin. I kiss him, light and quick. Once, and again. When I dip my tongue between his lips, I taste the coppery salt of my own blood.

His dick is rigid under his swim trunks, and every muscle of his body is taut with want.

"Do it, Jay." I skirt perilously close to that persuasive tone, but

I don't go there, because all I want is his pure, unbridled consent. "Take me. Right now. Right here."

With a growl, Jay lunges, gripping my thighs and hitching me onto the desk. His kiss is brutal, a thick lash of tongue through my mouth, lips bruised against teeth. He clutches me with half-restrained force, runs his palms up my neck and then over my shoulders, dragging down the scant triangles of fabric over my breasts. I reach between my legs and tug aside the material there, and then I yank down his shorts.

For another tangled, heated second we kiss, while the burning tip of his cock drags along my center; and then I hitch myself forward and he drives in. We notch together perfectly, the fit so tight and smooth that I release a broken sigh from the pure pleasure of it.

"This is how it's supposed to feel," I whisper against his cheek. "I didn't know."

"I was made for you," he says. "I always knew it. You and I were inevitable, Daisy. And I'll do anything—" His voice cracks with emotion, and he thrusts harder, hands braced on the desk while I wrap my arms around him for leverage. The angle is just right for me—his pelvis grinding into mine—and I feel myself starting to convulse, quivering right on the edge.

"Yes, yes," I gasp; and then Jay's claws emerge, and he circles the tip of my breast without slackening his pace one bit. I shatter into blissful fragments, clutching him desperately, releasing my cries into his parted lips. He crashes into me a few more times and comes hard, his claws screeching against the desk, leaving long grooves.

This is what I was missing before, a trust that's bone-deep, immovable. It's the foundation for everything—adventures and quiet moments, blood and kisses, cuddles and kink. I love him beyond sense, beyond expression. He's the complement to every side of me, from the Daisy who likes to curl up poolside with a fruity drink to the Daisy who wants to be chased naked through gardens at night. He loves me aimless or determined, scattered or focused, cautious or reckless. And I love him the same.

Jay is kissing me through the ebbing pleasure—sweet, earnest kisses with wicked little dips of his tongue into my mouth. I think I'm crying a little from the sheer joy of us. Yes, I'm definitely crying. Great, now I'm *that* girl.

I hop off the desk, swiping at my cheeks and tugging my swimsuit back in place. "I need to clean up and change."

"Go," he says. "I'll get that shot for you, and you need to hydrate."

I escape as quickly as I can, hopeful that he didn't notice the tears.

Once I'm done changing, I lean on the counter in the women's locker room and stare at myself in the mirror. "Get a grip, Daisy," I whisper. "No more crying during sex."

Jordan sweeps into the bathroom at that moment. "You okay, babe? Jay sent me in here to check on you. Thinks he hurt you or something. And he wanted me to give you this." She holds up a tiny syringe.

I lower my voice, glancing around to make sure there's no one within earshot. "He drank from me just now, and I kind of ran away afterward."

She frowns. "I know it takes some getting used to..."

"That's not why I ran. We also did...other stuff, and I started crying." I bite my lip. Damn it, why are the tears welling again?

"Oh, honey." Jordan circles my shoulders with a lean arm. "But you like him, don't you?"

"It's not that. I'm just... I'm sad about the whole Tom thing, you know? I wasted so much time on him because I didn't know what I really needed and wanted. What I have with Jay is just... It's..."

My face crumples, and Jordan hugs me, patting my shoulder with awkward sympathy.

What I have with Jay is beautiful. It's healing. He makes me feel valuable, wonderful, strong—all the things I haven't felt for a long time.

I just have to keep letting myself realize that my future isn't dark anymore. It's brightening, flooding with warmth, because of Jay. Because of my strengthening friendship with Jordan. Because I'm allowing myself, finally, to be fully and wholly *me* without those dark voices in my mind holding me back.

Sighing, I nod to Jordan, and when she releases me, I splash my heated face with cool water. "I'm good now, thanks."

"Damn, your cheeks look tasty when you're flushed." Jordan draws a glossy nail down my face. There's a flicker of white in her eyes, the hint of hunger. "I should go find a donor."

"You mean go drug someone and then bite them."

"Let's not start, okay? Jay has some of the guests wearing red bands if they're hopefuls—vampire candidates—and willing to donate, so I'll look for one of them first. But yeah, if I can't find one, I'll be taking blood from someone else. You can just put your judgy face away."

"Fine." I swipe my hand over my face. "There, it's gone. Go have fun. And thanks for checking on me."

"Always, babe." She breezes out of the locker room.

I take another second to pat my cheeks with a paper towel. Then I inject my thigh with the contents of the syringe and leave the locker room.

Jay is dressed again, staring at the people clogging the pool and lazy river. When I touch his arm, he jumps. "Daisy! Are you all right? Did I scare you, hurt you? Jordan said you're fine, but—"

"I really am fine. Just got a little overwhelmed, but in a good way."

His brow is still furrowed, so I reach up and pretend to smooth it out with my fingertips. "Stop worrying. You did nothing wrong. I started tearing up because of all the deep emotional stuff I was feeling, and I didn't want you to see me ugly cry after sex, okay?"

"If you're sure that's all... Because if I did anything to upset you or hurt you, Daisy, I'll fix it."

"No, Jay." I cup his face between my palms. "You sweet, gorgeous man. I'm good, really. And... Wait, why is your pocket buzzing?"

He pulls out his phone, and his eyes light up. "I set an alarm so we wouldn't miss it. Come on!"

We hurry through the crowd, up some stairs and along hallways and through a bedroom, passing through some French doors onto a small balcony at the back of the house.

"We should have a perfect view from here. Have a seat." Jay gestures to a couple of padded chairs. On the floor nearby is a bucket of ice, with a bottle of champagne and a bottle of sparkling juice nestled inside. Two glasses stand on a tiny table. "Champagne for you, sparkling cran-grape for me," Jay says.

"Is it heresy if I mix cran-grape with my champagne? I don't like the taste of champagne by itself."

"It is, but since it's just the two of us, who cares?" He pops the cork and pours me some of each.

I sip the concoction and nod approvingly. "So, why are we back here?"

"You'll find out in about"—he consults his phone—"one minute. Or less. I'd better put these in." He tugs a pair of noise-canceling earbuds from his pocket and tucks them into his ears.

A handful of seconds later, a great swell of music envelops the place, echoing across the lawns and gardens. There's a general murmur of expectation from the crowd, and then something bright rockets into the sky, cracking through the night like a thunderclap and splitting into a shower of golden sparks. Another burst of fire, pink this time, and then an explosion of blue.

"Fireworks," I breathe. Jay can't hear me, of course, with the noise-canceling buds protecting his sensitive vampire ears—but he looks way too pleased with himself. I twine my fingers with his and sip my drink while the fireworks spray and shatter across the sky, painting it in sizzling color and lingering smoke. The show goes on for a full fifteen minutes, ending with a series of enormous white fireworks with yellow centers. Wait a second...

Those are daisies. For *me*.

I tighten my fingers around his.

When the last glimmer fades, Jay removes the earbuds.

"You need to stop being so over-the-top romantic," I chide him. "Men your age don't do this stuff."

"Daisy, darling, you have to stop thinking that everything I do is for you," he says solemnly. "This show was for my wonderful guests. Think of how many vampires were able to slip away for a drink from their donors while it was going on."

"Right. And those daisies at the end?"

"Just a coincidence. Is it my fault that you see yourself in everything I do?"

"Yes." I trail my fingertips over his knuckles. "It's absolutely your fault."

He watches my hand wandering over his skin. "Did you like it?"

"I loved it."

"Anything you don't like, I'll change. Immediately."

"I told you, I don't expect perfection."

"Then you're a rare soul." He rises, looking off the balcony into the gardens. "When I look down there at all the guests who come to my house every Friday night, do you know what I see? I see a bunch of people starving for perfection. They all curate their social media with it in mind. Even their 'real' moments, their messy moments, are carefully chosen. They come here in search of the perfect night, the perfect entertainment, and they expect me to be the perfect host and provide the perfect experience. Anything less is my fault, even if it's really theirs. And they're not forgiving. Sure, they'll ignore a guy like Tom, mouthing off while drunk. As long as I'm shelling out free booze and food and fun, they'll claim to love me. But if I ever stop giving them what they want, all it would take is one rumor, and the whole rotten crowd would cancel me in a second, no proof required."

"When did you get so cynical?"

"I've always been cynical. It's what happens to dreamers who get their hearts crushed. And you're no optimist yourself."

He's right, of course. "I've had my rough spots," I admit. "First it was losing you and transitioning to a new social sphere, a new school. And then it was struggling through college while my relationship with Tom got...really dark. Even before he cheated on me, I was suffering with him, even though I didn't fully realize it at the time. He was constantly cutting into me with his words."

Jay's face darkens, his frown turning thunderous. He looks as if he might go hunt Tom down and drain him dry.

Quickly I continue. "It wasn't all bad, though. The best part was early high school, when Tom and I were still flirting, before we really started dating. I missed you a little less then, and everyone at school seemed to love me. I've tried a lot of new things during these eight years, you know. Money lets you do that, lets you try skiing and skating for the first time, gives dance classes and self-defense lessons."

"And people say money can't buy happiness." Jay gives me a sardonic smile.

"It can certainly contribute to happiness. Although it's not the only factor."

"That's for sure." He runs his knuckles along my cheek.

"And what were you doing all this time?" I ask. "Besides surviving as a runaway and plotting your vampire takeover of the world."

He snorts. "Not a takeover, Daisy. But to answer your question, I hung out with Cody, finished high school online, got a degree in chemistry, also online, took some medical courses, learned to dance. I taught myself how to talk more formally, with less of a southern hick accent. And I worked on the vampire transformation problem, to make the process safer and less excruciating."

"Jordan told me. But you never explained how you managed that."

"By piggybacking off the work of some other researchers and adapting it. And I had help from a doctor Cody knew. Basically, we designed an injection that dulls the pain receptors and keeps the body from fighting so hard against the formation of the new organs. That's the biggest problem, you see—the body's natural defense system, its tendency to reject new matter that's introduced."

"Like what happens when people receive donated organs," I interject.

"Exactly. My formula calms everything down, puts the body in a more receptive state so the change doesn't place so much stress on its systems. If you just drink a vampire's blood, straight up, your transformation puts you at huge risk of stroke, heart attack, and organ failure, not to mention the strain on the nervous system because of the sheer agony of the change. A lot of traditionally made vampires have white hair because of the trauma their bodies went through when they changed."

"Cody doesn't have white hair."

"No. But he still wakes up screaming from nightmares about his transformation. In the past, only twelve percent of traditionally turned vampires survived the process."

"Oh wow. I had no idea it was that low. No wonder people pay you extra for the safer and less painful way." I shudder.

"Exactly. I got my startup money for this place by testing the formula on some rich folks in Charleston."

"So, how much do I have to pay you to get my shot and my little cup of vampire blood?"

He looks at me, his upper lip lifting just enough to show the tips of his canines. "Nothing at all. For you, it's free."

"Lucky me." My voice is thinner and wispier than I'd like. "So can we do it now? Or—wait a second—I just gave you my blood, so wouldn't I just be pouring my own blood back into myself?"

"Once human blood enters a vampire's system, it's mixed with all the other blood that carries the genetic catalyst. But we do recommend that the blood for a transformation not be drawn until twenty-four hours after a feeding."

"You sound so official and proper." I try to laugh, but it comes out as a nervous giggle.

"Daisy, you don't have to change if you don't want to."

"No, I want to. I honestly do. I just—"

"You haven't thought it all through yet, and you need time." His voice is gentle, soothing, and I breathe a sigh of relief.

"Thank you for understanding."

"I would never push you into this," he says. "I want you to know exactly what to expect. Speaking of which, we have gatherings of recently turned vampires where they can chat, ask questions, exchange stories. Would you like to come with me to one of those meetings on Thursday night?"

"Wait a second." More nervous giggles bubble up in my throat. "You're saying that you have vampire support groups?"

He grimaces. "Yes?"

"Oh my gosh. Do you realize how funny that is?"

"No..."

"So what do they do? Sit around in folding metal chairs with their fangs out swapping blood-drinking stories"—I'm laughing so hard I can barely manage words—"and like, commiserating about having *two* stomachs that growl during classes or board meetings, and how two heartbeats confuses the hell out of their Fitbits..."

Jay is laughing too, with a kind of helpless surprise. "You're ridiculous."

"You should have the blood bracelets track people's steps, too," I add, wiping my eyes.

"They already track location, so I guess that would be easy enough."

My laughter fades. "You track their locations? Isn't that an invasion of privacy?"

"Everyone has to agree to it when they sign the paperwork. If someone goes glutton, murders a human, or gets dangerously low on blood, we have to be able to find them."

"I guess that makes sense."

Jay sits beside me again, gathering my hand in his. "I won't abuse the privilege. You'll go where you want, whenever you want. If you break up with me and decide to go off somewhere else with someone else, I won't follow you."

"Says the guy who followed me all the way here and bought a house up the road from my cousin."

He laughs nervously. "Okay, fine. If I follow you, I'll keep some distance. I'm not going to stalk you like Tom."

"You could never be like Tom."

A shadow crosses his face. "In some ways, I'm worse. I've killed people, Daisy."

"Because you had to."

"Yes. Gluttons who got out of control."

"How frequently does that happen?"

"It can happen to anyone, honestly. That's part of the reason we do interviews and research on our candidates. We have to make sure that they have some measure of self-control that will hopefully carry over into their vampire existence. But as you saw with Slagle, sometimes those precautions don't work. Sometimes people surprise you. That's why we have support groups, because like anything else in life, when you're stressed, you're prone to overindulge in the things that bring you pleasure—drink, food, games, drugs, sex, blood, whatever. So if any vampires are feeling anxious or stressed, we like to monitor that."

I stare at him, realizing again the scope of what he has undertaken. "And what about you? You've taken all of this on yourself—are you stressed?"

"That's like asking the Hulk if he's angry." Jay grins. "I'm stressed all the time. But I manage it. Mostly by having goals and staying focused on the things that matter the most to me."

He's looking right into my eyes. He's talking about me. And I want so desperately to tell him how much I care about him, too, but instead I'm shrinking shyly into myself, letting the words die on my tongue. Withdrawing into that place I go when I'm struggling to handle my emotions.

It's a coping mechanism, sure, but my gut tells me it isn't healthy. There's something not right with letting myself recede, especially now, so I struggle against it and force myself to stay grounded. I focus on the ribbed metal arm of the chair I'm sitting in, and the warmth of Jay's fingers, and the bitter scent of the fireworks smoke melting into the burnt sugar aroma of cotton candy from the snack station somewhere below us.

It works, for once. I manage to stay whole.

"I should tell you something before you change me," I say quietly. "You mentioned that I'm good in a crisis, but sometimes when traumatic things happen, I kind of separate myself into two people. One of them is in charge, doing all the right things, and the other one, the real me, is hiding. So I'm kind of both outside, doing the actions, and inside, watching myself perform them."

Jay rubs his thumb over the back of my hand, his eyes thoughtful. "I think that's called disassociation. One manifestation of it, anyway."

"It's not good."

"Maybe not. But it's not bad either. You've experienced a lot of trauma, and maybe your mind needs to do this occasionally. If it keeps up, you can talk to Miriam about it. She'll probably have some tips."

"*I've* been through trauma?" I lurch from the chair, suddenly frustrated. "Jay, you were abused and neglected your whole life. Your parents were literally the worst. I have a loving family, plenty of money, lots of friends, and you. I shouldn't have to do this disassociation thing, whatever it is. I shouldn't have this broken piece inside me. Earlier you said I was strong... I'm not. You've been through so much more and look at you—perfectly whole and mentally healthy—and look at me, collapsing inside over a failed relationship and a couple traumatic incidents. It's pathetic. I'm pathetic."

"Stop." He takes my face in his hands, tilts it up to his. "You are *not* pathetic. And don't compare yourself to me, or anyone else. I have my own unhealthy coping mechanisms, okay? I withdraw from people. I barely let anyone in, even you, sometimes. I may look like I have it together, Daisy, but I don't. And I'm not saying that to make it about *me*, okay, but to help you see that you can be broken *and* strong. You can be hurting *and* powerful. That's what I want for myself, and for you. Our pain and problems don't define us. We don't have to relive the past. We aren't cursed to repeat what we've done, or what our parents have done."

He pulls my head to his chest and holds me. My arms slide around his waist, and for a while we just stand together. With my ear pressed to his chest I can hear his heartbeat, strong and regular, and the fainter echo of that second smaller heart, lower down, somewhere on the right side.

He's a literal vampire. Not the kind from myth, exactly, but close enough. Maybe that would unnerve me more if I wasn't supernatural myself. I can't seem to get my head around it yet, to fully realize what I am. Which reminds me... I haven't told Jay about my chat with Dad yet.

"Speaking of things our parents have done." I sigh against him. "I should tell you about the talk I had with my dad. About what I am, and what he is."

When I've repeated the conversation for Jay's benefit, he asks a bunch of really specific questions, which annoys me a little because I didn't think to ask them myself. Since I don't have all the answers he wants, we spend the next hour poring over odd little folkloric blog posts online, trying to glean additional information about my powers, without much luck. Eventually a text pings on my phone— Jordan, telling me she's heading out. It's one thirty in the morning.

"I should go." I rise from the balcony chair and stretch, while Jay's eyes trail along my body. Then I touch the side of my neck. It's faintly sore, but all I can feel are two small indentations. "How's it looking?"

Jay peers at the marks. "Looks good. Try to keep it covered when you get home, though, or your dad might ask questions. A normal parent probably wouldn't notice, but since he's already familiar with supernatural entities, you never know."

"I want to tell them about you soon. About the vampire thing."

His brows contract a little, and anxiety tightens his mouth. "Do you think they'll accept me?"

"It doesn't matter if they don't. I'm a grown-up, and I get to choose who I'm with."

"I know. It's just...your parents are special to me." His lashes droop, and his brow furrows deeper.

"Hey. It'll be fine, Jay. They love you, too, you know."

"Not enough," he says quietly.

"They messed up with you. I know it, and I think they know it, too. But as you say, we can't go back. And we're not doomed to repeat our mistakes, not if we learn and do better."

"I hope you're right."

When we descend to the first floor, the party's still going strong. We pick our way over glitter and paper streamers, gold-painted plastic cups and a discarded shoe or two.

"Who loses their shoes in someone else's house?" I kick one of them aside.

"It's not the weirdest thing the cleaning crews have found," says Jay, but he doesn't elaborate.

Jordan sidles up and pinches me lightly. "Ready to go?"

"Yeah. What about Nick?"

"Staying over with Cody again. They're such lust fiends, those two." She smirks.

"What about you and the muscly hottie who twirled you around?"

"Michaelis? He's fun, but I'm not sure if I'll keep him. I've got my pick of the pack, you know. I'm surprised you're not staying over, considering how infatuated you are with this guy. But I guess you got your fill for the night, huh?" She winks.

My face turns into a raging inferno. "Jordan, I know you're a vampire, but I will find a way to kill you."

"I'm terrified." She pats Jay on the cheek. "Good night, Mr. Gatsby."

22

"WHAT DO I WEAR TO VAMPIRE SUPPORT GROUP?" I MOAN, staring into my closet.

Nick is lying on his stomach on my bed, scrolling through Instagram. "Something sexy."

"Why? So they'll want to bite me?"

"So they'll want to bone you."

"Ew. Seriously?"

"Precious, you've got a boyfriend again. An actual monster boyfriend. You better shake off that prim little attitude. It's not like you didn't get kinky with Tom the Terrible."

"I'm not talking about this with you."

"Fair enough." He scoots off the bed and flips through my clothes. "You need something new in here. You live in the same three pairs of shorts and six shirts all summer."

"I like what I like."

"So go buy more of what you like." He falls back onto the bed. "I'm not going to be your stereotypical gay fashion consultant, okay?"

"Too late for that," I mutter into the clothes.

"What's that?"

"Nothing." I yank a sundress and a cardigan out of the closet. "This?"

"Nope."

"You didn't even look."

"Your first choice is never the right one."

With a groan I return the outfit to the closet and select another, a baby-doll top and capris. Nick blows a raspberry. Narrowing my eyes, I pull out a slinky red top, knotted at the shoulders, and a black miniskirt. "This?"

"Bingo."

"No! Not bingo. This is the opposite of bingo. This is like wearing a big sign that says, 'Drink My Blood'!"

"He's picking you up in, like, two minutes, isn't he?"

"Crap."

"Put it on."

The doorbell rings a minute later, while I'm still in the bathroom changing. Every minute that passes is another minute Mom gets to grill Jay about what he's been through the past several years and what he's doing now, so I struggle into sandals as fast as I can and grab my bag.

"See ya." Nick salutes me.

"You better be gone when I get back."

"Love you too."

But when I rush into the entry hall, ready to save Jay, there's no interrogation in progress.

My mom is hugging him.

And she's crying.

He looks up at me over her shoulder, and his eyes are swimming with tears.

"Hey," I say softly.

Mom turns around, sniffling. "Hey, honey. Sorry, I didn't mean to, it's just—"

"It's okay. You all right?"

"I'm fine." She plucks a tissue from the box on the hallway table. "Just fine. It's really good to see you again, honey."

And this time the "honey" is for Jay.

She lingers in the doorway as we head outside to Jay's car. "You two have a good time tonight! Text if you won't be back by twelve thirty!"

"I will."

The car starts itself as we climb in, and we head out of our development onto the main road.

"So. Mom gave you quite the welcome." I sneak a side glance at Jay.

"She apologized for not stepping in more and addressing the situation with my mom. I know I asked them not to, because I didn't want to go into foster care, but she said they should have tried harder to figure out something else. And she said she was sorry you guys left so suddenly." He clears his throat. "It was exactly what I wanted to hear. And I couldn't say anything, so I just...hugged her. And she started crying. Do you think she'll be okay?"

"I think she'll be just fine." I squeeze his shoulder briefly, and he looks over at me.

Humor sparks in his eyes. "Interesting choice of outfit. You look like a tasty little blood snack."

"That's what I said! But stupid Nick made me wear it."

"Ah, the old 'Nick made me do it' excuse. I'm starting to hear that a lot from Cody, too." Jay's lips twitch up at the corner.

With a gusty sigh, I lean back in my seat. "Outfit aside, are you sure this is okay? I mean, I'm not a vampire yet. This group might not want me hearing their little vampire secrets and knowing their faces."

"When I emailed them about it, they said, and I quote: 'We'd be thrilled to have you and your girlfriend at the meeting.'"

Inside I'm squealing because he told them I'm his girlfriend. I'm Jay Gatsby's *girlfriend*.

But I say coolly, "That could just be politeness."

"But it's not. They all love me. When I go to these things, they give me the best snacks."

"Ah, so that's why you attend."

"Daisy. I have, like, a billion dollars. I can buy any snacks I want, or have Hestia order them online, or ask Henry to run out and buy them, or hire a personal chef to make them—"

"Okay, I get it. You're super rich, and you're also kind of a cult leader."

A passing car's headlights flash over his face. He looks deeply revolted and offended, and I can't help giggling.

"I know you think you're being funny," he says slowly, "but that's one reason I don't always participate in my own parties. I don't want that kind of treatment. It's weird. And if you knew how the First Gens act—Wolfsheim in particular—you'd understand the difference. He demands complete obedience and unquestioning worship. He views himself as a messiah or a prophet, a divinely appointed emissary to the chosen few."

I roll my eyes. "That's so cliché."

"Maybe so, but Wolfsheim actually believes it. And his followers—the other First Gens and their Progeny—are intensely fanatical."

A trickle of fear runs through my heart. "And these are the people you and Cody pissed off? The ones you keep defying over and over?"

He winces. "Yeah. But Wolfsheim is in Colorado, and he's got his own business to handle. He might fuss, but he won't bother us. And even if he does pay us a visit, we'll just show him our operation and tell him about the precautions we're taking. I mean, it's not like he and his people don't turn humans into vampires, too. They just do it on a very limited scale, and they don't charge money for it. Each First Gen is allowed to turn one human every five years. The candidates for Progeny are carefully selected, and they must serve their progenitor for five years after their transformation—if they survive."

"And the First Gens use the more brutal method. The one with all the agony."

"The drinking of the vampire's blood." He nods. "They believe old vampire legends are actually prophecies to be followed in the present. To them, transformation by drinking raw blood is the only pure way to create a new vampire. Like a test of the human's worthiness."

"That's total bull."

"Of course it is. A lot of religious traditions are. You've got to cut away all the extra crap people have added to get anywhere near the truth." He takes a sharp turn on the dark mountainside, and I gasp as the trees fall away on the right side of the car. A few feet from my window, the road drops into a deep gorge. There's no guardrail here.

"This is really dangerous. I should have let you turn me already," I mumble.

"I'm being careful. I'll go slower if you want."

"Yes, please."

He decelerates, taking the next hairpin curve with a precision that eases my nerves a little.

"You really are the best boyfriend." I stroke his thigh lightly.

He sucks in a quick breath. "Are you trying to distract me? I thought you wanted safe driving."

"Sorry." I withdraw my hand. "How close are we?"

"Nearly there."

The car lurches to the left again, up a dirt road I couldn't even see in the dark. "Do you have better night vision than a human?"

"Nope. But I've been here before."

"They must have really good snacks." Or someone hot he likes to see. No, I shouldn't even be thinking that way. That's the Tom baggage talking. Jay loves me; he's proved it time and time again. Still, I can't help myself. I try not to ask but it slips out, way more pathetic-sounding than I intended. "There's no other attraction, right? No hot little vampire girl, or guy..."

"You know I'm straight. And you also know I'm yours. Helplessly, devotedly yours." The car grinds to a stop in front of a house so nestled in trees and darkness that I can't tell its size. Orange light glows from the windows, warm and welcoming.

"You sound like a book again," I say wryly, releasing the latch of my seat belt.

"Fine. You want it straight up? I'm your damn slave, Daisy. And that's not going to change. It wouldn't change, even if you stayed human and got old and soft and whiskery and white-haired. You'd still be beautiful to me. It wouldn't change even if the hottest woman on earth strutted in front of me naked and begged me to sleep with her—I'd say no, and I'd go find you instead. No one else will ever be to me what you are. No matter how sick or sad or mad you get, no matter how bad you mess up or where you go, it's only you, and that's it. You never, ever have to be afraid that I'll stop loving you. Okay?"

"Okay," I reply in a stunned whisper. I want a moment to hold the gift he just gave me, to tuck it deep inside myself where it will keep me warm forever.

Jay leans over and gives me a quick kiss. "Come on, let's go inside. They have really good snacks."

"You're impossible." I shove myself out of the car, and he does the same. We crunch across the gravel, up weather-beaten steps, and across the creaky porch to the front door where Jay knocks. "The bell doesn't work," he explains.

The night is full of music, the sawing and chirping and singing of a million tiny creatures. Night is never black, not really. It's deep blue, sugared with stars, fringed with the silhouettes of trees, frosted with scraps of dark-gray clouds.

Jay knocks again, louder, and leans toward the door. "I don't hear anyone talking."

"Do we have the wrong night?"

"No." There's an edge to his voice. "This is the right night. See the other cars, there, and over there? There are people here, but they're not talking, or moving, or—"

His nostrils flare and his face changes, as if he has scented something that horrifies him. "Oh god."

He flings himself against the door, ramming it with his shoulder, but it's a solid piece of wood and it doesn't yield. "Fuck. I have to get in there. I'm breaking a window."

"Wait..." Tentatively I reach out and try the handle. It moves down, and the door swings open, flooding us both in amber light.

The smell hits me first. Raw, meaty, coppery, tinged with ammonia.

23

"Don't look, Daisy. Don't look." Jay's voice is a shattered plea, as if his words can erase the scene already pressing into my memory. He's braced in the doorway, rigid with emotions I can't fathom, because he knew every one of the bodies crumpled in the room beyond. He made them all.

"If you have to look at it, so will I." I wrap his fingers in mine and step inside, pulling him with me.

We've entered a cozy living space, with a cluster of couches around a thick wooden slab of a coffee table. Slumped on the couches and sprawled on the floor are headless bodies, leaking blood into the brown upholstery, into the shag carpeting.

A dead body is one thing—a headless body is something else. A deeper atrocity, the symptom of a vile hatred and disrespect.

Jay stands helpless and motionless while I walk forward, drawn into the center of that terrible room. Beyond the seating area there's an open kitchen with a broad island, where trays of snacks filter savory smells through the reek of death. The stuffed mushrooms, bowls of herb-flecked dip, dishes of chips—they're all splattered with blood.

Two more bodies lie behind the island on the floor. One of them slipped down in front of the open refrigerator, propping its door open, and the cold pale light casts an uncanny glow over the shoulders and the severed neck.

I'm going to be sick.

I race back outside and heave the contents of my stomach onto the grass. The acid sears my throat, burns in my sinus passages. I spit and cough, my shaking hands braced on my thighs.

I can't fall apart, not now, because I can hear Jay in the house, gagging through great broken sobs. So I suck my emotions back into myself, into that secret place where I can't be harmed, and I let my autopilot take over. It's not a healthy way to deal with a crisis, but it's the only one I have.

Slowly I mount the steps and return to the carnage.

Jay is leaning against the wall, his head sagging.

"Do we need to call someone?" I ask calmly.

"Daisy," he whimpers. "Daisy, my people."

"I know. Give me your phone."

"I should... I should be the one to—"

"You can't call anyone, not in this state." My fingers trace his spine, travel between his shoulder blades. "I can calm you down, if you want. I can make it hurt less, for now."

"No." He chokes on the word and repeats it, louder. "No. I need to feel it."

"Any idea who could have done this? Maybe humans, afraid of what you guys are?"

"It's possible, but we've been careful."

"There's no way word hasn't started to travel around, though, with as many people as you've been turning." Even as I say it, my cool, objective self knows that's not the cause of this massacre. No mob of terrified humans did this. Vampires are stronger and faster, and if humans had been the attackers, Jay's people would have fought them off or killed at least some of them. In that case there should be a few dead humans here too, but everybody I can see is wearing one of Jay's special bracelets.

No, these vampires were killed by someone who knew exactly what they were, why they were meeting, and how to kill them. Brutal as the scene is, there's a surgical precision to it, too.

"Who do you need to call, Jay?" I repeat.

"Cody first." He swallows hard. Sweat films his forehead, and his lashes glimmer wetly. "Then the other group leaders. And my contacts with the police. They can help with this, create a cover story."

"Serial killer or mass murderer is pretty much the only cover story at this point." My knees are starting to tremble, pulling together like magnets. I want to sit down, but there are splatters and sprays of blood everywhere.

"We need to get out of here." Gently I tug his elbow. "There's nothing we can do for any of them. We'll call from outside."

The night air whisks cool across my face as we leave the house. Jay pauses on the porch, tilting his head slightly like he's listening. "I don't hear or smell anyone else around." He sits heavily down on the steps.

I close the door and join him. He hands over his phone and I call Cody, who answers with a gruff "What?"

"Something's happened." My throat is sore from the acidic vomit, and my voice is starting to shake in spite of my superficial calm. I grip my kneecap painfully tight to steady myself. As I start to explain, Cody lets out a string of swears, tossing one in every time I take a breath, until I've finished telling him everything. "Jay is kind of overwhelmed," I say. "What should I do?"

"I'll call the police and the group leaders. You take care of my boy." His voice is tight and hard.

"I will."

"And then, when it's cleaned up, we're going to make somebody pay."

"I'm with you on that."

After ending the call, I set the phone on the step above us and move closer to Jay. "Cody is going to make some calls. Jay, who else knew about these meetings?"

"A lot of people," he says helplessly. "Once you're turned, you get access to the website with the group calendar and other info."

"Could someone have hacked into your website? Or faked the credentials? Maybe stolen log-in information from another vampire? Or—"

He stares at me with red-rimmed eyes.

"I'm sorry. Too many questions." My fingers tangle together, knuckles grinding hard and painful as I try to keep myself split, to keep the calm, logical Daisy at the surface, unaffected, while terrified, weeping Daisy stays deep inside. I have to be strong, for Jay. He's been through so much in his twenty-four years—so much terror and pain. I want to soak all his grief and agony into myself so he doesn't have to feel any more.

"My people," he whispers.

These weren't just clients to him. They were members of a family, a community he was building.

I cup his shoulder with my hand. "It's Wolfsheim, isn't it?" I murmur.

"No, he wouldn't go this far. He wouldn't resort to such drastic measures. Killing our own... It's beyond anything I—" He shakes his head. "He would have come to me first. Confronted me in person, talked to me."

"Really? Hasn't he been confronting you and talking to you and

Cody for weeks? Maybe he figured this was the next step. An unmistakable message."

"That's not a message," he says through gritted teeth. "It's terrorism."

"I agree."

"It can't go unanswered. If it's really him, we have to retaliate."

We have to retaliate. He means himself and the other vampires. At least Cody is on the same page about that. They can rally their remaining vampires and—

A cold finger of dread runs the length of my spine.

"Jay," I whisper. "Were any other support groups meeting tonight?"

"One, I think. Ewing's group."

"Call them." I rise from the steps. "Call them now."

Horror pools in his eyes. "You think—"

"Just call, Jay."

He leaps up, too. "They aren't due to meet for another half hour. We're going there, right now."

We race for his car and fling ourselves in. Jay tears down the mountain at a terrifying speed, his jaw rock-hard with tension. He uses hands-free mode to call the number of the support group leader, but no one answers.

"There must be someone else you can call," I urge.

"The group we're going to... Jordan was assigned to it."

My stomach drops. I jab my thumb at her name on my screen and hold the phone to my ear, aching for her voice. *Please, please pick up...*

"Hey, babe," she answers.

"Jordan! Thank god. Are you at your vampire support group thing?"

"Um, right. Like I'd go to that. You know support groups aren't my jam."

"Good! Don't go. And stay inside tonight. Are you inside? Lock your doors, maybe have a weapon handy. Ugh, I wish you could keep them out by not inviting them in!"

"Girl, you're not making any sense," she says, yawning.

"Jay and I were just at one of the support groups—"

"Seriously? Why? You're not even a vampire. Oh, is it because you're considering membership in the Vamp Club? You should totally be one of us. It's so freeing, not having to worry about death."

"Jordan!" I shriek. "Shut up for a second."

She goes quiet instantly.

"Everyone at the meeting was murdered. Their heads were gone. Completely gone. Sliced off by something sharp, and then taken away."

"What?"

"They're dead, Jordan. All of them. And we're afraid your support group might be next on the list. The leader isn't answering his phone."

She doesn't answer for a minute. Coping with the news in her own way. I bite my lip, waiting.

"I have numbers for a couple other people in the group," she manages at last. "I'll call them."

"Tell them we're on our way."

I end the call and tuck my phone back into my bag. I'm not shaking anymore or disassociating. I'm wholly myself, buzzing with adrenaline, every nerve and muscle in my body screaming *go, go, faster, faster.*

Jay takes a tight curve too quickly and swerves into the opposite lane. There's a flash of headlights and an earsplitting horn blast, and I scream, louder than I ever have in my life.

We swerve back onto on our side of the road just in time. The truck whips past us, honking again.

"I'm sorry, I'm sorry, Daisy. I'm sorry." Jay slows down. "Are you okay?"

My throat was already raw, and after that scream it feels like I scraped it with sandpaper. "I'm fine," I say hoarsely. "I thought we were dead."

"I'm turning you tomorrow. I can't live like this, with you so human and weak."

"That offends me."

"You know what I mean. Not weak, but vulnerable. Easy to hurt, easy to kill. I can't live with that."

"I'd rather not live with that either," I rasp. "Especially if I'm going to be in cars with someone who drives as fast as you do."

"So we're agreed. When we get there, you'll stay in the car, and I'll turn you tomorrow."

"Wait a second, I never agreed to stay in the car. Don't be that guy."

"The guy who wants to protect the love of his life?" He throws me a blazing look.

"You think that's gonna work, calling me the love of your life? No, Jay. You can't go in there by yourself. You were shaking and crying like ten minutes ago, and you're in no shape to face it alone if someone already attacked—"

"We'll probably get there just in time for the attack, which means I will have to vamp out and fight. What are you going to do?"

"I'll use my—" My heart sinks as I feel the raw scrape of the words past my vocal cords. "My voice. Crap. I don't know if I can get the right tone now. Why'd you make me scream like that?"

"I didn't make you do anything."

"You almost smashed us into pulp with your reckless driving."

"You'll stay in the car," he snaps.

"Fuck you." It's a stupid thing to say, but I'm so mad and sad and frustrated I can't think of anything else.

We don't speak again, not until he's careening into a neat little suburb, his tires shrieking around a bend.

"You're going to draw a lot of attention," I mutter.

Jay speeds up, sweeping into the cul-de-sac and straddling the curb, one of a curving row of cars in front of a two-story colonial. I'm out of the car before he can try to lock me in, and he actually snarls at me, fangs and everything.

"Down, boy," I tell him. I'm still hoarse. If only I had a little more time, or some water—

Jay marches around the car, wraps a stiff arm around my shoulders, and hustles me onto the front porch. His gaze darts into the deepest shadows with the practiced ease of someone who spent his childhood ducking, and hiding, and waiting for the next bad thing to jump out of the dark. He rings the doorbell, and there's a scuffle and a murmur of quick panicked voices that even I can hear. Which means the vampires inside are alive and aware of the danger.

The door creaks open a crack. "Yes?"

"It's me." Jay wraps a clawed hand over the edge of the door.

"It's Gatsby." The voice is drenched with relief. "Y'all, it's just Gatsby. Come on in. We just got a call from Jordan. What's this about some people bein' killed?"

The man who let us in is the one who twirled Jordan at the last party. His broad, handsome face is seamed with worry. He shuts the door behind us and bolts it.

"Cheadle's group was killed," says Jay. "All of them, including him. We were afraid whoever attacked them might come here."

"It's almost time for the meeting now." A thin woman with gray hair steps forward. She's in scrubs—probably one of the medical personnel Jay turned for free. "Are we still in danger? Should we leave?"

"I don't think you should leave right now. If they're out there, they might pick you off."

"Pick us off? Who's doing this?"

Jay hesitates, swallowing hard. "There are some First Gen vampires who don't like what Cody and I have been doing here, turning people like you. They believe humans should be turned rarely, using the old way—the way that usually ends up killing the candidate. Cody and I have tried to explain our reasoning, and I wanted to believe that it worked, but...I can't fool myself into thinking they will live and let live, not after what I've seen tonight. These First Gens are like a cult—fanatical, and they won't listen. We suspect they've decided to take drastic action to stop us."

"First Gens? Angry, fanatical First Gens?" exclaims another woman. She's tall, red-haired, dressed in a crisp pantsuit. "And this is the first we're hearing about this problem, or the potential danger?"

"We didn't think they posed a serious threat, Keziah. Nothing like this."

"Obviously you underestimated them," says Keziah. "You and Cody should have warned us. I've had enough of your secrecy and need-to-know crap. From now on, the whole community needs equal access to any information you have that pertains to the rest of us."

Jay's arm slips from my shoulders, and his hand finds mine. He's all claws and sweaty palm, but I hold his hand anyway. He's already emotionally fragile, and the accusations are making it worse. His worst fear is coming true—that he'll do something wrong, make a mistake, and everyone will turn on him.

I try for my special tone, low and smooth and musical, but I'm too hoarse. "Cut him some slack, okay?" I tell the woman. "He had no idea these people would escalate to violence so fast. We're here now, to warn you and to help you."

The woman releases a brittle laugh. "You're not even a vampire, are you? You're not one of us. You don't have the right to weigh in here."

"She has every right," Jay says, straightening. "Now why don't we get ready to defend this place in case someone does show up to kill us?"

Jay is no military strategist, but there's a former sergeant in the group and he directs us to various hiding spots around the first floor. I'm given a pair of kitchen knives and ordered to hide behind the kitchen island, so I can run out the back door or up the stairs if I need to. I don't like being viewed as the most vulnerable one, but I don't protest because my hiding spot puts me close to Jay, who is covering the back door along with the guy who likes Jordan—Nicholas or something? He's crouched near the fridge, a shotgun gripped in his big hands.

"I'm Daisy," I whisper to him.

"Michaelis." He nods and gives me a quick smile. "Hey, you should put your bag in one of the cabinets. That way it won't get all bloody if there's a fight."

"You're so right! Thank you. I'd completely forgotten about it." I sling my purse off my shoulder and into the nearest cabinet. I like this Michaelis guy. He's down-to-earth, practical, and good-hearted. Just what Jordan needs.

"I got your back, girl," he whispers. "No worries."

I want to tell him not to say things like that, because the nice guy who talks that way is always the first to die in horror movies. But I hold back the words and wait for the scritch of claws against the window, or the slow revolving of the lock on the back door, or the hiss of fanged voices.

Seconds tick past like bombs, each one an explosion in my ears until I want to snatch the stupid loud clock off the kitchen wall and smash it against the tiles.

Tick.

Tick.

Tick.

I feel like we should be hiding in the dark, but we left the lights on because the sergeant said turning them off would give the advantage to the enemy and also tip them off that we've been warned. Although the lack of chattering voices in the house is probably enough to let them know they're expected.

If they ever show up.

Maybe they only planned to kill Cheadle's group as a warning.

Maybe it's all going to be fine, and I won't have to use the stupid kitchen knives. My palms are as sweaty as Jay's were earlier, and the handles keep slipping. I've never stabbed anything before. Well, I stabbed a beef roast once, just to see how it would feel. It was satisfying, but tougher than I expected, what with all the muscle and sinew. How will it feel to stab a vampire? Or will I die before I have to find out?

Jay keeps looking over at me. His face is salt-white and he looks way younger than twenty-four. I want to run to him, to hug him, to protect him. I've always wanted to protect him, ever since the day I met him. He was hiding behind one of the dumpsters at our ratty apartment complex, his knees tucked up to his chin and his face tearstained. I gave him a green Jolly Rancher from my pocket and sat down beside him, and later he followed me home and Mom asked him to stay for dinner.

I'm not as familiar with this Jay who can take care of himself. The old Jay always supported me and listened to me, but he usually needed me more than I needed him. It felt good, being needed. Even now, scared as I am, I'm strengthened by his fear, by the knowledge that he needs me to be strong and brave.

"Jay," I whisper. "It's going to be all—"

The kitchen door blasts inward, carried to the floor in splinters by a hulking body. Dark-clad figures pour into the house, wielding long, shiny blades.

Michaelis lifts his shotgun and fires, and I release a panicked scream. I can't help it. Pain flares in my throat, and one of the attacking vampires whirls at the sound. She leaps forward, brandishing a machete.

There's a terrible moment when I think I might detach from myself, but miraculously I stay whole and clearheaded. I claw at the stored memories of my few self-defense classes and dodge the incoming swipe of the blade. In the same moment, I drop my knives, duck in past my attacker's arm, and grip her elbow and wrist, wrenching them at a painful angle like my instructor taught me. I can't remember what to do next, how to get the machete away from her—but it doesn't matter because Jay crashes into my attacker's body, roaring like a demon, and plunges all ten of his claws into her throat. With a ripping crack, he tears outward.

The vampire's head tumbles to my feet with a dull thud, and I'm doused in scarlet spray.

Jay's gone again, lunging for someone else's throat. He's not afraid anymore, or if he is, he's using the terror to fuel his ferocity.

I retrieve my attacker's discarded machete and wait, with my back to the kitchen sink. I don't dare try to enter the fight, because unlike Jay and Michaelis, I don't know all these faces, and the last thing I want to do is slice the head off one of the good guys. I try looking for the bracelets so I can tell who's who, but with everyone moving so fast, I can barely see.

There are so many flying limbs and flaying claws and slashing teeth, so much blood, I can't—I might be sick.

I cringe away, but I don't dare stop watching, because what if I miss my chance to help?

Michaelis's big body crashes to the floor near me, and another vampire sinks a long knife into his throat. He's about to saw his way through Michaelis's neck—he's going to kill Jordan's guy—

I lunge forward and swing the machete as hard as I can. My scream comes out as a hideous croak through my ravaged throat as the blade bites into flesh.

It's hard to cut someone's head off. My blade sticks, and I struggle with it while the vampire screeches, raking his claws along my arm. He reaches up, scrabbling for my face—

And then Jordan is there, her eyes stark white and her pale claws extended. She grips the struggling vampire's head, and with a surge of inhuman strength, she rips it free. The body tumbles forward onto Michaelis.

Jordan crashes to her knees beside him. She shoves the dead vampire aside with a vicious, "Get off him, bastard." Her fingers flutter over his chest, like she's not sure where to touch him without causing more damage.

Michaelis lies limp and motionless, blood flowing freely from the stab wound—but even as I watch, the blood flow lessens, slows to a trickle as his flesh seals itself again.

The rigid tension eases from Jordan's limbs, and she exhales, her fingers curling into the wet fabric of his shirt.

He blinks and stares up at Jordan. "What happened?"

"Daisy saved you. And then I took care of the rest." She winks at Michaelis. "You stay here, big man. I'm going to help finish this fight."

"Right on."

Jordan darts away, and I help Michaelis drag himself to a sitting position.

"Thanks." He runs a finger over his bracelet. "Don't suppose you could spare any blood, Daisy?" He shows me the indicator hovering in the yellow area, right above orange.

I flinch a bit at the thought of anyone but Jay biting me. Still, it might be best to let Michaelis drink now, before he gets too desperate. Not that I think he'd hurt me, but I don't know him well enough to be sure.

"Is it safe?" I ask. "With all the others in here... Will it attract their attention?"

"They're occupied," he reassures me. "And I'll make it quick. Trust me, I wouldn't do anything that puts Jay's girl in danger. He'd have my head if I let you get hurt."

"That's true." I take a deep breath, preparing myself. "Just take a little. Jay might need some later."

Where is Jay? I can't pick him out in the blur of slashing claws and flailing limbs and snarls.

I hold out my wrist to Michaelis and he champs down eagerly. I barely feel the pain as I rake the room with my gaze, hunting for Jay, my stomach coiling tight and sick. If anything happens to him—if they kill him—

The melee is settling down slowly, figures collapsing in weariness or death. And then I see Jay, with his head blessedly in place, holding down one of the attacking vampires with the help of Keziah, the red-haired, pantsuit-wearing woman. From what I can see, that vampire is the only attacker left alive. The others are all headless now.

"Put the kitchen door back up," Jay shouts. "Daisy—has anyone seen Daisy?"

"I'm here." My voice is a quiet croak, but he hears it anyway and his head whips toward me. When he sees Michaelis fangs-deep in my arm, his eyes go whiter and he snarls.

"It's fine," I say quickly. "I offered. He was badly hurt."

Michaelis pulls his fangs out of me. "I only took a little, Gatsby. Chill out, man." He licks the punctures and pats my arm. "Thanks."

"No problem." I cup my fingers over the wound.

"How many did we lose?" Michaelis calls, rising. He sways and grips the island for support. Jordan hurries over and loops his arm over her shoulders, helping him stand.

"We lost two of ours," another man answers. "And we got all of them, except that one." He points to the vampire Jay and Keziah are holding down.

I stand shakily, scanning the bodies. One of the headless vampires is wearing scrubs. She wears a blood bracelet on her wrist.

I didn't even know her, but tears prickle in my eyes.

"Who are you?" Jay growls at the captured vampire. "Who sent you to do this?"

"Meyer Wolfsheim," the vampire answers. "And this is just the beginning, unless you bow to the Progenitor and follow the Codex. Those who follow will be blessed, and those who resist will be cut off and their blood will be spilled as a warning to all who practice impure transformation."

"Wow," says Michaelis slowly. "That is some serious cult talk right there."

I pick up the machete—better safe than sorry—and sidle closer, until I'm within arm's length of Jay. The vampire under him has hollow eyes and a shock of white hair. His fangs are receding gradually. Bloody spit flecks from his mouth with every panicked breath.

"What happens if I refuse?" says Jay.

The captured vampire looks confused. "Those who resist will be cut off and their blood—"

"I heard you the first time." Jay's clawed fingers tighten on the man's throat. "What's Wolfsheim's next step? Tell me, and I'll let you live—for now."

The vampire hesitates, probably weighing his options, then says grudgingly, "Wolfsheim is coming here himself. To your house. Tomorrow."

"That'll be at night, right?" I say. "Because he's too old to handle daylight well."

"He can probably handle it for a few minutes at a time, but yes, I'd say night is a good guess." Jay pushes himself off the vampire. "Let's tie this one up and take him back to my place. It looks like we need to prepare for a few extra guests at tomorrow night's party."

"Jay, you can't have the party," I say. "Think of all those people."

"Those people would show up even if I tried to cancel." He scrubs at his bloodstained mouth with his even bloodier sleeve. "Honestly, they're probably our best insurance against a big scene. Wolfsheim wants to keep vampirism a secret, remember? So they won't come in and start killing humans right and left."

"That would be a good way to ruin you," I tell him. "Suppose they send someone in with a gun to shoot up the place? Then people wouldn't come back to your parties, and your vampires wouldn't get their blood supply."

"But if that happened, we'd just find another way or another venue. No, Wolfsheim's going after the source of the problem."

"You and Cody."

"Exactly. And they're going to want—" He looks as if he's about to say something else, but then he shakes his head. "With all this noise, it's likely someone in the neighborhood will have called the police. Michaelis, I'll stay here with you and talk to the cops. Everyone else, go on home. Wash up first if you need to. Jordan, would you take Daisy home for me?"

"No problem."

"Good." Jay points to the sergeant and Keziah. "You two tie up this guy and take him to my house. Henry will show you where the dungeon is."

They obey him immediately, even though both of them are much older than he is. Do they know he's only twenty-four? Or do they think he's been around for decades, like Cody? Either way, Jay commands an astonishing level of respect. Maybe his post-battle appearance has something to do with it, too. His shirt is soaked with blood, his pants are spotted with it, and more blood drips from his hair and gloves his fingers. The entire lower half of his face is coated with red, like a half mask over his jaw and lips. I can barely look at him, but I force myself to. Anything less could hurt his feelings. After all, he was only protecting his people.

"Michaelis, I'll have a cleaning crew come by tomorrow, and I'll replace anything they can't clean," he says.

"Thanks, Gatsby." Michaelis gives Jay a grin that would be pleasant if he didn't also have fresh blood glistening all over his face and neck. "Hey, sorry about drinking from your girl."

"She agreed to help you." Jay's eyes slide to mine. "Her choice. And I'm good with that." He surveys me, and I'm suddenly conscious of how short my skirt is, and how much blood-spattered leg I'm showing off right now, and the fact that I'm still holding the machete. Tie my red-streaked hair into a couple of pigtails, and I'd be a distant cousin to Harley Quinn.

His gaze is still threaded with pain, but there's pride in it, too, and relief.

"You did so good," he says softly. "I'm glad you're all right. Now go get some rest...and take care of that voice. We might need it."

24

JORDAN HAS A BAG OF SPARE CLOTHES IN HER CAR, FOR WHEN she gets her outfits dirty during video shoots. We scrunch into her back seat and change into them, then scuttle into a gas station bathroom to rinse the blood from our faces and arms—and legs, in my case.

It's the same gas station we always seem to stop at, the one where Myrtle works. And when I come out of the bathroom and walk up to the counter to buy some chocolate—much deserved after the night I've had—there she is.

Her hair still has that crimped curl to it, but she's not wearing her usual lip gloss or eyeshadow. And she looks so tired.

I almost run back outside to Jordan's car, but Myrtle's bone-weary expression draws me in. I'm not afraid of her, not here. I knew Jay couldn't keep her in the hospital for long. The goal wasn't to lock her away, after all, but to get her some help.

Maybe seeing my face is less than helpful, but it's too late now. She has noticed me.

Slowly I approach the counter and lay down the candy bar. "Hey, Myrtle."

She narrows her eyes. "What happened to your voice?"

"Um, laryngitis. Not contagious."

"Hmm. Will that be all?"

"Actually..." I glance around to make sure no other customers are within earshot. "I was wondering... I wanted to know if you're okay."

"Okay?" She chuckles grimly. "Let's see, my ex convinced me to kill someone, so I shot your boyfriend through the heart and he didn't die, and then my ex came and smacked that information out of me. Oh, and my brother's still dead. So there's that." She glares as she rings up the candy bar. "Will that be all?"

"You're talking to someone, right?" I fish in my bag for my credit card. "Like, a therapist?"

"Yeah." She sucks in her cheeks, like it's a sour truth. "Gatsby is paying for it. He sent a bunch of money to my account, too, like he thinks he can pay for what happened to George. Or like he's trying to shut me up."

"If he wanted to shut you up, he'd go about it differently," I tell her. "And what happened to George wasn't his fault. I hope you'll see that eventually. Jay really is trying to be nice to you. Sometimes he's too generous—or generous at the wrong moments—but it comes from a good place."

"I guess he does seem nice," she admits. "He came to see me in the hospital."

I didn't know that. But it sounds like something he would do.

"Maybe I was wrong about him," Myrtle says. "I still hate you, though."

"Feel free." I tuck my card back into my purse and grab the candy bar. "Just do yourself a favor and stay clear of Tom. He's bad news. Twists you up inside until you're not sure who you are anymore. And it hurts."

Myrtle holds my gaze. We'll probably never be friends, but we have one thing in common—we are both survivors, hopefully wiser for the pain.

"Take care, Daisy." She points to a bit of dried blood on my thumb. "You missed a spot."

"Shit. Thanks."

I hurry back to the bathroom to wash my thumb, then I run out to the car.

"You took a while," Jordan comments as I swing in and shut the door.

"I was talking to Myrtle."

Her eyes widen. "No way."

"Yup." I lean back against the headrest. "And now, I'm done for the day."

"You need something to help you sleep tonight?"

"I'll be fine. Mom's got wine in the fridge if I really need to knock myself out."

"Don't give yourself a hangover, though. You never know when Jay might need us tomorrow."

"I don't do hangovers." I yawn until it feels like my cheeks will split. "Any idea what the party theme is for tomorrow night? You always seem to know that stuff."

"Jay posts it on his party Instagram. He puts pictures on there too, like the ones from the Met Gala night."

"Seriously?" My hand dives into my bag and comes out with my phone. "What's the handle?"

She tells me, and I do a quick search. The account has rows and rows of gorgeous images and suggests several hashtags people can use to tag their own photos from Jay's parties. Right at the top is a post with a stock photo of a regal, dark-haired woman in a fur-trimmed robe, wearing a crown. *The theme is Royals*, the caption reads. *Put your own spin on it. We'll take everything from Lorde to Game of Thrones.*

"I don't think I have anything to wear," I groan.

"Really, Daisy? That's your big concern?" Jordan side-eyes me.

"No, no it's not. I just... I fixate on small things when I'm worried. Sorry, that sounded super shallow, especially after people died tonight. Ugh, I'm the worst."

Jordan sighs. "No, it's fine. I get it. It's hard to take it all in. At least, that's how I felt after the thing with George. I didn't really feel sad, you know? Just kind of distantly sorry. He was someone I didn't really know. But the people being threatened now—these are my people, other vampires, and they're being massacred by someone who doesn't think they should have a choice about their own mortality, their own bodies."

Her words hover in my mind even after she drops me off. Sometimes the world feels so exhausting, so full of pain, like a great chorus of agonized souls all crying together, and I can't stop it, and if I try to feel it all, I'll crumble into nothing. But shutting it all out isn't the answer either.

When I enter the kitchen to make some tea for my throat, Mom and Dad are there, sitting next to each other at the island, holding hands.

"Are those *your* clothes?" Mom arches an eyebrow.

"No, they're Jordan's. Mine got dirty."

She doesn't ask how, which is a relief.

"So..." I drag out the word. "What are you guys talking about?"

"Your father explained about his gift and how he used it."

"Oh." My heart thumps harder as I set the Keurig to heat some water. Are they going to give up Dad's job and the house? Is he going to try to go back, to rewind and untwist the past, to undo the choice he made?

What will I have to give up?

God, I'm so selfish. I need to be better.

"We've decided to let the past be the past, and move on from here," Mom says carefully.

Relief surges through me, mingled with guilt. "Okay. That's good."

"Do you want to talk about it?" Dad asks.

"I'm pretty exhausted, honestly, so I'm going to bed."

"You sound hoarse, sweetie," says Mom.

"It's nothing. I'm making tea."

"Be sure to add some honey."

They continue talking in low voices, but I don't try to decipher the words. When the tea is ready, I give them each a side hug before heading to my room.

My brain isn't capable of navigating moral complexities right now. My main takeaway from all this is that bad decisions, once made, result in a whole bunch of effects—like dominoes falling in rippling rows, like cracks spiderwebbing through glass. You can't unbreak what's been shattered, and you can't go back.

You can only go on.

25

I WEAR MY RED DRESS TO THE ROYALS PARTY.

I bought it a few Halloweens ago, hoping to be Juliet to Tom's Romeo. He hated the gown—said it was too stuffy and not sexy enough. He said red looked better on people with dark hair. So we went to the costume party as half-naked Batman and slutty Catwoman instead, like he'd wanted, and he spent the night hooking a finger into the choker around my neck and pulling me around with him.

My only excuse for putting up with that is... Well, I have no excuse. At the time, I was so enamored with him and anxious to please that I sublimated my own self-esteem.

I never have to do that with Jay. So tonight, I'm rocking the Juliet dress like a freaking queen. The gown is a big, heavy, rich thing, all bustles and embroidery, scored secondhand from a theater near Asheville. What can I say? You can't take the bargain-hunter out of the poor girl, even after she's got money.

I don't have a tiara, but Mom does my hair and puts pretty crystal combs in it. I'm not even sure where she got them. They look old, and they're heavy, too. Might make decent weapons if it comes down to that. Weird that a few weeks ago my only summertime worries were chlorine damage and sunburns.

After the hair and the combs and some dangly earrings, I hunt through four different drawers before I find the little charm bracelet Jay gave me when I was fourteen. A couple of the charms are worn through the silver coating to the cheap brass underneath, and it doesn't go with my outfit.

It's perfect.

Jordan and I barely speak when she picks me up. She's dressed in some flamboyant purple thing with a slit up her thigh, showing off an actual knife sheath, with an actual knife in it. It looks very hot and dangerous. Senior year of high school, Jordan took knife-throwing lessons from a guy so she could do a couple stunts with daggers, and I'm betting she could still do some damage if she had to. Not to mention that, as a vampire, she now has her own set of ten retractable knives on the ends of her fingers.

We stop to collect Nick, who looks every inch the dazzling prince in a royal-blue suit. I notice a tiny hole under one of the arms and a little fraying around the cuffs, but I don't mention it. He deserves to feel like royalty.

I took the back seat so as not to wrinkle my dress, and Nick turns to look at me as he slides into the front passenger side.

"How's the voice?" he asks.

"Way better than last night. Did Jay call you?"

"No, Jay told Cody and Cody texted me. It was a whole thing." He hesitates, then says, "Cody also told me that Jay wants to turn you."

For some reason, a blush heats my cheeks. "He does."

"Are you gonna say yes?"

"I already did. We're doing it soon. If we all survive."

"I'm surprised Jay didn't tell you to stay home where you're safe."

"He learned his lesson about that last night, when he told me to stay in the car," I mutter.

"Nobody puts my girl in a corner when her man's in danger," says Jordan. "You know I want you safe, babe, but I think you're doing the right thing by coming to the party tonight. We might need you."

I moan, setting my forehead to the cool glass of the window. "It's a lot of pressure, guys."

"Maybe you won't have to do anything." Nick's smile is so drenched with worry that it doesn't have the effect he was probably hoping for. "Cody said they've been busy all day, setting up more cameras and hiring more security. Jay even got sensors for the doors to detect weapons or bombs."

"Bombs? Are you serious?"

"When you think about it, it would be the easiest way to take everyone out. But Cody says that's not how Wolfsheim usually does things. He says Wolfsheim will try to talk first. And they'll want Jay alive."

Why does that sound worse than them wanting him dead? "Um, why do they need him alive? Not that I'm complaining…"

"They need Jay to tell them where he stored all his research, including the stuff he uses to ease the vampire transformation," says Nick. "They'll want to destroy it all, so no one can use it again. But Jay keeps it hidden. Could be at the mansion, but maybe not. They won't kill him until they find out where it is."

"Well, aren't you a fount of information." I slump in my seat, a little miffed because I've barely heard from Jay all day—which is fine because I know he's been busy—but I've been worrying and pacing and wondering for hours, while Nick was apparently in constant contact with Cody, getting all the juicy details. Beyond a few messages about our backup plan, which involves my voice and an inordinate number of earplugs, all Jay texted me was "Rest up" and "Are you sure you should come tonight?" which was his delicate way of suggesting I stay at home without actually saying "Stay at home."

"What about you?" I ask Nick. "Are you turning into a vampire?"

"I'm not sure. Cody and I have talked about it, but I like my sunshine, and I'm kinda squeamish about blood. You know how I get during horror movies. I don't mind Cody drinking from me—it's pretty hot—but as for drinking blood myself, I don't know. No offense, Jordan."

"None taken."

"The blood-drinking thing *is* kind of hot," I murmur to myself, but of course Jordan hears, and she casts me a smirk over her shoulder.

"Maybe you'll have time for a quickie when we get there." She waggles her eyebrows.

"Oh my god, stop. I'm not screwing Jay when his mortal enemies could show up any minute."

Thankfully Jordan doesn't have time to say anything else, because we've arrived.

Jay's house is an explosion of lights, a defiant blaze against the pink-and-orange sunset. Jordan navigates to the back of the house through archways of sparkling lights curved over the drive, and then the valet takes over while she, Nick, and I walk up to the entrance. It's early, and we're among the first to arrive, because we have no idea when Wolfsheim and his crew will show up, and we have to be ready.

I kind of wish I was already a vampire, because I have a very human fear of bodily harm—but I'll be bedridden for a week during the change, and there's no way I can sit this out. I can't be lying in bed puking while Jay is here with his people, fighting for his life.

As we circle the house and head to the back, I notice the arches installed over each doorway. They're painted with gold and heavily embellished, but once we're out of the car and walking in, I can tell that they're only frames hiding some kind of metal detector or scanner. There's no annoying beep when people pass through, but a few guys in suits flank each archway, and one of them holds a tablet, looking up from it now and then to inspect the people entering the party. Right before we reach the arch, a burly guard pulls a man aside and makes him turn in the handgun under his jacket. The gun guy isn't a vampire, just some redneck who thinks it's cool to tote his piece everywhere. He makes a fuss, but the guard with the tablet pays no attention. As Jordan, Cody, and I pass through, his eyes flick from us to the tablet screen and back. He gives Jordan the slightest nod, acknowledgment of her status as one of Jay's vampires.

The music that rolls through the house and grounds is different tonight—sweeping, epic, the stuff of fantasy shows and blockbuster movies. It makes me feel tall, and splendid, and important, even though Jordan is way taller than me and Nick. She glides ahead of us, apparently not nervous or frightened at all. She even kisses her fingers playfully and wiggles them at a cluster of girls she knows. Nerves of steel, that one. I wish I could say the same. I keep swallowing, trying to moisten my cottony mouth and throat.

"Gonna talk to my girls," Jordan says. "Join you in the dance hall in a bit."

She sashays off. I'd love to take a photo of her right now, with the gold chains dripping down her spine and those angular shoulder blades setting off the sweeping purple glory of her dress. The need to capture that image spikes inside me, oddly strong.

Maybe I should take a photography class sometime. Or an art class. Eventually I'm bound to find something I love, right? A career option beyond "traveling and hanging out with people," which is not viable for collecting a paycheck. Maybe art could be my thing.

If I live through the night.

"I need a drink." I clutch Nick's arm, and because I can't be alone with my nerves, I add, "Come with me?"

"Sure, precious."

But as it turns out, we don't have to find a drink station, since costumed servers are circulating with medieval-looking goblets and tankards on trays. It's a tiny bit too Renaissance faire for my taste, but the decor elevates the vibe—huge urns of fresh flowers, neatly shaped boxwood trees in every corner, tapestries hanging from the balustrades, and greenery twined around the light fixtures. There are actual suits of armor, sans weapons, and statues gilded with gold paint placed here and there. I touch one experimentally, and it's surprisingly lightweight.

"Styrofoam," Nick says. "Like they use for plays and movie sets. Cheap and effective."

"Jay must plan these things weeks in advance. Think of the time and the expense."

"Hey, as long as I get to attend, I'm not complaining." Nick swallows a huge gulp from his tankard. "Come on, let's find our men."

It's not tough to pick them out, since the interior is still mostly empty, with just a sprinkling of guests. Cody and Jay are standing beside the open double doors of the dance hall, directly in front of a royal tapestry of scarlet and sparkly gold, imprinted with a random coat of arms. They're both dressed in dashing princely outfits— Cody in dark green and Jay in blood red. Jay even has a gold band around his head, nestled in the brown waves. I swear it's like he's trying to say, "I am the leader of the new generation of vampires. Come and get me."

Maybe that's exactly what he's doing. Painting a target on himself to draw attention away from his people.

Cody steps forward, sweeping his velvety green cape aside and bowing to Nick. "I'm being banished to the security office," he says sourly. "Come with me?"

"Sure," says Nick. "But why?"

"Because I know what Wolfsheim looks like." Cody takes Nick's drink and tosses back a swallow of it. "Jay insists I sit there and watch the security feeds. I'm to let him know if I spot my fucking progenitor. It will be incredibly boring, but if you come along, I suppose it will be bearable." He returns the drink and squeezes Nick's shoulder.

Nick gives me an apologetic look. "Will you be all right, Daisy?"

"Sure. I'll be with Jay."

"All right then." Nick waves and lets himself be towed away.

With a deep breath, I face Jay. His jaw is tight with anxiety, and he stands rigid, like a doll posed in place. But his eyes soften when I meet them, and he reaches for me. "You look beautiful."

"You too." I sidle in close and whisper, "Are you standing here waiting to be shot or beheaded? Because you look ready for the firing squad."

He chuckles faintly. "All my people will be gathering in the dance hall. That's what I told everyone in the messages I sent out today."

"And you explained about the earplugs?"

"I didn't exactly tell them about you, if that's what you're asking. I just gave the order to be prepared and said there might be a powerful sonic weapon involved." He sucks in his cheeks, avoiding my eyes.

"Powerful sonic weapon, huh? So they expect you to have this great secret weapon up your sleeve, and all you've got is me."

"Don't be mad." Jay's brown eyes carry a plea I can't resist. "I had to tell them something. A lot of them were reluctant to come tonight."

"But if they stay home, Wolfsheim wins. He'll destroy you and

Cody, then pick off the rest. Your people understand that, right? They need to fight now, or be killed off later."

"That's what we tried to explain. But I'm not sure the message got through, and I don't know how many will show up." He rubs a hand across his forehead and sighs. "Some of them will probably come because they're desperate for blood and they don't know where else to get it safely."

"I hope so. The good news is that while my voice is no sonic blast, it is better today than it was last night."

"I don't think you should use it at all. Not even if we get into trouble. Once people know what you can do, that puts a target on your back."

I can't help a little shiver of apprehension, and Jay notices.

"You don't have to do this, Daisy. You said you weren't going to save me, and I completely understand that."

"Maybe I changed my mind." I weave my fingers with his.

"I never intended for you to be in this much danger."

"You're too smart to believe that being a vampire would never expose me to danger. Really, Jay."

"Fine, maybe I knew there would be some minor danger until you were turned. I didn't expect Wolfsheim to take issue with my methods so strongly, or go this far. What is *wrong* with him, anyway? Why can't he just live and let live?" He shakes his head in frustrated disgust. "But seriously, Daisy, you're human right now. You can't let the First Gens know what you can do. They'll try kill you, and I might not be able to stop them."

"Aren't you going to promise that you won't let anything happen to me? That I'll be safe as long as I'm with you?" I fake a pout, and he rolls his eyes.

"You and I always used to mock movies with those lines," he says.

"False promises that can't be kept. I can't promise you'll be fine, or that I'll protect you. I *can* promise to get between you and anyone who wants to hurt you."

That's not much comfort to me, because it puts him in harm's way, and just the thought of seeing him torn apart sends me straight back to the way I felt kneeling by that pool, staring at what I thought was his corpse. I never want to feel that way again.

"I'll stay back while you try to work it out," I concede. "But if things get really bad, and it's looking like they won't listen, and your people can't win, then I have to try to help. Though I'm not sure how effective I'll be."

I've never controlled more than two vampires at once. I've never asked them to do anything more complex than pat their heads and restrain themselves to drinking only what they need. Speaking of which—

"How's our glutton doing? Slagle?"

"Better," Jay replies. "Miriam has been to see him a couple of times, and they're working on his deeper issues. I let him out for tonight, under close observation. I figured it couldn't hurt to have an extra body if there's a fight. I also fitted him with a shock bracelet, in case he tries to shake his guard or harm a human. Did you know that electricity slows our cells' regenerative abilities? If you mortally injure a vampire and run electricity through his system continuously, he can't heal, and he dies."

"That's horrible." I shudder. "How do you even know that?"

"Cody watched Wolfsheim do it to vampires who didn't follow his rules."

"And you thought Wolfsheim wouldn't turn violent if you defied him?"

"Well, I was wrong. And stupid." Jay flushes, and I stop myself from saying anything more. Pointing out the mistakes he made isn't helpful when he's already stressed about tonight. He's so focused on perfection, on fixing anything that's not quite right, on making sure he's above reproach that I can only imagine how painful this situation must be for him right now. Though he's far from perfect, he has an astounding imagination and an incredible skill for accomplishing big things once he's given the tools to do so. I wish he could see how amazing he is, despite the errors he's made getting here.

To distract him, I flutter my hand in front of his face, shifting my wrist so the charm bracelet slides along it. "What do you think of my accessory?"

Jay's eyes lock on the bracelet. "Why did you wear that?"

"Because I love it."

"That's sweet, but it's so cheap, Daisy. I could buy you something much better now. Something with diamonds, maybe."

"Don't you dare. I would refuse to wear it."

His mouth quirks. "I highly doubt that."

"Okay, maybe I'd wear it if it was extremely pretty. But this one is special, and I will always cherish it."

He gathers my hand in his and starts to say something, but his attention travels to a trio of guests wearing blood bands. They move into the dance hall, nodding to him, and he acknowledges them with a nod of his own.

More people are trickling in, some vampire and some human. The epic music swells suddenly into a waltz, and I peek through the doorway near me. There's a mini orchestra in the dance hall, stationed on a low stage that's swathed in red fabric and lined with tall, golden pillars. Tiny origami swans, crowns, and dragons hang from the ceiling, twirling on glittering strings.

"It's beautiful, Jay. Did you think of all this yourself?"

"Some of it. I have party planners to help me." He holds out his hand. "I can't stand still any longer. Would you dance with me?"

"Always."

He whirls me into the waltz, and as we dance, more and more vampires enter the room. Jordan and Michaelis, Slagle and his burly female guard, redheaded Keziah from the other night, dark-haired Sloane, and the guy who wanted to show me the hedge maze. My stomach thrills with frantic triumph every time another vampire comes in.

"They listened, Jay," I whisper. "They're here for you."

"Not all of them, but more than I expected." His palms are clammy against mine. "I was afraid no one would come."

"I know." I scramble for something else to distract him, and my mind latches onto a familiar cadence. "Hey, I know this song. It's—"

"The theme from *Howl's Moving Castle*." A faint smile crosses his mouth. "Your favorite Studio Ghibli movie...or it used to be."

"It still is."

He brightens, delighted at discovering another bit of me that's still the same. We've both embraced the differences that the years have made, but finding those nostalgic links between us is just as precious as exploring all the new ways we can be together.

I smile back, moving with him through the dip and sway of the waltz.

"This is unbearably romantic," I say soberly. "I don't think I can handle it."

He laughs, but it's a quick, nervous sound. I only distracted him for a few minutes, and his anxiety is surging again. "You're clear on the plan?" he asks.

"Yes."

Movement near one of the doors draws my attention—it's

Henry, Jay's house manager, struggling through the growing crowd. His face is stark, his eyes wide with warning.

"Jay," I whisper.

"I see him." Jay releases my hands and moves toward Henry, his lithe figure slipping between the guests with ease. I dart through the gap he makes and follow him all the way to Henry.

"Mr. Gatsby, Cody has spotted Wolfsheim," Henry says. "And the men at the entrances have noted several individuals carrying weapons under their clothing—long knives and such. The guards did not attempt to disarm them, but directed them here, as you ordered. You have two minutes before they arrive."

26

"Tell the orchestra to go play in the garden," Jay says. "And have the staff get the humans out of this room and start the prize drawing outside."

Henry hurries away, and Jay steps over to say something to Jordan and Michaelis. The orchestra stops playing, with a squeak of dying instruments and the final thud of a drum, and everyone in the room murmurs nervously. The silence feels raw and dangerous. As the staff begin to herd the humans out of the room, Jay's vampires shift and mutter among themselves. They're anxious, nerves strung tight, and the ominous silence is not helping the mood. Several of them look as if they might break and run.

Quickly I step to the wall panel by the door and request the first cheerful song I can think of—a silly thing my mom and I danced to when I was little. "Hestia, play 'Pink Shoelaces,' by The Chordettes."

The music starts, bold and brassy, and the spirit in the room brightens immediately. Several couples start dancing again, and I marvel for a second at the power of music.

Jay comes back and slides his fingers around my wrist. "Come on, we need a place for you to hide. Also, 'Pink Shoelaces'? Seriously?"

"It's a great song."

"No arguments here." He hurries me over to the abandoned stage. "Get behind the keyboard. And for the love of god, Daisy, don't show your hand unless you absolutely have to. Please."

"I know." A panicked pressure builds in my chest, and as he's turning away, I seize the lapel of his princely coat. "Jay, listen. I sort of admitted this to you before, but I haven't actually said it—"

Jay catches my mouth with his, a hard, swift, passionate kiss that leaves me breathless. "Don't say those words to me because you're afraid," he whispers. "I've waited, and I can wait longer. Now hide."

I crouch behind the keyboard. It's shrouded in sparkly fabric that hangs down over the stand, concealing me from view. About an arm's length from me is a tall stand with a bedazzled cordless microphone in a holder at the top—probably intended for a singer later in the evening. It might come in handy if I need to use my voice.

Under the keyboard, there's a loop of space where the sparkly material has slipped down a little. It's just enough for me to have a limited view of the center of the room, where Jay stands with his back toward me. He's still as stone, an anchored boat in the sea of dancers bobbing and sweeping around him.

My thighs are already aching from the crouch, so I adjust my position and lay aside the little clutch I've been wearing on my wrist. My phone is inside, turned off—no rookie horror movie mistakes for me. I won't have my hiding spot betrayed by an ill-timed ringtone.

The Chordettes are still singing about Dooley's polka-dot vest when a man walks into the dance hall through the door across from Jay. At the same moment, I hear movement from the other doors, more people coming in. Probably the First Gens' Progeny. The bad guys. The ones who plan to kill every person Jay and Cody have turned.

The man approaching Jay is not what I expected. When I heard

"Wolfsheim" and "Colorado," I thought of someone wolflike, big and burly and hairy, kind of a backwoods Wolverine type in plaid flannel. But this guy is medium height, midthirties, with a neatly trimmed goatee and thin eyebrows, perfectly arched. He has straight, shoulder-length hair, dark brown shot through with gold. His crisp white shirt stretches tight over the muscles of his arms and chest, and through its open collar a silver chain glints—a heavy, jeweled cross. His fingertips are tucked into his pockets. There's a hardness to his eyes, a brutality in the arch of his upper lip. He radiates power, self-assurance, and charisma; but not the way Jay does, not with that charming, open hopefulness, that sunny generosity. This man oozes danger from every pore. His very aura sends my heart into double time and sets my nerves screaming *run, run, run*.

Every step Wolfsheim takes into the room feels like a violation.

"Hestia, turn off the music," Jay says.

"Thank the Maker." Wolfsheim's voice is reedier than I expected. I thought his tone would be dark as a tar pit in hell. "An odd choice of music for this theme. Royals, eh?" Wolfsheim sweeps his hand to encompass the decor and Jay's costume. "You think you're some kind of vampire king?"

"Not at all," Jay says. "I'm just a guy providing a service. Helping people out."

Another figure moves into my narrow view, taking up a position at Jay's side. Someone in a velvety green cape, with glossy black hair.

"Ah, Cody." Wolfsheim smiles, all teeth and triumph. "My little runaway lamb. I have let you wander from the fold long enough. It's time for you to return."

"He's not going anywhere," Jay says coolly. "This is a safe place for everyone. A place where we can live in peace. You're welcome here, unless you intend violence."

"I think you know exactly what we intend," says Wolfsheim. "You boys have had your fun, but it's time to grow up now. The Blood Gift is not meant to be distributed so liberally. And offering it in exchange for money is sacrilege of the worst order. Cody will be coming home with me, and as for you, Gatsby, if you help me destroy the heretical work you've been involved in, there might be hope for your rehabilitation."

"And my people?" says Jay.

"They are abominations. They should not exist. We'll be rectifying that problem now." Wolfsheim raises his hand, and there's a faint *shing* of blades being drawn all along the edges of the room. "Have your house close the doors please, Gatsby. We don't want humans involved in our business, do we?"

"Most of the humans are out in the gardens for the prize drawing," says Jay. "But just to be safe... Hestia, close the doors to Ballroom One."

The house obeys, doors closing and sealing all around the room, one after another. I bite my knuckle hard to center myself, to stave off the rising panic of being the only human trapped in a room with so many vampires.

"Before you massacre innocent people, I will speak," Jay says. "Cody and I have explained to you repeatedly what our purpose and plan are here. We feel that it's wrong to withhold a gift like this from humanity. I know you want to keep our existence a secret, and trust me, we're being discreet with our operations. If you'll agree, I'd like to show you our contracts, our orientation materials, the precautions we take to ensure—"

"Enough!" Wolfsheim's roar shatters the quiet. "You've sent us volumes of paperwork already. I had one of my people hack into your ridiculous website where you schedule the *support groups* and offer *therapy* sessions. As if the Blood Gift is an addiction. Which is it, Gatsby? A problem or a product? You can't seem to make up your mind. I'll tell you what the Blood Gift is—it's an *honor*. It is a rite, and a church, and a destiny."

"A cult, you mean." It's Jordan's voice. I can't see her from where I am, but Wolfsheim turns his head, apparently inspecting her. His lip curls with disdain.

"A cult is a label too readily applied by those who dislike exclusivity," he replies. "You are one of Gatsby's abominations. Do not speak to me again."

"I'll speak to you however and whenever I want, asshole," Jordan says. There's a laugh in her voice, the confident glee of power and freedom, and I'm suddenly, passionately grateful to Jay for giving my friend that extra strength and protection. Jordan has always been fearless, but becoming a vampire has unlocked her truest self.

"Brave speech from one who is about to die," Wolfsheim says coolly. He lifts his hands, turning his head slightly toward his people. "Let's end this, my friends. Kill them all except Gatsby and my former pet."

"Weapons," Jay calls, and his people draw knives and short swords from beneath their clothes. From what I can glimpse, some of the weapons look like collectibles, not actually meant for fighting. I'm pretty sure one guy is holding a replica from The Lord of the Rings. It's pitiful. Sure, they've got their fangs and claws too, but judging by the speed and efficiency of the vampires who attacked the support group, Wolfsheim's people have training and better weapons. Jay's group is going to be slaughtered.

Talking didn't work, and the backup plan is me.

For half a second—one horrible, nightmarish instant—I think about what would happen if I ran away. If I turned and left this house, retreating back into my parents' money and my summer and my normalcy. Jay and his vampires would be killed, and all of this—the parties, the blood, the kisses—would fade like a dream. I could go on as if none of it ever happened. I could go back to being fun, flirty, popular Daisy, and find a normal human boyfriend and a regular job, and never think about scary supernatural crap again.

But I've been the fun girl, the easygoing girl, the one who smothered my anger so I could keep up friendships with people who hid terrible secrets from me. I've been the person aching to fit in, to fill the hollow inside me, to wedge myself into the prescribed mold—the life I'm expected to have. But here in the quivering space between threat and bloodbath, none of that matters, and the knife-sharp clarity that floods my mind is a beautiful thing.

I took the first steps into my new self when I knocked Myrtle out, and when I threatened Tom. Wolfsheim is just another Tom, selfish and proud, lusting to impose his will on others. I don't need to split myself in two and create some façade to shield my emotions. I don't need to bow to false friends or cower from men like him.

I just need to be me, real and whole and powerful.

Adrenaline races through me from shoulders to fingers to toes, bathing my body with burning ice.

I rise, collect the cordless mic from its stand, switch it on, and hold it to my lips. Slowly I stalk down the steps of the platform.

"This isn't your house, Wolfsheim," I say quietly, and my voice echoes through the room. "You don't own this space, or this world, for that matter. I don't think you have the right to dictate the choices anyone else makes."

I'm still working on clearing away the lingering rasp in my throat, ratcheting down my tone to the right timbre, controlling my nerves enough to find that lyrical rhythm. It's terrifying to be visible to everyone, to have all the First Gen vampires and their Progeny staring at me, to have every eye in Jay's group fixed on my face. But it's empowering, too. And their surprise gives me the time I need to find my voice.

"Who the hell are you?" says Wolfsheim, his lip curving scornfully. His gaze flicks to my wrists. "Not one of Gatsby's pets."

"I'm the person telling you all to calm down and lower your weapons." I'm there now. I'm in that silky space where the words just flow, undulating from my mouth and twining around the vampires like slithering cords. Every gaze locks on me—Jordan and Cody, Jay and his people, the First Gens and their Progeny—even Wolfsheim himself. Their eyes glaze over, lips parting as if they're listening to the most beautiful song in the world. I keep talking, scarcely conscious of what I'm saying while I recover from the shock of all those minds tethered to my words. I have to stay focused. I have to figure out how to defuse this situation safely.

"That's much better now, isn't it?" I croon. "Let's have no more bloodshed. Why don't we put down all the swords and knives, okay?"

The vampires obey, and a clatter of blades rains onto the dance floor. For a panicked moment, I fear the sound has disturbed their trance—they're beginning to frown and glance around—so I keep talking, keep weaving my voice around them, low and thrilling and irresistible. "Let's all be friends, because that's so much nicer than fighting, don't you think? Now, everyone, put your hands in your pockets, and if you find a pair of earplugs there, go ahead and put those in—and once you have them in, you're free to do what you need to do, to follow the instructions Gatsby has given you."

Jay's people find their earplugs immediately and insert them, slowly coming back to themselves and remembering the plan, what they're supposed to do next. Wolfsheim and his vampires fumble desperately with their clothing, raking their fingers through their empty pockets.

Time for the next phase of the plan.

"It's all right if you don't have earplugs," I tell the Progeny softly. "There's nothing to worry about, nothing at all. Let yourselves relax. You're perfectly safe. Your fangs are receding, your claws are disappearing. You're doing just fine. Everything is going to be fine. Softly now, quietly, move to the center of the room, and hold out your hands, because you're going to be getting some lovely bracelets."

The bracelets are reinforced zip ties, some type of enhanced polymer Jay developed for restraining gluttons. Jay's vampires move in, zip-tying the intruders' wrists one at a time. The thrill of my power zaps along my nerves, an electric ecstasy beyond anything I've ever felt, as every Progeny vampire remains stock-still and glassy-eyed, mildly holding out their hands to be bound.

Jay's people keep quiet, because we haven't explored my voice power thoroughly and we don't yet know what sounds could break our enemies out of the trance. My palm is sweating against the microphone. I'm running out of things to say, but I keep repeating myself anyway, maintaining that low, melodic tone, terrified that if I stop, the Progeny will break free of my control.

This room is a death trap, and my voice is the golden chain, the thin border between peace and carnage.

"It's hard to imagine that this room is the place I first saw him again," I say softly. "It looked so different then, dark and wild, shuddering with music, lights strobing back and forth. Keep holding out your wrists. It's all right if the bracelets are tight."

Jay finishes securing a Progeny vampire's wrists and glances up at me before moving to the next prisoner. I know he can't hear me because of the earplugs, and for some reason that knowledge frees me to speak words I normally wouldn't say.

"If anyone is worth following, it's Gatsby, not Wolfsheim. Is Gatsby perfect? Hell, no, but he tries. He learns, he grows, he's willing to listen and do better...and sometimes I think that's all any of us can ever do. Listen, and change. Like you're listening to me right now."

My gaze travels the group again, and another thrill hits my stomach as I realize I can sense them all—each mind tethered to my voice, each will bound by my words. The connections are smooth, silken, no hint of resistance...except...

No, there's one thread that's taut and threatening, pulses of conflicting energy rolling along it.

Wolfsheim.

The longer I talk, the more fiercely his frown deepens. He's fighting me, revolting against the influence of my voice, and I'm not sure how to lure him back in without losing my grip on the others.

He was the first one they zip-tied, but there's a power rolling through our connection that frightens me. I'm not sure one set of cuffs is enough.

I wave my hand to Cody, miming the act of reinforcing the zip ties. He nods and steps in, adding another set to Wolfsheim's wrists.

"Stay where you are," I tell the older vampire. It's command, no less forceful despite my crooning tone. "Give in to me, and surrender."

Sweat beads on Wolfsheim's forehead, and his fangs are growing longer again, spit flying from his lips with each harsh breath. The link between us shudders violently, and I gasp at the strain of holding it in place.

I can't warn Jay because he has earplugs in and he won't hear me, and I can't stop talking or the other vampires might break free and not all of them are handcuffed yet—

Shit, I'm losing him.

Wolfsheim's body seems to swell larger, muscles straining and swelling, tendons standing out along his neck, arms bulging against his shirtsleeves. Claws longer than any I've seen on a vampire extrude from his fingertips. He rips through the zip ties as if they're twigs, and his jaws clamp down on Cody's neck, ripping out a massive chunk of flesh, and Cody goes limp, sliding to the floor in a quick-flowing pool of his own blood.

I try to hold the mesmerizing rhythm of my words, but my voice rises to a shrill cry of alarm—and my control over the vampires snaps, like a guitar string breaking. Protected by the earplugs, Jay's people don't hear the change, but the Progeny vampires stir, waking from their daze, and the ones who weren't bound yet leap to attack Jay's vampires. There's a roar of alarm and a horrible cacophony of thudding bodies and savage snarls.

Wolfsheim charges me, his eyes stark white, bloody slaver swinging from his fangs. This is the devil of myth, the monster Jay never wanted to be, rocketing out of hell, bent on my destruction.

If I die, at least I gave Jay and everyone else a fighting chance.

27

WOLFSHEIM'S INCOMING WEIGHT KNOCKS ME DOWN, AND pain stabs through my spine and neck. Nothing broken, I don't think, but I can't seem to make my lungs work. One of my arms is trapped under his knee, and he pins my other arm above my head with his left hand. His sharp teeth rake along my cheek, nearly nicking my eye. He's stronger than I expected—stronger than Jay, stronger, I suspect, than any of the others.

Desperately I struggle to inhale through the shock and the pain. When I finally manage a breath, Wolfsheim's scent invades my lungs, mint and cold iron and violence.

I can't speak. His right hand clutches my jaws, an aching pressure. He's holding my mouth shut, keeping my voice in check.

But he hasn't killed me yet.

"What are you?" he hisses.

The vise grip on my jaw keeps me from answering. It makes me mad when people do that in movies—ask questions while their victims are gagged or screaming. So ridiculous. And the anger of being in that very situation myself gives me a moment's relief from fear—a few seconds of clarity.

One of my wrists is pressed to the floor right by my head, near my hair comb. My fingers writhe, twisting, finding the edge of the comb. But Wolfsheim is pinning my wrist too tightly—I can't pull the comb free or use it. And with his weight crushing my chest and his hand covering my mouth, I can hardly breathe.

I'm going to die. Here, on the floor, voiceless and powerless, while Jay and the others are being slaughtered by vampires much stronger and more violent than any glutton.

I don't want to die. Not when I finally started to figure out what I want in life. Not when I've barely had the chance to explore who I am.

Wolfsheim tips up my jaw, baring my throat, sniffing along my neck.

Jay.

He would be here if he could. He's fighting somewhere in this room.

Jay—

Wolfsheim draws back and inhales, and his jaws part wider, ready for the plunge into my neck.

No no no—

Arms lock around Wolfsheim's throat, and a blur of cinnamon curls and blue eyes appears over his shoulder.

"You get off her!" Nick roars.

Wolfsheim chokes, his eyes bulging with surprise and the pressure on his throat. With a yell, Nick tightens his arms and twists, like he's trying to snap Wolfsheim's neck.

The vampire releases me and reaches back with wicked claws to slash at Nick. With a scream, Nick lets go. Wolfsheim slams a fist into my cousin's chest, and Nick flies off the platform, his head rebounding off one of the pillars before he slumps to the floor—dazed, unconscious, or...

No, Nick, no—

I can't help him yet, but he bought me a few precious seconds—
enough time for me to yank one of the combs from my hair. When
Wolfsheim turns back to me, his gaze flaming with vengeful hate, I
ram the tines into his eye.

He shrieks with pain, and I twist the comb deeper. He grabs my
hand, half crushing my fingers, and shoves it away. With a roar of
anguished rage he pins me again, claws poised to dive into my heart.
But his weight isn't on my lungs anymore, and he's not covering my
mouth. Even though my pulse thunders in my throat, I try my com-
pulsive voice anyway, pushing through the tremulous fear.

"Submit," I say, and Wolfsheim freezes midstrike.

One word, and in it I feel the dominant force of the billion times
that word has been spoken to women like me from the mouths of false
leaders like him. I know the terror of silence, and I silently praise the
ancestors who passed their gift to me so I could use it in this moment.

"You will not touch me again," I continue, soft and venomous,
and he winces, recoils, fighting me. But I'm back in control, and I
refuse to give up that control again. Not to him, not to anyone.

"You should never have come here. You have no right to tell
anyone else how to live." I sit up, and he shrinks, snarling, as if he
wants to flee from my voice, but I continue weaving the spell, swiftly,
softly, and inescapably, just for him. "You will stay, and you will listen
to me. You think you're a big, scary bad guy, don't you? A Blood
Messiah, a god or a prophet, with the power to sway others, to make
everyone bow to you and your rules, when really, you are nothing
but a sad, sick man in love with control. You wanted to know what
I am? Well, if Jay Gatsby is the vampire king, as you called him, that
would make me his queen." My voice dips lower, a primal tether
binding him to my will. "You might think you're a wolf, but honey,
I'm your alpha."

Wolfsheim shudders over the word, straining, sweat filming his skin; but his ears are too full of my voice—he can't break free. I lean closer and talk to him, softly, menacingly, winding long sentences around his consciousness. I pour into him all the poisonous things I ever wanted to say to Tom, all the vindictive words I've saved up for the friends who betrayed me, every curse for the predators with bruising fingers and bladed tongues. I can't let him go. Can't risk him breaking out again, becoming a threat again. He's the worst monster in this room, the biggest danger to all of us, so I push him deeper and deeper into himself, farther from the surface, until his consciousness is a fragmented thing floating in the vast darkness of his pitiless heart.

As the rush of power fades from my body, weariness washes over me in a dizzying tide. I'm not sure when I stopped talking, but it's all right. Instinctively I know that Wolfsheim is beyond resistance now, nothing but a hollow shell. I'm not exactly sure what I've done to him, but I'm not sorry. I hope it's permanent.

It was foolish of us to hope that I could maintain control over so many vampires—especially one as old and powerful as Wolfsheim. One-on-one, though, I was more than a match for him. I think that should terrify me, but I can't feel anything but exhaustion and a gnawing worry about the others.

I'm swaying where I sit, blinking, trying to focus on the scene behind Wolfsheim's catatonic figure. I can't seem to latch onto anything in the blur of movement, but I think the conflict is waning. I think we won.

Jay's anxious, bloodied face appears in front of me, and a few of his people haul Wolfsheim off the platform and drag him away.

Jay slumps down beside me, pulling out his earplugs. "Are you all right? Did he hurt you? There's blood—"

"It's his, not mine."

"Oh good." And then he keels over, limp and unconscious. He's bleeding heavily from three deep gashes across his abdomen and another on his thigh.

Panic stirs me out of my fog, sharpening my focus. A quick swipe of my finger over his bracelet shows his blood levels in the orange zone.

"Jay!" I cradle his head in my lap and tuck my wrist against his mouth. "Drink, Jay. Come on."

His fangs are still out, but he makes no move to drink. His lashes form ashy smudges against his pale skin.

"Jay," I say, low and soft. "You need to drink now."

But my voice doesn't work. He's unconscious—he can't hear me.

"Jay!" I smack his face sharply, and then I shove my wrist deeper into his mouth, prodding my skin with the tips of his fangs. When I smack him again, he stirs, and his hands drift up to hold my arm in place. With a sigh that goes straight to my heart, he begins to drink.

I sit there, stroking the soft brown waves of his hair with my free hand. He looks so pretty and young and helpless right now, and I love him just as much like this as when he's facing off against a powerful First Gen vampire. I can't spare too much blood—I'm tired, and Jay warned me about letting my blood volume get too low—so I gently disengage his teeth after a couple minutes, once he's inched into the yellow zone. His wet tongue glides over the marks, halting the flow of blood.

The fight is nearly over now. Wounded Progeny litter the room, most of them still zip-tied—which means I did play a helpful role in the conflict, even if the plan didn't go quite as smoothly as we hoped. Several of Jay's vampires are still battling Progeny, but they're gaining the upper hand, so I don't interfere. There's a strain in my mind when I think about using my voice, a warning that I've exercised my power enough for one day.

Some of Jay's staff enter the room, offering their own wrists or necks to Jay's injured vampires. Lillian bustles up to us, rolling her sleeve up her plump arm. "Here, Mr. Gatsby. You should drink some more."

"Did the humans see anything?" Jay asks weakly.

"They are mostly in the garden. Very smart of you to have the prize drawing out there to distract them." She nods approvingly. "A few of the guests saw the Wolfshcim folks being taken to the dungeon, but I told them it was part of a special role-play experience that people paid extra for."

"You're a genius, Lillian." Jay smiles at her before carefully biting her arm.

Watching him drink from her doesn't bother me. She treats him with such motherly affection that I can't help liking her. She's part of the family he has built around himself.

Speaking of family... "Lillian, would you stay with him? I have to find Nick."

She nods, and I jump up, scanning the room frantically. Nick isn't lying by the pillar, but I spot him not far away. He's kneeling with his back to me, bowed over Cody's limp body.

"Oh, no." I run to him, crouching at his side.

But Cody is awake and drinking from Nick.

"Is he healing?" Nick asks. "I can't watch. It's too weird. You look at him for me. Tell me what's happening."

Cody rolls his eyes, still sucking from Nick's wrist. The flesh of Cody's neck is knitting itself back together tendon by tendon, muscles reforming. Even as I watch, the skin smooths over the wound and it's seamless again.

"He's healed," I say. "Careful not to let him drink too much."

Cody extracts his fangs and licks the wound he made. "Don't worry, Coffee Beans. I won't let your cousin die. I'm rather fond of him."

"The healing took a while because Wolfsheim tore such a big chunk out of him," Nick explains. "I thought he was really dead. Worst few minutes of my life."

"I thought *you* might be dead, dork." I ruffle his hair, and he bats my hand away with a chuckle.

"Nah, just dazed for a few minutes. I've got a nice big lump on my head, like some character in a cartoon."

"We should get you checked for a concussion." I wince as he points out the swollen bump. "So you were in the room the whole time? I thought I was the only human in here."

"I slipped in with Cody and stood in the corner, behind one of those boxwood trees. Nobody really paid any attention to me. But hey, I got to save your ass, and I have the battle wounds to prove it. Check this out." He lifts his other arm, where Wolfsheim's claws left four shallow slashes.

"I would absolutely be dead if you hadn't jumped in," I tell him. "Thanks."

"Oh, I won't let you forget it. You owe me a life debt now, precious." He grins.

"Give me that." Cody drags Nick's clawed arm to his mouth and licks the wounds tenderly. "That should help with the healing."

Jordan saunters over and sprawls beside us. Her full lips are slick with blood, and her gorgeous purple gown is nearly shredded. "I drank from one of those Wolfsheim vampires," she says, grimacing. "She nearly chopped my arm off, so I figured it was only fair that she help with my healing. She'll probably die in her cell later—I drained her pretty good. Serves her right." She pushes my shoulder. "What about you, Miss Vampire Queen? I don't remember exactly what you said—it's pretty hazy—but you were a freaking rock star! If rock stars talked really quietly, instead of belting it out."

"It wasn't perfect, but it worked out okay, I guess." I lean into her shoulder. "I just wish I'd been able to hold them longer, so you guys wouldn't have had to fight at all."

"So Wolfsheim resisted? He broke free?"

"Yeah. I think my influence was spread too thin, and with him being a First Gen, he was more powerful. But I took care of him in the end."

"I'll say. His eyes looked completed empty." Jordan shudders.

"Since all the baddies are locked up now, I think we deserve hot baths and rest." I climb to my feet, suddenly feeling very bruised and manhandled.

Strong arms travel around my waist, pulling my body against a firm chest. Jay smells like blood, metallic and sour, but there's a spicy freshness under that smell. I revolve in his arms and press my face to his blood-soaked shoulder, not even caring when my cheek comes away wet. His mouth grazes mine, driving a wild spike of need straight through my exhaustion. I grip him around the neck and throw myself headlong into the kiss, and for a few minutes our desperate relief manifests in a storm of blood and teeth and tongues.

"Get a room," teases a voice, a grinning Michaelis on his way to Jordan. "Never mind, I'll join you." And he dips her for a dramatic kiss.

"You were amazing," Jay whispers in my ear. "So brave. When you came down from that platform in that dress, I thought my heart was going to explode."

"Mine too. With terror." I smother a chuckle against his shoulder. "Can I go home now? I want a bath."

"You think I'm going to let you out of my sight after what Wolfsheim almost did to you?"

"He's locked up now."

"But won't your parents freak the fuck out if you come tramping in all covered in blood?"

I narrow my eyes at him. "You want me to take a bath here? In your house?"

"It's not the worst idea." His mouth curves at the corner. "I could use a bath myself."

A tingle rolls through my body at what he's suggesting.

"As much as I want to, I think tonight has been exciting enough," I tell him. "But you're coming to my house for dinner tomorrow night, right? What if you stayed over?"

"Your parents..."

"I'm an adult, Jay. And they won't mind. It's you."

He tilts his head. "Are they real, your parents? They've always been too cool."

"My mom's just that awesome. And my dad... Well, he's literally the stuff of legend."

He grins. "You should still wash up before you go back. Don't want to push your luck with them. They might kick you out, and then you'd have to come live with me."

My heart flips. "Is that an invitation?"

"Absolutely."

I return his smile, but then I hesitate. "I want to, I really do. But I think I need to stay with my parents through the end of the summer. I need to get comfortable with myself again, Jay, and you're a part of that, but I want to have some alone moments, too. And time with my parents before I become a vampire. Does that make sense?"

"So much sense." He curls my fingers in his. "Just know that you have a home here, anytime you want."

His eyes glow with so much love that I flush, dropping my gaze, a smile of ridiculous joy spreading over my face. "I think we should tell my parents about the vampire stuff when you come over. I've made some iffy choices in the past several years, and I want to let them know that I'm becoming a vampire. Not for their permission, but for their input."

Jay cups my hands in his. "Whatever you need." And he kisses my forehead.

The forehead kiss stays with me while Henry drives me home. I love all Jay's kisses, but that one in particular felt special. It didn't ask for anything, or want anything. It was simply a gift, a sign that he sees me. And loves me.

28

WE HAVE A FORMAL DINING ROOM AT MY HOUSE, BUT WE never use it. We prefer the big table in our enormous kitchen, which offers quicker access to second helpings and condiments and feels more comfortable and friendly. Jay's visit is no exception. He's family, after all, as I remind myself repeatedly, every time my stomach twists and turns over the big revelation we're planning. Somehow I manage to eat enough roast chicken and creamed corn to stave off any concerned looks from Mom.

After dinner, Jay dives right into his confession. He tells them everything, from the moment he ran away, through the entire showdown with Wolfsheim at the party. I cringe through parts of it that I personally would have chosen to soften a bit, for my parents' sake.

Jay concludes with wanting to turn me into a vampire. And then he goes perfectly still, and waits.

My mother is as white as the flour canister on the counter behind her. My dad starts to swear, and then bites it back, as if he still thinks we're kids and he needs to set an example or something. It's hilarious.

"So you...um... Sorry, I'm not sure where to start." Dad looks over to me. "You say your ability works more powerfully on vampires? Is that why you were asking me about it the other night?"

"Yeah. With humans it's just a strong sort of persuasion, but with vampires it's total compulsion."

"My ability allows me to compel humans," Dad admits, with a glance at Mom. "I've sworn not to use it," he adds hastily to Jay. "And it doesn't last more than a day or two, though usually that's enough time to secure the results I want."

Like when he secured the job he wanted. He's always been my mild-mannered, super-nerdy, scientist dad, but now I'm seeing this ruthless edge to him, and while it's a little scary, it's also kind of cool.

"I wouldn't judge you, sir," Jay says.

"Oh, but you should. See, I'm judging you right now, son, based on your decision to involve my daughter in all of this."

"It wasn't his fault," I protest. "You heard how it happened."

"Yes, and I'm wondering if we're getting the whole story. Forgive me if I don't trust you both on such an important topic. They say the ones with something to hide are always the most suspicious, and as you know, I've been hiding my power for years, so I have become a very suspicious person. I'm curious about how my ability would affect a vampire, and I'm vested in finding out the whole truth. So in the interest of doing both—Jay, would you be willing to help me with a little test?"

Spoken with that firm tone and steely gaze, it isn't really a request.

"Of course," Jay says.

"Come into the other room." Dad is smiling, but it's a faintly menacing smile. "I've also got a few questions about your intentions toward my daughter."

"Dad! Seriously?"

"It's fine." Jay rises from the table. His throat bobs as he swallows. It's kinda cute that he's nervous.

They go into the living room, and Dad tells Serenity to close the sliding pocket door—which pisses me off, because I wanted to listen. I've never been so jealous of vampire hearing.

"Jay will be just fine," says Mom, standing up and stacking plates. "Help me load the dishwasher."

She clinks the dishes extra loudly and runs the water longer than normal, just to keep me from hearing the voices in the other room. By the time Jay and Dad return—after fifteen freaking minutes— I'm a mass of nerves and frustration.

"Well?" I snap.

"I can compel vampires," Dad says smugly. "Don't look so ferocious, Daisy. He's fine. Right, son?" He slaps Jay on the back.

"I think so?" Jay looks a little dazed, like vampires usually do after they've been compelled. "I can't really remember what we talked about."

"It was better than truth serum." Dad yanks the fridge open. From my angle, I can see that he reaches for beers before grabbing two Cokes instead. Because Jay doesn't drink. The whole men-sharing-beer ritual is kind of old-fashioned, but it's also a little endearing that Dad wants to do that with Jay. What did Jay say to him in there? It must have been good.

"You have to tell me what you guys talked about," I say.

"Nope." Dad opens his Coke with a satisfying hiss. "But I'll tell you later, sweetheart," he says to Mom.

"No fair. He's my boyfriend and I deserve to know—"

"You deserve to know?" says Mom crisply. "You're the one who's been stacking up secrets this summer—things your dad and I deserved to know, since you're living under our roof and all. So while we're talking about knowledge that people deserve access to, maybe you should apologize for that."

I glance at Jay, but he only sips his Coke with a sheepish expression like *This is all you.*

"Fine," I mutter. "I'm sorry. I thought if you knew about Jay, you wouldn't want me dating him while I was, as you say, living under your roof. And I couldn't risk that. I needed him. Especially after Tom. I never told you all the things Tom said to me, the things he did—"

"What did he do?" Dad's face darkens.

"Nothing you need to worry about now. He's out of my life. But Jay is different. I'm...I'm kind of my best self when I'm with him, if that makes sense. And he's my... He's... I need him." My stupid voice is trembling. I have nowhere to hide the oncoming tears. I'm naked and exposed and vulnerable.

Until my mother wraps me in her arms. "I love this for you," she says quietly.

I can't answer. I'm too busy blinking hard and trying to hold the sobs in.

"We wouldn't ask you to stop seeing him," says Dad. "You're an adult now. And after what Jay told me... Well, it would just be cruel to separate you. But please try to stay out of dangerous situations. And about the vampire thing—"

But Mom interrupts him. "I'll take this one, Liam, if you don't mind. I've been thinking about it while Daisy and I were cleaning up." She hesitates, releasing me from the hug and gripping my hand instead. "The happiest moments of my life are when all three of us are together, on the couch or in our beds. When we're all under one roof, safe and healthy. That's when I feel like I can actually relax, like all the pieces of me are in place. And Jay, you're telling me you can keep Daisy safe all the time, that if she gets into a wreck it won't kill her, that if someone attacks her she'll be strong enough to fend them off, that she won't ever have to be sick again?" She drags in a shuddering breath. "And you want to know if I'm okay with it? Hell yes, I'm okay with it."

"The side effects—" Jay begins.

"Drinking blood, photosensitivity. I still say yes."

I squeeze her hand. "You're literally the coolest mom. And Jay can turn you guys too, if you want... Maybe?" I glance uncertainly at Jay.

"If we decide we want that," my dad interjects. "I'm not sure we do. It's something we'll have to discuss."

"I'm not sure why anyone wouldn't want to stay young and disease-free forever," I say. "But okay."

"What if your voice ability doesn't work after you turn?" Dad asks.

Shit. I hadn't thought of that.

"Even if I lose my ability, I want this," I say slowly. "I was thinking we could take a beach vacation first, as a family—maybe save the transition for the end of summer. But I'd like to do it soon, before any other weird crap comes our way. I want Jay. Forever." I dig my nails into my palms to fend off more tears. God, what is wrong with me tonight?

"Forever?" Jay's voice is threaded with hope. I risk a glance at him; his brown eyes glow into mine, brimming with a passion that heats my very skin.

My parents exchange delighted glances, and Mom seizes my dad's hand, tugging him toward the hall. "Why don't we let you and Jay talk it over?" she says. "Whatever you decide, you have our support. Right, Liam?" Dad hesitates, and she elbows him, still smiling broadly at Jay and me.

"Absolutely." Dad gives us a wry smile. "Whatever your mother says. Talk among yourselves..."

Mom drags him away, and a few seconds later I hear the distant thump of their bedroom door closing.

Jay circles the kitchen island, trailing his fingertips along its smooth surface. The blood bracelet on his wrist catches the light, turning to silver flame. His eyes are hooded now, dark and intense. Hungry. He has never looked more like a beautiful predator.

"Are you cool with this?" I ask, sidestepping to keep the island between us. "Turning me, I mean?"

"It's your choice."

"Good answer, but I actually want your advice."

"Part of me wants to keep drinking your human blood and no one else's, because you're delicious." His slow, sharp-toothed grin sends a tingling thrill between my legs. "But a bigger part of me wants you protected. You're so vulnerable as a human, Daisy. So easily broken, so slow to heal. I want you to have strength and speed and regenerative powers. I want this for you, as long you're okay with being supernatural."

"If we're being technical, I was supernatural first. I just didn't realize it."

"True. Once you're a vampire, we can still exchange blood occasionally, for fun. If you want to. We'll do anything you like, whenever you want." His gaze softens with longing. "And if, in a few years, you'd like an enormous diamond ring, I'm down for that, too."

My pulse kicks up, and he tilts his head as if he can hear its new rhythm. He's coming closer, and my insides are hollow with craving, desperate and vulnerable and *his*.

"You said you want me forever," he whispers.

"I know, and I'm sorry—that's ridiculous and overreaching—I assumed too much, and honestly who says that when they're twenty-two? We're too young—"

"Didn't your parents marry right out of college?"

"Yes, but—hang on." I'm breathless, dizzy. "Nobody said anything about marriage."

"Calm down, klipspringer. I'm not proposing to you yet."

"Good, because I don't want you to think I'm jumping into this because of the money. It's not that. I mean I want to travel and party and research with you, but I didn't say forever because I want all those things. I don't plan to mooch off you for the rest of my existence—"

"Daisy." He's right in front of me now, and his tone stops my nervous chatter. "Daisy, I thought you understood. Everything I have is already yours. I accumulated this *for you*. There's no mooching." He laughs, sounding a little breathless himself, and the realization slows my heart rate to a bearable speed. "It's yours, sweetheart. All of it. All of me. And the sooner you move into *your* house, the happier I'll be."

"Oh my god, Jay," I whisper tearfully.

"Hey." He sweeps his thumb along my cheekbone. "I know this is big, for both of us. But right now, all we're talking about is timing. When you want to turn."

"Sometime in August." I sniff a little.

"You're sure?"

"I am."

"Sounds perfect. When the time comes, I'll email your mom a list of the supplies she'll need to help you transition. You'll be sick for about a week while the new organs and fangs are developing. There will be nausea, headaches, body aches, fever. I wish I could make it more pleasant, but trust me, with my special cocktail, it will be a lot more comfortable than the old way, and less risky, too."

"I trust you."

He hesitates, meeting my eyes. We both know what those three words mean. For me, they're more powerful than the other words couples usually say to each other.

That's why I say them again. "I trust you, Jay Gatsby."

His lashes lower, and his jaw works briefly.

"And I'm not going anywhere this time," I add.

"I know." He looks up at me, joy shining in his brown eyes. "I trust you, too."

We collide then, his mouth slamming into mine, and I'm devouring him, drinking him whole. Impossible to know how we find our way to my room without ever removing our hands or lips from each other. But somehow we do.

As I sink onto the bed with Jay, lost in the sweet fire of his mouth, I remember what my mother said.

That in her happiest moments, we are all together. All under one roof. Safe and healthy, even if it's just for one night.

And then I almost forget my mother exists, because Jay is shucking off his shirt, and I'm admiring the expanse of perfectly carved abs that now belong to me. I discard my own clothes in trembling haste, eager to be pressed right up against his warm skin, thrilling because *we did it*, we leaped the hurdle that was my family. I would have forged ahead anyway, but it's so much more satisfying to have their support.

Jay hesitates a few steps away from me, devouring me with his gaze. White stars swirl in his eyes, a galaxy of thirst, of craving. With clawed fingers he undoes the button of his pants and draws down the zipper, easing them off his hips.

"We'll have to be quiet." His voice slides through the fangs, slightly distorted.

I nod, breathless. "I can be quiet. I think." I climb on my bed and scoot backward, until my spine is pressed to the padded headboard. Then I move my thighs apart, letting my legs fall open, baring my pussy to Jay. I waxed thoroughly because there's something I want to try. Something daring and dangerous. Something I wouldn't trust anyone else to do, but with him—god, the risk is exhilarating.

Jay stares. Swallows. I can tell he's trying not to drool, and it makes me laugh.

"I want you to bite me," I say softly. "Right here." I tap my pussy invitingly.

"Shit, Daisy," he breathes. "Are you sure?"

"Please."

"Oh god..." His voice thickens into a growl, and he leaps onto the bed, his eyes whited out entirely. Watching him crawl toward me, his nostrils flaring, teeth bared—it's unbelievably hot. I'm trembling, so sensitive that the first breath he exhales over my clit makes me jump.

Jay smiles, licking his fangs. "Hold as still as you can."

Tilting his head aside, he moves in, grasping my thighs, and licks through my folds, a long, slow, lazy caress of his slick tongue.

"Shit..." I whimper.

"Bite the pillow, sweetheart," he advises.

I grab one of my pillows and clutch it to my bare chest, stuffing one corner into my mouth as Jay continues to bathe my sex with his tongue. He laps at my clit, then slides his tongue through every delicate crease, every little bit of me, savoring it all. I'm whining into the pillow now, trembling, half-embarrassed at the wetness gushing out of me.

"I think you're ready," says Jay, with a tender kiss against my clit. I try not to squirm, quaking on the edge of an orgasm.

Jay carefully takes one of my labia between his teeth, and sinks in his fangs.

I squeal into the corner of the pillow. It hurts, yes, but it's a brilliant, sensual, clarifying pain, pure and addictive. Jay's lips close on my flesh and he drinks, while his claw-tipped fingers sweep along my inner thigh. The side of his thumb brushes over my clit, and the startling friction almost makes me come right then.

I spit out the pillow and whisper, "Shit, shit, shit," like a litany, like a prayer, while the vampire I love sucks on my pussy. He releases me after a few moments, licks the punctures, and bites into my inner thigh, drinking more deeply.

When his bracelet vibrates, he pulls back, fangs glistening scarlet, his eyes reverting to their usual brown. But he's not done with me. He moves between my legs again, nibbling at my clit with an enthusiasm that makes my head fall back and my eyes close. I have to squeeze and bite the pillow even harder as Jay shakes his head between my legs, his tongue whipping across my hypersensitive bud until I snap—I break—I'm writhing, silent, un-breathing, dazzled by the whip-crack of ecstasy still lashing through me.

Jay strokes me with his tongue until I can't bear it and I push him away, cupping my hand over my quivering sex. He covers my fingers with his, a reassuring weight, while I gasp through the rest of the orgasm and then fall apart under his hand.

I've slid halfway down onto the pillows, and I lie there, blissful and undone, while he kisses me between satisfied grins.

"Sure, you can give it out," I say blurrily after a few minutes. "But can you take it?"

"Oh, I'll take it." He rocks his hips, running his hot length between my folds, its hard underside passing right over my clit. The wet tip of him touches my stomach.

"Not like that. Not yet." I pull myself upright. "Lie on your belly. Now."

With a muffled groan of reluctance he flops down, his long legs stretched out and his round ass presented to my view.

I crawl over one of his legs and settle myself between them. "You may want to bite the pillow."

"I don't think I need to—God!" he barks out as I lean down and bite the fleshy cheek of his ass. "Fuck, that felt...amazing."

"Pillow," I warn him, and he gathers it against his upper chest, both arms banded over it.

This time, I trail one hand all the way up his leg, from ankle to ass, and I reach between his legs and cup his balls while I sink my teeth into the other cheek.

He jumps a little this time, a groan vibrating through his body. I smack his butt lightly. "Hush!"

"If you keep doing that, I'm going to come on your sheets," he hisses. "You should stop."

"You shouldn't have such a tasty-looking butt," I retort. But I do want him inside me, so I give him one last nip before I let him roll over. "I'm doing this again once I'm a vampire."

"I'll hold you to that. Fuck." He's panting, his cock standing straight up.

I take hold of him and guide him in, settling into place. He holds my waist with his left hand and cups my breast with his right, his thumb stroking my nipple.

The way he's looking at me now, with such grateful adoration, makes me feel more like a goddess than I ever dreamed possible. But I'm the one who should be grateful.

"Thank you for not giving up," I whisper. "Thank you for finding me. Shit, I'm crying again... I told myself I wouldn't do that... I'm sorry—"

But his eyes are glistening, too. "Don't apologize." His voice is tight, thick with emotion.

I watch those lovely brown eyes flutter shut as I ride him, as we breathe softly together in a quiet, lascivious hymn of moans and sighs, as we transform each other into the creatures of power and passion we were always meant to be.

EPILOGUE

"Wolfsheim," Jay crows in a singsong voice. "You have a visitor."

He opens the top hatch of the cell door while I approach slowly, cautiously. Nervous energy cascades through my new body, the untapped potential of freshly toned muscles and systems operating at peak fitness.

An incredible feeling, but I'm still adapting.

It's been two months since the showdown with the Wolfsheim and his Progeny. After that night, I made a bucket list of sunshiny things I wanted to do before turning into a vampire, the first being a long beach vacation with my parents.

Since the Glassy Mountain vampires were pretty freaked out about my ability, it wasn't a bad idea for me to get out of town while Jay stayed behind to manage the aftermath. He had to reassure all the anxious vampires that I'm not a threat, that I would only use my powers to rehabilitate gluttons or protect the vampire community.

Yeah, that took some convincing. But being Jay Gatsby, he managed it somehow.

Two weeks ago, I drank Jay's blood and took the serum he developed to ease the transformation. I spent six days sweating, moaning, and dry-heaving. It felt like the worst flu I've ever had. Jay spent as much time with me as he could while I recovered, holding cool washcloths on my forehead, putting on my favorite shows, coaxing me to drink sips of ginger ale, or, toward the end, donating blood.

By the seventh day the aches and gurgles in my body had settled down, and I was left with a hollow, ravenous hunger. Jay explained that I couldn't drink from him right away—new vampires need human blood. He taught me how to carefully drink from my mom and dad, which was super awkward. But my mom just laughed and said, "This isn't the first time you've depended on my blood for survival."

I raised my eyebrows at her. "Geez, Mom. That makes this all better. Just like old times, in utero."

After a week or so of drinking from her and Dad, it's a little less awkward. But I still haven't gotten used to licking their wrists afterward to heal the puncture marks.

Other than that, I've adapted seamlessly to the whole blood-drinking deal. No gluttonous urges so far. I'm adjusting to my stronger, faster body and my superior hearing. The best part of it all? My dewy-fresh, practically poreless skin.

I haven't tested my voice power yet. My voice was hoarse for a while after the change, but it's nearly back to normal. We're testing it today on Wolfsheim.

I slink closer to Wolfsheim's cell, listening to his slow, heavy breathing. Jay stands quietly by the door, watching me. Behind him is the house manager, Henry, one sleeve rolled up to the elbow. Jordan's here too, as both my friend and a representative of the Glassy Mountain vampire community.

"The prisoner has been catatonic for weeks," Henry says coolly. "We've had to use an IV to get blood into him, since he won't drink. And I've been forced to...clean him." His nose wrinkles slightly.

"It's like you scraped out his brains, Daisy." There's a wariness to Jordan's expression, and I don't blame her one bit. I'd be a little scared of me, too.

"Open the door to his cell, Jay," I request.

"Are you sure?"

"He's catatonic, remember? He won't hurt me."

There's a facial recognition panel near the door, and after Jay completes the scan and enters a code, Wolfsheim's cell unlocks.

Fists clenched, I step into the doorway.

Wolfsheim is greasy, drooling, staring into space with vacant eyes. None of his magnetic presence or commanding power remains.

"Maybe I should try my power on one of you first." I glance back at Jay and Jordan. "I don't know if I can do anything with him."

"Try," Jay urges. "If you can restore even a little of his mental faculties, just enough so he can take care of himself, it would make life a lot easier for my staff. Besides, we may need him eventually. He brought a lot of his people with him to confront me, but Cody suspects there are more of the Progeny out there. If they ever decide to come knocking on our door, I'd like to have their leader functional yet still under our control, so he can call them off."

I draw in a long breath. "Earplugs in, just in case."

Jordan and Jay insert the earplugs, while I crouch in front of Wolfsheim. The rank stench of him nearly knocks me over.

"It's been a while since you tried to kill me." I start in a normal tone, gradually notching my voice down into the familiar, soothing register. "The strangest thing is, I haven't needed to dissociate since that night. I don't have terrible dreams about Tom or George anymore. Breaking you healed me, I think. Isn't that ironic?"

I'm there now, in that space where my words carry the deceptively silky weight of an irresistible command. "Wolfsheim, I need you to wake up, just enough to drink blood like a normal vampire and take care of your body's needs. But you're not going to attack me, or Jay, or any of his people, human or vampire. And you'll keep following these rules even when I'm not here, speaking to you. Do you understand? Nod if you understand."

Wolfsheim lifts glazed, bloodshot eyes, and his shaggy head bobs.

I motion for Henry to come forward. He moves past me, into the cell, his arm extended.

"Wolfsheim, you're going to drink a little from Henry. Just enough to show you can understand and obey me."

His head lolling heavily, Wolfsheim pushes himself upright. His fangs extend slowly, and he manages to bite Henry's wrist and suck a little blood.

"That's enough," I tell him, and he stops immediately.

Goose bumps break out over my skin at the instant obedience. My thrilling, terrifying voice is still here. Still mine.

I thought I'd be fine with it if my power went away. But now that I know I still have it, I'm beyond glad. I'm ecstatic. Maybe that's evidence of my lingering insecurity. I'm clinging to any power I can grasp to keep myself safe.

Or maybe I just like being dangerous.

"I think we're done for today." I glance back at Jay and nod. "We'll see how long my influence lasts."

Once Henry and I exit the cell, Jay secures the door. He removes his earplugs and stares at me, half-awed, half-triumphant. "You can still do it."

"Yeah." I can't help smiling.

Jordan plucks her earplugs out too, looking less pleased. "Well... it makes things more complicated, for sure. But it's cool to know that you've got our backs if any more First Gens come nosing around."

"I don't think there are enough left to challenge us," Jay says. "But it doesn't hurt to have a secret weapon."

I meet Jay's eyes. We haven't told anyone that my dad has the ability as well, and that's how it's going to stay. Dad tested it on Jay just that once, but he has vowed to himself and my mother not to use his power again, especially since his voice affects humans much more strongly than mine does. Neither Jay nor I would ever ask him to break that vow. But I do plan to learn from his example of restraint.

"Thank you, Henry. Thanks, Jordan." Jay nods to them both, a mild dismissal. "I'm going to take Daisy down the hall to the lab. Dr. Cheznick will want to run some blood tests and do a body scan to check the placement of her new organs."

Henry gives a slight bow and walks away, but Jordan steps toward me, her face tight with repressed emotion. Stiffly she holds out her arms.

"Oh my god, I get a hug? From a death-defying goddess?" I fan myself. "I can't believe it."

"Shut up." But she breaks into one of those magnificent Jordan Baker smiles.

I hug her tightly, while Jay turns and walks on, giving us a moment.

"You know I would never hurt you, right?" I say.

"Yeah, I know." She squeezes me tighter. "You're good people, and so is Jay. Whenever I'm scared shitless about what you can do, I'll remind myself of that."

"If I ever get out of line, you can decapitate me. Cool?"

"Cool." She laughs, pulling back.

"Thank you, by the way. For texting me that first night about the party. Why'd you do it, anyway?"

She shrugs, tracing the toe of her Puma sneaker along the

concrete floor. "I heard about Tom. A lot of us did. And I saw some people taking his side over yours, kissing his ass on their socials, believing his lies. Pissed me off, I guess. I wanted you to know you still had someone in your corner. Even if we weren't as close as we used to be."

Tears swell in my eyes. "You'll never know how much that meant to me."

"Damn, girl." She swipes at her own eyes with the back of her wrist. "Go get your body scanned or whatever. Text me later. I've got a new idea for a stunt."

"Can't wait to hear it."

With a wink and a wave, she follows Henry toward the exit, while I head up the hall after Jay.

Past the prison cells, this underground complex contains a small medical facility and one of Jay's numerous research labs. It's also home to the vault where Jay keeps his vampire serum. I've been to the medical center before, when I got my special dose.

I find it ironic that Wolfsheim is incarcerated not far from the lab he wanted to find and the serum he wanted to destroy. Serves him right.

Even if I could, I wouldn't ever completely restore Wolfsheim's mind, not after he ordered the slaughter of Jay's people. At first, I was surprised Jay left him alive at all. But it makes sense to keep him around, just in case we need him to give orders to the remaining members of his vampire cult.

That's the reason Jay always gives, but I suspect he has another motive as well. Despite the killing he's had to do, Jay is kind. He knows Wolfsheim isn't a threat now, and he's being merciful. It's one of so many things I love about him.

Impulsively I take his hand, and he looks down at me, delighted.

Such a simple thing, holding hands. Walking together. But after eight years apart, neither of us takes it for granted.

"We made a breakthrough with the blood substitute last week," Jay says. "We're doing preliminary testing on the captured First Gens, with some very encouraging results. Soon we might be able to switch over entirely to synthetic blood." His brown eyes shine with eagerness, with hope.

"That's good news. I'm really looking forward to the whole fake-blood thing. Drinking from my mom is just way too awkward."

He shrugs. "I've drunk from so many people it doesn't feel awkward anymore...but I get it. Once you're a little further past your transition, you can drink from me sometimes. Occasionally you'll still need a nice fresh human, though." He winks at me. "Here we are, darling. Time to play doctor."

"If only." I give him my best sultry smile.

He chuckles. "Maybe sometime you and I can play in here. For today, you get Dr. Cheznick. She's the world's first specialist in vampiric health."

After the blood tests and body scans, Jay and I leave the underground complex behind and head upstairs. It's a rare rainy day in late August, a welcome respite from the pounding glare of the southern sun.

I wander through the screened porch that leads to the pool area, and I place my hand against the cool glass of the back door, watching plump raindrops chase each other and merge into flat streams. I can hear the patter of every distinct drop against the concrete patio.

And I can hear the faint rustle of Jay's crisp dress shirt and neatly pressed slacks as he comes up behind me.

"I used to hate this time of year," I murmur. "It meant I had to go back to college."

"And you didn't like college?"

"So much of it seemed pointless. Learning facts I couldn't see myself using in the future. I guess Jordan's attitude about high school kinda rubbed off on me. But I never had the same drive she has, you know? That passion for something, that purpose."

"Hmm." He cups my shoulders lightly. Kisses my hair.

"I think I have a purpose now. And it's wrapped up with you, but it's not *just* you. It's also about the other vampires—helping them. Protecting them. Using what I have to do some real good."

I turn in his arms, facing him. "When I was younger and more vulnerable, before I had all of this, Dad used to tell me to check my privilege. I think that's going to be even more important now, for both of us. We've got to be aware of our privilege and power, and use them the right way. Once the blood substitute is ready and supply is less of an issue, we can start thinking about saving more lives. There are so many hurting people in this world, Jay—people who could use what we have."

"Not everyone should live indefinitely." Jay's eyebrows pull together. "We have to be careful about whom we choose."

"So you and I are the gods who select who's worthy? Sounds a little too much like Wolfsheim and his cult."

Jay winces. "But we're benevolent gods. Well-meaning gods."

"Some of the cruelest gods in human history have called themselves good." I reach up and brush aside a stray lock of his brown hair. "And most real-life villains are convinced they're the good guys."

"Well, I'm counting on you to let me know if I stray into the villain zone."

"Same, though." I slip my fingers behind his neck. And then, because it finally feels as right and natural as breathing, I murmur, "I love you."

His eyes widen. "I love you, too." He kisses me tenderly, like he's savoring the taste those three words left on my lips. "Look at us—dirt-poor kids from Easley, and now we're rich supernatural beings. Makes you wonder, doesn't it? What else could be out there?"

"Who knows?" I wiggle my eyebrows at him mysteriously. "Faeries, banshees, demons, werewolves, things from myths we've never heard of. Scary, isn't it? And kind of exciting."

"*You're* exciting," he murmurs, swaying his hips against mine.

But I wriggle out of his arms, struck with a sudden, wild idea, and I dart out the back door onto the patio.

The pool is a rain-speckled dusky gray under the cloudy sky. I strip down to my skin while Jay watches from the doorway.

"Daisy Faye Finnegan, what the hell are you doing?" There's a helpless laugh in his voice.

"Come swim with me."

He hesitates, staring at the pool.

The pool where he died.

Barefoot, I stalk up to him and take his hands in mine. "We're going to live a long time, you and I," I tell him, through the warm rain streaming down my face, soaking my hair. "Bad things are going to happen to us sometimes. But we're always going to move past them. That's what we do. We heal, and we try again. Now come on, Jay Gatsby. You haven't used this pool all summer."

The reluctance on his face quivers and melts away. He smiles the kind of smile that makes me feel more whole, valued, and trusted than I've ever been in my life.

"Fine." He shucks off his shirt. I run ahead while he's taking off his pants, and I crash into the pool, a glorious cannonball shattering the memory of Myrtle's gunshot and Jay's blood.

Jay leaps into the pool too, sending up a wave of spray to collide with the raindrops. When he surfaces, he catches my wrist, pulls me in for a kiss. He's laughing against my mouth, and his smile tastes like moonlight.

And I laugh with him, because we never have to be sick again. Not a head cold, not some nasty new virus—nothing. We don't have to be afraid of cancer, or heart disease, or aging.

Who wouldn't sacrifice everything for that assurance?

That's exactly what makes all of this so dangerous, and vital, and beautiful. We are moths, feathery and fragile, dipping ourselves in titanium and gold to survive a decaying world.

And by some miracle, we can still fly.

BONUS FEATURES

You are cordially invited to step into the
world of *Beautiful Villain*, containing
exclusive bonus content including:

Gatsby & Daisy's Playlist

A bonus (spicy) scene of Gatsby & Daisy
in the novel's original roaring 20s

An extended excerpt from *Charming Devil*,
the story of the darkly mysterious Dorian Gray

GATSBY & DAISY'S PLAYLIST

"Green Light"—Lorde

"Heat Waves"—Glass Animals

"Hallucinate"—Dua Lipa

"gold rush"—Taylor Swift

"We Used to Be Friends"—The Dandy Warhols

"Anti-Gravity"—RUNAGROUND

"everything i wanted"—Billie Eilish

"Here We Go"—Mat Kearney

"Don't Start Now"—Dua Lipa

"Young and Beautiful"—Lana Del Rey

"Closer"—Lemaitre, Jennie A.

"Trust"—Boy Epic

"Complicated"—Avril Lavigne

"One Day At A Time"—UNSECRET, Tim Halperin

"Throne"—Bring Me The Horizon

"Speechless"—Rachel Platten

"Howl's Moving Castle—Merry-Go-Round of Life"—
Vitamin String Quartet

"A Little Party Never Killed Nobody (All We Got)"—Fergie,
Q-Tip, GoonRock

"Pink Shoe Laces"—The Chordettes

"Speechless"—Naomi Scott

"Alpha"—Little Destroyer

"Animal"—AG, MOONZz

"Born for This"—CRMNL

"This Is Why We Can't Have Nice Things"—Taylor Swift

"Champagne Supernova"—Oasis

"Clean"—Hey Violet

THE JAZZ AGE

DAISY & GATSBY

Jazz music blares across the lawn, its brassy notes filtering through the trees, softened by whispering, green foliage and delicate darkness.

I pause by an oak, bracing myself against the trunk while I take off my T-straps. Leaving the shoes there, I continue in my stockings, not really caring if they're full of runs tomorrow.

The champagne I drank sparkles in my head, punctuating my dark thoughts like the fireflies winking on and off across the shadowed expanse of the lawn. I round the corner of a hedge, taking a last backward glance at the up-lit pinnacles and glowing gables of the great house from which I'm fleeing.

Tonight's party is a masquerade, so I'm wearing a half mask covered in faux pearls, lent to me by my best friend, Jordan. Now that I'm away from everyone else, I could take the mask off, but it feels like a shield, like protection. A layer of mystery between me and whomever I may encounter.

I had to escape the party—"Gatsby's party" they said. A man named Gatsby, though no one could tell me his first name and no one seemed to know where he was or what he looked like. I've never been to a party where the host was so scarce—it's rude, I think, not to make oneself known to one's guests. Especially when someone has a name like "Gatsby."

I knew a Gatsby once, years ago. He went off to war, and I waited...I waited so long, until Mama and Daddy insisted I marry *someone*. It was odd, they said, for a young woman of twenty-two to be unmarried. I was on my way to being a dried-up old maid, they told me, and we couldn't have that in the family, no we couldn't. It wouldn't do for a dynasty such as ours, old money with a name to uphold.

So I let Tom Buchanan tether me to him with a long string of pearls, roping me as surely as any pretty heifer being led to market. The wedding is in one week.

My family and I are staying with Tom's parents at their Long Island estate until the big day. Afterward my parents will go back to Georgia, and I'll stay here, to be Tom's fire bell, his devoted wife, his dutiful escort to all business dinners and society affairs.

The world is changing. I know it. I feel it—I can taste it. But I'm being left behind. Once I'm married, I'll be trapped in Tom's family, and they're high society, old money, like mine. That sort of wealth comes with expectations—rules I'm expected to follow, etiquette I'm supposed to know.

Sometimes I think the poor girls working as typists or clerks in the city have more freedom than I do. That's why I let Jordan sneak me out of the house tonight so we could attend this party. It's more than just a dance—it's my last gasp of liberty before I resign myself to married life. The music is wild, the place is hopping, and the whole event is a speakeasy right out in the open—'shine flowing in fountains and damn the snoopers. I suppose someone with a house like that and money like that can just pay off the cops if they come poking around.

It was fun at first…and then as time passed and I saw nothing of the party's host, I began to feel hollow. I could hear the clock in my head, ticking down the minutes until dawn, when I'd have to hobble home on weary feet and give myself up to the inevitable reality of being Mrs. Tom Buchanan, the oven in which the next generation will bake.

Mama hates it when I talk like that, but it's true. To Tom, I'm a pretty little fool, a lovely trophy to be admired when I'm with him and to be used whenever he feels the urge. Of course, I say none of this aloud. I keep it in my head, where it belongs. That's what good girls do. They know their place, and mine isn't among the glad whirl of people howling and laughing and dancing their shoes to ribbons in Gatsby's courtyard and halls. My place is amid huge rooms of silent, deadly elegance; endless beauty rituals to keep myself perfectly polished and pleasing to my husband; lawn parties and teas and occasional trips into town, where I must smile and keep my voice low and never speak out of turn.

And my alternative? Without any education or training, no money of my own? I'd have to rely on friends like Jordan, and she's tied to her own family. She'd be shunned in our circles for helping me, and I can't destroy her like that. Which means I have no choice. To survive, I have to marry, and I've said no to far too many suitors— waited far too long, hoping one person would return and ask me.

He never did, and I can't put this off any longer. That string of exquisite pearls is constricting around my neck. It'll be over soon, and then I won't feel anything.

While I wait for the noose to cinch tight, the green gloom behind this hedge is a decent place to hide.

I pluck idly at the leaves of the bushes as I walk, snatching, tearing, sprinkling the bits like confetti over the grass.

I don't know what I expected from this party tonight. I knew its host couldn't be the same Gatsby—my Gatsby. That Gatsby was a soldier with no family or fortune. Penniless and perfect. He had the sweetest face, the warmest brown eyes, and a smile that said I was the most important soul in his world—the most exquisite being in the universe.

I miss that smile.

Something rustles behind me and I whirl around. I suppose I shouldn't be out here in the dark without a companion—some grifter could be lurking around, looking to do mischief.

"Is anyone there?" I ask.

Another rustling step, and a broad-shouldered, suit-clad figure emerges from the gloom. I can't see his face, but he's big—a regular bruno. His mask is carved in the shape of a leering, fanged face, like a demon I once saw in a stage performance of *Faust*.

"I was just going back to my friends," I murmur, backing away.

"Were you?" His voice is a low rumble.

"If you'll excuse me, I'll be leaving."

"Or you could stay."

There's something familiar about the way he speaks. I wish he would say more, so I could listen and try to remember who he reminds me of.

He moves closer, corralling me against the hedge. He doesn't touch me, but he's enormous, magnetic, swallowing all the air around me until I can hardly breathe. I'm not scared, not really. Or maybe I am—wonderfully, wildly scared.

His scent is rich, heavy, spicy—a cologne of pine, leather, black pepper, amber. I inhale deeply, savoring the scent because there's something familiar in that too. Like the lyrics of a song you can't quite remember but you wish you could because it always made you want to dance.

"You remind me of someone." The man's jawline and lips are the only features visible below the edge of his mask, and even those features are softened by the night.

"Do I?" I say vaguely, conscious that he's coming closer, reaching for me.

He speaks again, thrillingly low and tempting. "May I touch you?"

No. The word trembles on my tongue. No is what I owe to Tom, to my family, to the white wedding and the pallid life that have been planned for me.

No is what they expect me to say to anything *I* might desire, anything that deviates from the plan. Always no.

But maybe, just this once, in the darkness, under the champagne stars, I can say a quiet yes, just for me. Just once, before the pearly noose tightens and my neck snaps.

Yes.

I say it with silence, and with the release of tension from my shoulders. I say it by leaning toward him, yielding.

He reaches down, cupping his hand around the back of my thigh right above my knee. His fingers glide upward, scrunching up the glittering fringes and the silky fabric of my dress. His hand skims across my garter strap and moves higher, sliding over the left cheek of my bottom and the lacy panties covering it. He pauses there, splaying his fingers. A tingling thrill skitters between my legs.

The stranger squeezes my ass lightly, and I shiver with pleasure. His hand moves higher, along my spine, dragging my dress upward.

Cool air flutters across my lace-covered center, but even that slight chill can't suppress the warm glow in my lower belly. I'm dizzy, delighted, flush with need.

Music from the party echoes across the garden, a hectic rhythm matching the heat of my blood, the speed of my pulse. The stranger bends, his masked face pressing into the curve of my neck. I tilt my head to give him better access. His warm breath bursts against my sensitive skin...and then his wet tongue trails over the pulse point of my throat.

My breath catches.

His lips seal to that tender spot, a brief kiss with firm suction. He folds his arms around me, gathering me close, engulfing my slender frame. I sense his fierce need in the heat of his mouth, the strength of his grip, the rush of his breath.

He kisses my throat again, and I'm motionless, mesmerized as each press of his lips sends a tiny bolt of ecstasy between my legs. The music is thumping faster, faster, a frenzied rhythm shuddering through the summer night...and as a trumpet wails, bold and brassy, soaring over the rest of the band, two small pricks of pain register at my throat. Twin needles of sharp discomfort melting swiftly into thrilling suction, into a mind-softening warmth.

One of the stranger's arms is clasped across my back, while his other hand travels lower again, clawing my skirts up and slipping into my panties, over my bare bottom. Those devilish fingers roam my skin, smoothing and squeezing, and then they delve deeper, between my thighs, finding my slit. My face is a furnace, shock and desire mingling as he strokes one finger through the slippery folds, discovering how wet I am.

His mouth is still latched to my throat, and he's sucking, sucking... I start to frown, to wonder...but then two of his fingers slip inside me, and I release a faint moan, sinking into the bliss of his touch.

Deep in my soft, slick channel, his fingers twitch and stroke, then begin pumping rhythmically. At the same moment, he breaks the long kiss on my throat—I'll have a mark there for sure—and he licks my skin several times, as if he adores the taste of me, as if my skin is dusted with powdered sugar and he can't get enough.

He eases his fingers out of me, and when I whimper a protest, he chuckles. "Greedy little kitten." He runs his hand up my front, fondling my breasts through my sparkly fringed dress. I can't help hating the dress, wishing it would disappear so I could feel his bare palm skimming over my nipple, his fingers kneading my flesh. The dress is going to be ruined now, stained with my arousal—his fingers are wet from me, from the liquid need soaking through my underwear.

I plunge my hands beneath his suit coat and rake his shirt up, dragging it out of his pants, working around the suspenders. Greedily I run my hands beneath the cool cotton of the loosened shirt, devouring the smooth, sculpted heat of his body. He's beautiful, this man—I can tell that much, despite the dark. The body of a god, or the loveliest of monsters.

My slim fingers travel over his pectorals, nails scraping lightly, and he responds with a huff of barely contained lust, groping beneath my skirts again and sliding his hand into the front of my panties this time.

Sensation explodes through my body. Dazzling little bursts of electric delight dance along my nerves as he teases that small bud between my legs. Mama would never tell me its name; she called it the devil's doorbell once. Not sure that's a suitable name—he's making me feel like I've died and gone to heaven, not to the other place.

I've played with myself a few times, when I dared to, but I've never been this aroused before, except once. My first time. The only time I've been with a man, and he touched me just like this.

It isn't him. Couldn't be. If he didn't die in the war—if he really made it back, he would have come to me, found me...

He's massaging that spot swiftly now, expertly, and I'm so close, I can't help exclaiming a quiet "Shit!" And then I bite my tongue because Mama would die if she ever thought I knew that word, much less spoke it aloud.

The masked man laughs softly and presses his mouth to mine, as if to savor the taste of the profanity on my tongue.

The edges of our masks collide, but it doesn't matter. I spin away into the sweet midnight darkness of that kiss, while moths burst into a fluttering frenzy in my belly and every bit of my skin comes to incandescent life.

I'm barely aware when his hand leaves my panties, when he picks me right up off the ground, still kissing me, and walks us both to the deeper shadow of a live oak tree farther down the sloping lawn. He ducks beneath a low-hanging bough, still holding me, still kissing me, and strides forward until he can set me against the trunk. Only then does he break the kiss and toss away his mask.

I can't see his face in the dark. I don't need to. With a trembling hand, I discard my mask too, and we wrap ourselves together, limbs locked and bodies grinding urgently. I hook my knees over his hips, lock him in with my ankles, haul him closer. My dress is scrunched around my waist, the fringe tickling my thighs. There's a mere scrap of lace between my center and his pants—I rub myself against the hard bulge shamelessly, until, with a fractured groan, he reaches down and undoes the belt one handed. His pants are the new kind, with a zippered front. He rips the zipper down and pulls out his length. I reach for it, curling my fingers around it. Satin-soft and burning hard.

Desperately I rake my panties aside, uncovering my opening. His dick presses against me there, warm and urgent.

There's a heady danger in doing this bare and unprotected. I think I know who he is, but I can't be sure. I don't *want* to be sure. I want to be a rebel, to be reckless. I want something wicked and dangerous that is mine to remember forever.

"Please," I whisper.

He goes in easy, I'm so wet. Pushes himself all the way in...deep, so deep.

A gasp rips from my lungs at the sensation of that thick, hard column filling me up. My body welcomes him, like it recognizes his shape.

He groans, slow and heavy, like he's been restored and unmade at the same time. It's exactly how I feel.

Tonight, when I left Tom's house, I abandoned my pearls in favor of a string of ebony beads I borrowed from Jordan. The beads bounce lightly against my chest as the stranger fucks me against the oak tree.

I don't care about the grating of the bark against the back of my dress. Don't care that my stockings will be ruined. This is what I need. This is everything.

I wind both arms around his neck. "More," I plead breathlessly. "More. Faster."

He redoubles his pace, driving sharp, little moans from my throat with every thrust. It's the perfect rhythm, the perfect amount of friction, and I come with a breathless squeal under the boughs of the oak, under the canopy of the stars, under the sweet strains of the dance tune echoing from Gatsby's party.

He pulses inside me, flooding my body with his release. He's been holding my waist, keeping me steady, but when he comes, he shifts one hand and plants it against the trunk of the tree. His hips thrust forward once more, shoving into me harder, deeper. I suck in a breath of pleasure at the new angle, the solid feel of him. He comes a little more, with a ragged gasp.

When he pulls out, I'm sloppy and dripping. Without a word he sinks to his knees. Holding up my dress and pinning my panties out of the way, he begins licking me clean.

I tilt my head back against the tree, fingers splayed against the trunk, while he buries his face deeper into my sex, bathing every bit of me with his tongue. He growls softly, a predatory vibration that drives me blissfully mad, and I squirm, moaning for more.

A sharp prick of pain startles me, and I look down with a gasp. "Did you...bite me?"

He doesn't answer, but I can feel it now—two sharp teeth piercing the lips of my pussy, gentle suction on my clit, growing stronger by the section. I should be screaming. I should be terrified, but the tiny pinpoints of pain are enhancing the pleasure. Everything between my legs is deliciously warm and wet, except for those intense points of painful clarity. I'm molten, mindless, prey to the exquisite sucking sensation over my clit and the slow, lascivious sweep of his tongue into my folds. I let my eyes close, succumbing to the swell of bliss, not caring how it's happening, just yielding myself to it as it expands, wider, wider, a beautiful rolling wave that *crashes*, explodes into ecstasy. I half scream, biting the back of my wrist to stifle the sound.

When he gets to his feet, I'm coated in a light sweat, fragrant with sex, panting and sagging against the tree, trembling from head to toe, and completely satisfied.

He kisses me with damp, warm lips, and I taste coppery blood and salty cum on his tongue. It's obscene and terrifying—and I love it.

When I swirl my tongue through his mouth, I feel the keen tips of his teeth, and in a moment of silent, blinding realization, I understand what he is.

Jordan and I read *Dracula* at the same time, one winter two years ago. A story, a myth, yet it seems more believable to me than the other truth about him—that he could be Jay Gatsby, the soldier I loved. The soldier who left me.

I don't know how he became *this*—a vampire. But if being *this* helped him survive the war and brought him back to me, I accept it. Monster or not, he is mine.

He ends the kiss and zips up his pants, then fixes my underwear and pulls my dress down to cover my thighs.

My eyes have adjusted to the dark, and I can see his face a little better now—strong lines, high cheekbones. Handsome and hauntingly familiar, though the leafy shadows playing across his features make it hard to be sure.

He reaches up to fondle the ends of my carefully combed blond bob. Well...it *was* carefully combed. Now I'm fairly sure it's been mussed six ways to Sunday.

"I just had it cut this morning," I blurt out. "It's the fashion, and I needed a change."

He smiles. "It's fucking adorable."

"My fiancé won't like it."

I wait for his reaction to that terrible word—*fiancé*.

After a few seconds of silence, he says, "What's not to like?"

"Tom prefers my hair long. He hates it when I do things without asking his permission."

"And you do them anyway." He nods his approval. "Good girl. You should always make your own choices."

"Maybe I shouldn't, if they're wrong choices that lead me astray."

"Astray?" He laughs. "Doll, there's only one path worth following, and that's the one that takes you straight to what you want."

"And if I'm not sure what I want?"

"Then you must try new things until you find your passion in life."

"Try new things," I say dully, finger-combing my hair into better shape. "Since my engagement to Tom, he's taken me to so many places and we've done so many things—always with my family or his along as chaperones, of course. Yet I couldn't seem to stir up much enthusiasm about anything. I think I've become quite cynical."

"Maybe the problem wasn't you or the places you went, but the people you were with," he says. "With the right person, even a ruined shack in a mossy clearing can be exciting."

And there it is.

A paralyzing joy floods my brain, blurring everything else.

Years ago, I gave myself to a young soldier as we lay in a broken-down shack deep in the heart of Georgia, in a clearing thick with Spanish moss.

No one else knew about that tryst. No one except—

"Gatsby?" The word cracks from my lips.

"Daisy," he says softly.

So it's him after all. I knew it, and yet the admission makes me angry.

I shove a fist against his chest. "You didn't come back. I thought you *died.*"

"I sent letters."

"I never got them."

"Your mother." He practically snarls the word. "She never liked me."

"She hated you."

"Because I was penniless and nameless, and yet I dared to love her daughter." Anger and contempt color his tone. "I'm richer than your parents now, with a name I've made for myself."

"Yes, but how, Jay? How did you do all this?"

He starts to reply, but I take one swift step forward and clamp my hand over his mouth. "No... Wait. You don't need to tell me— not right now. Maybe you're a bootlegger, a hatchet man, a thief or a sharper—you're definitely a vampire, and I don't care. All I care about is that you're here, just in time." I grip his collar in both hands, pulling his face to mine, brushing my lips over his.

"Just in time," he echoes. "You know, I've been following you everywhere. They've been dragging you from place to place without any warning, almost like they knew I was trying to find you. I was always a step or two behind—couldn't catch up. But I saw your cousin Nick in Boston a while back, and he was kind enough to let me know you'd be coming *here*, to prepare for the wedding. So I bought this place, I started throwing parties, and I let my name be known. If you were really in love with Tom, I didn't want to interfere—but I thought, if you wanted me, you'd come find me. And you did."

"So..." I hesitate, because despite everything he just said, I'm scared to ask the question that's searing my very soul. But I need to know what my options are: a secure, socially approved marriage or whatever he's offering. "So...what now?"

"Now," says Gatsby, his voice low and intense, "now you leave that bastard and you come live with me, in this house. It's all ready for you, furnished with you in mind. If there's anything you don't like, we'll change it."

My heart sinks. "I can't live with you here, Jay. Not so close to Tom and his parents—not here, where people know them, know *me*. If we're going to do this, we have to run away. We have to leave everything and just *go*."

"But you don't understand." He clasps my hands. "I did all this for you. We can stay here, close to this wild, wonderful city, and we can hold our heads high. If they try to ostracize us, damn them all. I have money now. Money will pave the way. It can *buy* their acceptance, you'll see."

Slowly I withdraw my hands from his. "You wrote to me all those years, wanted me, followed me, collected all this wealth for me—and now you won't do this one thing? You won't *leave* with me? That's cruel, Jay, cruel to both of us. I'm willing to abandon everything for you—I always was, even before you had all of this."

I turn and walk away, out of the tree's shadow. After the darkness beneath the boughs, it feels brighter on the open grass...but it's a cold, cheerless light from distant, unsympathetic stars. Far away, the band is playing a haunting melody, like a serenade to lost love.

He can't do this. He can't come back to me and then make me live here, under the ruthless scrutiny of the people who will judge us both for being together. It's not right. If he loved me like I love him, he'd understand why I can't bear that, why I need to be far away from them all.

Strong, gentle hands cup my shoulders, and his voice surrounds me, steady and comforting. "Of course I will."

"Of course you will *what*?"

"I'll run with you, Daisy. Anywhere you like. What I've started here can be continued elsewhere. I only ask that when we find a place you love, where you're comfortable, you agree to putting down some roots. I've been without a family for years, kitten, and I want one. I want a home, with you."

A glow spreads inside me—better than lust, better than champagne. This is pure joy.

I turn around, looking up into his face. Fondly I trace his jawline with my finger—such a strong jaw, even more defined than the last time I saw him. "We had sex, fought, and made up all within the first hour of meeting each other again."

He chuckles. "Does that worry you?"

"Not on your life. Though you have some explaining to do about your new set of chompers. You plan on ripping my throat out?"

"Never," he says earnestly. "I would never hurt you. And I wouldn't hurt anyone else unless I had to, to protect you."

"Good enough." There's a frantic urgency in my blood, a warning that simmers through my veins—the knowledge that if Tom gets wind of my leaving, he'll try to stop me with everything he's got. I suspect he'd kill me before he'd let another man have me. "Let's run right now."

Gatsby nods. "I've got cash and a fast car—everything else can be sent to us later, once we get wherever we're going. What about you? Anything you need?"

Mentally I review the contents of the trunks lined up in my bedroom at Tom's parents' house. Strangely, I'm not attached to a single thing in any of them.

"I don't want anything from the past," I tell him. "Just you."

"Then come on, Daisy Faye." He flashes me that sharp-toothed grin again. "Let's go for a ride."

Minutes later we're in his big yellow Rolls-Royce, hurtling down the road, heading through New York City and on to anywhere. Disappearing, both of us—dissolving into gossip and then into legend. I can practically taste it—love and liberty, the sweetest of pairings, a liquor no law can ever deny us.

CHARMING DEVIL

PLEASE ENJOY THIS SNEAK PEEK, COMING SOON!

I DON'T PAINT PORTRAITS. EVER.

Which is why I have to respond with a gentle no to the commission request in my inbox.

Sometimes people get pissed about being denied. Like they have a right to my talent and my time. They come back with a faintly belligerent "Why not?" which I usually brush off with "I'm just no good at faces" or some such excuse. Never the real answer.

Others simply don't understand. They love my style, and my refusal makes them want it more. They give me sweetly emotional reasons why they want a portrait of this person or that. It's tougher to say no to the nice ones.

But in the end, everyone gets the same answer—including this latest potential client.

My thumbs fly over the screen, spelling out one of my usual

excuses. I push send and lay aside my battered iPhone. It's several generations old. I'm hoping to replace it soon.

People think I'm a rich girl because I own a studio near downtown Charleston and a house close to the waterfront, on Wentworth Street. Thing is, I inherited both of them.

When you lose something in life, you almost always get something in return. I recently lost my last living relative—an aunt I barely knew. In return I was able to pay off my college debt, and I got an adorable, squashed-looking house on Wentworth Street, along with a tiny shop on the corner of Columbus and Meeting Streets.

Inherited houses and retail spaces come with all kinds of chains, like super-pricey insurance, heavy taxes, repairs, you name it. Home insurance near the beach, in a hurricane-prone area? Yeah, it sucks.

What I've dubbed my "studio space" used to be a secondhand clothing store. It's a dingy room with carpet that curls up in the corners, which I have to keep stomping down. The lighting isn't great, but I've got lots of thrifted lamps around the place, so I make do.

I dab another blob of Mixing White into the Ultramarine Blue on my palette and absently swirl it around with my brush. The resulting shade is almost right for this coastal painting—the kind of art tourists gobble up. When they come to Charleston, they want pretty, beachy paintings and sketches, not the art of my heart, the creepy gloriousness I keep tucked away at the back of my shop. That stuff is too morbid, too "weird."

I have to force myself to paint the art that sells. Usually I arrange a mental bribe, like if I finish two beach vignettes, I can work on one of *my* paintings.

The bell on the shop door jingles, and I startle, my surprise blending with an inner thrill because I have a *bell* now. After four

years of slogging through college, I'm finally doing this art thing
for real.

The slim young man who saunters in is so tall, his hair almost
touches the top of the doorframe. To be fair, the door is shorter
than standard, and his blond, shoulder-length hair is thick and wavy,
adding another inch or so. Still, his height is impressive.

And *god*.

He's obscenely pretty. I mean really...how *dare*.

Slanted cheekbones designed for slicing open soft little hearts.
Plump lips, as red as if they were glazed with the blood of said hearts.
Perfect nose. Neatly arched eyebrows over electric-blue eyes.

His mouth tilts in a little smirk, dark lashes hooding his gaze.
It's all I can do not to scoff as I look away. He's just the sort of self-
centered pretty-boy I despise. A walking TikTok thirst trap.

But he's wearing a Dior T-shirt and Escada jeans, so clearly he
has money to burn. Which means I can't tell him to fuck off.

Why the hell is he in *my* shop? He belongs in one of the fancy
galleries in the French Quarter.

As he breezes past me, a sage-and-lavender fragrance unfurls
from him—delicately masculine and metrosexual, probably an
expensive cologne. He smells damn good, like the incense I usually
burn at home.

Rolling an unlit cigarette between his ringed fingers, he inspects
the paintings on display—still lifes of shells and pebbles in vivid
blues and rich browns; a scene of bristling boat-masts against a
peach-colored dawn; waves crashing on cliffs; gulls with cruelly
blank eyes. Everything's priced lower than it's probably worth, but
hey, there's a lot of competition in this city, and a girl's gotta eat—
and pay for hurricane insurance.

He scans them all, his eyes hooded as if none of them meet his standards. There's an insolent slouch to his posture, a casual care-lessness I've come to associate with rich, gorgeous assholes. I knew a couple, distantly, at USC.

I swallow my inner resistance and force out polite words. "Can I help you with something?"

"I'm looking for Baz Allard." His voice is low, smooth, musical, with the faintest hint of a British accent. A voice designed for melt-ing hearts—or panties.

I pretend I'm immune to such voices. "That's me. I'm Baz."

He cocks an eyebrow.

I'm not about to explain the history of my weird name to this guy, or the fact that staying gender-neutral online and refusing to post pictures of myself have spared me from a lot of unwanted attention by random incels. "Are you looking for something specific?"

"I've seen your work on Instagram. Some of it is like this"—he gestures dismissively at the ocean-themed art—"but other pieces are much more interesting."

I waffle between offended and flattered for a second before I reply. "I keep my darker stuff back here." Hopping off my stool, I walk to the back of the shop, sliding a huge oceanscape aside and pulling several smaller canvases out from behind it. A cockroach scuttles across the carpet, and I bite back a scream before crushing it under the chunky heel of my Blackcraft Cult boot.

These paintings are my babies—my beautiful Gothic children. Fish swimming through a rib cage while light glances down through the water, sparkling on a diamond ring that encircles a rib. A spider spinning a web across the jaws of a skull. A hawk lying dead at twi-light beside a country road, one wing jutting brokenly upward, a moth perched on its half-open beak.

The customer scans the paintings briefly before shaking his head. "I'm talking about your character art."

The only people I let myself paint are entirely fictional, created from my head. I barely glance at reference photos. Too risky.

I nod to my customer and walk over to a battered dresser, tugging on the sticky top drawer. "I've got some samples here. You have a D&D character or something you want art of?"

Another smirk. "Do I look like I play Dungeons and Dragons?"

"Um..." I turn, prints in hand. "Maybe? It's anyone's game. I do art for authors too. Any original characters, really."

"I need a portrait."

My heart sinks. "A character portrait?"

"No, an actual portrait. Of me." He's still smiling, but his jaw goes tight, a muscle flexing near the sharp corner.

Great. There goes my one chance at making some replacement-iPhone money. "Sorry, I only paint fictional characters."

"Why?"

"I don't know." I shrug, putting the prints back in the drawer and pushing it shut. "For some reason I'm just no good with real faces. The results are crap every time." I give an airy little chuckle.

"Bullshit." His white teeth bite off the word crisply.

"Excuse me?" I frown at him.

His debonair attitude drops like a coat falling to the ground, leaving behind a naked intensity, a steely desperation that's palpable in the taut air between us.

He steps toward me, and I back up against the dresser. I'm immediately angry at myself for retreating. But he closes in before I can undo the recoil.

"Look, man, I've got pepper spray," I tell him.

"Where?" His gaze travels the length of my bare legs, sheathed in tattoos—skims over my tight black shorts, faux leather and clearly pocketless—then roams my black vest and cropped white tank top.

"Maybe it's hidden in all that hair," he muses.

The left side of my skull is shaved, and the rest of my hair spills over my right shoulder in an abundant pink-and-black waterfall.

I wish I had pepper spray hidden in my hair. But of course it's back home, where it's useless.

"Fuck you," I hiss.

He shutters the predatory light in his gaze, shifting back a step. "I don't mean to frighten you. I just want honesty."

"And I told you honestly that I can't do your portrait." I sidestep, snatching a palette knife from my worktable. "I think you should leave now."

"I'll pay you ten thousand dollars."

Sweat breaks out on my palms and the back of my neck. "Come again?"

His rosy lips stretch in a catlike grin, a dimple popping into his cheek. "You heard me."

Shit.

Maybe I could—

No. I can't. Not for any sum would I ever consider painting someone's portrait. Not after what happened to Dad. Not after—

I took a fucking vow before the goddess and the spirits and whatever else exists out there. I won't break it. I can't.

The guy is watching me. There's no trace of threat from him now—his face is so serenely beautiful, it's almost innocent.

"You think about it." He tucks the cigarette between his lips and pulls a wallet from his back pocket. He extracts a business card and hands it over, pinned between two long fingers. He's got a few silver rings—not as many as I usually wear, but his are fascinating. Antique for sure, maybe ancient.

His business card is a smooth, silvery gray, printed with two words and a number in an elegant, black font.

I take the card, still gripping the palette knife in my other hand.

He strides to the door and pushes it open as the bell jingles. "Let me know when you change your mind."

"I won't, though," I respond.

"Sure." He gives me a wink.

The door closes, and I watch him stroll past the window.

Only then do I read the name printed on the card.

Dorian Gray.

ACKNOWLEDGMENTS

I've had this "green light" dream ever since I was a kid. I wanted to write a book and have it published. I wanted to see a book of mine on shelves, in bookstores.

When you reach the green light, you realize how many hands pushed you toward it—some gently, some forcefully, some without even knowing the part they played in your growth as an author, as a person.

My dad read aloud to my siblings and me every night, and often made up his own stories to tell us. My mom taught me to read and encouraged me to write. I have complex feelings about my childhood, but I am truly grateful to my parents for teaching me to love books.

I also have to thank the creators and actors of the movie *Begin Again*. In early 2018, I had two young kids, and I'd been feeling like my author dreams were probably done for good. I broke down crying while watching that movie for the first time, and that night I determined to go after what I wanted. *The Greatest Showman* movie and Holly Black's *The Cruel Prince* also inspired me around the same time. After years of writing things I didn't enjoy, I could see my green light again.

Without the writing community of Twitter (yes, I'll forever call it Twitter), I wouldn't have known how to query properly, how to find agents, or how to take the first steps to make my dream come true. There are so many indie authors, so many readers, so many wonderful people who gave me bits of advice and encouragement, swapped beta-reads with me, and pushed me to keep going. If I tried to name them all I'd leave out someone important, so I'll just say a heartfelt *thank you* to everyone.

Thank you to my sister, who first introduced me to *The Great Gatsby* and who has been a constant encouragement with my writing.

Thank you to my amazing agent, Eva Scalzo, who offered me representation twice. I wish I'd accepted the first time, but I had things to learn about what I really needed from an author-agent partnership. I'm so glad she gave me another chance.

And thank you to Mary Altman, my wonderful editor, who understood my "Gatsby with vampires" book from the beginning and has been a dream to work with. It means everything to have someone who loves my characters as much as I do, whose vision I can trust.

Lastly, thank you to my kind husband and my sweet kids. Thank you for the hugs, the empathy, the cheerful smiles, and the words of encouragement that keep me going every day.

ABOUT THE AUTHOR

Rebecca Kenney writes spicy contemporary and fantasy romance about sassy, strong women and hot guys with tragic backstories. She is the author of the "Wicked Darlings" series (spicy Fae retellings of the Nutcracker, Wonderland, and Oz), the "Dark Rulers" series (standalone fantasy romances in a shared world), and the "For the Love of the Villain" series. Rebecca is represented by Eva Scalzo of Speilburg Literary. She lives in upstate South Carolina with her handsome blue-eyed husband and two smart, energetic kids. For updates and information about upcoming novels, follow her on:

Instagram: @rebeccafkenneybooks
TikTok: @rebeccafkenney